"A BROODING, INTENSELY READABLE NOVEL . . .

Antecedents like *The Exorcist* might flash through your mind, but in the end it will be Karen Hall's vision of evil that will color your nightmares."
—*Chicago Tribune*

"A riveting tale of the supernatural . . . Very entertaining, a perfect beach book."
—*Cemetery Dance* magazine

"A successful hybrid of Anne Rice and Colleen McCullough . . . Full of wit [and] romance . . . Genuinely entertaining."
—*Booklist*

"Gripping, much heralded horror debut by top TV scripter Karen Hall. The five years Hall spent on writing, revision, and deep research reap big rewards for the reader in this very serious (and spiritual) shocker . . . All set off by strong characters and witty dialogue."
—*Kirkus Reviews* (starred review)

"A page-flipping tale."
—*Publishers Weekly*

DARK DEBTS

Karen Hall

IVY BOOKS • NEW YORK

Ivy Books
Published by Ballantine Books
Copyright © 1996 by Karen Hall, Inc.

Grateful acknowledgment is made to the following for permission to reprint previously published material: Graywolf Press: Lines 14–17 of "The Other" from *The Selected Poems of Rosario Castellanos,* translated by Magda Bogin. Copyright © 1988 by the Estate of Rosario Castellanos. Translation copyright © 1988 by Magda Bogin. Reprinted with the permission of Graywolf Press, Saint Paul, Minnesota. Molly Malone Cook Literary Agency: Two lines from "On Winter's Margin" from *No Voyage and Other Poems* by Mary Oliver (Houghton Mifflin). Copyright © 1965 by Mary Oliver. Reprinted by permission of the Molly Malone Cook Literary Agency. Warner Bros. Publications: Excerpt from "Whatever Lola Wants (Lola Gets)," words and music by Richard Adler and Jerry Ross. Copyright © 1955 by Frank Music Corp. Copyright © renewed 1983 by Lakshmi Puja Ltd. and J & J Ross. All rights reserved. Used by permission of Warner Bros. Publications U.S. Inc., Miami, FL 33014.

http://www.randomhouse.com

Library of Congress Catalog Card Number: 96-95382

ISBN 0-8041-1655-5

This edition published by arrangement with Random House, Inc.

Manufactured in the United States of America

First Ballantine Books Edition: June 1997

10 9 8 7 6 5 4 3 2 1

For the guy in the flannel shirt

If only it were all so simple! If only there were evil people somewhere insidiously committing evil deeds, and it were necessary only to separate them from the rest of us and destroy them. But the line dividing good and evil cuts through the heart of every human being. And who is willing to destroy a part of his own heart?

Alexander Solzhenitsyn, The Gulag Archipelago

Too few dark debts are ever paid . . .

from a poem by Gary Gilmore

PROLOGUE

Michael sat on the witness stand, feeling like a six-year-old who'd just been informed that the nurse would be back momentarily with his shot. For what seemed like several weeks now he'd been watching the defense attorney pace and think. Scott Bender. Court-appointed. In the middle of his Andy Warhol fifteen minutes and milking them for all they were worth. Michael had developed a strong dislike for the guy somewhere around "nice to meet you," for no concrete reason. Something about his demeanor. Haughtiness with no money or breeding to back it up. Michael had come from plenty of money and breeding, and then chosen a career that necessitated downplaying them into oblivion. Which was probably his reason for resenting Bender—the way someone on an eternal diet resents fat people walking around with ice-cream cones.

"Father Kinney"—Michael was addressed as "Father" about every third question, lest the jurors lose track and suddenly begin to think of him as an insurance salesman in a Roman collar—"Father," Bender repeated, for the sake of the truly dull, "is Bishop Roger Wilbourne your immediate superior?"

"No, he's not."

"And who is?"

"Frank Worland. The Jesuit provincial."

1

"Can you explain to us how that works?"

If the jury was having trouble remembering his occupation, Michael doubted they'd be able to follow the intricate inner workings of the Jesuit hierarchy. Nor could he understand what difference it made to matters at hand. But Perry Mason should have thought of that before he asked. Michael explained. Provinces. Regions. Rectors. Provincials. Father General. Rome. The delicate balance of Jesuitdom. Forever and ever, amen.

"So, if you wanted to do something . . . out of the ordinary," Bender asked, "you'd need permission from your provincial?"

"In most cases."

"And that would be Frank Worland?"

"Yes."

Michael could see Frank glaring from his seat in the third row. It was a hard sight to get used to. Up until this insanity, he and Frank had been friends. Not particularly intimate, but close enough for the occasional dinner or game of racquetball. Those days were over, he knew. Their tense conversation from the night before was still churning in Michael's head like cerebral indigestion.

"Michael, the trial is less than twelve hours away."

"I know. And I can't do a thing with my hair."

"There's a very simple way out of this, you know."

"I don't consider lying simple."

"No one is asking you to lie. All you have to do is plead confidentiality."

"Frank, nothing that happened was told to me in confidence. Quite the contrary, and you know it."

"But the judge doesn't know it. And the defense has no way to prove it."

"Well, I'm glad you're not asking me to lie."

"All you're going to do is buy the Church another round of bad publicity. Is that what you want?"

"No. I'd much prefer we stop doing the things that bring on the bad publicity."

"Oh, for Christ's sake, Michael."

"What?"

"You're a little old to be self-righteously idealistic, don't you think?"

"And so," Bender continued, "was Frank Worland the superior from whom you needed permission in order to become involved in my client's . . . situation?"

Michael shook his head. "No. For that I needed permission from the bishop."

He hadn't even told Frank about it, until after the fact. Which was a large part of Frank's anger. But, as Michael had tried to explain, he'd gone into this mess thinking he was doing a small favor for an old friend. He'd certainly have mentioned it to Frank—and several other people— had he known it was all headed toward a triple homicide.

"And permission from the bishop was never granted, is that correct?"

"That's correct."

"You made a decision to act without the authorization of either your provincial or the bishop, did you not?"

"Yes, I did."

"And why was that?"

Michael took a moment to figure out a diplomatic way to put it. "I felt that the situation was . . . critical."

Bender nodded. Michael braced himself for the question he'd been dreading, which he assumed would come next. It didn't. Instead Bender returned to the defense table to check his notes.

Michael took the opportunity to scan the crowd. The courtroom was packed for the third straight day. People had been lining up in the mornings to get a good seat. The first two days had been pretty boring, but their persistence was about to pay off. Today they were going to get their money's worth.

Uh-oh.

That woman. The editor from *The New Yorker.*

Damn.

He hadn't seen her earlier and had decided God had taken him up on his offer: anything he owned (or would come to own in this lifetime) in exchange for her having some other pressing engagement today. It was bad enough to have to make a public fool of himself without her sitting fifteen feet away. What was her name? Tess something. Tess Mc-something. Pretty name. To say nothing of its owner. She was wearing an emerald green jacket, and her long red hair hung loosely around her shoulders. Gorgeous hair. It had been tied back every other time he'd seen her. He'd met her in the hallway the first day of the trial—overheard her asking someone about him and took the opportunity to introduce himself.

"You're Father Kinney?"

"Yes."

"You're kidding."

"What were you expecting? Bing Crosby?"

"I don't know, but I'm a lapsed Catholic and I spent a lot of years in parochial schools and I've never seen a priest who looked like you.... Never seen one blush, either."

"Well, I guess this is your day for firsts."

She'd asked him about doing an interview for the article she was writing on the trial. He'd said he'd think about it. Yesterday she'd left two messages on his answering machine, which he hadn't returned. Now she looked up at him and smiled. He didn't return that, either. He wasn't exactly in a mood to flirt. Besides, he knew how vulnerable he was right now. It wouldn't take much for harmless flirting to become anything but. Especially with a woman who looked like she did and, by virtue of her occupation, had a brain as well. That combination had been his undoing before, and he'd sworn he'd never go down that road again. The consequences were too devastating, for everyone involved.

Bender had reemerged from his legal pad.

"Father, we were talking earlier about this magazine that you edit. What kinds of articles would we find in this magazine?"

There was something subtly patronizing in Bender's voice. Michael wasn't entirely sure of its source, but had a feeling it was something along the lines of *"I spend my life fighting for truth and justice, and you spend yours in total devotion to a fairy tale."* There was probably a little bit of *"and you're a eunuch to boot"* thrown in there. Michael was used to that subtext by now, but it had never stopped bothering him.

"We publish scholarly articles," Michael answered, trying hard to have no attitude whatsoever. "Articles written by priests. Sociologists. Religious historians."

"So this is a serious magazine? People take it seriously?"

"I certainly hope so." *Yes, you condescending asshole. Amazingly, there are still a few people who take this God stuff seriously.*

"You don't print articles on things like the Virgin Mary appearing on someone's garage door?"

"If we did, it would be under the category of psychosis and religious hallucinations, and it would be written by a Jesuit psychologist."

Bender nodded. Michael took a breath. No amount of reminding himself could convince his brain that he and this jerk were sympathetic to the same cause.

"Father, would you describe yourself as a skeptical person?"

"In most respects."

"Meaning?"

"I'm a priest. I'm obviously selectively skeptical at best."

"All right. Let me ask you this. Do you believe in UFOs? Alien abductions?"

"No."

"Crop circles? Cattle mutilation?"

"No."

"The Loch Ness monster?"

"No."

"Spontaneous human combustion?"

"No," Michael said, finally losing his grip. "And I don't believe in Santa Claus or weeping statues or milk shakes that cure cancer and I think that Elvis is really dead and Bill Clinton probably inhaled at least once. If you're asking me if I'm gullible or easily misled, the answer is no, I am not."

"Well, that's certainly direct and to the point, Father," Bender said. He smiled, reminding the jury that (all evidence to the contrary) Michael was not a hostile witness. Then added, "You'd never make it as an attorney."

There were snickers from the crowd and Bender's illusion of dignity was restored.

"Okay. Let's say we go back in time, to the day before you met my client. On that day, did Father Michael Kinney, the nongullible-serious-Jesuit-magazine-editor, believe in the devil?"

A hush fell. Michael heard someone stop mid-cough.

"No. I did not."

"Okay. And if we move forward from there to the day my client was arrested . . . on that day, did you believe in the devil?"

Michael didn't answer immediately, allowing himself one last moment of respectability. He could already see his picture on the front page of tomorrow's *New York*

Post. He snuck a furtive glance at Tess Mc-whatever. She was taking notes.

"Father?"

Michael looked back at the lawyer. "Yes," he said. "On that day, I did."

Rustling. Mumbling. Reporters scribbling furiously. At least there was no laughter. No audible laughter, anyway.

"And did your encounter with my client play a part in your change of opinion?"

"Yes."

"In fact, it was your encounter with my client that was entirely responsible for your change of opinion, isn't that correct?"

"Yes. That's correct."

The attorney nodded and smiled. This was his idea of a good time.

"Okay, Father. Let's go back to the day you met my client. I want to ask you a few questions about that day."

Michael waited while the attorney checked his notes again. The courtroom was so quiet he could hear the sound of the sketch artist's pencil. He glanced over at Frank Worland, who immediately looked the other way—but not before Michael had a chance to read his face. Judas must have seen (and felt) a similar expression, right before the temple guards led Jesus out of the garden.

When the elevator door opened on the second floor of the Jesuit residence, Michael was accosted by the sound of a cocktail party coming from the lounge next to the dining room. There was always a cocktail hour before dinner, but it never involved more than the fifteen guys who lived in the house. From the sound of it, there had to be at least fifty people in the lounge. The conversation was animated and sprinkled with laughter.

Michael headed for his room. Whatever it was, he wanted no part of it.

Halfway down the hall, Larry Lantieri came out of his room, drink in hand. Michael knew why. Larry claimed he'd taken an extra vow: never to drink cheap scotch.

"He's back," Larry said, smiling. "And I'll bet he's in a great mood."

"What is that?" Michael asked, nodding toward the noise.

Larry's smile broadened. "Oh, Mikey. You've forgotten what day it is."

Michael thought for a second. He had to work to remember what *month* it was.

"It's July," he said. "End of July." It came to him. "Oh, hell." It was July 31. The Feast of St. Ignatius. Jesuit Fourth of July.

Michael sighed. "How bad is it?"

"Buffet dinner for the benefactors," Larry said. "You remember them. The people who give us money so we can keep publishing a magazine so we don't have to go to Louisiana and teach history to fourteen-year-olds."

Down the hall, strangers with wineglasses were examining the row of framed magazine covers on the wall.

"They're wandering," Michael said.

Larry nodded. "Frank removed cloister until ten o'clock. But it's not like you could hide in your room. You're technically the host."

"Tell them that a crazed gunman opened fire on the courtroom. I'm not expected to live." He patted Larry on the shoulder and started for his room again.

"Where are you going?" Larry asked.

"To check my messages, change my clothes, and hang myself from the shower rod."

"You're not getting out of this," he heard Larry say, as he closed the door of his room behind him.

After an entire day out of the house, he had exactly one message on his answering machine. Pretty typical these days. Except for his housemates, he didn't have a friend left. Unless he counted the Siberian hamster he'd won in a poker game.

He played the message.

"Hi. It's Tess McLaren. Again. The reason I've been calling is that it suddenly occurred to me that I'm not the person who should be writing this article. I've been reading some of your stuff and . . . well, if they end up defrocking you for this, you can come and work for me any time . . ."

The phone rang. Michael turned off the machine to answer it. He was deeply relieved to hear his grandfather's voice on the other end.

"So, how'd it go?" Vincent asked.

"I'll send you the *National Enquirer* clippings. I'm sure you'll be proud."

"I am proud. You did the right thing."

"Then why do I feel like shit?"

"The right thing doesn't have to feel good. It only has to feel right."

"Vincent, you've been trying that one on me for half a century and it's never worked yet."

"I don't discourage easily."

"So I've noticed." Michael sank into his desk chair. "Listen, can I call you back? I have to go to a damned party."

"Call me when you can. I want the sordid details."

"You can have them now: I no longer have any credibility as a journalist; I no longer have a relationship with Frank Worland; I wouldn't place big money on getting a hug from the bishop anytime soon, and the jury is still going to vote to convict. But I did the right thing. God's impressed as hell."

"Just send me the papers."

"I'll make you a scrapbook."

Michael hung up. He wasn't about to relive the day's events. Not even for Vincent. He stared through his blinds at the dirty windows of the building next door. The air was filled with the usual rush-hour din of taxi horns and the sirens of gridlocked emergency vehicles. This time of day, the city always depressed him.

Shedding the clerics would help, he realized. He hated them; never wore them when he could avoid it. The benefactors didn't care how he was dressed, as long as he talked to them so they could feel important.

He was halfway out of his shirt when there was a knock on the door. Someone wanting a trial update or Larry coming back to drag him to the party. The possibilities were equally repugnant.

"It's open," he called, making no attempt to sound hospitable.

The door opened a crack.

"Are you sure?" A female voice. *What the hell?*

He pulled the shirt back on. "Relatively," he said, mostly to himself. He was on his way to the door when it opened and there she stood. Still wearing the green jacket. With a short skirt. And legs that were a near occasion of sin without help from his imagination. Not good. This was not good.

"Hi," Tess said, smiling.

"How did you . . . ?" He stopped, searching for the question.

"How did I what?"

He tried to put it together. Had she been invited to the party for some reason? Or had she just dropped by to visit? Either way, how had she found him?

"I asked someone at the party which room was yours,"

she said, answering his question. "Why? Is there a rule against girls in the dorm?"

"Even if there were, I'm not a big fan of rules," he said. He hoped his voice sounded steadier than it felt. "As you'd know if you were paying any attention in court."

"Apparently you're not a big fan of returning phone calls, either."

"Do you show up on the doorstep of everyone who doesn't return your phone calls?"

"No." She let it go at that, but there was a look in her eyes that filled in the blanks.

"I haven't been avoiding you any more than I've been avoiding anyone else," he said. "I'm a little preoccupied right now."

"I know. I'm sorry. But if we're going to do this thing, we need to get started."

"Do what thing?"

"The article. Didn't you get my last message?"

He nodded. "Yeah. Something about me getting defrocked and going to work for you. I saved the tape. I'm pretty sure I can sue you for sexual harassment."

She laughed. She even laughed like a woman with a brain.

"So, do you have to go to the party?" she asked, nodding toward the noise. "Because if you want to escape it, I'll buy you a drink and we can talk about the article."

What if I just cut my heart out and toss it into the Cuisinart? Same end result.

"I don't think it's a good idea," he said.

"The article, or having a drink with me?"

He didn't answer. In truth, he liked the idea of writing the article. A lot. Almost as much as he liked the idea of having a drink with her. But both of them were minefields, and he was in no shape to be making life-and-death decisions.

"Look," he said. "I'm not opposed to the idea of writing the article. But, just for the record, I plan to remain frocked."

He didn't have to wonder if she'd understood. It was interesting to see a stunned look on her face. Michael doubted it was a frequent occurrence.

"I stand advised," she said, recovering.

"I realize I'm being presumptuous, but I'd rather be presumptuous now than uncomfortable later." It annoyed him that she was playing dumb. The vibes were so thick he was amazed he could still breathe the air.

"So what you're saying is, you're particular about *which* rules you break?"

Michael stared at her, speechless. She went on before he had a chance to recover.

"Since you're laying down the ground rules, does that mean you're saying yes to the article?"

"I'm saying maybe," Michael said, finding his voice. "Probably. But I want to sleep on it."

She nodded. "Good enough. You can call me in the morning."

"Okay."

She started out, then stopped and turned back to him.

"Are you always this skittish around women?" she asked.

"Only the ones who follow me home."

"I don't follow many people home. You should be flattered."

"I stand advised," he said.

She smiled, and then she was gone.

He woke up in the middle of the night, thinking about her. The last bad sign he needed. He'd call her in the morning and politely decline her offer. He didn't need to set a new record for how much trouble he could get into at once. Besides, there was nothing to be accomplished by writing the article.

Or was there? He was torn between the idea of letting it all die and the idea of explaining himself to the rest of the world. He was never going to accomplish that by testifying at the trial. In fact, he was never going to accomplish *anything* by testifying. He didn't know what was behind that compulsion. It wasn't going to change a thing that mattered. It certainly wasn't going to change what had already happened.

There was only one thing he knew for certain: everything was different now. His brush with Evil had done something to him. Nothing he could define, but he knew that he had not survived the confrontation unscathed. Even in one brief collision, it had seeped into him, body and soul. It had left behind a whisper of itself. Like a warning. Like a reminder. Like a threat.

That someday, at some unexpected hour, it would return.

And next time Michael had a feeling he wasn't going to walk away so easily.

Next time, in fact, he might not walk away at all.

BOOK
ONE

Fate is not an eagle; it creeps like a rat.
Elizabeth Bowen, The House in Paris

THE RAT

CHAPTER 1

Randa couldn't move. She could feel her weight in the chair and it was the only thing keeping her upright. How long was she going to have to stay here? It was three o'clock in the morning and she had to be at work by nine. Or did she? Was this a legitimate excuse to take the day off? Did she have a right to mourn? And would everyone see it as mourning, or merely as the final chapter in a neurotic obsession? She had felt uncomfortable at the paper ever since last summer. She knew a lot of people had bought the self-serving pile of crap Cam had spread around, in which she came off as a psychopath. If she told them about the phone call, would they even believe her? How far "out there" did everyone think she was? A question that had plagued her life. And the other question. How far out there *was* she?

"How long did you say you've known Mr. Landry?" It came from the older one, a doughy, middle-aged man wearing a shirt the color of Dijon mustard. Neither of them looked anything like she would have expected a detective to look.

I don't know a "Mr. Landry." Mr. Landry is someone's political science teacher. I know Cam.

"Seven years. Or eight." Then added, "I haven't seen him in a long time." She didn't know whether that was relevant or not. It was certainly relevant to her.

17

They had made her identify the body. A granite-faced
man from the coroner's office had lifted the sheet, while
a uniformed cop had supported her by the elbow in case
she collapsed. Apparently a fifteen-story fall onto the
concrete sidewalk had yielded all sorts of ugliness. She'd
have to take their word for it. All she had seen were
Cam's eyes. Truth be told, they were all she had ever
noticed when she looked at Cam. She noticed everyone's
eyes, but Cam's were unlike any she'd ever seen. An
ephemeral blue, the color of jeans that have faded just
right. But it wasn't the color that gave them their
haunting quality, it was the depth. A depth that knew no
context, like the light inside a prism. Somewhere near the
bottom, a crystal base of hope managed to send a trace of
itself to the surface. Along the way it was clouded over
by layers of pain and sadness and bitter defeat. That was
what she had always seen in Cam's eyes. The hope and
the bitterness, locked in mortal combat. Even now, she
knew something inside her would be forever scarred by
the outcome of that battle.

She glanced at her reflection in the dirty glass parti-
tion. Her eyes seemed to be sinking into her face. They
looked, as her mother would have put it, like "two little
pee-holes in the snow." She tucked a strand of thick
blond hair behind her ear, as if that would help. Was
thirty-five supposed to look this old? Had she looked so
old this morning? God, why was she worrying about how
she looked at a time like this?

She braced herself as another angry wave of pain
washed over her. *How can this be real? How can Cam be
dead? He's outrun it for so long.*

Outrun *what*? What part of her was talking, and what
was it talking about? She'd noticed lately (in the last
year, maybe?) that there seemed to be this voice inside
her head that would blow through, make some grand pro-

nouncement, and disappear without the slightest desire to explain itself.

"We've been trying to locate a relative to notify. Do you happen to know of anyone?" It came from the younger detective. His light brown hair had a waxy texture that made him look like a Ken doll.

Randa shook her head. "They're all dead."

"No aunts, uncles, anything?"

She could hear Cam's voice: *Not unless you count those fucking inbred third cousins in Macon.* She wondered if she should mention Jack. It wouldn't help, but it would give them something to write in their reports, which might get her out of here sooner.

"There's a brother somewhere, but you won't be able to find him. Cam's been trying for years."

The younger one clicked his ballpoint. "You know his name?"

"Jack. It's probably short for something, they all had fancy names."

"They all who?"

"Cam and his brothers."

"And all the brothers are dead except this Jack?"

"Yes." *I wouldn't hold out on you. I'm not trying to keep the corpse for a souvenir.*

"So where does this Jack live?"

"Somewhere around Atlanta, the last anyone heard from him. But that was ten years ago."

"And there's absolutely no one else?"

It seemed he was never going to let go of this until she told him something new. She tried to think. Who would have been called if she hadn't shown up? The answer slammed into her head. She took a deep breath.

"He has a girlfriend. Nora Dixon." *A lying bitch from some back corner of hell who'd better not show her sorry ass in here until I'm long gone if you don't want to add a homicide to your caseload.* "I don't know why she wasn't there, I thought they were living together." *She must have met someone who could do her career more good.*

"Wait a minute." The younger one again. "If she's his girlfriend, who are you?"

"I'll be damned if I know." Out before she could censor it. She immediately hated herself for the venom she could hear in her voice. How could she be mad at Cam *now*?

"What does that mean?"

"I'm sorry," she said, not sure why she was apologizing. "We used to be friends."

"Why'd you stop?"

She looked up in time to see Detective Ken wink. Wonderful, now he was going to hit on her. Just what she needed.

"I don't see how that's relevant."

"Whoa . . ." He made a show of looking around the room. "Are we in court already? Time flies."

Very cute. David Letterman is probably quaking in his Nikes.

"What time did you say he called you?" The older one showed no sign of noticing the sparring.

"Around one o'clock."

"Could you be any more precise?"

"One-oh-nine. Or nineteen. I remember a nine on the digital clock."

"You remember a niiiiine?" Detective Ken dragged it out, imitating her accent. "What part of the South are y'all from?"

The part where men talk to women the way you're talking to me, which is why I left.

"Georgia." She gave him the iciest look she could muster. *Say "peach." I dare you.*

"Georgia," he said, in a tone that implied there was

something remarkable about being from Georgia. He let it go at that. He seemed to be picking up on her unequivocal lack of interest.

The other one raised an eyebrow. "Did you know Mr. Landry from Georgia?"

"No. We met here. That was just . . . a coincidence." She trailed off, as she heard her father's voice in her head. *"Coincidence is a fool's defense."* Why she thought she needed to defend herself was another question.

Under all the paranoia, memories of Cam were starting to emerge, shooting at her like darts, too fast to dodge. She was surprised at what was coming back. It wasn't a montage of great moments. It was a montage of trivia. Holidays. Dinner parties, such as they were. (If there were at least four people present and they used breakable glasses, Cam called it a dinner party.) Concerts, everything from Bruce Springsteen at the Sports Arena to some don't-quit-your-day-job folksinger in the fifty-seat auditorium in the back of the guitar store. Getting lost everywhere. (Neither of them had the sense of direction God gave a banana squash.) Stopping to get directions from an old guy in a Shriner's hat who'd hopped into the car and pored over the Triple-A map with them without a second's thought about who they might be. (Funny, how people always assume they know what danger looks like.) Late-night dinners in funky little coffee shops. The one with the full bar. A grilled-cheese sandwich and a margarita, Cam's idea of heaven. Combing outdoor flea markets for antique Mickey Mouses. Following Cam through cramped, musty bookstores while he piled her arms with books she couldn't live a fulfilling life without reading. Tiny moments of unprompted warmth. A hug from nowhere, a present for no reason. Meaningless arguments that had turned vicious and personal, only to wind their way back to banality and dissolve in some black joke or a simple change of subject. Sitting here now, she couldn't remember the big events. (Had there even been any?) Instead, she just felt the time. All the mundane, directionless time that makes up a friendship.

A friendship. Was that what it had been? A friendship that had been hanging over her head like an oppressive cloud for more years than she cared to acknowledge. What would happen to that cloud now? Did Cam's death mean that it was gone, or that she was stuck with it forever?

"So when he called you, he didn't say anything that indicated . . ." Detective Mustard Shirt groped for a kinder, gentler way to put it.

"That he was about to jump out the window? No. And I don't know why he'd call me to come over if he was planning to kill himself before I could get there."

"Are you saying you don't think he jumped?"

"You said his door was locked from the inside. Obviously he jumped. I'm just saying if you're waiting for me to make any sense of this, we're going to be here for a long time."

"Had he been depressed lately?"

"I don't know. Like I said (*if you'd been listening*), I hadn't seen him or talked to him in a year."

If he'd been breathing, he'd been depressed lately. She'd never seen him go longer than a week without falling into a major funk. She had eventually learned to stop worrying about it. It was just a part of who he was. And who could blame him? Hell, it was a wonder he could tie his shoes.

"So why did he call you tonight?"

Jesus, how many times are we going to do this?

"I don't know. He said he needed to talk to me. And he said something about being in some kind of trouble, like I told you. He didn't say what the trouble was, he didn't explain why he was calling me specifically, and he didn't say he might kill himself if I got stuck in traffic."

The older detective nodded and wrote something down, completely unfazed by her impatience. He stared at the memo pad. This was how it had been going for the last hour. He'd ask a few questions, make a few notes, then stare at the pad for what seemed like an eternity. If there was a logic to it, Randa didn't know what it was.

Her head felt ready to explode. She pressed the bridge of her nose between her thumb and forefinger, trying to find the pressure point that was supposed to trigger nerve endings or reroute blood or some damned thing to get rid of a headache. Her holistic chiropractor had shown it to her. (It had never worked before, but what the hell.) Why was this taking so long? Why couldn't they just chalk it up as another suicide in the big city and be done with it? Surely they had better things to do. Wasn't Hollywood, all myths aside, the crime capital of the planet?

She glanced around the bull pen, taking a quick inventory. Probably pretty boring compared to a Saturday night, but colorful nonetheless. Her bleary eyes scanned the collection of prostitutes, dope peddlers, and other assorted rejects from polite society. She wondered if she could catch something unspeakable just by breathing the air. She wondered if she cared.

The older detective was looking at her as if she'd missed a major point and she realized he'd just made some proclamation.

"I'm sorry, what?"

"Couple of hours ago, someone robbed a liquor store a few blocks from Mr. Landry's apartment building."

Was that the big news flash? She knew the liquor store he was talking about. It was on the corner of Sunset and Vista, with a wide front door angled for easy access (and getaway) from both streets. None of the businesses

around it were open at night, so it really stood out. She
and Cam had joked that the owner should just put a sign
in the window that said ROB ME. ("*My brothers would
have used that place as an ATM,*" *Cam had said.*) But
what did any of that have to do with Cam's death?

"... Witnesses described the robber as a white male in
his late thirties, about six-three, salt-and-pepper hair,
wearing a nice suede jacket, sort of an odd shade of
green. He asked the cashier to throw in a bottle of Chinaca tequila. Not exactly your standard profile." He
smiled a little. "Your run-of-the-mill liquor-store robber
will usually settle for Cuervo Gold."

Randa just stared at him. Cam had a tequila fetish that
was not a secret to anyone who knew him or read his
books. And she had given him a sage-green suede jacket
two Christmases ago. But surely he wasn't implying ...

"I noticed an unopened bottle of Chinaca on Mr.
Landry's desk, and it rang a bell. Far-fetched, I know, but
I swung by and had one of the witnesses take a look at
Mr. Landry's driver's license, and what do you know?
Bingo."

It was all Randa could do not to laugh.

"That is the most asinine thing I've ever heard!
It's ... it's comical!"

"Yeah, well, I've got a nineteen-year-old stock boy
over at the county morgue with a bullet wound in his
chest and he ain't laughing very much."

"Well, if you think Cam had anything to do with it,
you're out of your mind!" The incredulity in her voice
raised it an octave.

"What makes you so sure?" the young one asked, in
his best Sergeant Friday voice. (Evidently trying to
redeem his manhood, in light of his two failed pass
attempts.)

"In the first place, Cam had more integrity, more

humanity, than anyone I've ever known . . ." For the first time she choked up. She swallowed hard and continued. "And he hated guns. He would never have touched a gun, much less shot someone. And then there's the fact that he'd just signed a book deal with a three hundred thousand dollar advance, which would pretty much alleviate the need to rob a liquor store!" She was practically yelling at them, which was a waste of adrenaline. This whole thing was from *The Twilight Zone.*

"Three hundred thousand dollars?" It was the older one who spoke, but the younger one's eyes glazed over with the sudden knowledge that he was in the wrong business. The older one recovered and continued.

"How do you know that if you haven't talked to him in a year?"

Because all of my so-called friends sent me every clipping they could get their hands on, just in case I hadn't heard.

"I read it in *Publishers Weekly.*"

The older guy nodded as if his subscription had just lapsed, then went on. "Well, be that as it may . . ." He looked down at his desk for a moment, then back up. His eyes met Randa's. He was obviously gearing up for something.

"The neighbors told us some interesting things about Mr. Landry's family history, which I assume you know . . ."

So, there it was. Randa had figured they would end up here eventually.

"That's exactly why I know this is crazy."

"Why's that?"

"Because it is. Look, I knew Cam for a long time, and I knew him well."

"You hadn't seen him in over a year."

"I don't think he had a soul transplant in that time."

Then why did he do what he did to you? And why did it catch you so off guard, if you knew him so well? And what on earth was that phone call about? What about what he had said . . . what had he said? "I'm in trouble I didn't even know existed." Well, he certainly knew that liquor stores existed. But what about the witnesses? Could they have been that mistaken? No one on earth looked like Cam.

"Maybe he just had you fooled." Detective Ken again. His arrogance was now enhanced by a patronizing sneer. Randa abandoned all efforts to hide her contempt.

"I don't fool that easily."

They locked eyes, and Randa did not look away as another man approached the desk. She could hear him talking to the older detective as he rustled something out of a brown paper bag.

"Back closet . . . under a pile of clothes . . ." She looked up. The older detective was holding a plastic bag. Inside, marked with a small cream-colored tag, she saw the gun. Her entire body locked with disbelief. The man was still talking.

". . . Forensics dusted it, we're waiting . . . Ballistics said send it over, they're not busy. I said there's no rush, the guy's dead . . ."

"Rush anyway."

Randa stared at the gun. Were they saying it came from Cam's apartment? Behind her, Captain Arrogance could barely contain his glee.

"Well, what do you know? Looks like you fool easier than you think."

It was nearly dawn by the time Randa got home. She sat on her sofa in a stupor, as the sun rose and the room lit up around her. She could only think, she couldn't feel. Her emotions were locked in the bottleneck of information— Cam's death, the police, the guy at the liquor store, the gun—it was too much, it numbed her. All she could do was play this strange night in her head, over and over, searching for any part of an answer.

She had finished filing her column by six o'clock—the latest in a series of tirades on the sorry state of the Supreme Court. It would be her last rant on that topic for a while, since there had been too many letters complaining that it wasn't a "local issue." *Really? LA is not going to be affected by the obliteration of the Constitution? Good, I'm living in the right place.* In LA, a "liberal" readership meant people who wanted to hear from other liberals on the subjects of where to eat and what movies to see. Next week she'd go back to comparing trendy shopping districts, giving everyone a break now that she'd forced them to think for ten minutes.

She had settled back to zone out in front of a true-crime miniseries that had sounded promising in the reviews. She gave it about fifteen minutes before deciding the critics all had brain tumors and turned it off. She had tried writing a letter to her sister, but when she thought about what she'd say (*work sucks; I'm on another stupid diet; it actually got below seventy here yesterday*) it didn't seem worth wasting stationery over. She flipped through the latest issue of *Rolling Stone* but couldn't bring herself to care whether or not Heather Nova's latest album was better than her last one.

It was one of those nights that reminded her she'd inherited her mother's nerves. She was consumed by a feeling of lurking doom. It made no sense, especially on a Wednesday night with her work done. The paper came out on Thursdays, so Wednesday was usually her night to relax. Not that she was someone who ever really relaxed.

Looking back on it now, it was like she'd spent the night waiting for the phone call, as if some deep, hidden part of her had known it was coming.

* * *

She had been sleeping on the edge of the bed with her
head near the nightstand, and the phone had scared the
hell out of her. She hated middle-of-the-night phone
calls. A wrong number or someone was dead—too wide
a spectrum to prepare for on a moment's notice with a
pounding heart.

"Hello!" She'd answered in a tone that demanded a
quick explanation.

"Randa?"

She'd recognized the voice instantly. Cam had a very
distinctive voice, smooth and almost lyrical, with traces
of an accent too watered-down to be placed. She'd
always loved his voice. She had thought she would never
hear it again. For a millisecond she considered hanging
up on him, then asked herself who she thought she was
kidding.

"Cam?"

"I have to talk to you. It's really important. I know it's
late, but I have to talk to someone and you're the only
person I know who might believe this."

"Believe what?"

"I can't do it on the phone. Randa, it's crazy, it's . . .
Look, you always said you'd do anything for me."

"Well," she said, "that was a long time and many erro-
neous perceptions ago."

"I know. We can talk about that, too. You don't
know . . . you can't believe the things you don't know."

"Hell, I can't believe the things I *do* know."

"DAMMIT, RANDA!" It was so loud and so unchar-
acteristic, she almost dropped the receiver. "I'm in
trouble! I'm in trouble that I didn't even know existed!
Now are you going to get off your ass and help me or are
you just going to send a nice wreath to the funeral?"

"Okay, calm down. I'll be over as soon as I can."

"No! Not here, you can't come here."

"All right. I'll meet you at Ray's."

"Okay. Hurry."

"Okay. Bye . . ."

"Randa!"

"What?"

The line was silent as he thought. "Nothing. Just hurry."

Ray's was a coffee shop where Cam all but lived. He ate there at least once a day, sometimes three times. His loyalty had mostly to do with the place's proximity to his apartment. Cam lived in Hollywood, in an area Randa had always referred to as the "hills above hell." She had tried repeatedly to talk him into moving to a nicer neighborhood, but he said he couldn't write the kind of stuff he wrote in an antiseptic environment. She had offered that there was a wide range between "antiseptic" and "very likely to meet death in the underground parking garage," but he never listened.

It was a little after two in the morning when she got to Ray's. It wasn't the first time she'd been there at that hour, so the clientele did not catch her off guard. Homeless people ("displaced persons," they preferred to be called now), rock-and-roll types, prostitutes of both genders taking a break from trolling, and an eclectic assortment of insomniacs. The "denizens of the deep," Ray called them, with a certain amount of affection.

Ray was in his early fifties, short and round with dark features and several visible tattoos. Where he had ever come up with the money to open a coffee shop was a mystery, as he was no businessman whatsoever. Half the regulars had running tabs they never paid, and whenever someone approached the cash register holding a bill, Ray always seemed pleasantly surprised. Randa was convinced he was in the Witness Protection Program. But he was friendly to her, and extremely fond of Cam.

Cam was nowhere to be found, and his car wasn't in the lot. Ray was sitting on a stool at the counter, poring over a racing form.

"Ray?"

"Hey, Randa! Where the hell have you been?"

"I've been around."

"You ain't been around here."

"No." The last thing on earth she wanted to do was explain it to Ray. "I'm looking for Cam, have you seen him?"

"Not since breakfast."

"Breakfast?"

"You know, noon. *His* breakfast. So does this mean he finally unloaded that spook?"

Ray called any woman with dark hair and a lot of makeup a spook. Randa had tried before to explain the racial undertones, but Ray wasn't interested.

"I have no idea. I haven't seen him in a long time."

"Yeah, I know. I always ask him about you."

He must love that. She wondered what Cam had said. She moved away? She got hit by a train? She grew a beard and joined the circus? Or had he told Ray the truth? Had the two of them had a good laugh and a moment of male bonding at her expense? And what would he tell Ray tomorrow? She guessed that depended on what he told her tonight.

She ordered a cup of coffee and went to use the pay phone. She hadn't dialed the number in so long, it took her a moment to remember it. She was amazed that it hadn't changed, but after two rings a machine picked up and she heard Cam's voice. *"No one's here. Leave a message after the beep."* It was his depressed voice. She knew it well.

"Cam? It's Randa. I'm at Ray's and you're not. Are you there?" She waited. "Well . . . I guess you're on your way. I'm giving it ten more minutes and I'm leaving." *Yeah, talk tough. You'll sit here until hell freezes over.*

She hung up and went back to the dining room. She could see a cup of coffee sitting at "their" table, where Ray had put it. There was also a Coke for Cam, and a chocolate-chip roll. Ray had never been an ally in her effort to get Cam to eat better. Still, it was a thoughtful gesture. She could have gotten all choked up over it, had she chosen to be dramatic. She didn't do that anymore.

She sat down and tried to collect herself. She wanted to be as stoic as possible by the time Cam showed up. Over the last year she had always dreaded the inevitability of coming face-to-face with him again, because she had no idea how to act. Part of her still felt the same way about him she'd ever felt, and another part of her wanted him to die slowly and painfully at the hands of skilled torturers, and there didn't seem to be any middle ground. She tried to will herself to stay conscious, to listen to whatever he said and react to that and nothing else. That might work. It just depended on what this was about.

What *was* this about? And why did it involve her? No matter what kind of trouble Cam was in, he had a million friends he could have called. People who lived closer, people who stayed up later, people he hadn't spent the last year trying to pretend he'd never met. Not to mention the lovely and provocative Nora. Where was she?

Half an hour later Randa had finished two cups of coffee and most of the chocolate-chip roll, and she was angry. Cam could have walked there three times since she left the message. It was obnoxious enough for him to have called her in the first place, but doubly tacky to tell her to hurry and then leave her cooling her heels among the night crawlers. She didn't share Ray's affection for them, or Cam's sense of belonging.

As soon as Ray's back was turned (she was not in the mood to answer any more questions), she put some money on the table and left, to drive up the hill to Cam's.

She remembered the drive well. It was only then that she had started to wonder if Cam really was in some kind of terrible trouble. Up until that point, she had been telling herself not to panic. Given Cam's flair for hyperbole, he could make misplacing a credit card sound like a matter of life and death. But he *had* sounded different. She had figured it was just that she hadn't talked to him in so long. Or maybe he felt awkward because of the nasty way they'd parted. Hell, he *should* feel awkward. But the fact that he'd called her at all was what made her worry. If there was one thing she knew about Cam, it was that he would go to any length to avoid something unpleasant, especially something unpleasant from the past. If he was suddenly willing to call her for help, knowing full well that it would mean he'd have to face some hard questions, then something must really be wrong.

But what?

She'd just begun to hypothesize when she turned onto Cam's street, and into a sea of flashing red lights.

CHAPTER 2

Jack reached over and turned off the alarm clock the second it started to buzz. He'd been awake for hours. He'd awakened around 4:00 A.M. with a pounding headache and a sense of foreboding so strong it felt like someone was sitting on his chest. He was used to vague, intangible fear. He'd lived with it his entire adult life. Fear left over from a time when there was a reason for it, the way amputees still feel pain in a missing limb. But this was different. It was as if he'd been jarred awake by a loud noise, but he couldn't remember hearing anything.

And then he'd had the most ridiculous urge to call Cam. Where the hell had *that* come from? He hadn't seen or talked to Cam in ten years. He rarely even thought of Cam, and when he did, he still felt an anger bordering on rage. Why would he think of calling Cam? What did he think he'd say? *"Hey, asshole, it's the Ghost of Christmas Past. How's your cushy fucking life?"*

As soon as he'd sent those thoughts packing, his mind had begun to bombard him with memories of things he'd completely forgotten. Vignettes from his childhood, random and meaningless. Like fishing trips with his mother's twin brother, Uncle Ryland, the only member of the extended family who had ever acknowledged their existence. Ryland had adored the boys and they'd adored him, even if he was a certified loon. It was Uncle Ryland who had taken them to the Rotary Club–sponsored "Huck Finn Day" at Lake Allatoona, the one summer they'd managed to attend that much-heralded event. It was one of his few pleasant childhood memories. Their mother had dressed the four of them in matching overalls and different-colored plaid shirts, borrowed from Ryland's kids (cousins they'd never met), and they had passed themselves off as a normal family. Tallen caught the biggest fish of the day and got his picture in the paper. Probably the only time in his life Tallen had his picture in the paper without breaking a law. There was something about Tallen and fish. Ryland used to say that all Tallen had to do was *call* them.

Their father had been unimpressed. Said fish liked Tallen because they had so much in common—their main thought in life was how to keep from being caught. He also said Tallen wasn't any better at it than the fish were. He always seemed to have even more contempt for Tallen than for the rest of them, which was saying something. Jack's theory was that it was because Tallen so obviously worshiped Will. Will Landry was not comfortable with anyone's affection, and made it a point to punish those who bestowed it.

It suddenly dawned on Jack why he was thinking about them. He'd had that damned dream again. It had been worse than usual, in some way he couldn't remember. It would come back to him, though. The bad stuff always did.

The phone rang. It had to be Rick, the guy who owned the temp company through which Jack usually worked. Rick was the only person who had his number; the only reason he owned a phone (let alone an answering machine) was to find out whatever he needed to know about his next job. The machine picked up. He cringed at the sound of his own voice, as always, and waited for Rick's.

"Yeah . . . Jack . . . this guy called here looking for you . . . I told him I'd check with you and call him back. He sounded kinda . . . official."

Jack picked up the receiver.

"I don't care if he was the fucking president, Rick. How many times do we have to have this conversation?"

"Well, he said it was important."

"What do you *think* he's gonna say? This is an asshole reporter calling to annoy the shit out of him?"

"I just thought . . . I mean, do reporters still call you?"

Jack sighed. No use explaining to Rick why that wasn't the point. "This year is the tenth anniversary," he said with forced patience. "Reporters love crap like that." He didn't finish. Knew he didn't have to.

"Oh. God. Sorry, I didn't think of that."

"Well, start thinking. And don't give anyone my phone number. Anyone. Ever. No exceptions."

Rick apologized again and hung up.

Jack wrenched himself out of bed. The day was off to a lovely start.

He headed for the bathroom, hoping there was a bottle of aspirin in the medicine cabinet. He should keep a record, he supposed. Did he always wake up with a headache after the dream? If the headaches got worse, he'd have to go back to the pain clinic in Atlanta, and they'd ask him about things like that.

There were two aspirin left in the bottle. He swallowed them without water. He closed the cabinet and glanced at his face in the mirror. He looked like he hadn't slept at all. Felt like it, too. At least he didn't have to be anywhere early. The job he'd been working had finished yesterday, and he didn't start another one until Monday. He might pick up something for today if he went and stood in front of the Western Auto with all the other day-labor candidates. He didn't have to worry about getting there early. The black guys might sit out there for hours, but the minute a white guy showed up (even him), half the town would remember odd jobs that couldn't wait. Blond hair was all the résumé he needed.

He really didn't care whether he worked today or not. It had been a good month, and it wasn't like he needed to save for anything. Maybe he'd go down to the coffee shop. Maybe a decent breakfast and half a pot of black coffee would be enough of a bribe for his headache. Besides, the thought of being around other people was not as repulsive to him this morning as it usually was.

Half an hour later he was dressed and headed down Route 36, hands in his pockets, his work boots crunching the loose gravel on the side of the road. The early morning sky was a dull gray, and the fine mist that was falling felt good on his face. If it turned into a steady rain, he'd have a guilt-free excuse for not working.

"Men in the Rain." A poem Ethan had written when they were in high school. Something in it about walking along beneath John Deere caps ... dirt disturbed ... a final destination ... His mother had taped it to the refrigerator door for a couple of weeks. (Lucy had always gone out of her way to encourage their artistic pursuits. Anything to keep them inside, out of trouble.) He remembered the title because the rest of them had given Ethan a hard time about it, had made all sorts of insinuations about Ethan's sexual preferences. (Tallen, home during one of his brief bouts with freedom, had said "Go steal a car, Ethan. You'd *love* reform school.") What a joke. There had never been a shred of real doubt about any of them, as far as that went. Even Cam was a raging heterosexual.

Why the hell couldn't he get his mind off his family today? Most of the time he didn't think about them at all. He stuck militantly to the safe subjects: what should he eat, what should he read, where was he working tomorrow? Lately, more and more of the other stuff was slipping through the cracks. Was he getting careless? Or was it somehow safer now? He couldn't figure why it would be.

The dream was coming more often, too. He used to have it about three times a year. He'd already had it twice this month. He couldn't remember when it had started. Was it right after Ethan died? Or his father? Or Tallen? Hard to remember, he got the funerals mixed up. Not something he felt great about, but it was the truth.

Whenever it had started, he'd been having the dream for years. Some things about it varied, others remained doggedly consistent. It was always dark. He was always walking down some lonesome stretch of two-lane. Desolate. The sky more purple than black. Angry mountains in the distance. The whole scene always looked like one of those gloomy landscapes Tallen used to paint. Jack would walk along, not knowing where he was headed or why, and suddenly he'd come upon some colossal, gruesome accident. There were always red lights flashing everywhere. Sometimes he would see dozens of cars piled on top of each other, smashed and twisted, shards of glass and metal covering the ground like confetti. Other times, there would be no cars. Just the bodies. Bodies lying everywhere. Horrible-looking bodies— bloody, with limbs twisted or missing, some of them decapitated. And no one seemed to be helping them. He'd walk through the carnage, recognizing people from his past—old friends, teachers, distant relatives. At the end of the line, he'd always find them—Ethan, Tallen, his father, and later his mother. All badly mangled, reaching out for him, calling him, as if he could do something. He'd stare at them, and more than fear or horror or anything like that, the strongest feeling he'd have was always his wonder that he wasn't with them. Cam was never with them either, but that made sense. Cam had never been with them.

Even after it had become familiar, the dream would cling to him for days, like a filmy coat of something old and sour. He was sure the dream was symbolic as hell, and that it recurred because he didn't know what it meant. Sooner or later his subconscious would get the message that he didn't give a fuck what it meant, and would leave him the hell alone.

The coffee shop was not terribly crowded. He sat at the counter, where he was least likely to draw attention to himself.

"I knew you were gonna be here today." Sherry, the new waitress, was already pouring him a cup of coffee. She was an energetic redhead in her mid-twenties. Pretty, in a J. C. Penney's sort of way, but she talked too damned much.

"Why?"

"I don't know. Maybe I'm psychic." She fished her guest-check pad out of her apron pocket. "Let's see if I can guess. Two eggs, scrambled. Bacon. Wheat toast."

"Over easy, sausage, Sunbeam. Don't hang out your shingle just yet."

"You did that to be ornery."

"And a side of grits."

"I knew that."

She left to take the order to the kitchen. Jack watched her go, almost smiling to himself. She had only been working there for a couple of months. He guessed that she was new in town. It was the only possible explanation for the fact that she flirted with him. He responded mechanically. On those rare occasions when someone tried to engage him in conversation, his basic rule was not to piss them off. Easier to stay invisible if he just went with the flow.

Jack poured a little cream into his coffee and watched as it turned a smooth caramel color. From an unseen radio Reba McEntire was wailing about whatever man had done her wrong this week, over which floated all the usual country small talk. *"What ch'all know good? How's your mamma'n'em? Carter Rae, sit down in 'at chair fore I wear your tail out."* From somewhere else he could hear his mother's voice. *"Jackson Landry, would you please write the word* once *and show me where there's a* t *at the end of it? There aren't many things in life that I can control, but I will not have my boys talking like a bunch of ignorant country hicks."*

Sherry returned from the kitchen and went down the counter collecting saltshakers. She came back with a handful and stood in front of Jack to refill them.

"So, is it gonna rain?"

"You're the psychic, you tell me."

"Smart ass." She smiled as she said it. A plump, dark-haired waitress brushed by Sherry and nudged her with an elbow.

"I gotta talk to you." The woman disappeared into the kitchen without waiting for an answer.

"That's Darlene. She usually works the dinner shift."

Jack nodded, although he didn't know why she felt the need to explain it to him.

"She probably broke up with her boyfriend for the fifth time this week. Sonny Reynolds, you know him?"

Jack shook his head no, which he would have done even if he had known the guy.

"He's a prison guard over in Jackson." She leaned down and lowered her voice. "It must not take brains, he ain't got the sense God gave a June bug."

Jack stared at his coffee cup, lest his eyes yield any

clue that he didn't need to be told about prison guards. Sherry prattled on.

"I know she's no beauty queen or nothin', but she could sure do better than that ignoramus."

The door to the kitchen opened, and Darlene stuck her head out.

"Sherry." She gave Sherry a look that meant business and disappeared again. Sherry looked at Jack and rolled her eyes.

"I don't know how *I* got to be Dear Abby, neither."

She screwed the top on a saltshaker and, with an exasperated sigh, headed into the kitchen.

Jack took the opportunity to survey the breakfast crowd. The usual eclectic mix. Lawyers. Farmers. A couple of housewives and their kids. The janitors from the courthouse. He knew most of them by name—the lawyers and the janitors. He'd gone to school with them. The coffee shop divided into the same cliques the high school had. He'd felt so alienated from them all back then. He hadn't known anything.

Shit.

His least favorite coffee-shop regular—the priest from the postage stamp–sized Catholic church at the north end of town—had just situated himself a couple of stools away. As usual, "Father" was dressed in jeans and a plaid shirt over a thermal undershirt, sleeves rolled just right, like he thought he was a fucking lumberjack. The guy never wore his collar, and Jack wouldn't have known who he was except that it was impossible to move to Barton without being the buzz of the coffee shop for a couple of days. The previous priest had died three or four months ago—of a heart attack, a stroke, liver cancer, or AIDS, depending on which rumor one chose to believe. Father Casual had made his appearance a few weeks later. Jack had heard he'd transferred from New York

City and figured he must have screwed up royally to have been exiled to rural Georgia.

Jack rarely had the emotional energy to hate someone on sight, but he'd made an exception for Father. It was partly the clothes. It was also the John Lennon glasses and way too much hair for a guy who looked to be in his late forties. The thing that really iced it, though, was that this clown had taken some kind of personal interest in Jack that made his skin crawl. He couldn't count the number of times he'd looked up from a meal to find the guy staring, mesmerized.

Like now. Jack could feel the guy's gaze. He looked over, purposefully.

"Is there a reason you're staring at me?" Jack asked. He was not in the mood for this crap today.

The priest smiled and shook his head. "Sorry," he said. "I was thinking about people who sit at coffee-shop counters. You could divide the world that way. Like people who wear hats and people who don't."

Jack stood up. He walked along the counter, stopped at the empty stool next to the priest. "Look," he said, in his calmest voice, "I don't know whether you're trying to save me or fuck me, but either way the answer is 'no.' "

Without waiting for a reply, Jack turned and went back to his seat. He pushed his coffee down a couple of stools, just to emphasize his point. He didn't look back to see how Father was taking it.

The door to the kitchen opened, and Sherry returned, no longer smiling. She put his plate in front of him.

"Can I get you anything else?" she asked. The perkiness was gone from her voice.

"No. Thanks."

She tore his check out of her pad and laid it on the counter in front of him. He watched her as she went back to refilling saltshakers. She was spilling a lot more than she had been before. She glanced up and their eyes met. She quickly turned and busied herself checking coffee filters. Jack watched her with growing anxiety. A hazy suspicion was trying to form, but he pushed it away.

Suddenly Sherry was in front of him again. She crossed her arms and sighed as if she were disgusted.

"This is so dumb."

"What?"

"Darlene telling me how to run my life."

Jack relaxed a little. This was just some tiff between a couple of waitresses. He reached for his coffee cup and Sherry dropped the bombshell.

"She thinks I shouldn't talk to you."

Jack felt the muscles in his stomach contract as his dark fears were confirmed. Something in Sherry's eyes triggered an old anger. He caught it, turned it off.

"Fine." His voice was calm and quiet. "Don't talk to me."

"So, is it true, what she said?"

"I don't know what she said."

"You know. About your family."

"What about them?" He'd be damned if he was going to make it easy for her. If she had the nerve to bring it up, she was going to be the one to say it out loud.

"You know."

He stared at her, unflinching. She looked around to make sure no one was listening, then looked back at him and spoke quietly.

"She said you had a brother who was executed."

It had been a while since Jack had heard those words. They went through him like a cold wind. He didn't answer.

"She said it was a few years ago."

Ten. A decade. Another lifetime.

She looked at him, apparently waiting for a reply. When none came, she tried again.

"She said it was in Alabama."

"Well, Darlene's handier than *The World Book Encyclopedia,* isn't she?" His voice was still calm and steady, but it was an effort.

"He musta done something terrible."

Jack stood up and dropped more than enough money on the counter.

"You mean she left that out? Get her to fill you in, I'm sure it'd make her day."

Heading back down the road, he told himself it was his own fault. He never should have let himself get drawn into all of that. He could hear Tallen's voice from long ago: *"Why do you talk to them? They don't care about us, they're just looking for more gossip. We're their fucking entertainment."*

No matter where they'd lived, the Landrys had always been the family in town whose name was never spoken without *those* in front of it. Actually, Will Landry's name was usually spoken alone, in a tone that said all anyone needed to know. And most people felt sorry for Lucy, for all she had to endure. But the boys were *those Landrys.* A blight on the community. The kids everyone warned their kids to stay away from.

Jack couldn't even remember, really, how he and his brothers had first come to be disenfranchised youth. He remembered the earliest deeds, but not the compulsions. Maybe it was as simple as the fact that "juvenile delinquent" was an identity within their reach, and a negative identity was better than none at all. Or maybe it was because they'd all inherited Lucy's pride, and they simply couldn't stand the way people looked at them. Maybe they evoked people's ire to be spared their pity.

This notoriety had not been easily won. In rural Georgia, adolescent wildness was given a wide berth before it was looked on as anything other than good-old-boy-in-training behavior. Smoking and drinking and poaching a deer or two were hardly enough to raise any eyebrows, and getting laid at an early age was a matter of course. Drugs were a right step in the wrong direction—a step that all of them had taken as often as they could afford it. Upon realizing that the Landry brothers hurting *themselves* was not going to keep anyone up nights, they began to go that necessary extra mile. They hot-wired cars for joyrides, leaving them wherever they happened to get bored. They vandalized property. (Turning over the Coke machine in the basement of the courthouse was one of their favorite minor pastimes, as it provided just the right "fuck you" to the proper authorities.) They committed all sorts of petty thefts and burglaries. Nothing hard-core in those early years. They left themselves something to aspire to.

None of this, of course, applied to Saint Cam. It wasn't like he openly sided against them, or ratted on them when he knew something. He mostly stayed in his room and ignored them. But whenever he'd have occasion to meet their eyes, he'd give them a look that left no doubt as to the degree of his scorn. They'd made his path difficult, and he made sure they knew he hated them for it. Meanwhile, he studied hard, kept his nose clean, and walked around with his put-upon attitude, as if nothing short of some great cosmic blunder could have landed him in a house with these people.

The truth was, Cam knew better than that, he just chose to ignore it. He was too bright and too close to the source to be able to write them all off the way the rest of the world did. He couldn't look at them and say "white trash lowlife, end of story." He knew damned well that wasn't the end of the story. It wasn't even the beginning.

Jack wasn't really sure where it began himself. Maybe

it had to do with the polarity of his parents: Lucy, a sensitive and delicate beauty from an old Savannah family that no longer had any money, but whose remaining forty acres allowed them to keep thinking of themselves as landed gentry. (They'd all disowned her when she'd married Will.) And Will, a lone hellcat of a man whose only parent had been a mentally unbalanced daughter of sharecroppers; he'd never known anything but poverty and rejection—a fact he did not accept quietly. The two of them had been attracted to each other because of their vast differences, and then spent the rest of their lives trying to kill each other for them.

The boys had grown up caught in the middle. Lucy did everything to encourage the artistic inclinations they all seemed to have inherited from her—Cam's prose, Ethan's poetry, Tallen's painting, Jack's love for reading. Will thwarted her efforts at every turn; he was violently opposed to anything that made his sons look unmanly. He'd never managed to beat the art out of them (though God knows he'd tried), but he'd successfully trained them to sabotage their own efforts. All of them except Cam.

As far as Jack was able to figure, the difference was that Cam had used his talent to pull himself out, and the rest of them had clung to art as a source of comfort in the prison they thought they had no hope of escaping. Was it really that simple? he wondered, thinking about it now. Did it all boil down to the fact that Cam had felt hope and the rest of them hadn't? And, if so, where had that hope come from? Was it something a person was born with, like blue eyes? Had the rest of them just been born without it? Where was the justice in that?

He chuckled to himself. Justice. What in God's name was it going to take for him to stop considering the possibility that somewhere, somehow, the world was fair and life made sense? The truth didn't have to be fair. The truth could be that Cam had been born with a chance and the rest of them hadn't. Cam wouldn't have liked that theory much; it would have deprived him of the right to feel superior.

Well, none of it mattered now. The accident-waiting-to-happen they'd called a family had exploded. Jack and Cam had been the surviving debris, hurled in opposite directions, landing intact, but not whole. Now Jack spent his days going through the motions of living, never really sure why he bothered. And somewhere out there, Cam was busy turning his life into a quest for vindication. Maybe he'd even gotten it. Well . . . fine. Good for him.

The drizzle had turned into a steady rain, and Jack could feel the wet chambray of his work shirt beginning to stick to his back. He'd be drenched by the time he got home. What the hell. This day had never had any intention of being on his side.

Suddenly it came to him. The thing that had been different about the dream last night. He didn't know why it had left him so upset, but he knew what was different. Last night, for the first time, Cam's body had been on the pile, too.

CHAPTER 3

Randa managed to get a couple of hours of sleep before it was time to go to work. She woke with a fuzzy knowledge that something dreadful had happened, but for a moment she couldn't remember what it was. When she did remember, she had a moment of hope that it had been a nightmare. She saw the jeans and blouse she'd worn draped over the chair and that hope dissolved, leaving her with the crushing reality.

Cam was gone. Even more than he had already been gone. She wondered how many years it would take before she wouldn't even remember what he'd looked like, or the sound of his voice. Or the tiny scar on his chin she'd never asked him about. Or the way he crinkled his nose when she said something that annoyed him. Or the way he stared at his hands when he lied.

She wished, like she'd wished a year ago, she'd had a chance to say good-bye. The man from the coroner's office had told her that they wouldn't release Cam's body until after they had spent a reasonable amount of time trying to find Jack, so Randa knew there was no funeral planned. There would probably be some sort of a memorial service that she could go to if she made an issue of it; but whenever she imagined it, she could see herself alone in a corner, watching people console Nora. No thanks.

She decided to go to work, since the alternative was sitting around in her apartment making herself crazy. She showered and dressed in layers of black—black leggings, black boots, black oversized turtleneck sweater. The contrast between the dark clothes and her crop of shoulder-length, wheat-colored hair might compensate for something. She stared in the mirror at her pale, sleep-deprived skin and exhausted eyes, and decided any energy spent on makeup would be wasted. She brushed some peach-colored blush over her cheekbones and said to hell with it.

She dialed the paper and asked to speak to Roger Eglee, the managing editor. She had to start somewhere, and Roger was a friend. At least, he seemed to be. She no longer put her faith in things like that.

"Okay," Roger said as soon as he picked up the phone, "what creative excuse have you come up with for missing the staff meeting?"

"It's pretty creative," she answered in a flat voice. "Cam's dead."

"What?"

"He killed himself. Last night."

"Oh, my God." Roger was one of Cam's poker buddies, although he'd been quick to side with Randa when everything had blown up. "Oh, my God. Randa. I can't believe it. What happened?"

She proceeded to tell him the whole story, including the part about the police station and the liquor store, which sounded even more preposterous as she recounted it. She asked him to spread it around the office before she got there, so she wouldn't have to go through telling it again. Told him she'd be in soon, then hung up before he could argue with her about it.

Half an hour later, Randa parked her five-year-old Volvo behind the ratty two-story building that housed the *Chronicle*'s offices and printing presses. The building was on the east end of Sunset, in a neighborhood where Randa definitely had to get in her car and drive if she wanted anything other than a greasy burrito for lunch. But she had always liked the old building. It wouldn't have made sense for the paper to be in some spanking clean, architecturally barren building on Ventura Boulevard. Creativity thrived in an underdog environment, and this old firetrap certainly provided that.

They were an odd bunch, the people who wrote for the *Chronicle*. Like most members of the alternative press, they thought of themselves as "real" writers. They tolerated rival journalists (barely), but looked down on their peers who sold out for the big bucks (and bigger compromises) of Hollywood. (The *Chronicle* writers thought of the screenwriters as whores, the screenwriters thought of the *Chronicle* writers as permanent adolescents, and neither group was entirely wrong.) For Randa's part, the job provided her with two things she craved—freedom and respect. She knew that she wasn't likely to find either anywhere else.

There was an eerie feeling in the air as Randa made her way through the newsroom. There were no radios blaring, no laughter coming from the offices, none of the "we're-not-the-stuffy-Republican-*LA-Times*" atmosphere that usually prevailed. Randa could see people looking at her out of the corners of their eyes. She stared straight ahead and walked quickly to the relative security of her tiny, cluttered office.

The call to Roger hadn't ended up buying her much. The minute she sat down at her desk, her office was filled with people who wanted all the gory details—gawkers chancing upon a grisly car wreck. She'd given them a few perfunctory answers, but made it clear she didn't enjoy talking about it. Finally the vultures cleared out, and she was left with a couple of Cam's actual friends. Barely an improvement, all things considered.

Tom Heller, the paper's film critic, sat in a corner and stared at the wall. Ever since Randa and Cam had parted, Tom had been actively avoiding her, wasting little energy on subtlety. He had adopted Nora's version of the story like it was the latest software upgrade. (According to Nora, Randa's only reason for being attracted to Cam was the criminal history of his family. Randa supposed that made her a first cousin to those fat-women-prison-groupies. A wimpy first cousin, though, who didn't even have the guts to go for the real thing.) In truth, Tom had never liked her anyway, and now he had something concrete to pin it on. She was sure he was currently unhappy about the fact that the pseudo-wake had ended up in her office. It made her grateful for Roger, who was sitting on the corner of her desk, picking the eraser off a pencil and shaking his head over and over.

"I just can't believe it," he said for the dozenth time. He looked ill; but then, Roger was a man who, under the best of circumstances, looked like he was on his way to a CAT scan. "This must be awful for you," he said to Randa.

She nodded, a bit embarrassed. Since Tom considered her grief to be psychotic, it wasn't a topic she wanted brought up for discussion.

Tom looked at Roger as if Randa weren't in the room. "I must have left him ten messages this week. I should have gone over there. I just never would have thought . . ."

"No one would have," Roger assured him.

"I don't get it." Tom shook his head. "Why now? His career was taking off, he had finally gotten into a decent relationship . . ."

Randa winced. *You vindictive asshole.* Roger sensed the tension and jumped in.

"Do you have any idea why he would have called Randa out of the blue?" Roger was diplomatically trying to acknowledge Randa's existence.

"No." Tom looked at her, finally. "He hadn't mentioned you in a long time."

It was another shot. Roger didn't notice this time. He was lost in his own thoughts.

"This whole liquor store thing is from Jupiter. The LAPD branches out, now they violate your rights posthumously."

Tom nodded. "They had some candy-assed case they wanted off the books, they found out a little about Cam, and they just used him."

"They said they found the gun in his apartment," Randa offered. She wasn't trying to incriminate Cam, but an explanation would be a nice thing to live with.

"They did?" Tom's tone was mocking. "Well, that clinches it. The LAPD certainly wouldn't lie."

Randa told herself that Tom was extremely upset about Cam and held her tongue.

George Maynard appeared in the doorway. George was the paper's insufferably conceited music critic, whom Cam had always described as "the most obnoxious person I know who I like anyway." Randa agreed with the first half of that.

"What the *hell* is going on? Is it true?"

Roger nodded glumly. "Yeah."

"Christ. I don't believe it." George removed his wire-rimmed glasses in a gesture that seemed calculated. He and Cam had never been particularly close, but there was no way he was going to miss the melodrama. It fascinated Randa, the way people vie for custody of the friendship of anyone who dies young or tragically. George, putting in his bid, came into the office and pulled up a chair. "So . . . what? Does anybody believe this?"

"No one believes he robbed a liquor store," Roger answered. "I mean, come on . . ."

"Well, maybe he did." George had an endearing habit of switching positions the minute anyone agreed with him. "Maybe it was like Attack-of-the-Runaway-Gene-Pool."

"George." Roger gave him a look of contempt.

"Well, I'm sorry, but this shit is just too weird." He looked at Randa. "Somebody said you were there."

"No. I mean, I was, but—I got there, right after . . ." She didn't know how to finish, so she didn't.

"What were you doing there?" George asked, as if he were conducting a senate hearing.

"She thinks he called her." Tom answered for her. Randa looked at him, stunned.

"What is that supposed to mean?" she asked, trying to stay calm.

"Maybe it was someone else, you were half asleep and you thought it was Cam."

Randa could barely believe what she was hearing.

"Why on earth do you need to come up with some far-fetched theory like that?"

"Because it doesn't make any sense that he would have called you, not after . . ."

Randa knew exactly what he had stopped himself from saying.

"Not after he had finally gotten rid of me?"

Tom did not appear embarrassed. He said, simply, "I wasn't going to put it like that."

It was all Randa could take.

"Dammit!" She picked up a notebook from her desk and hurled it at the wall, where it crashed and sent paper flying. The guys were all too stunned to move. "What is it with you people? I have a right to my own damned emotions!"

Tom was the first to find his voice. "Randa, calm down! Jesus!"

"I'll calm down when you stop treating me like I'm some fifteen-year-old who got a crush on Cam and followed him around like a lovesick sheepdog!"

"I never said—"

"Don't tell me what you never said! Do you think the things you said didn't get back to me?"

"What things?"

"That I'm weird, I'm a nutcase, that I was only attracted to Cam because I have some kind of sick obsession with his family! All that shit you bought from Nora because she batted her fucking eyelashes at you, and who

could blame you, you'd known her a good fifteen minutes, how could she be lying? All that shit you needed to
tell yourselves or tell Cam so you could all erase me and
never give it a second thought! I heard every word of it
and you knew damned well that I'd hear it!" She grabbed
her purse and stood up. "How I felt about Cam and why I
felt it was nobody's fucking business a year ago and it's
nobody's fucking business now!" She marched out,
slamming the door as hard as she could.

She sat in her car and took deep breaths. Now she'd done
it. It might have felt good for five minutes, but those five
minutes were not going to come cheaply. Now Tom was
really going to be after her scalp. Well, to hell with it. If
she got fired she could go find herself a job with a salary
she could tell someone with a straight face.

Truth be told, she had no idea what the fallout from
this was going to be. She had no history of outbursts. To
the contrary, she usually chewed her nails and internalized and, she presumed, planted the seeds of future
ulcers. Or she'd take all she could and march off to confront the source of her distress, only to have her throat
close and her eyes well up the moment she tried to speak.
That was why she had become a writer in the first place.
It was the only way she'd ever found to have a voice. It
wasn't enough, but it was a valve that let off enough
steam to keep her from exploding.

Randa didn't want to sit there in the parking lot, but
she didn't know what to do with herself. She didn't want
to go home and be alone, but she didn't feel up to being
around other people, either. She'd drive. She'd just drive.

Driving always made her feel better. It was a way to
have a connection to the world without having to participate. She especially loved to drive in LA, where the landscapes changed vividly from one neighborhood to the

next. The lost souls wandering down Hollywood Boulevard. Overdressed agents lunching with disgruntled clients at the outdoor cafés on Sunset Plaza, all of them happy enough to see and be seen; breathing carbon monoxide was a small price to pay. Tanned, muscular guys in tight jeans, strolling down Santa Monica Boulevard with their arms around each other. Beverly Hills housewives dressed in their Chanel suits, on their way to lunch at the Beverly Wilshire before the Ferragamo trunk show at Saks. The Santa Monica promenade, with its bizarre mix: yuppies; beach bums; panhandlers; an occasional schizophrenic preaching fervently to a nonexistent congregation.

Randa had never been able to understand how anyone could hate LA. Smog, traffic, and earthquakes seemed minor concessions for a place that offered so much freedom. She had grown up in Asbury, Georgia: one stoplight, one drugstore, two gas stations, fifteen churches, ten of which were Baptist. Twelve hundred people, the majority of whom imposed a strict code of ethics on the rest, and saw to it that anyone who tested its limits paid a heavy price. As far as Randa was concerned, LA was the promised land.

She drove aimlessly for about an hour, then paid a guy in a red vest three dollars for the privilege of parking at the Santa Monica pier, where she could stare out at the ocean. She did that until she was bored, then leaned her head back on the headrest and closed her eyes. She gave it a moment, then made a conscious decision to let herself remember.

Cam had come into her life eight years ago. More precisely, she had come into his. She had happened upon a book he'd written during one of her book-buying orgies (her regular cure for depression). She usually avoided mysteries (she drove herself crazy trying to figure them out);

but she had seen his book on the "Recommended" shelf at Book Soup and had been intrigued by his name. "Cameron Landry" seemed far too poetic for a mystery writer. When she read on the jacket flap that he was also from Georgia, she decided to give it a shot. The book had startled her with its complexity and insight. She was also drawn to its darkness—its bleak themes and haunted characters.

Randa had been attracted to darkness from an early age. Maybe it was just from having grown up in the South, where people clung to morbid fascinations and superstitions as if they were consolation prizes from the Civil War. (A just God would never have tolerated Sherman's rampage, so there had to be powerful dark forces at work that protected Yankees and other agents of evil.) Or maybe it was growing up in her family, where everyone practically worshiped at the altars of depression and morbidity. (The only song Randa could ever remember her mother singing to her was called "Put My Little Shoes Away"—a song about a child who knew he was dying.) Whatever the reason, something about the darkness soothed her like a lullaby, and she sought refuge in it by whatever safe means she could find.

The darkness in Randa's soul had been quick to respond to the darkness in Cameron Landry's prose. She immediately bought his other three books and read them, then pestered everyone at the paper until they let her write a story about him.

She scheduled an interview through his literary agent, then went online and ferreted out every article ever written about him and every interview he'd ever done. The reviews of his books were consistently effusive. People who cared about such things compared him to Ross Macdonald, Raymond Chandler, Dashiell Hammett. A reviewer in one of the magazines for mystery

buffs swore that Landry would leave them all in the dust
before it was over.

Very little had been written about the man himself.
He'd grown up in several small towns in rural Georgia, the
youngest of four brothers in a working-class family. He'd
read a lot, he was good in English, a teacher had encouraged him, he decided to become a writer, and so on. No in-
dication of where that dark vision had been born.

As she continued to search the computer indexes for
anything more enlightening, she came across another
Landry, one whose name had an even more poetic lilt:
Tallen Landry. She didn't know if it was a man or a
woman, but she loved the sound of it. When she saw it
the second time, she decided to detour and find out.

She typed the name into the computer and brought up
the first citation. It was an eight-year-old article from
Texas Monthly entitled "The Impact of Capital Punishment on the Families of Death Row Inmates." It had been
written by an SMU sociology professor, a Dr. Karl
Wiedergott, who had interviewed fifty families of condemned men and women and compiled a study about
their emotional and physiological reactions. Near the end
of the article, Tallen Landry was identified as a convicted
murderer who had been executed in Alabama a couple of
years before. (What an irony, she thought, for a murderer
to have such a lovely name.) The professor had interviewed a couple of Tallen's cousins and some family
friends, but said that members of the immediate family
had refused to talk with anyone. Randa was about to exit
the article when something in the next paragraph caught
her eye. Tallen Landry was more specifically identified
as the second of four sons from a working-class family in
rural Georgia. Randa stared at the paper, amazed. Surely
it was a coincidence? *Landry* wasn't a particularly
unusual name, and Georgia was not a small state. Still, if

there was any connection at all, it would certainly shed some light on the workings of Cameron Landry's mind.

A week later, at the appointed time, she sat at a table at Musso & Frank, poring over her notes and nervously chewing the ice from her water glass. She was surprised to see the maître d' showing a tall guy in a brown leather jacket and black Ray-Bans over to her table. She had certainly not expected him to be on time. He smiled warmly and offered his hand (*"Hi, I'm Cam Landry. I'm not late, am I?"*), then slid into the booth across from her. He didn't look anything like she'd expected, although she didn't know what she had expected. His hair was very dark brown, almost black, just long enough to look artistically unkempt. It had a lot of gray in it for a man his age (which, from the articles she'd read, she knew to be thirty-one). His face was perfectly shaped, with sharp features, and his skin looked as if it had never seen the light of day. And then he had taken off his sunglasses and she'd seen those eyes, and all other physical attributes were rendered unimportant.

When they started to talk, she was amazed at how they found an instant rhythm, and it seemed to have nothing to do with their common heritage or the fact that they both had cousins in Polk County. By the time the food came, they were finishing each other's sentences.

The one thing he didn't want to talk about was the content of his work. Whenever Randa tried to get into the material in any depth, Cam would quickly and adroitly change the subject. No wonder the articles she'd found had not gone beneath the surface.

After dinner they ordered margaritas and swapped war stories from their careers. When it had started to get late and he still hadn't mentioned his family, she finally asked about them. He shrugged. "They're all dead."

"Well, who were they when they were alive?"

He shook his head. "A sorry bunch of people. Don't waste your time."

"A lot of great writers have come from sorry bunches of people."

"Yeah, well . . ." He looked away. "Actually, my mother was okay." He seemed to be saying it to himself. "She just . . ."

"What?"

"She thought she was very selfless, and maybe she was . . . but she put all her effort into maintaining her dignity in a horrible situation instead of trying to get *out* of the horrible situation, you know?" He looked away again. The energy had definitely shifted. Randa decided to go for it.

"By any chance, are you related to Tallen Landry?"

He didn't move, but she could see the muscles in his jaw go tense. Finally, without turning back to her, he said, "How did you know that?"

"I came across an article. I saw that you were both from Georgia and both had three brothers, so I thought there might be a chance . . ."

After a long moment he turned and looked at her again. He didn't look angry. Maybe a little defeated.

"I don't suppose it would do any good to ask you not to mention it."

Randa didn't answer. God, this stroke of luck, this great angle, and he wanted her to just ignore it. She didn't know him. She didn't owe him anything. So why did she feel she couldn't betray an unspoken loyalty?

He picked up his sunglasses. "I know, it's a ridiculous thing for me to ask. You're obviously very good at your job." Before she could figure out what to say, he was gone. She watched him go, knowing it would do no good to call him back.

For days after that she'd found herself missing him.

How she could miss someone she didn't know was a mystery to her, but she did. She'd almost managed to clear it from her mind when, about a month after their dinner, she was surprised to get a phone call from him at her office.

"What happened to the article?" he asked, without any preamble.

"I scrapped it."

"Why?"

"I didn't think I could write it honestly if I didn't go into your background, and I didn't think I could sleep well if I did." He didn't say anything, so she added, "I'm sure you've been through enough."

"You don't even know me." He sounded incredulous, and impressed.

She thought about it and decided to risk him thinking she was nuts. "I know, but I feel like I do. I know it sounds crazy, but the minute you sat in that booth, I thought, 'Oh yeah, there's Cam.' I can't explain it, it was weird."

"I know. I felt the same way. It wasn't like we just met, it was like we were . . . reunited. I almost said something about it, but I was afraid you'd think I was coming on to you."

She might as well go for broke. "Maybe I wouldn't have minded that."

"Yeah, but my wife probably would have."

Damn. Of course he was married. She felt like a fool. But then, he hadn't exactly mentioned it at dinner.

"Are you still there?" he asked.

"Yes."

"Listen, let's get together again. I'll give you the real interview."

"Why?"

"I don't know. I guess I trust you not to turn it into a

three-ring circus. And it's probably time for me to stop hiding from it. Maybe that's why you came along."

They had met for dinner a few days later, and he'd told her the story (*"In broad strokes, okay? I can't go through it in detail, I just can't."*). It was a fascinating story, if relentlessly disturbing. Cam told it without much emotion; she guessed it was a self-preservation instinct. He told her about his father, Will Landry, a violent drunk who had brutalized the family. His mother, Lucy, a classic martyr/enabler who was more terrified of Will than of what he was doing to the rest of them. His brothers, marauding delinquents who had terrorized the neighborhoods in which they had lived. Each of them, however, had been artistically gifted in one way or another. He told her about Ethan, who was almost as talented a poet as he was a cat burglar. Tallen, who had grown up in reform schools and graduated to prisons, painted mesmerizing, melancholy landscapes that screamed of loneliness. He had been the most sensitive, and therefore the most troubled. (The rest of Tallen's story, Cam had said, she could read in the papers.) And then there was Jack, his oldest brother, who had always been a complete mystery to Cam. It was partly because of the age difference, but mostly because Jack had hated Cam too much to reveal anything to him. Jack was the only one who hadn't done anything artistic, although he'd been a voracious reader. Jack had never *done* much of anything, but he seemed to turn observing into an art form of its own.

Ethan and Will had both died the same year. Ethan had drowned (Cam supplied no details), and Will had committed suicide a few months later. Lucy had also killed herself, on the anniversary of Tallen's execution. Jack still lived in Georgia, as far as Cam knew. Cam hadn't seen him since Lucy's funeral. They had gotten into a bitter argument just as Cam was leaving, and he'd said some things he later regretted. He had written Jack a long, apologetic letter. It had come back marked MOVED—NO FORWARDING ADDRESS. He had tried to find Jack a couple of times, with no luck. He knew Jack didn't want to be found and figured he'd never see Jack again. It didn't bother him, or so he claimed.

Cam wouldn't offer much about how he had managed to escape unscathed. He attributed it to the age difference between him and the next oldest (five years) or the fact that Will had been kinder to Cam than he had to the others, probably because Will knew it was his last chance to have a son he got along with. Cam said he remembered realizing at a very early age that his family was crazy and saying, "I'll be in my room until I'm eighteen, then I'm out of here." He had kept that promise and had not done a lot of looking back.

The article about Cam had turned out to be one of the best things Randa had ever written. It caused a bit of a stir for a while, but Cam kept reassuring her that he was not sorry he'd given her the interview. He said it had been very "freeing." It had also bought him a lot of free publicity, but he didn't seem to think like that, as far as she could tell.

Not long after her article appeared, Cam's marriage had broken up. She never knew if there was any connection because he never wanted to talk about it. He just kept saying that it had been coming for a long time. Randa never even met Cam's wife. All she knew was that her name was Terri and she was or wanted to be an artist. Through a couple of cryptic comments he'd made, she also suspected that Terri had never been very faithful (although, by his own admission, neither had Cam) and that she had some kind of chemical dependency. All in all, it sounded like Cam was better off without her.

When Cam and Terri broke up, Randa was living with

Evan, a screenwriter who made a fortune writing movies that were never made. The first time Randa had asked Evan if he loved her, he'd said he didn't know what love meant. When he was still saying it two years later, she moved out. The irony was that she wasn't sure she loved him either, but she wanted the option.

Next she'd taken up with David, a studio musician who'd fascinated her because he was brooding and mysterious. When it had finally become apparent to her that he was merely brooding, she decided to chalk up another waste of time and move on. David hadn't minded much. It gave him something new to brood about.

While Randa was with David, Cam went through a country singer, a publicist, a freelance photographer and, for the sake of cliché, several flight attendants. Not necessarily in that order and not necessarily one at a time.

Through all of this, Randa and Cam remained fast friends. They got together at least once a week to share their successes, bemoan their losses, or to critique movies they'd seen, books they'd read, or to vent about the state of the world in general. They also took each other to anything their mates didn't want to go to, since they both always seemed to hook up with people with whom they had little in common. Their mates were always required to live with this arrangement, and only the most insecure of them had ever felt threatened by it.

Randa wasn't sure when she had realized that she was in love with Cam. There wasn't any specific moment, just a sort of growing awareness; she'd admitted it to herself so gradually that at some point it simply became a given that she was in love with Cam, that she had been in love with Cam since the moment she'd met him. It didn't really matter *when* she'd known it, because there was nothing to be done about it. Cam had never shown even the slightest glimmer of being romantically interested in her, and there was no way in hell she was going to make a fool of herself by saying or doing anything to call his attention to the fact. As long as they were friends, he'd be in her life. She wasn't about to give him a chance to reject her.

When Randa and David broke up, three days before her thirty-third birthday, Cam took her out to dinner, to "mourn or celebrate, whichever you want." They'd gone to an Italian restaurant on Melrose whose only distinction was that it was possibly the darkest restaurant in the greater Los Angeles area. Randa always complained that every restaurant in LA was lit like a Kmart, and Cam wanted to prove to her that she hadn't been going to the right places. They'd sat on the same side of a large red-leather booth and picked at whitefish while Randa complained about her lousy luck with men.

"You don't have bad luck," Cam informed her. "You have bad taste."

"Gee, that cuts so deep, coming from someone whose entire romantic history combined couldn't produce the IQ of an Irish setter."

"We're not talking about me, we're talking about you." He was swirling the ice cubes around in his margarita; he seemed oddly serious. "Do you think you ever really loved this jerk?"

Randa didn't have to think. "No. I loved the idea of being in love with a tortured artiste. I figured that out months ago."

"Then why didn't you break up with him months ago?"

"I don't know. I guess I didn't feel like going through all the drama. Not to mention having to find another apartment." Randa was still living in the apartment she shared with David, sleeping on the couch. Not a comfortable arrangement on any level.

"Why don't you buy a condo in my building? There's one for sale right below me."

"Right. All I need is to move into your lovely, crime-infested neighborhood."

"We could see each other more often."

"Translated: I could feed your cat when you go out of town."

He smiled. "You're such a cynic." He put his fork down and stared at her for a moment, suddenly quite serious. "You really look pretty tonight."

She smiled back. He was just trying to make her feel better, but she appreciated it. "Thanks. I guess self-pity becomes me. Enough of my stupid life. How are you?"

"Oh, you know. My usual cheery self."

"How's Patty?" Patty was Cam's latest girlfriend. She was a waitress at a health-food restaurant (which didn't explain where Cam had met her) who fervently believed there wasn't a problem on the planet that couldn't be cured by the right combination of herbs. Randa and David had gone out with them a couple of times. Randa was still trying to be open-minded.

"I don't know," Cam answered. "I guess you'd have to ask Richard."

"Who's Richard?"

"The New Age weight trainer she dumped me for."

"Oh, no." Randa could not possibly bring herself to say she was sorry. "Are you serious?"

Cam nodded. "She doesn't know if she loves him, but she thinks they have karmic debts to settle. And he's going to teach her how to have an out-of-body experience."

"Cam, Patty has never had an *in*-body experience. I always thought someone should hire her to plug that hole in the ozone layer, as long as she was up there anyway."

"Yeah, well . . ."

"Don't."

"Don't what?"

"You're just trying to figure out what you can do with 'plug' and 'hole,' and I don't want to hear it."

Cam laughed, confirming her suspicion. "You know me too well."

"Yeah, I probably do."

They sat in silence for a moment, then Cam got that serious expression on his face again. "Do you realize this is the first time since we've known each other that we've both been single at the same time?"

Randa hadn't thought about it. "Yeah, I guess it is."

Cam picked up his fork, then put it down again. He looked at Randa, then shifted to face her. When he spoke, his voice was different, almost tentative. "Have you ever wondered what we'd be like . . . you know, as a couple?"

Randa had to remind herself to breathe.

"Yeah, I've wondered. But I thought you . . ." Her voice trailed off.

"What?"

"I thought you didn't think of me, you know, like that."

"I thought *you* didn't think of *me* like that." They both smiled at the irony. "So, what do you think? How would we be?"

"I think . . . we'd be great." Randa said it in a quiet voice, wondering if that was the answer he had expected. Cam smiled, and reached down and took her hand. She didn't have the presence of mind to feel awkward about it.

"See, I think the reason I keep getting into these stupid relationships is that I don't care who I'm with if I can't be with you." He smiled self-consciously. "I never said anything because I was afraid of what your reaction would be."

Randa heard the words, but she kept waiting for the punch line. This couldn't possibly be real.

"Cam," she'd managed to say, "tell me this isn't a joke."

"Of course it's not a joke." He reached up and pushed a strand of hair away from her face; she felt the back of his hand brush her cheek. Her eyes were beginning to well and Cam's face was a blur. He kissed her, before she even had time to wonder if he was going to. Then he'd smiled and said, "God, I've been wanting to do that for so long."

"Me too," she'd whispered, afraid saying it out loud might jinx something. She could have died happily on the spot. Many times since then, she'd wished she had.

She hadn't gone back to his place. It was too much at once, she had to let it settle. They made a date to have dinner the next night and she'd been like a zombie all day, checking her watch every fifteen minutes until it was time to go.

She still couldn't think about that night without her throat tightening up. When she'd knocked on the door, Cam had opened it instantly and pulled her inside. He'd thrown his arms around her and they'd stood there and made out like teenagers for what seemed like ages. Randa would try to make herself pull away, but she couldn't. To be kissing Cam after all these years; she couldn't believe it long enough to know what it felt like. Dinner hadn't happened. Neither of them had ever mentioned it.

The scene in Randa's mind vanished suddenly, as if the film had snapped in the projector. She couldn't bear to think any farther than that. The tears she'd been holding back broke through and slid down her face; they felt like an invasion, but she couldn't bring herself to wipe them away.

She sat in her car for a long time, watching the ocean, trying to lose herself in the waves that rolled onto the sand one after another, effortlessly, as if this were any normal day.

CHAPTER 4

Nick Varella answered the door with a scotch in his hand, very obviously not his first of the day. He had a two-days' growth of beard and his dark hair looked as if he'd just been in a strong wind. Randa had heard about Nick for years, but had never met him or even seen him before. He was the best friend Cam had, but not in a conventional way. They only got together about four times a year, but Randa knew that Cam told Nick things he never told anyone else. (Probably because whenever they met the main objective was to see who could consume the largest amount of alcohol in the shortest amount of time.) Even though their careers were roughly parallel (Nick's science fiction novels were as respected in that genre as Cam's crime novels were in theirs), Cam considered Nick a mentor. Or maybe a surrogate brother. At any rate, Cam had thought of Nick as some sort of soul mate, and had talked about him until Randa felt she knew him. At least, she had until he had answered the door and she was faced with having to explain her presence.

"I'm sorry to bother you. I'm Randa Phillips." She saw no reason to beat around the bush.

"Oh. Wow. Hi." He was staring at her, his eyebrows arched in a way she couldn't interpret. Maybe it just had to do with being thrown a curve when he was too drunk to handle it. Or maybe no one ever dropped in on him; he was a notorious hermit. She could hear loud music coming from the back of the house, and it suddenly occurred to her that he might not be alone. That possibility hadn't entered her mind when she'd decided to go to see him. *God, can't you ever think anything through?*

"I wondered if I could . . ." What? She hadn't really thought about what she'd say. *Don't go unconscious and act like an idiot. Just tell him the truth.* "I know you don't know me and I know this is a bad time, but I have to talk to someone. I can't stand another minute alone with this."

He just kept staring at her. She suddenly felt very foolish. "I'm sorry, this was a stupid idea." She turned to leave, but he grabbed her elbow.

"No. Don't go. I'm just . . . I'm not very good at spontaneity." He held up the drink by way of explanation. "I'm also not thinking all that clearly, thank God." He finally smiled. "Wanna join me?"

She managed to smile back. "With all my heart."

He opened the door wider and motioned her inside. He led her down a narrow hall into a room that, judging by the advanced degree of clutter, was where he spent most of his time. The music was coming from an elaborate stereo system against the back wall. It was loud, angry heavy metal; raspy voices screaming unintelligible lyrics.

Nick went straight to the makeshift bar and started tossing ice cubes into a glass. "If you don't mind a drunken observation, you're even prettier than I'd heard."

It stung, the thought that Cam had told Nick that she was pretty. She forced a smile. "Thanks."

"What can I pour you, given I don't have anything dainty?"

What difference does it make? "Do you have any tequila?"

He shot her a look. "Now, what do you think?" He had

already picked up a bottle of Cuervo Gold. "You're not expecting me to mix it with anything that would require concentration, I hope."

"Straight is fine." The music was already wearing on her nerves. Nick poured the glass half full and handed it to her. He lifted his glass in a semi-toast.

"Well . . . Life sucks." With that he downed half a glass of scotch. Randa sipped the tequila. The slow burn felt great; she followed it with a healthy slug.

"I've always wanted to meet you." It would have sounded dumb even if she hadn't had to shout.

"Yeah. I wanted to meet you, too. Just not bad enough to go to one of Cam's parties. He probably told you I can't be in a room with more than three people. With special dispensation for strip joints." He polished off the rest of the scotch with ease. "Guess I'll have to add funeral parlors to the list."

She couldn't decide whether she liked him or not, but straining to hear made it hard to think. She pointed to the stereo.

"Could you maybe turn the music down a little?"

"Why?"

"So we won't have to shout."

"It's good for you."

She'd had this exact conversation with Cam, more times than she could count. She wasn't in the mood for it.

"I'm really not up to fighting with anything."

He shrugged and went over to the stereo. "This is very controlling behavior," he said, as he lowered the volume. Randa burst into tears.

Nick immediately turned the stereo off, came over and put his arms around her. "I'm sorry. I was kidding. I'm really sorry."

"Cam used to say that." It came out in a choked whisper.

"I know," Nick said, rocking her gently. "That's where I got it." Now that she was close enough to tell, his eyes were none too dry either.

They sat in a booth in a tiny Spanish restaurant on Alameda and shared a pitcher of something that was supposed to be sangria. Randa felt pretty sure it was actually cheap burgundy someone had poured into a pitcher along with a can of fruit cocktail, but if it would anesthetize her, she didn't care what it was.

"So, what's the agenda?" Nick asked as he refilled his glass. So far they had only been rehashing what Randa already knew.

"I'm not really sure," Randa answered. "I thought maybe you could shed some light on it all."

"You're going to be disappointed."

"Well, I hadn't seen him in a year, you surely know more than I do. Had he been more depressed than usual? Had he called you up and said 'Guess what, Nick, I just robbed a liquor store'? "

"I haven't . . . hadn't . . . seen him in a couple of weeks, so I don't know what his most recent frame of mind has been . . . had been . . ." He stopped. "Christ." He stared at his wineglass for a long moment. He finally sighed, then continued.

"He certainly didn't call me and tell me he robbed a liquor store, not that he would have. But . . ." He bit his bottom lip and shook his head.

"What?"

"Nothing. It's just . . ." He looked up, directly into her eyes, as if he'd made some sort of decision. "I wasn't terribly surprised when I heard that."

Randa stared at him, shocked. "You weren't?"

"Look, I want to say a couple of things before we talk about this."

Randa braced herself for whatever was coming.

"I've heard all about what happened with you and Cam, all the different sides, except yours, but it's pretty easy to connect the dots. I just want to say so we can get rid of the undercurrents. I know what you meant to Cam."

A cynical chuckle escaped her before she could stop it.

"No, I'm serious. I know you loved Cam, I know he loved you. I also know that if the last thing he did was call you, he was probably going to tell you everything I'm about to tell you, so that's how I'm going to justify it to myself."

What was he going to tell her? Randa wondered. He had an odd look on his face, as if he were about to confess something that embarrassed him.

"I just want you to promise me this will stay between us. I can't stand the thought of all the *Chronicle* nerds taking this and running with it. I think that would be horribly unfair to Cam."

Randa nodded. "You don't have to worry," she said quietly.

Nick picked up the pitcher and refilled Randa's glass, as if she were going to need it. She waited.

"Cam had been acting very strange. I think he just . . ." He stopped; seemed to change direction. "A couple of months ago, he ditched Nora, out of the clear blue sky." Randa listened, trying not to have any opinion that would show on her face. "He didn't tell her why, and he didn't even tell anyone else that it had happened. I only found out because I ran into her at the Beverly Center." He smiled. "Oh, yeah. I make an exception for that, too. But only on weekdays, and never when there are sales."

Randa smiled and forced back all the questions she wanted to ask. *What was she wearing, how did she look, was she devastated, I hope?*

Nick fished a square of peach out of his glass with his spoon, popped it in his mouth, and went on.

"Anyway, I asked Cam about it, he just said he had to be alone. I never could get any more out of him than that, but I didn't really care that much anyway. You know Cam, they come, they go . . ."

Randa winced a little. Nick caught himself.

"I'm sorry. Jesus, I didn't . . ." He seemed genuinely embarrassed. "See, I don't put you in that category, so I'm not careful."

"What category do you put me in?" Randa asked, genuinely interested.

"I don't know if I could name it," he said, speaking slowly, as if stalling for time. "There's one thing, I don't know if this will help you. Cam used to say something to me, over the years, every time I'd ask him why the two of you weren't together, if he was so crazy over you. He'd always say he couldn't be in a romantic relationship with you, and I'd ask why, and he'd say 'I love her too much.' "

Randa felt her brow furrow. "What does that mean?"

Nick looked at her for another long moment. He seemed to be playing this conversation like a game of chess.

"He never would tell me what it meant. Except for one night . . . It was very late, we'd all been over at Roger's, playing poker. Cam and I went back to his apartment to see how much drunker we could possibly get, I guess. Anyway, it was about three in the morning and we were both several sheets to the wind, and Cam started talking about you. I don't know why. I think it was right after you guys had started to . . . date." He smiled. "I'll be a gentleman."

He paused to take a sip from his wineglass, and seemed to weigh the decision to tell her these things one more time. He looked back at Randa. "Cam told me that he thought, he truly believed, there was some kind of a curse on his family. Not like spells and witches and devils and all that, but some real thing that was like this black cloud of bad luck. And he was convinced that if he got very involved with you, it would infect you and ruin your life."

Randa stared at him. "That's crazy."

Nick nodded. "I know. I didn't say this was going to make sense. I just said I'd tell you.

"Anyway," he continued, before Randa could figure out what to say, "that's just a digression. Although it may have been the beginning, and I just didn't see it."

"The beginning of what?"

"Like I said, Cam had gotten really weird. Even for him."

"Weird how?"

"First, he started calling me all the time. Three or four times a day. Only me, from what I can tell. And he was saying all these bizarre things."

"Like what?"

"Like, he was having these nightmares, but he was convinced they weren't dreams. He said he thought he was 'going somewhere' in his sleep."

Randa frowned, trying to follow. "What does that mean?"

"I don't know. He didn't know. But he just became more and more insistent that these dreams were more than dreams, and he thought they were going to end up hurting him somehow. I guess he got sick of trying to convince me, he finally stopped talking about it. But then he started to get very paranoid. When we would go somewhere, anywhere, even during the day, he'd always look around, like he was afraid someone was following us. I'd ask him why he was doing that, and he'd either deny he was doing it or just say 'no reason.'

"He'd call me late at night, and he'd just talk forever about nothing, or he'd try to get me into some long, complicated argument. I always felt he was trying to keep me from hanging up. Or he'd show up at night, unannounced, and stay until very, very late, and then sleep on the couch. He'd claim he was too drunk to drive." He stopped, looked at her. "Does that sound like Cam to you?"

Randa shook her head. It didn't. "What do you think all that was about?"

"I don't know. But I haven't even gotten to the best part." He picked up his wineglass and emptied it. He filled both their glasses with the last of the alleged sangria. Finally he was ready to resume. He looked at her.

"A couple of weeks ago, he told me that he had seen Tallen."

Randa stared at him. The restaurant suddenly seemed eerily quiet. "He *what*?"

"That's what he said. He was adamant about it."

Randa was still struggling to understand. "You mean, he saw someone in a crowd who looked like Tallen?"

Nick shook his head. "No. Tallen. In his apartment. He woke up one night and there was Tallen. He swore it. He saw Tallen, they talked, Tallen told him things . . . We never got to *what* Tallen told him. By that time, I had stopped him, I just couldn't listen to it. I told him I was worried about him and I thought he should find a better shrink. He got furious and stormed out of my house." Nick was quiet for a moment; he looked pained. When he spoke, his voice was different. "That was the last time I saw him."

Randa didn't know what to say, what to do with any of this. Nick shook his head a little, as if coming out of a trance.

"So," he continued, "all in all, the liquor store thing just didn't shock me."

"You think he was . . ." Randa couldn't bring herself to say any of the possible words.

Nick was nodding. "There's that tiny line between eccentricity and insanity . . . Somehow, when we weren't paying attention, he just crossed over." He looked away, and spoke as if he were talking to himself. "Let's face it. How long could anyone expect him to keep it up— walking around, pretending to be normal, pretending he lived on the same planet with everyone else, like they . . . like *we* had *any* way to comprehend what he'd been through, what he had to live with. . . ." He paused for a moment, and shook his head. "In my humble opinion," he said quietly, "the question we should all be asking ourselves is not 'how could this happen,' but 'why did it take so long?' "

Randa sat back in the booth, dazed, trying to take it in, and wondering how much a pack of cigarettes went for these days. Nick motioned the waiter to bring them another pitcher of wine.

The door to Cam's apartment looked perfectly normal. Randa had expected there to be police tape, or at least some kind of a note. She opened the door with the key she had never returned (not that he'd ever asked her to, that would have required acknowledging her existence) and stepped inside. She closed the door behind her and locked it.

Nothing had changed. It looked exactly the same as the last time she'd seen it. She was sure that if she looked hard enough, she'd see signs of Nora's having passed through, but she didn't plan to look that hard.

She had decided to come here halfway through the second pitcher of sangria. She told herself she wanted to pick up the things that were hers, but she knew the real reason had little to do with two Pyrex casserole dishes and a spare hair dryer. Now that she was here, she realized that all she really wanted was some sort of closure. She had lived without it for the last year, but she couldn't go on without it for the rest of her life.

She did have one real quest. There were a couple of scrapbooks—the last remaining vestiges of Cam's family, except for Jack, assuming he was still alive. Randa didn't know what she'd do with them, but she knew she'd make sure they were kept safe. She didn't know why that felt so important, but it did. Just the thought that generations of people had been whittled down to two tattered books of yellowed paper and faded black-and-white photos. The books seemed sacred to her; they were the only remaining evidence that any of these people had ever lived.

Randa looked around, trying to remember where Cam had kept the scrapbooks. She checked the hall closets, but all they contained were clothes and boxes of old magazines. She would have to check the bedroom, something she'd hoped to avoid at all costs—she was sure she would find the scrapbooks there.

The bedroom looked the same, too. The door to one of the closets was open, and there were clothes strewn on the floor in front of it, where the cops had plowed through. They'd obviously found the gun without much trouble. She didn't see any sign of the scrapbooks. Without giving it a lot of thought, she went over and opened the other one. There were a couple of shirts hanging on a hook inside the door; they brushed her face as the door opened. They smelled like Cam. She hadn't expected this, and the full force of the pain made its way through the wine and the denial. She bent over, as if from a sudden cramp, as a sob hit her. She let herself sink to the floor, buried her head in her knees, and gave herself up to the misery.

She cried for a long time. When she finally stopped, she felt as if something inside her had given way, like a fever breaking. She wiped her eyes with the sleeve of one of the shirts—a faded red brushed silk, from Traffic at the Beverly Center. She had been with Cam the day he bought it. (*"Randa, what about this red one? It matches my eyes."*) She took a couple of deep breaths and was about to stand when she saw the scrapbooks on the floor next to her. They looked the same as when she'd last seen them, which somehow surprised her. She gathered them in her arms and pulled herself to her feet.

On her way out, she noticed something on the night-stand: a pen and a sheet of paper. The paper was covered with doodles: trees; dollar signs; a skull atop a mound of bones. A couple of phone numbers. One was hers. The other was an 800 number. Unable to resist, she picked up the phone and dialed it.

"Thank you for calling Delta Airlines. All of our agents are busy at this time . . ."

Randa hung up. She looked at the pad again. Cam had written "#178" in the middle of all the pictures and cir-cled it. Randa dialed Delta again. When she got an agent, she was informed that 178 was one of the morning flights from LA to Atlanta.

Why would Cam have been planning a trip to Atlanta? He hadn't been home since his mother's funeral, and he'd always sworn he'd never go there again.

She folded the sheet of paper and tucked it into one of the scrapbooks. She could figure it out later.

Halfway to the front door, a sound caused her to stop.

An old man was standing in front of the window, look-ing down at the street. He looked up and saw Randa. His face showed no sign of surprise, or any other emotion.

"It's a long way down, isn't it?" He had a soft voice, and a refined Southern accent, as smooth as old scotch.

"Me, I'd go with pills. It wouldn't hurt, it wouldn't make a mess, and it wouldn't bother anybody else's life."

He was dressed in a charcoal gray suit, white shirt, and maroon tie, all of which looked expensive. He was an attractive man for his age, with a full head of white hair and a neatly trimmed beard. There was a calmness in his eyes that would have been comforting under different circumstances.

"I'm sorry," Randa said, putting the scrapbooks down. "I didn't realize anyone was here." It sounded stupid, but she had to start somewhere.

"I'm Ryland Parker," he said, simply. "Cam's uncle."

Lucy's twin brother. Now she recognized him from the photos she'd seen, although he was much older. She had completely forgotten about him when the cops were asking about Cam's relatives. Actually, it had never dawned on her that he would still be alive.

"Oh, yes. Of course. I'm sorry, I guess the detectives wondered why I didn't tell them about you, but I didn't remember . . ."

"Well, I'm sure Cam didn't talk about me very much. We weren't close."

She wondered how the cops had managed to find him, but there was no polite way to ask.

"I'm an old friend of Cam's," she said. "I was just . . ." *Just what? Just sitting on the floor of his closet, sobbing?*

"What were you planning to do with the books?" His tone wasn't accusatory, but Randa felt guilty just the same.

"Oh. I thought someone in the family should have them. I guess that would be you." She picked up the books and started to hand them to him, but he waved her off.

"No, not me. Jack should have them."

"Well, that's what I thought, I'd try to find a way. . . . Do you know where he lives?"

"Yes."

"Then I guess you could take them. . . ."

He was shaking his head. "No." He didn't offer an explanation. He turned toward the window again, this time looking straight out, at the lights of the city. "Cam would have to have a place with a view, wouldn't he? Always *looking* somewhere. Looking in, looking out, looking back. Where did all that looking get him, except looking in a rather unfortunate direction when he finally decided to follow his own gaze."

Randa suddenly remembered what Cam had said about Ryland. *"He makes my mother look sane."*

"But," he went on, "he was doing the best he could, all things considered. Like they all did." He looked back at her.

"You have to take the books to Jack," he said, suddenly.

"Me?"

He nodded. "And tell him about Cam's death. Everything you know about it."

"That's crazy. Why can't you tell him?"

"He wouldn't see me," he said, shaking his head.

"Then leave them at his door with a note. I'm not going to fly three thousand miles to hand two scrapbooks to someone I never met, when you know him and you'll be there anyway . . . that's crazy."

He was suddenly right beside her, staring intently into her eyes. "Listen to me. This is not about the books. It's about getting through Jack Landry's thick skull, and I can't do it."

"What on earth makes you think I could?"

"In the first place, you're the only person left who might want to. And you're a very attractive young lady, and there must be *something* alive in him that would take note of that fact."

Randa was sure she was offended by that last statement, but she couldn't isolate the reason to call him on it.
Before she could figure it out, he was talking again.

"I want you to give Jack one message for me. Word
for word, please." He was looking her dead in the eye.
"Tell him that the thing is real. You have to make him
believe that, no matter what it takes."

With that, he turned and headed for the door.

"What thing?"

Let him go, idiot. He's a nutcase.

"He'll know," Ryland said, then turned to look at her
again. "If you ever cared about this family, you'll do
this." Then he left.

Randa waited, giving him plenty of time to get out of
the building. She tried to figure out why he'd been able to
upset her so much. So Cam's crazy Uncle Ryland was in
town for the funeral, and she'd met him and he'd talked
nonsense, as crazy people have a tendency to do. So what?

HE'S TELLING THE TRUTH.

The voice. *The* voice. The one that had been drowning
the others out for a while now, even though its messages
usually made about as much sense as Uncle Ryland.

She headed for the door. She'd track Jack down and
mail the books to him. She'd include a note about her
conversation with Ryland. That would be that. She'd be
done with the Landrys for good; she could move on to
another obsession.

She waited for the elevator, unable to get Ryland's
face or voice out of her head.

"*... doing the best he could, all things considered83
...*"

What was that supposed to mean? Cam had been doing
the "best he could," but the best he could was pretty
damned impressive.

"*... like they all did ...*"

The elevator door opened and she got in and pressed the lobby button, eager to get away.

"... *if you ever cared about this family* ..."

What? She was supposed to care about them enough to fly clean across the country to deliver a nonsensical message to the surviving member? Assuming she could even find him, why would he listen to her? What did any of this have to do with her?

IF YOU EVER CARED ABOUT THIS FAMILY ...

I didn't even know them.

IF YOU EVER CARED ABOUT CAM ...

Not fair. Now the damned voice was going to play dirty. Well, what the hell. Everyone else did.

Back home, she sat on her bed and sipped straight tequila and flipped through the scrapbooks. There they were, in time-faded black-and-white photos: Will and Lucy, Jack, Tallen, Ethan, and Cam. She knew who everyone was, from having gone through the books with Cam so many times. Randa wondered once more why her heart was so torn by these sad people she'd never met.

She picked up the piece of paper from Cam's nightstand and looked at it again. Asked herself again why Cam would have been going to Atlanta.

"*I want you to give Jack one message* ..."

Was that it? Was Cam trying to go to Atlanta to look for Jack? To tell him something? Would Ryland's nonsensical message convey whatever Cam had wanted Jack to know? If so, then Ryland was asking her to do something that Cam would ask her to do, if he could.

If you ever cared about this family ...

"Oh, hell," Randa said out loud. She picked up the phone and dialed the Delta number.

CHAPTER 5

Jack knocked lightly, rattling the screen door of the trailer. He knew Cathy had seen him come up the walk, but she would take her time about answering the door. She always did.

The storm had moved on and the smell of wet pine filled the crisp night air. Jack looked across the way at the other trailers. The lights were on in almost all of them, and he could hear a radio somewhere, tuned in to a country station. He hated having to think about people living in tin boxes, and wondered why it always took Cathy so long to answer the door. Did she still bother to primp for him? If so, he couldn't imagine why.

The light came on above his head and he heard her slide the lock, then the door opened. She was smiling, the honest smile of a woman who has long since stopped trying to be coy. The lines around her eyes surprised him, once again. In his mind, she was always young.

"I thought it was gettin' to be about time for you to roll in here." Cathy had never put a final *g* on a word in her life. In fact, everything about Cathy belied her intelligence. Jack had always suspected it was all deliberate. Or habit, from having been taught young that smart women lead lonely lives.

He offered his version of a sheepish smile. "Is it okay?"

"Well, I was expectin' Tom Cruise, but I guess I can call and put him off till tomorrow night."

She opened the screen door and he stepped inside. He looked around a little, as he always did, to get his bearings. Everything was neat and as stylish as she could afford for it to be on what she made at the truck stop. There was a half-finished afghan on the sofa that she must have been working on.

"Why do you always look around like you've never been here?" she asked.

"I don't know." He glanced down the hall, toward her son's bedroom. "Where's Tommy?"

"Who knows? Out with his hoodlum friends. A couple of 'em got their driver's licenses and I haven't seen him since."

"You better watch it."

"He's just sowin' his oats. You were a little hellion when you were his age."

"I wasn't a little hellion. 'Little hellions' steal hubcaps. Besides, do you want him to grow up to be me?"

"In some ways." Cathy spoke quietly, reaching for his jacket, then added, "He'll be okay. He's got a good heart."

"I know," Jack said, nodding. "I don't want to see him end up with two thousand volts through it."

Her eyes narrowed a little; she hadn't seen that coming. "I'm doin' the best I can do, Jack," she said, without sounding defensive. He saw the sadness in her eyes and he felt guilty. He sighed.

"I know. I'm sorry." He shook his head. "I've been in a foul mood all day."

"How come?"

"I don't know. I woke up with it and I can't shake it."

He kissed her on the back of her head—his version of an apology—and walked back into the bedroom.

* * *

She was the closest thing Jack had to a friend. They had
known each other since high school. They had never
really dated. Cathy had a boyfriend when they met—
a genuine creep whom Jack, who loathed the term,
couldn't help thinking of as white trash. But even if she'd
been available, in those days Jack was spending too
much time on the streets or in the juvie courts to have
much of a social life anyway.

They had both left school at the end of their junior
year. In unrelated incidents, Cathy had gotten pregnant
and Jack had been expelled. (He and Ethan had been
expelled on the same day. *"Mrs. Landry, it's very clear
that your sons are not interested in anything but
causing trouble, so let's just stop wasting everybody's
time."*) Cathy had married the creep. He stayed with her
for six years, to his credit, Jack supposed; but he'd left
her to raise a son on minimum wage and tips, with an
occasional child-support check, although Jack doubted
she'd seen one of those in a while.

Cathy and Jack had drifted apart after they left school;
and especially after he went to the state prison in Reids-
ville for ten years, although she had visited him there a
few times. When he got out, they would run into each
other in town every now and then; they'd make a lot of
noise about getting together for dinner or something
sometime, but they never quite got around to it. Then
Jack had moved to Atlanta, had thought he would have a
life there. The Ritz-Carlton Buckhead had just opened
and, thanks to a brilliant piece of fiction disguised as an
application, he got a good job as a waiter in the dining
room. Between his deceptively wholesome looks and
whatever he'd inherited of his mother's breeding, he had
really been able to charm people in those days, and he
made a small fortune in tips.

He met a woman, Paula, who worked at the registration desk, and started going out with her. Maybe he even fell in love with her. Back then it was still possible. He'd confessed his entire sordid past to her. When she'd found out about the BA he'd earned by correspondence while he was in prison, she'd encouraged him to go for his master's, to arm himself to fight his past. He'd been in the process of filling out grad school applications when all hell had broken loose with Tallen. He moved back home to be with his mother during the trial. He handed his savings over to the court-appointed attorney to spend on a psychiatrist for the jury to ignore. He never returned to Atlanta; never saw Paula again; never gave another thought to grad school or anything resembling a career.

He and Cathy had become romantically involved (if you could call it that) the day Tallen was sentenced. She'd called him as soon as she heard. Jack had been out of his mind, and she had come to comfort him. He couldn't remember how they'd ended up in bed. (Surely he hadn't been trying to seduce Cathy a few hours after finding out that Tallen had been sentenced to die?) Even if he hadn't instigated it, it seemed heartless and incongruous, thinking about it now. But at the time it had seemed very natural, perfectly in keeping with the desperation he had felt.

Even after that night, Jack and Cathy had never been anything approaching a couple. Jack didn't have the stamina to be in a relationship, and Cathy had never had the stamina to stay out of one. The two of them would get together from time to time, whenever one of them needed the other for anything. That almost always meant sex, since that was the only thing either of them needed that the other could supply.

These days they never wasted time with small talk, so Jack had everything off but his jeans when Cathy came out of the bathroom, still dressed. She went over and sat on the bed and looked at him. "I want to talk to you."

"About what?"

"About us. About this."

Jack looked at her, worried. Surely she knew him well enough to know he wasn't going to talk about "them" and "this." He'd be a streak of light out the door.

"Stop lookin' so petrified. It's not gonna kill you." She patted the bed. "Come here and sit down."

He sat on the end of the bed. She frowned at him.

"Up here," she said, patting the bed right next to her. He didn't move. "Jack, come on. I'm not tryin' to throw you a curve. I just need to talk for a minute." She smiled. "You don't even have to speak, you can just nod every now and then."

As usual, her voice calmed him a little. He moved up next to her, and relaxed, as much as he could. He still dreaded this conversation, whatever it was.

"You're a nervous wreck," she said, starting to massage his shoulders. "Do you see what a nervous wreck you are?"

"I don't think I've ever tried to deny being a nervous wreck, or any other kind of wreck."

"I know you don't deny it, but I'm not sure you really notice it, either. Let me tell you what happens when you come here. . . ."

"I know what happens."

"I'm not sure you do. And even if you do, you need to hear it out loud. Do you know how often you show up here?"

He didn't answer. She leaned over and kissed him on the cheek, then continued. "You come here roughly every three months. Unless it's been rainin' a lot, then you come more often. I think that's because when it rains, you're not outside, you're not workin', you don't have any way to let off steam. Because that's what most of this is about. Lettin' off steam. And I'm not sayin' that's bad. I just want to make sure you know what you do and why you do it. It's gonna be important to you later."

"I know what I do and why I do it," he said, trying to be patient. "Why can't you trust me on that?"

"You come here when you can't stand it anymore," she said, ignoring his request. "The rest of the time, I seriously doubt you even think about sex. You don't think about it until you have no choice. What happens when you start thinkin' about comin' here? How do you feel?"

"Cathy . . ."

"Just tell me, the simplest way you know how."

He thought about it for a minute. He knew she wasn't going to let him out of this. "I feel . . . like I can't stay calm." He looked at her. She was nodding.

"Okay. That's good."

"Great. I passed. Is it over?"

She leaned over again and kissed him, on the lips this time, and stroked his cheek with her fingers. Then she continued.

"Look at how you're breathin'."

"*Look* at how I'm breathing?"

"You know what I mean."

He didn't answer her. His breath was short and shallow; tense.

"By the time we hit this room, you're always breathin' like that. You're half-crazed."

He winced at her choice of words, but she didn't seem to notice.

"It's not just about sex, Jack. It's about that volcano you sit on all the time. You're always so gentle with me, but it's not what you really want. I can tell by . . . I don't know, I can just tell. The minute you let yourself feel the tiniest thing, it just reminds you of how much is still there, and it scares the hell out of you. So you can't even stop bein' careful when you go to bed with me." He started to speak, but she cut him off. "Let me finish." He leaned back and closed his eyes. He might as well let her finish, she was going to, one way or the other.

"So you make love to me, and you're slightly less careful, but you're still careful. You only allow yourself a little bit of passion. You don't make a sound, because it's too dangerous to let anythin' like that out. And you hold back, you don't come until you absolutely can't help it, like you think that keeps it from bein' your fault that it feels good. And then you go home, as fast as you can without bein' completely rude to me, because you want to get out of here and pretend none of it happened. And then you forget all about it, until you can't forget it anymore." She looked at him, gave it a moment to sink in. The silence was too heavy. He broke it.

"You've given this a lot of thought."

"I've had a lot of years to think about it. Isn't it all true?"

He didn't say anything. He knew his silence answered her question. She went on.

"Jack, I don't think any of that . . . any of what you do . . . is goin' to change. I wish it would, but I don't see how it can." She shook her head a little, pushed her dark hair away from her face. "God, I wish I knew a simple way to say this. Just don't . . ." She stopped; sighed.

"Don't what?" He wanted to know what she was trying to say.

"I love you to death. You're my oldest friend, and I'd love to think it could ever be more than that, but you . . . you know . . . your life is what it is and I think it's a stupid waste, but it *is* your life."

He suddenly knew what she was going to say. He kept quiet and let her say it.

"I've been seein' somebody. I mean, *really* seein' somebody. . . . I think we're . . ." She stopped. She shook her head, then looked away, toward the wall.

He got her drift. He'd been through lots of boy-friends with Cathy, and while there may have been occasional problems of logistics, it had never altered their relationship.

"Where'd you meet him?" He didn't know why it mattered, but he wasn't ready to say anything else.

She looked back at him. "He's the night manager at Winn-Dixie. He transferred from Columbus about six months ago. I kept seein' him in there. . . . One night I had to get a check approved and we started talkin'. . . . He asked me out and we just . . ." Her voice trailed off. "God, I hate this. . . ."

"Cathy, it's okay," he said quietly.

She was starting to cry. He pulled her to him and held her. She tried to go on.

"I want a life, Jack. I want a house, I want to get Tommy out of this fuckin' trailer . . ." Jack handed her a tissue from the box by the bed and she dried her eyes. "I know I'm probably just headin' for another disaster—"

"You don't know that. It could be fine." He kissed her cheek, then rubbed a stray tear away with his thumb. "Don't cry. You've told me, it's over, everything's okay."

"I'm worried about you."

"Cathy, I'll be okay. I'm not going to go nuts, I'm not going to . . ." He stopped. "Look, if I didn't know how to take care of myself, I wouldn't be here, would I?"

"I guess not." She didn't sound very convinced. "Just be careful."

"I'm always careful. You just said that."

She smiled through the tears. She hugged him, kissed the side of his face. "When I die, I'm gonna beat the shit out of God for everythin' he's done to you."

"I'll help you," he said, feeling guilty about the fact that he was really ready for her to stop talking. He knew her well enough to know that she would never have told him to sit on the bed unless she was planning on allowing him one for the road. And she was right. He *was* half-crazed.

As if she could read his mind, she pulled away and gently pushed him down on the bed. She stretched out on top of him and kissed him, hard, from her soul. He kissed her back, from whatever was left of his. Then she raised up and looked at him; she still had tears in her eyes.

"Will you at least make some noise?" she asked, smiling a little.

"No." He smiled back, and reached to unbutton her blouse.

By the time he got back home, Jack was much calmer. A long way from mellow, but at least the tension was bearable.

He went through the nightly routine like a robot: got undressed, brushed his teeth, set the clock. He got into bed and tried to read, but he couldn't keep his mind focused. It kept going back to everything Cathy had said. What was he going to do three months from now, when he was coming out of his skin again? In his wildest days, he'd never slept with a hooker. Back then, it had been a matter of pride. These days, it was a matter of staying alive. As always, when confronted with it, he was surprised to discover that some part of him did have a strong will to live. Or maybe he was just too afraid of the possible alternatives. At least this was a familiar hell. There was no reason to assume that whatever was waiting would be anything other than worse.

Was he that volatile, he wondered, that a prolonged period of celibacy was such a threat? But Cathy was right. It wasn't just about sex. Sex was only relevant because he couldn't afford any additional stress. She understood that, and she kept him grounded. In his clear-thinking moments, he knew this. It had to do with her honesty. Sometimes he needed to be around that just as much as he needed to get off. Maybe more. He had to touch base with something he knew was pure and good. And someone who knew him, knew his nature; knew it wasn't all bad, but didn't fool herself into thinking it was nothing to worry about, either.

It took his mind a while to settle down, but he finally felt himself slipping into unconsciousness, and was deeply grateful.

He was walking down a shady residential street. Broad daylight. Up ahead he saw a girl walking toward him. She was in her late teens, pretty, with long blond hair and tan legs in cutoff blue jeans. She smiled and motioned for him to come to her. He went, stood in front of her, and waited to see what she wanted. She looked at him, oddly, like she could hear his thoughts and was pausing to listen. And then, without warning, she was kissing him, with a strength that amazed him. He could barely stand up. And then he realized she was pushing him down. He felt his knees give way and he was on the ground and she was on top of him, still kissing him, his face cupped in her strong hands. He kept his eyes closed and tried to just go with it, but he couldn't stop wondering why it didn't feel as good as it should. Something told him to open his eyes; he did, and instantly he knew something was wrong. The girl's hair, hanging down around his face, was not blond anymore. It was gray and coarse. He pushed her away, so he could see her face. It wasn't the girl.

She was the most grotesque thing he'd ever seen. Her skin was a transparent, slimy white and covered with open, runny sores. Her eyes were blue, but the whites of them were laced with red, and the look in them was pure hatred. She smiled at him; her mouth was full of sores and half her teeth were missing. The ones she had were yellow and pointed, like a vampire's. She looked at him like she owned him.

He tried to push her away, but it was like pushing a brick wall. He tried to roll himself out from under her. She laughed, a howling, mocking laugh. The more he struggled, the louder the laugh became, until the woods were echoing with it. He screamed at her to leave him alone, and she stopped laughing. The silence was almost worse. She looked in his eyes, and he couldn't move. Somehow her gaze had the power to paralyze him. He couldn't do anything but watch as she wrapped her bony hands around his throat and started to squeeze. He tried to move, but he couldn't. He could feel her fingers digging into his throat with a strength that was not human. In seconds, he couldn't breathe at all. She started that laugh again, and as she leaned her head back to howl, he was suddenly able to move. He grabbed her hands, but her grip was like iron. He thrashed, trying desperately to throw her off of him. He had to breathe. His chest felt like someone had run a hot knife through it. In a wild attempt that he knew would be his last, he summoned every ounce of his strength and shoved himself to the side. Her grip slipped just enough, and he managed to shove her off and roll away. He sat up, gasping for air. He looked around quickly, to see where she was, and realized he was awake.

He sucked air into his lungs in visceral gasps. His eyes scanned the apartment. The sun was just coming up and he could see enough to tell that there was nothing wrong.

He lay back down on the pillow and took deep breaths. His head felt like someone had it in a vise.

The phone rang, making him jump. He glanced at the clock, to make sure he wasn't late. The machine picked up. He heard his own voice; the one that followed the beep was not Rick's.

"Yes, I'm trying to locate a Mr. Jack Landry. This is Bill Warren at the LA County Coroner's office and I need you to return my call at your earliest convenience. The number here is (213) 343—"

Jack turned the machine off, then stared at it in disbelief. There was only one reason he'd be getting a call from the LA County Coroner's office.

Cam is dead.

He didn't move for a long time. Just lay there, staring at the phone.

Cam is dead.

What the hell was he supposed to do about it?

When he finally picked up the receiver, it was to call Rick and ask for the day off, pretending he had the flu. Then he dressed and headed down the road, on the two-mile walk to the liquor store.

He sat in the vacant lot behind the train depot, where he and Ethan and Tallen used to play. He took the pint of Jack Daniel's out of the paper bag and looked at it. He'd felt as nervous buying it as a kid with a fake ID. He hadn't gone near alcohol in ten years, no matter how much he'd needed to escape; but he'd always told himself it would be there if things got bad enough, and that it would be okay as long as he was careful. He twisted the cap and broke the seal, and was halfway amazed that there was no ensuing clap of thunder.

He opened the bottle and tilted it, letting half the contents spill onto the ground. He watched the copper pool soak into the dirt, until he was satisfied the right amount remained in the bottle—enough to spread a soothing fog over him, but not enough to do any real damage. He put the bottle to his lips, paused for a moment, then tipped his head back and felt the welcome burn slide down his throat. A few minutes and a couple of ounces later, he let himself think about Cam.

What on earth could have happened? It was hard to believe that Cam and death could travel the same axis, much less collide. It made him think about nights when he was a kid, lying in bed, fantasizing about smothering Cam with a pillow and letting everyone think Cam had died in his sleep. His plan included comforting his mother with a theory he thought she'd buy—that the angels had decided they just couldn't live without Cam another day.

The whiskey dulled the pain in his head, but it was getting back at him in other ways. It stirred the old voices and, as always, brought him closer to the anger. Pictures flashed through his head. His father holding Cam by the hand, waving Cam's report card like it was the goddamned flag. Looking at the rest of them like he wished the ground would open and swallow them. *"At least I've got one son who's gonna amount to something. The rest of you combined ain't worth the breath it'd take to cuss you."*

And now the Boy Wonder was gone. Jack suddenly saw clearly what he'd known since the moment he'd heard the message. The LA County Coroner would have to move on to Plan B. Even if Jack had loved Cam the way he'd loved the others, he couldn't do it again. He couldn't do one more funeral.

At least he could comfort himself with the knowledge that it was all but over. There was no one left to die. No one but him. And when he died, there would be no phone call, no stricken faces, not even one ambivalent drunk wrestling with his conscience. Just a quiet end to the chain of misery.

He drained the last of the whiskey. He put the cap back on the bottle, stared at it for a moment, then hurled it at the side of the depot, where it shattered and fell to the ground in a thousand pieces. It was the closest thing to an act of violence that Jack had committed in ten years. The sound sent a cold echo through his hollow soul.

CHAPTER 6

Driving her rented car down I-75, Randa began to feel it—the almost tangible poignancy she always felt in Atlanta, and had felt ever since she first came there on a second-grade field trip. Memories whirled over her, and she could feel her throat tighten into what she had come to think of as the Atlanta knot.

There was a bank of black clouds on the horizon, and every now and then a streak of lightning would split them. Randa was driving right into the storm, and had to force herself not to look at it as an omen. Thunderstorms were high on the list of reasons she had left Georgia. She reminded herself of all the reassurances she'd heard about a car being the safest place to be, and how statistically slight her chances were of being struck by lightning. Those statistics never calmed her though, since those same statistics had applied to anyone who ever *had* been struck by lightning.

The storm seemed to be stalled somewhere. By the time she was within three exits of Barton, it was still off in the distance. Maybe it would stay wherever it was until after she was safely back in her hotel room.

Barton was a little town about an hour south of Atlanta. It was also the town where Will Landry had finally done his version of settling down, and the town the Landry boys had spent their youths terrorizing. Randa had never been there. It was one of those towns there was no reason to visit. Its biggest claim to fame was the country's oldest still-standing buggy factory. Once a year everyone got decked out in antique clothes and celebrated "Buggy Day" by riding buggies up and down Main Street. But that event was hardly worth the time it would have taken her to drive down there when she was growing up in Asbury, an hour and a half on the other side of Atlanta.

Chances were slight that anyone in Barton would know where Jack lived now, but she had to start somewhere, and it seemed like the logical place. (Not that any of this had anything to do with logic.) She took the first of the two exits, followed the signs to the downtown area (such as it was), parked in one of the diagonal spaces on Main Street, and surveyed the landscape. Typical small-town Georgia. A little row of shops that hadn't been updated in decades. The lawn in front of the courthouse was dotted with silver historical markers and a large statue in honor of the Confederate war dead. She'd been gone long enough to find it all quaint.

She spotted a small coffee shop, always the best place to go for information in a small town. A sign painted on the window read TILLIE'S GOOD FOOD COFFEE SHOP. Randa left her car unlocked and headed inside.

Tillie was not doing a booming business. A few customers, mostly elderly ladies, were beating the dinner rush. As Randa passed them, they stared hard at her, their eyes squinting with the intense mistrust of strangers only rural southerners can muster. Randa ignored them and made her way to the counter, where a pudgy waitress greeted her with a forced smile.

"Do you need a menu?"

"No. Actually, I'm trying to find someone. I wondered if you could help me."

"I'll try. Who is it?"

"A man named Jack Landry. He grew up here and moved away. He's in his late forties, probably blond . . ."

"Yeah, I know who he is."

Randa stopped, a bit surprised. "You do?"

"He eats here sometimes." She lowered her voice. "Is he in some kinda trouble?" Her tone was not one of concern.

"No, no. Nothing like that." Randa tried to hide her amazement. "Does he live around here?"

"I think he lives in that boardinghouse out on thirty-six. That's what I heard."

Randa was too stunned to know what to say. If Jack still lived here, why hadn't Cam been able to find him? Had Cam lied about it? Why would he do that?

"Do you know where that's at?"

Randa managed to shake her head.

"The road that goes past the courthouse is thirty-six. Go east, it's about half a mile."

Randa thanked the girl, who had already gone back to filling the napkin dispensers. As she turned and headed for the door, the early diners seemed to be glaring even harder. Evidently they'd overheard. Evidently the Landry reputation had not diminished with time.

The boardinghouse was an old Victorian two-story, sitting by itself out on one of the two-lane highways that ran into town. The place had obviously been a nice old house at one time. Now it was badly in need of a paint job and a new roof. Randa parked her car by the road. The wind had begun to pick up and the thunder was sounding closer.

She took a moment to breathe deeply, bracing herself. She hadn't expected to have to face him so soon. She wondered what he would look like. She'd only seen photos of him as a child. She'd been intrigued by him since the first time she and Cam had gone through the family albums. Jack stood out because he was cutting up in every photo—sticking his tongue out, rolling his eyes, making devil horns behind someone's back. Looking at the photos, anyone would have picked Jack as the one who would wind up where Tallen had. Randa had made that observation aloud once, but Cam had disagreed. "That's just it. Jack got it all out of his system."

Randa took another look at the dilapidated boarding-house and told herself that Jack must have gotten a lot of things out of his system. She picked up the shopping bag containing the scrapbooks and headed for the front porch.

There was an elderly woman sitting on the porch swing. She eyed Randa suspiciously as Randa made her way to the front door and knocked.

"He ain't in."

"Excuse me?"

"Mr. Overby. He works during the day, at some bank over in Griffin. His wife is usually here, but she had to go to the store. I don't think there's any rooms available anyway, except that attic room and nobody in their right mind wants that thing."

"Well, I wasn't looking for a room, actually, I was looking for a boarder."

"A what?"

"Someone who lives here."

"I live here."

"No, I mean . . . I was looking for Jack Landry. Do you know him?"

"Know him? Don't nobody know him." She cocked her head a little, seeing Randa in a new light. "You kin to them?"

"No. I'm a friend of his brother."

"Which one?"

"Cam."

"Is that the one in California?"

Randa nodded. Her clothes must have given her away.

"That's the only other one still alive, ain't it?"

"Yes." Randa was in no mood to get into it. "Could you tell me which room is Jack's?"

"Basement. It's got a separate entrance back around the other side of the house."

"Thank you." Randa turned to go.

"He ain't there, though." Randa stopped, discouraged. "I seen him go out about an hour ago and he ain't come back."

"Oh. Well . . . I guess I could leave a note."

"Why don't you go on in and wait?"

"Go in?"

"He never locks it. Mr. Overby told me he wouldn't even take a key."

"Well, I can't just go into someone's place."

"Suit yourself. It's comin' up a bad storm."

"Still . . ."

Raindrops were beginning to strike the tin roof. There was a flash of lightning and a crack of thunder that was sharp, even if still in the distance.

"Lord!" the old woman exclaimed. "That was bad somewhere."

Randa looked at the car. She was debating going back to it when it suddenly started to pour. The old woman was watching her.

"Car's the safest place to be, unless you're sitting under a power line. Or a tree." Randa's car was sitting under both. She was starting to rethink the ethics of going into Jack's apartment. How could he be annoyed with her for wanting to come in out of the rain?

"I'm gonna get myself inside," the old woman said, standing up. "They're worse if it takes them a long time to get here, and this one's been coming all day."

She gathered her needlepoint and headed for the door. "I wouldn't stay out here under this tin roof if I were you."

As soon as the screen door slammed behind her, Randa headed for Jack's apartment.

The door was indeed unlocked. Randa made sure no one was watching, then went inside. She closed the door behind her and stood facing it for a moment, savoring the last few seconds of not knowing what the place would look like. She shivered with a chill that was not from the rain, and turned around slowly.

She had told herself to be ready for anything, but nothing had prepared her for how utterly bare the place was. The room she had entered served as the bedroom and living room. It was furnished in Early Yard Sale. There was a chair and coffee table that almost matched. Behind the sofa there was a double bed with an old iron headboard, graced by a nondescript grayish-blue blanket and a couple of pillows in plain white pillowcases. The dresser beside it was bare. There was no television, no radio, not even a window, with the exception of the one in the top half of the door, which was covered by a faded blue curtain. On the nightstand there was a telephone and an answering machine. She couldn't imagine why he would need either.

She wanted to sit down, but it seemed wildly inappropriate. Not that her being here at all wasn't wildly inappropriate. But the bareness of the apartment made her presence feel like that much more of an intrusion. At least it was dry in here. And clean. That was the other thing that surprised her. Everything was so clean.

A brilliant flash of lightning lit up the room, followed immediately by a sharp crack of thunder. The lights flickered, but stayed on. If he'd been working an outdoor job, they would have packed it in and he'd have had time to get home by now. He must have stopped somewhere to get something to eat. Deciding that she had a little time, Randa gave in to the irresistible urge to snoop. She slid one of the closet doors back and looked inside. A few pairs of jeans in various stages of disrepair. Work shirts, work boots, a gray sweatshirt, a pair of khaki pants permanently stained with white paint. The only thing even remotely personal was a tan corduroy shirt that looked as if it had been hung hastily, the sleeves still rolled up. The shelves were empty.

Sliding the closet door back into place, she tried to put it all together. She thought about the cute blond kid in the photographs, always eager to draw attention to himself, always looking so full of life . . . how had that kid ended up in this apartment? It was as if he had sentenced himself to his own prison. But what was his crime?

She had only glanced into the darkened kitchen. Now she turned on the light and looked inside. A small white wooden table, bare. Two chairs. Inside the cabinets were plain white dishes; a couple of pots and a frying pan that had seen some years but were otherwise nondescript. A bottle of Ivory liquid on the counter was the only sign that any of it was ever used.

She was about to check out the refrigerator when something caught her eye. There was a small hallway that led to the back door. It was obviously a service porch—just enough room for a small washer and dryer. Instead—she moved closer to make sure she wasn't imagining things—there was a desk and chair. It was a nice desk, obviously an antique and made of some rich wood like mahogany or cherry. In front of it was a matching Windsor chair with a worn maroon cushion, and on the desk there was a beautiful Tiffany lamp. It all looked so incongruous, shoved back into this dim corner like a secret hideaway. Which, she guessed, was exactly what it was. She felt vindicated. She had been sure there was no way a person could live without giving a single sign of who they were, or where they had come from. The desk definitely spoke to the latter. She was sure it had belonged to Lucy. She gave the drawer a slight tug, somehow convinced that it would be locked. It wasn't. She fairly collapsed into the chair and pulled the drawer to her. It was full of all sorts of odds and ends. She reached for the first thing she could find—an old yellow photo, torn around the edges. She recognized it immediately: it was almost identical to one she'd seen in Cam's photo albums. It was a picture of Jack, Tallen, and Ethan as kids, dressed in cowboy costumes and posing proudly beside a large, crudely carved pumpkin. In spite of all the holiday trappings, there was something tentative in their faces, as though they were afraid they'd get into trouble for smiling.

She put the picture back. She was dying to go through the entire drawer, but she thought she'd better check the window first and make sure it was safe. She stood up and turned, then froze in place.

He was standing in the kitchen doorway, glaring at her in a mixture of anger and confusion. His hair had darkened with age to a sandy blond, and all the mischief was gone from his face. He was wearing dirty jeans and an equally dirty blue work shirt. He was wet from the rain. He folded his arms across his impressive chest and continued to stare at her, waiting silently for an explanation.

Randa forced herself to meet his eyes. They were the same shape as Cam's eyes, except they were a strange pale olive color. And they were keenly alert—not the zombie eyes that often accompanied such a physique. *Cam's soul in a construction worker's body. What more could you ask for?*

"I'm sorry. I didn't hear you come in." It was the best thing she could come up with under the circumstances.

"I don't generally knock on my own door." His voice was a deeper version of Cam's and flat with restraint. The fact that he wasn't yelling at her was giving Randa the creeps.

"My name is Randa Phillips." She figured the best defense was to pretend there was nothing wrong with what she was doing. Any other option was too embarrassing to even consider. "I'm a friend of Cam."

"If you're here to deliver the sad news, the coroner beat you to it, so I guess you wasted a trip." There wasn't a trace of emotion in his voice.

"Well, I can at least offer you my condolences, I can see you're devastated."

He nodded toward the drawer. "Were you looking for anything specific?"

"No." She didn't bother to defend herself. "Look, I happened to be in Atlanta visiting my family (*not that I wouldn't have flown 2,000 miles for the pleasure of your charming company*) and I drove down here to bring you some things I thought you might want."

"I don't want anything of his."

"Fine. But I'm sure *I'm* not the person who should end up with your family albums. I left them on your sofa. I don't give a damn what you do with them. Have a nice life." She made a beeline for the door. Faced with the prospect of spending another minute with him, she suddenly felt the storm seemed a lot less threatening.

For some strange reason, her main thought as she brushed past him was that she hoped he caught a whiff of her perfume.

If she'd caused a disturbance when she'd stopped at Tillie's to ask questions, Randa was about to shut the place down by having dinner there alone. The place was packed now, and there was hardly a person in the room who hadn't stared blatantly at her at least twice. Some kept staring, as if thinking if they stared long enough, she'd get up and tell them who she was.

She was still shaken from her encounter. She didn't know what she had expected. Certainly not open arms, but at least some sort of connection, however brief. She didn't know *why* she'd expected that, but she had. At least he could have acknowledged the fact that this trip had required some degree of effort, not to mention money. But then, she'd told that lie about being in Atlanta. She wondered how he would have reacted if she'd told him she'd come all this way just to meet him.

She looked up to signal the waitress for her check.

Uh-oh.

There he was. Dressed in clean but paint-spattered jeans and a denim jacket she didn't remember seeing in his closet. He was looking at her. He turned away the minute she met his eyes and stepped over to the end of the counter, where a sign said TAKE OUT.

Now what? She couldn't bolt. Well, she could, but she'd have to walk within three feet of him to get out the door, which would be extremely uncomfortable. She ordered a cup of coffee and decided to wait. She fished a pen out of her purse and started making notes on a napkin, as if she'd just remembered a few crucial things she'd forgotten to do. Actually, she made a list of the ten albums she'd take on a desert island, and the ten singles she'd die before admitting she liked. All the while, she prayed he hadn't ordered anything hot.

You have a right to be here.

Right. She knew damned well she shouldn't be here. It was his territory, and he'd made it clear that she wasn't welcome.

From the corner of her eye, she saw him leave with nothing but a cup of coffee. She doubted he'd walked all this way for that. Well, she'd soon be gone and out of his hair for good. She would pack the Landrys in the back of her mind with all the other embarrassing memories—all those things that present themselves like flash cards during moments of low self-esteem. This entire episode would just be another card in the deck.

Outside, the storm had left the air chilly, reminding her that in places other than LA, it was the middle of winter. She tried to remember what clothes she had packed. She had decided to stay for a few days. She might even call her mother and admit to being in town. *(Yeah. JUST what you need, Mom on your heels with: "Cam? Cam . . . isn't he the one whose brother killed all those people?")*

She wasn't sure whether she was truly nostalgic and homesick, or just trying to justify the airfare. Not that it mattered. She'd paid for it out of the Hostility Fund—the money her father had left her. Her rule of thumb was that she only spent it on things she knew he'd disapprove of. This trip would certainly qualify. Irrational, impetuous, and definitely on the wrong side of the political fence.

She turned the corner on the side street where she'd left her car.

Jack was leaning against the wall of the Western Auto, sipping his coffee, waiting for her.

She walked closer, then stopped. They stared at each other for a moment before he spoke.

"How did he die?" His tone was different. Quiet. Not as icy as before.

"Well . . . they say he killed himself."

"They say?"

"He did kill himself, it's just . . ." She sighed. "There was a lot of weird stuff going on and I'm not sure how much of it was true."

"Such as?"

"Well . . ." How was she supposed to tell him like this? "Do you want to go someplace where we can talk?"

"Aren't we talking?"

"I meant for a while. It's all very complicated."

"Just give me the bare bones."

The lack of emotion in his voice made her wonder why he even cared. "Okay. I hadn't seen him for some time. We had kind of a bitter parting, and—"

"This doesn't sound like bare bones."

Randa glared at him for a moment, then rattled it off. "People who'd seen him right before he died think he was having some sort of nervous breakdown. And the cops think he robbed a liquor store and killed a guy."

For the first time, Jack looked nonplussed. "What?"

"That's as bare as I can do it. If you want the rest, we're at least going inside the car because I'm cold."

He thought about it, as if it were a monumental decision. "Okay. Let's go sit down somewhere."

Randa had a sense that it wasn't so much a social leap of faith as a desire not to be enclosed in such a small place as a car with her. That was fine, as long as they didn't have to go back to that damned coffee shop.

"Is there a bar around here?"

"I don't drink."

"Is there a reason you can't have a Coke and watch *me* drink?"

He stared off down the street. He looked like he might just start walking that way. Instead, he looked back.

"All right." It sounded like some sort of surrender. "There's a bar a couple of miles down the road."

The "bar" was more like a truck stop with a liquor license. It was a brick building with no windows and a neon sign above the door that read COUNTYLINE TAVERN. It looked like the kind of place where if you didn't have a gun going in, they'd give you one at the door.

They had found a booth in the back, away from the jukebox. Other than wanting to be away from the commotion, Jack had shown no signs of having an opinion about the place one way or the other. He was completely focused on wanting to hear the story. By the time Randa had finished with the basics, he was on his third Coke and Randa was on her second bourbon, and wishing she didn't have to drive to Atlanta so she could order about five more. She wondered why he had made such a point of telling her that he didn't drink. It was the only bit of personal information he had offered. He certainly didn't impress her as a proselytizing former alcoholic.

When she'd finished the story in as much detail as he would allow, he repeated it to her, like someone unsure of a set of directions. She answered by rote, and took the opportunity to study his face. It looked softer in the glow of the cheap red patio candle on the table. He had high cheekbones and a square jaw. Perfect teeth, which she knew had to have come through the grace of God and not as the result of years of expensive orthodontia. She sensed he had the kind of smile that would change the entire nature of his face, and wondered when was the last time anyone had seen it. There was something about his face that made it more than the sum of its parts. The kind of face that would have been fascinating to stare at while he slept. She wondered when was the last time anyone had done that, too.

She nodded as he finished recounting the story. He shook his head. "There's no way in hell Cam robbed a liquor store." It was the first sign of any emotion other than anger she'd seen from him. Maybe it was all the sugar and caffeine.

Randa nodded. "I have a hard time with it myself. But if he was . . . crazy . . ."

"I don't care how crazy he was." He polished off the Coke. He didn't volunteer anything else.

Randa stared at her cocktail napkin. She was sick of carrying the conversation, but the silence was cloying.

"So which county is dry?"

He looked up. "What?"

"I grew up in Georgia. If this is the 'Countyline' Tavern, it's because the next county is dry."

He came very close to smiling. "Henry County. Next door. You think my father would own a house in a dry county?"

Randa was startled. It had never occurred to her that Will Landry had ever *bought* a house. Cam had certainly never mentioned it.

"So . . . what happened to the house?"

He suddenly looked pained, realizing he had disclosed something. He shifted his weight. "It's still there."

"Does it belong to you?"

"Technically."

"But you don't live there?"

"Obviously not."

"How come?" She knew he was hating this, but she couldn't resist.

"Look, are we done?"

"Well, no." She paused and sipped her drink, giving

him time to recover from having accidentally stumbled into normal human interaction. "There's one more thing."

"What?"

"Well, when the cops couldn't find you, I guess they called—" She stopped, remembering. "You know, you're living right here where Cam last saw you, but he told me you had vanished off the face of the earth."

"Did he?" His tone was snide.

"He said he sent you a letter and the P.O. sent it back, moved-no-forwarding-address."

Jack looked vaguely amused by that. He shook his head.

"It came back return-to-sender, addressee-wants-to-be-left-the-hell alone."

"Why did Cam lie to me?"

"How should I know?"

"Well, it doesn't make any sense."

"Don't expect anything about my family to make any sense." She could see a flash of anger in his eyes, but it seemed to vanish as quickly as it had appeared. When he spoke again, his voice was quiet and he was perfectly composed. "So . . . what's the rest of it?"

She got the feeling he had been in the company of another person for as long as he could tolerate it.

"When I went to get the scrapbooks, I met your Uncle Ryland. He was at Cam's. I guess he came to go through Cam's things and . . . you know, make all the arrangements. But he was weird. I mean, Cam had told me that he was a little bit fruity—"

"What paper do you write for?" he asked, cutting her off.

His voice was angry and Randa could see the tension in his jaw. She looked at him, puzzled. She hadn't mentioned her career to him once.

"How did you know I was a writer?"

"What paper?"

"The *LA Chronicle*. It's a—"

"I don't know what the hell you're trying to pull. Obviously Cam told you just enough that you can smell a story."

"What are you talking about?"

"Oh, cut the act." He was standing now, pulling money out of his wallet. He threw it on the table. "I don't know how you people sleep at night."

"I don't know *what* you're talking about."

He didn't show any sign of hearing her. He headed for the door. She ran to catch up to him.

"Would you please tell me what is going on?"

He ignored her and kept walking. Annoyed, Randa reached out and grabbed his arm. He stopped and turned, jerking his arm away. He stared down at her with an anger that was almost palpable.

"You shouldn't have relied on Cam for your information. He never knew or cared about anything that went on in the family. That's why I didn't even bother to tell him."

"Tell him what?"

"That Ryland died. He had a heart attack, he's been dead for three years. Nice try, though."

He was out the door before Randa even realized what he had said.

CHAPTER 7

All he wanted out of life was for nothing else to happen to him. Good, bad, indifferent, it didn't matter. He couldn't deal with one more thing.

He lived his life as invisibly as possible. He did nothing to draw attention to himself. No driver's license, no credit cards, no checkbook. He'd even had his phone and utilities listed in the landlord's name and paid his bills in cash. No doctors, no prescription drugs. He didn't want his name in any fucking computer. He just wanted to be left alone. He'd felt that way most of his life. It didn't seem like a lot to ask.

"It doesn't work that way, Jack," Cathy said, as he finished giving her that speech for the zillionth time. "Life's not juvie court. It doesn't cut you a deal everyone can live with and then lose your address if you never fuck up again. Life is a serial killer. It just keeps comin' back for more."

"I don't have any more to give. You can't get blood out of an onion."

"Turnip," she corrected him.

"Whatever fucking vegetable. You know what I mean."

He sighed and leaned back in his chair. Cathy was at the sink, washing a large pot that had been the focus of her attention ever since he'd arrived.

"Let me know when you need me to leave," he said.

"It's okay. How many times do I have to tell you?"

He continued to stare at the yellow Formica on top of her kitchen table, and traced a crack with his index finger. No matter how much she denied it, he was sure his presence was making her nervous. Otherwise she would not have declined his offer to help with the dishes.

"Is what's-his-name coming over after work?" It probably sounded pissy but he was too tired to care.

"His name is Ben and he's at a friend's deer camp in Locust Grove till next week sometime. He'll never know you were here."

"And it doesn't bother you?"

"That you're here?"

He nodded. She dried her hands with a dishtowel and looked at him.

"Jack, I wasn't tellin' you not to come to my house anymore. Is that what you thought?"

"We didn't discuss the new rules."

"Do we need to?"

"No, I get it. I'm still welcome in the kitchen."

"So your short reign of bein' a prince about this is over?"

"I'm still a prince. I'm just . . ."

"What?"

"A tired prince."

"When was the last time you had a decent night's sleep?"

"I think I was in junior high school." He mustered a feeble smile, which she ignored.

He ran a hand through his hair and stared at the blackness out the window. "I want a drink like I can't tell you."

"Well, if you don't have the sense to keep your butt out of a bar . . ."

"Where should I have gone? Her hotel room?"

"So is that why you came over here? So I'll make sure you don't drink?"

"I haven't needed a baby-sitter in a long time, thank you."

It was as icy as he'd meant it to be, although he had only himself to blame for bringing up a sore subject. He should never have even told her about the bar, but he'd been in too much of a huff when he got there to be careful.

"I just think you've got enough to worry about without lettin' somebody drag you into a bar."

"She didn't drag me. And I hate to break it to you, but

I'd want a drink right now if I'd spent the last two hours in a church."

She turned away from him, back to the sink. He didn't know why he was sniping at her, except that the AA crap annoyed the hell out of him. Still, the last thing he needed was to alienate the one person he could talk to.

"Cathy, I'm sorry."

"Okay." She didn't look at him. She was about to scrub the enamel off the sides of the pot, which had never been very dirty to begin with.

"I mean it."

"It's okay. I know what you're doin'."

"What?"

"You're takin' it out on me because you're upset about Cam."

"Thank you, Dr. Brothers."

"Jack, it's okay if you're upset. I hated my father's guts and I was still a wreck when he died."

"I am *not* upset about Cam."

Quoting the "Big Book" was one thing, but he drew the line at the fucking *Good Housekeeping* psychology. Especially when she was right.

"Do you have any aspirin?" The best defense being a change of subject.

"Yeah." She didn't make any move to get them; just stared at him to let him know she saw through the ploy.

"I would get them, but I'm too grief-stricken to move."

"Jack, you're right on that line." She tossed it over her shoulder as she headed for the bathroom.

He smiled. It was a bit left over from high school. In earlier days it was preceded by "You know that line where you stop charmin' people and start pissin' them off . . . ?"

He wondered what she'd think if she knew what was

really eating at him. Randa. Randa's face. The fact that he couldn't get it out of his head.

As angry as he had been to find her sitting at his desk, rummaging through his drawer, the moment she had turned around something had stirred beneath the anger—feelings so long buried he'd forgotten they existed. He had no idea what had happened. She was certainly not the first pretty woman he'd seen in ten years, and it wasn't like she was cover-of-*Vogue* gorgeous. But there was something in her face—a beauty that was straightforward and unpretentious. Real. And those eyes. Such a deep shade of sable it was impossible to tell where the pupils began. And blond hair that had obviously grown out of her head that color. Back when he had cared about such things, he'd always been a sucker for blond hair and brown eyes.

It all went beyond the way she looked, though. He loved the fact that she'd simply refused to offer any bullshit excuses for what she was doing, as if that would be beneath her dignity. In fact, everything about her implied a code of personal ethics (ethics, *not* morality) that she refused to violate; an authenticity that would shatter any pretext, even her own, by sheer force of its own purity.

Then why did she lie about Ryland? It doesn't fit.

I don't know. When did I claim to have all of the answers . . . ANY of the answers?

He'd been able to admire it all from a safe distance until she'd grabbed his arm in the bar; but then he'd felt it in every cell of his body, even though he was furious with her at the time. He wasn't sure now whether that rage had been aimed at her or at himself for not being able to keep her out.

Well, it didn't matter. It was over. She was probably already on her way back to LA to break the bad news to her editor. In his own life, she'd been nothing more than a signal, like the dreams and the headaches and the home movies flashing through his head. All of these things were a warning that some strange tide was eating away the seawall, and it was time for some shoring up. Where he was going to get the sandbags was another question.

Cathy returned with a small bottle of aspirin and a Dixie cup full of water.

"I'm only givin' you these if you swallow 'em like a normal human. It makes my skin crawl when you chew them."

She put the cup down on the table and handed him the bottle. He shook a few pills into his palm.

"How many are you takin'?"

He looked at her. "I don't know. How many do I have permission to take?"

"I don't understand why you refuse to get a prescription. It couldn't be any worse than livin' on aspirin."

He popped four into his mouth and made a big display of chewing them.

Cathy made a face. "Thank you."

"Spite is my natural reaction to nagging." He handed the bottle back to her.

"No, keep it. You might get hungry later on."

She moved behind him and began to massage his temples, which surprised him, given the tense undercurrent since he'd walked in the door. He closed his eyes, tossing her the olive branch of letting her know it felt good.

"How did you know where it hurts?" he asked.

"I know all your headaches. The press always gets you right here."

She was right, which was amazing, since it had been years since he'd had any problems with the press. But then, Cathy had been through the thick of it, so it probably shouldn't surprise him that she remembered.

(The day of Tallen's execution, she had chased a reporter from the *Atlanta Constitution* off Lucy's front porch with a baseball bat. Called him a "selfish insensitive chicken-shit jackass." It made the front page, in a sanitized form.)

He could smell her perfume. She'd always had a knack for finding cheap perfume that didn't smell like cheap perfume. Still, hers paled in comparison to the memory of Randa's, which had been light and crisp and, he'd bet money, French. Reminded him of the perfumes he used to smell on the women at the Ritz-Carlton—the ones who dripped Chanel. It had been off-putting then, the scent of a wall he'd never scale. But without the Chanel and the jewelry and the hair that wouldn't move in a wind tunnel, the effect was different. French perfume on a woman wearing faded jeans and a baggy sweater was an alluring incongruity. At least, it could have been.

Cathy's voice saved him from his thoughts. "It doesn't make any sense."

"What?"

"That Cam would kill himself. He was always the survivor."

Jack opened his eyes. "You don't think I'm a survivor?"

"I guess that depends on your definition of survivin'."

Jack refused the bait. "I don't know why he killed himself. What difference does it make?"

She shrugged. "I just always thought Cam was safe."

"Yeah, well. Nobody's safe."

He hadn't told her about the liquor-store thing, not wanting to endure the barrage of theories sure to follow. In fact, he'd only told her about Cam's death at all because it would hit the local paper sooner or later, and she'd be insulted if she hadn't heard it from him first.

She moved away, back to the sink. She leaned against it, facing him. The look on her face made him feel like he was in the crosshair of a deer rifle.

"Was she pretty?"

Damn. How had he given himself away? He picked up the Dixie cup and drank the water slowly.

"Jack?"

He put the cup down. "Yeah, for a bloodsucking, lying, scheming, self-obsessed journalist who dragged me to a bar, I suppose she was pretty. What are you really asking me?"

"Just wondered if you noticed any signs of life below the waist."

"Mine or hers?"

"You're avoidin' the question."

"Well, that's my one true talent." He shifted in his seat. Next she'd be dissecting the Ryland story. Cathy shared his mother's ready belief in anything that defied the laws of nature, and it was a miracle she hadn't done the whole "what if it really happened?" thing yet. Apparently she realized he wasn't in the mood for that kind of nonsense, and so far she'd been able to resist the temptation. His luck wouldn't hold out forever, though.

He looked at the clock on the wall above the sink. It was almost midnight. "I should go home."

"You've been sayin' that ever since you got here. Why don't you go home?"

He didn't answer. He didn't know how to tell her, and it was getting to the point where he'd have no choice.

"Jack?"

He stared at the table for a long moment. She sat down in the chair across from him.

"Jack, what is wrong?" Her voice was full of concern that he knew was genuine. He continued to rack his brain for a way to go from *A* to *C* without passing *B*. After a long moment, he looked at her and shook his head. "It's crazy—"

"What?"

"The stupid dreams—" He had told her about the dreams yesterday, although not in any kind of detail. There was no way to describe them that did them justice.

"What about them?"

"They're not just bad dreams. Not like nightmares. They're like—" He shook his head again.

"What?"

"I don't know."

There was no use trying to explain. He didn't understand it himself. He might as well get the worst behind him.

"Can I stay here tonight?"

She gave him a look that was about what he'd expected.

"Jack . . ."

"To *sleep*."

"I can't keep you from havin' bad dreams."

"I know that."

"Then what's the point?"

He couldn't believe she needed to ask. Maybe she just wanted to hear it out loud. Hell, he'd give her that.

"I don't want to be alone."

She looked at him like she was waiting for the punch line; then, realizing there wasn't going to be one, she shifted to thinking out loud.

"All right . . ." she said, weighing it carefully. "Tommy's in the woods with Ben . . . you can sleep in his room."

"No way."

"What do you mean, no way?"

"I'm not sleeping in Tommy's room. Are we back in high school?"

"So, Jack . . . what are we solvin'? I mean, what are you gonna do *tomorrow* night?"

"I don't know. How long are they gonna be in the woods?"

"I'm serious."

"So am I." He smiled a little. She didn't return it.

"Cathy . . ."

"What?"

"Am I sleeping here?"

"I guess so. I'm not big enough to throw you out."

"Why is this such a big deal?"

She shook her head. "You're really thick sometimes."

"So tell me."

She sighed, shook her head a little; finally spoke. "You never once slept here when I asked you to, you know? When *I* needed *you*."

It landed where it was thrown. He waited a couple of respectful seconds, then decided he should at least go through the motions of defending himself.

"Look, you know—"

"Don't, Jack. Save it for somebody who doesn't know it by heart."

She got up and left the room.

He sat bolt upright in bed and reached for Cathy in the dark, but he was alone. He could hear the sound of the TV in the other room, and a dog howling in the distance. He took deep breaths and waited for his heartbeat to slow down.

The dream had been the same as last time, only more vivid. He could still see the hag-woman's face. He could still feel her hands around his throat, her thumbnails piercing the skin on his neck. He could remember the putrid smell of her sour breath. He half-expected to see her step out of the shadows. He looked around the room, though he didn't know what he was looking for.

He lay back down and closed his eyes, trying to clear

his head. He felt foggy and disoriented, as if he'd *left* reality instead of returning to it. Or like he'd come back from someplace far away—farther away than a person's mind could travel in a dream. It didn't make any sense, yet the feeling was strong. He felt drained by it.

He had a throbbing, maddening headache. He pulled himself to his feet and went to look for the bottle of aspirin Cathy had given him.

Cathy looked up from the TV.

"What's wrong?"

He shook his head and headed for the bathroom.

"Did you have a bad dream?"

"It didn't kill me. Don't worry about it."

He went into the bathroom and closed the door. He didn't care if she knew he was annoyed, even if he had no right to be. To him, it had been implicit in the unspoken deal that she would go to bed when he did, to be there if he woke up. He wanted her to hold him and tell him it was just a dream and it couldn't hurt him. He had offered her a rare glimpse of his vulnerability, and she had opted for David Letterman. On second thought, he had every right to be angry.

He popped a couple of aspirin, then turned on the cold water and splashed it on his face until he felt better. He wiped his face on a towel without bothering to take it off of the towel rack, then looked in the mirror, as if to check for damage. His heart stopped.

What the hell?

On his neck, just where he had felt her thumbnails, were small red crescents, surrounded by a cluster of purple bruises.

He blinked hard, then leaned closer to the mirror. They were still there. He touched one of the crescents and could feel a slight indentation.

Suddenly he felt a hand on his back. He gasped and swung around wildly, almost knocking Cathy over. She jumped out of the way.

"Jesus, Cathy!"

"I'm sorry. I thought you saw me."

He closed his eyes and winced as a pain shot through his head, sharp and hot. He felt Cathy's hand on his shoulder. Her skin felt cool against his. He shook his head and she pulled her hand away.

"Are you okay?"

He opened his eyes, slowly, and looked at her. "You're not going to believe this."

"What?"

He was surprised she hadn't already noticed. He pointed to his neck.

"What?" she asked again.

Maybe he wasn't pointing to the right place. He turned and looked in the mirror.

Nothing.

He put his hand to his neck.

"They're gone."

"What's gone?" she insisted, impatiently.

He looked at her. What was he supposed to say? *"A witch-woman tried to choke me in my dream and it left marks on my neck; they're gone now, but you have to believe me."*

He shook his head. "Nothing."

He moved past her, trying to look annoyed, like it was her fault she didn't see anything. He slammed the door to the bedroom—not hard, just enough to keep her from following him. He made it to the bed before his legs gave way.

What the hell was going on? Had he still been asleep when he saw the marks? Hell, no! He'd been wide

awake. Then what had he seen? He must have made the
marks himself. He'd somehow pressed his own hands on
his neck so hard that even his bitten-down-to-the-quick
nails had made the marks. And somehow they'd vanished before Cathy could see them. That had to be it.
Might not hold up to a lot of scrutiny, but it was stone
solid compared to the alternatives.

He lay down, in hopes of calming the pain in his head.
It had spread from his temples to the base of his skull, as
if someone were tightening a steel band. He definitely
had to do something about the damned headaches. They
were getting worse along with the dreams. He felt he was
under siege. Maybe Cathy was right. Maybe it was time
to break down and trek to Atlanta in search of someone
with a couch and a prescription pad. Unloading the
family secrets couldn't be any worse than this. (Although
he could just imagine his first visit. *Let's see. There were
four brothers, three with impressive criminal records,
which, by the way, includes me. One brother was executed
by the state of Alabama. One supposedly drowned,
although I've long suspected that my father killed him.
My father killed himself, which was the only good thing he
ever did for the world. My brother the token success
story just killed himself, but first he had a nervous
breakdown and killed someone else. My mother was basically psychotic and delusional by the time she died, and,
oh yeah, she killed herself, too. Me, I've never had the
guts to kill myself, but I'm working on it. I haven't been to
a therapist before now because I didn't think I needed it.*)

The lighted dial on the clock by the bed said 1:10,
which meant Cathy would probably be watching the
stupid television for at least another twenty minutes.
He'd just have to stare at the ceiling and think. Not something he relished, but he didn't have any other choice.

Something moved.

He raised his head and looked in the direction of the movement.

There's something there.

In the corner, by the dresser. It wasn't really a *thing* so much as a *shape*, but it was moving—a constant, fluid motion. Swirling. It was colorless—shades of black, somehow. The darkest parts were a vile black, like wet tar; and yet it was transparent. Looking at it was like staring through gasoline vapors.

Jack closed his eyes tightly, then opened them. It was still there. It was floating now, slowly, across the floor, still swirling within itself. For reasons that made no sense, he had the strange sensation that it was *watching* him.

It knows who I am.

It was moving toward him, slowly but steadily. He opened his mouth to call Cathy, but the dry scream lodged in his throat, making it even harder to breathe.

And then it was gone.

Gone. It didn't dissolve. It simply wasn't there anymore. He turned his head enough to make sure that the room was empty, although he knew without looking. The air around him was warm.

Oh, God . . . What was it? WHAT was it?

His mind grasped furiously for an explanation. There was only one.

It didn't happen.

Of course it happened. Why am I shaking?

You think it was there, but It wasn't. Just like the marks on your neck.

Fuck the marks on my neck! There was something in here just now! I saw it!

Right.

I'd swear on my life!

That's just what Mom used to say.

Jesus . . .

He could feel a mist of cold sweat on his chest and his forehead.

Jesus . . . could I be . . .

Yes. Of course you could be. Why the hell not?

He forced himself to stand and reached for his jeans from the back of the chair. He pulled them on. His hands were trembling so, he could barely zip them up.

There was a tap on the door, then Cathy pushed it open. "Jack?"

He couldn't look at her. He kept dressing.

"Jack, what is goin' on?"

"Nothing," he said quietly.

He was losing his mind. It was that stark and that simple.

Cathy came over and put her arms around him; kissed him on the shoulder, a gesture that was far too intimate for him in his current state. He pulled away from her. "Sorry," she said, under her breath. She was too used to it to get offended.

I'm losing my mind. Isn't that just fucking perfect?

He reached for his shirt.

"Where are you goin'?"

"Home."

"Are you mad at me about somethin'?"

He shook his head and fumbled with the buttons.

"Then why are you goin' home? I thought you wanted to stay here."

He stopped buttoning. "You know what she told me?"

"Who?"

"Cam's friend. She said he had some kind of a break-down . . . he lost his mind . . ."

Her face slowly softened as she began to understand.

"Jack . . . you're not losin' your mind. You're just havin' bad dreams." She put her hand on his arm and gave it a gentle squeeze. He kissed her on the forehead and finished buttoning his shirt on the way out the door.

Back home he turned on the shower and let the hot water pour over his head, as if it could wash away the events of the last forty-eight hours, and he could start over somehow.

What was happening to him? The onset of schizophrenia? A brain tumor? Or just a garden-variety nervous breakdown? Was that what had happened to Cam? Did things like that run in families? Would the imaginary sights and sounds turn into a sudden urge to rob a liquor store? Or was he just going to gradually disintegrate until he wound up living on a heating grate in downtown Atlanta, shouting to passersby that aliens were controlling his brain?

Out of the shower, he dried his hair with a towel and made a point of looking (*really* looking) at his face in the mirror. He hadn't cared what he looked like in ten years, just as long as he looked clean-cut enough not to threaten anyone who might want him to paint their house. Now all of a sudden, in the middle of a nervous breakdown, he found himself wondering what he looked like. He didn't look crazy. Did crazy people look crazy when they first started to go crazy?

He made his way to the bedroom and lay down on top of the covers. He folded the pillow and propped his head on it, in an effort to keep from nodding off. He did not want to know what his subconscious had in store for him next.

He knew why he was thinking about his looks. That damned woman. What was there about her that brought back thoughts that hadn't troubled him in years? He couldn't shake the feeling that he was going to see her again. Like they'd made some date he had every intention of keeping. What if they *had* made some arrangement to get together again? Where would they have met? What would they have talked about? Would she have apologized for the Ryland story and begged him to forgive her? Would he have? (He knew the answer to that one, although he'd have made her work for it.) Would he have told her that he'd been hallucinating; and, if so, would he have told her before or after he slept with her? God. What would it be like, after all this time, to sleep with a woman he was actually strongly attracted to? He was, he realized, making the gigantic assumption that *she* was attracted to *him.* It had been a very long time since he'd tried to capitalize on his looks, so he had no idea what, if anything, remained intact. (*Slightly aged but formerly extremely good-looking schizophrenic wishes to hook up with beautiful, understanding single white female, preferably recently deceased brother's ex-girlfriend . . .*)

He suddenly realized what he was doing and winced. He told himself that it was just easier to fantasize about her than to wonder about what was happening to him. In fact, if she hadn't hit him at a vulnerable time, he probably would never have given her a second thought.

The clock said 3:16. He should probably try to get some sleep, even if it meant risking the dreams. When he lost sleep he just got more depressed, and he needed to keep his head as clear as possible, to deal with whatever the hell was going on.

He reached over to turn off the lamp and for the first time saw that the red message light was blinking on his answering machine. He thought for sure he'd checked it when he came in, but he must not have. He debated leaving it for morning, since he knew it was Rick with Monday's work schedule. But every once in a while Rick found weekend work for him, and the idea of having something to do tomorrow appealed to him. Anything to keep his mind off his encroaching insanity. He pulled himself to his feet, made his way to the phone and hit the "play" button.

For a few seconds there was only static, and Jack had decided it was a hang-up and reached to reset the machine when he heard the voice.

". . . Jack . . . you have to get help . . ." The line crackled for another second, then the voice returned. *"She was telling you the truth . . ."*

Jack felt his legs give way and he collapsed onto the chair.

More static. Replaced by a dial tone, then the machine's robot voice: *"End of messages."*

He reached for the machine. His hand was shaking so that it was all he could do to rewind the tape. He heard the static again and waited. It went on and on, long after the message should have started. The dial tone cut it off again. *"End of messages."*

Jack rewound the tape again and hit the "play" button. The machine beeped at him. *"End of messages."*

He pulled the tape out and made sure it had rewound all the way. It had. He snapped it back into the machine and pressed the button, hard, as if that would help. *"End of messages,"* the machine insisted.

Nothing. There's nothing on the damned tape!

Jack put his face in his hands and tried to breathe. His eyes were welling up and his throat had closed so tightly it made his chest hurt.

The voice was still echoing in his head. He hadn't heard it for a long time, but he knew it well.

It was Tallen.

CHAPTER 8

Randa stared at Tillie's breakfast menu through unfocused eyes, the result of a hangover that rivaled anything she'd ever done to herself at a freshman mixer, and tried to remember why it had seemed like a good idea to stay and have two more drinks last night after Jack had stormed out.

Could it possibly be because you apparently had an in-depth conversation with a ghost?

I did not have a conversation with a ghost. There are a million logical explanations.

Name one.

Maybe it was someone pretending to be Ryland. Cam had a respectable amount of money and, as far as anyone knew, no locatable next of kin.

The man you saw was the man in Cam's scrapbook, and you know it.

Maybe Ryland isn't really dead. Maybe Jack lied.

Why would he lie?

Well, Cam seems to have lied to me all over the place. Maybe they're a family of pathological liars. They're certainly a family of pathological somethings.

The breakfast crowd had not paid her a lot of attention, with the exception of the occasional scowl she was getting from the little old woman who owned the guest house she had checked into upon discovering she was too drunk to drive to Atlanta.

She looked out the window and was just beginning to worry about the possibility of Jack showing up when she saw him, a blur of old denim, making his way up the highway, his hands in his pockets. He was walking briskly, as if he were late for an appointment. Barely checking for traffic, he half-ran across the road. He came through the door and headed straight for her booth, sliding into the seat across from her like she'd been waiting for him.

"I called every hotel in Atlanta looking for you."

This was a long way from what she'd expected; it took a herculean effort to conceal that fact.

"Why?"

"I wanted to talk to you."

"You could have fooled me last night." *Watch it. Not too frosty. He'll think you care.*

"Will you just hear me out?"

"Why, certainly. You were so patient with me, the least I can do is return the favor." *Frosty and sarcastic is different.*

"Let me know when you've gotten all of this out of your system," he said, without emotion. He was untouchable behind the fortress of that blank expression, and he knew it. She wanted to kick him.

"Okay," she said. "What is it?"

"I need to know the truth."

"About what?"

"What you said, about talking to Ryland. I have to know if that really happened."

"How could it have happened? You said Ryland's been dead for years."

"Forget that. Let *me* worry about it."

The redheaded waitress appeared, Bic poised above her guest check.

"What can I get y'all?"

"Coffee. Black," Randa answered, mechanically.

"Two," Jack added.

"You don't want nothin' to eat?" It was directed to Jack, as if Randa weren't there.

"No thanks."

She pocketed the guest check, took Randa's menu and was gone.

Jack went on. "The guy who said he was Ryland. Where did you see him?"

"Cam's living room. He said I should find you and give you the books. I asked him why he didn't do it himself. He said he couldn't get through your thick skull." She paused for effect, then added, "I can't imagine what he could have meant by that."

Jack remained stoic. "So what was it that a total stranger was supposed to be able to get through my thick skull?"

"He seemed to think you were in some kind of trouble."

"What kind of trouble?"

"I don't know. He wasn't making a lot of sense. But then, the poor guy's been dead for three years, I guess I shouldn't pick on his syntax."

The waitress returned with two mugs of coffee.

"Are y'all sure you don't want breakfast?" It was again aimed at Jack. Randa had a sneaking suspicion the girl had a greater interest in eavesdropping on their conversation than any genuine concern over Jack's nutritional needs. He looked at her, annoyed.

"We're sure," he said. "Hadn't you better stop talking to me, before you get Darlene all upset again?"

Her face turned sheepish, so Randa assumed Jack had hit a nerve. Whatever he'd done, it had worked. She was gone. Jack turned back to Randa.

"How can I know?" he asked.

"Know what?"

"That you're not just trying to trick me into something."

"Oh, come on. Are we going to do that one again?" It came out louder than she'd meant it to, and Randa was drawing stares, but she was too annoyed to care. "Look, if I wanted to write some tabloid exposé on your sacred family, I would have done it a long time ago and I wouldn't have needed you. Cam's followers will have a new messiah by the time I get home, so a story about his childhood wouldn't even be an easy sell, much less a hot property. And in case you haven't noticed, this country has been executing people at far too rapid a rate for anyone to give a fuck about Tallen anymore. So if I'm trying to trick you into a story, *you* tell *me* what the hell story I'm trying to trick you into."

He was quiet for a long moment, staring into his coffee. When he finally spoke, he didn't look up.

"Then why are you here?"

"I don't know."

He looked at her.

"I really don't know. The man who said he was Ryland told me that I'd do this if I cared anything about your family."

"Why do you care about my family?"

"Apparently I have a pathological obsession with them, if you want the unsolicited opinion of your brother's girlfriend."

He looked at her, startled out of his shell. "I thought *you* were . . . I mean, I assumed . . ."

Randa shook her head. "Nope. My stint as Playmate of the Year was cut down in its prime by Nora Dixon, formerly my closest and most trustworthy friend."

"Cam ditched you for your best friend?" He seemed mildly amused by that.

"Well, from what I heard, Nora wasn't exactly a passive participant. And I'm the idiot who introduced them, so it's hard to come up with a blameless party in the mix." She didn't know why she was telling him any of this. It was none of his damned business. "I don't have an answer. My current theory is that I was very bad in another lifetime, and for punishment, God has made me obsessed with your family."

He smiled. He actually smiled. She'd been right, too. It took years off his face, and the hardness was replaced by something close to warmth.

"Well, whatever you did, I must have done something worse. At least you didn't have to grow up in the house with them."

He sounded like Cam when he said it, down to the tiniest inflection. It made Randa wince. She was grateful when he didn't seem to notice.

He shook his head. "I don't get it. If Ryland's still alive, why wouldn't he just come to me?" The smile was gone, as quickly as it had appeared.

"Is it possible that Ryland's still alive?"

"I guess so, technically. I didn't go to the funeral. Mainly because he'd been dead for a year before my aunt bothered to tell me."

"Why would she tell you he was dead if it wasn't true?"

He shrugged. "To be rid of me, I guess."

"It doesn't make sense. Why would he go along with it?"

"I don't know." He sipped his coffee and stared out the window. "Nothing in my life makes any sense anymore." He hesitated, then looked back at her.

"The reason I tried to find you in Atlanta"—he paused and took a breath—"I know how crazy this sounds, but last night when I got home, there was a message on my answering machine from Tallen."

Randa stared at him, waiting for him to explain. He didn't.

"You're serious?" she finally asked.

"It's not something I'd joke about."

Randa remembered Cam's claim that he'd seen Tallen, and she had to work to suppress a shudder.

"Are you sure it was Tallen?" she asked.

"It was Tallen's voice," he said. "You probably wouldn't have any trouble convincing me that I'm losing my mind, but I know Tallen's voice." He choked on the words, and stopped, stared down into his coffee cup. "It was him," he said, quietly, to no one.

"Well . . . did he . . ." *Did he what, Randa? Leave a number where he could be reached?* She tried again. "What did the message say?"

"That you were telling me the truth."

So, his ghost believed that she saw her ghost. That helped.

"Do you still have the tape?"

"There's nothing on it."

"What do you mean?"

"I mean I rewound it, there's nothing on it," he said. "Look, it's probably just—my mother was ratshit crazy when she died. My father was not even human, and Tallen had to have been at least temporarily insane to do what he did, I don't care what the fucking jury said. And if even Cam could lose it, there's no reason to think I'm somehow exempt." He sighed. "I've been coming unglued lately. I've been having these migraines, one right after another. It keeps me disoriented. And these dreams . . . I can't even describe them. They're unreal. I mean, even for dreams. It's like . . ." He groped for a word.

"Like you're going somewhere in your sleep?"

His face tensed with disbelief and went ashen. "How do you know?" he asked, in a tight whisper.

"Cam was having weird dreams, too. That's how he described them to someone."

"That's exactly how it feels," he said, still half-whispering. He put his coffee cup down and shoved it aside.

"Was there something your family referred to as 'the thing'?" Randa asked. "That's what Ryland was saying. He said, 'Tell Jack the thing is real.' "

Jack froze. He looked numb, like someone who had heard one too many bits of bad news.

"Are you okay?"

He stood up. "Let's get out of here."

Before she could answer he was up, on his way to the door. Randa signaled the waitress for the check.

She found him outside, pacing in front of her car. Randa wondered what land mine she'd stepped on this time.

"Where are we going?" she asked, bracing herself for whatever came back at her.

"I don't know," he said, quietly. "I just . . . couldn't breathe in there." He took a few steps away from the car, stopped, and stared down the road.

Randa had a sudden idea.

"Could I see the house?" she asked.

He looked back at her. "The house?"

"Your family's house. Is it near here?"

He nodded. "About five miles down thirty-six."

"I'd really love to see it," she said. She was surprised by her brazenness, but none of this felt real anyway. She was sure that any minute she'd wake up, Cam and Nora would be announcing their engagement and she'd be working on a story about where to find the best soft tacos in the San Fernando Valley.

"Well . . . okay," Jack said. "I guess we could go there."

Randa unlocked the car door quickly, before he changed his mind.

As was usually the case anywhere in Georgia, as soon as they left the town they were in the boondocks. They rode in silence. Jack stared out the window, but Randa doubted he really saw anything.

The two-lane wound them through the gentle landscape. Rolling hills dotted with grazing cattle; miles of pastures bordered by tall Georgia pines and huge old oak trees. Randa had forgotten how beautiful it was, and how deceptively peaceful. She could never look at those pastures, though, without envisioning them obscured by smoke from cannon fire, awash in carnage and chaos.

"What do you know about me?" Jack asked suddenly.

"Not much," Randa said. She wondered why he was asking. He didn't say anything else.

"I know you've done time," she said. "Cam told me."

"I'm sure he did," Jack said. He had no attitude that she could pinpoint.

"He didn't tell me what for."

"Overdue library books," Jack said, without smiling.

Randa glanced at him. She thought she could detect the tiniest trace of a smirk.

"What was it really?"

"Armed robbery."

Randa was stumped for a response. *How interesting. I've never driven down a deserted country road with an armed robber before.*

"Don't worry," he said, breaking the silence. "I gave it up." He pointed at something up ahead. "Turn left at those mailboxes."

She turned. There were pastures on either side of the gravel road, enclosed in barbed-wire fencing. In the pasture on the right, a herd of white-faced Herefords were all lying down, feet tucked neatly under their bellies, watching the car with great indifference.

"Guy down the road owns the cows," Jack offered. "He tends the fence, fertilizes and bush-hogs the pasture, in return for running his cattle on the land."

"This is your land? All of it?"

"It's not that much. Forty-five acres."

"Where's the house?"

"Other side of those trees. It's about half a mile off the road."

"How on earth did your father afford this?"

"He didn't. Ryland paid for it. My mother had this stupid theory that my father would settle down if they had their own place, so she talked Ryland into buying this place for us. It went cheap. No one around here wanted it."

"Why not?"

"Family who lived here right before we bought it . . . guy went nuts one night and took an ax to his wife and three kids, then shot himself. Nobody was in a big mood to live here after that."

"I'm surprised your mother would."

"What my mother wanted more than anything else was a permanent address. I guess that won out over potential ghosts."

"Did anything weird ever happen?"

"If I ever heard anything go bump in the night, it was generally my father slamming my mother's head against the wall."

The road curved and suddenly the house was in sight.

There was nothing about the house that offered any

hint of its ugly past. It was the standard white clapboard story-and-a-half farmhouse with a front porch, the roof of which was supported by concrete and brick pillars. The place wasn't immaculate, but it wasn't in a state of disrepair either. The only thing that would even verge on gothic was the fact that it was so isolated. It was impossible to see the road from the house, and empty fields stretched out beyond it on all sides. Will must have loved that—plenty of room to wreak havoc on Lucy and the kids, and no one within miles to hear anything and call the cops.

"Forgive the obvious question, but why don't you live here?" Randa asked.

"Too many bad memories, I guess. As trite as that must sound."

"Then why don't you sell it?"

"Partly because I don't want to deal with all that."

"What's the other part?"

"I have this fantasy of striking a match to it." He didn't smile when he said it. "Burn the fucker to the ground, just sit here and watch."

"So why haven't you?"

"I guess I'm waiting for the right moment."

He nodded toward a small barn a few yards away. "I'm going to get something for the ducks." He was gone, disappearing inside. Randa looked around, wondering what ducks he was talking about. He returned with a small red plastic bucket full of dried corn.

"You don't mind walking, do you?"

She shook her head and followed him. It was chilly, but the quiet was intoxicating, worth any discomfort. The sky was gray from the storm front that had not quite moved on, and it gave the place a touch of the ominous atmosphere it deserved. Jack led her up a hill, down a shallow valley and up over a ridge, beyond which there was a small lake. The silence was broken by a frenzy of quacking from the half-dozen mallards on the lake, who had seen them coming. Randa smiled. Ducks always seemed like cartoon animals to her. Cute, but surely not meant to be taken seriously. Jack reached into the bucket and tossed a handful of corn to the shoreline. The ducks waddled out of the water and all dove after the same kernel, not noticing that the ground was yellow-speckled all around them.

Randa watched Jack watching the ducks. No matter how he felt about the house, he and the land suited each other nicely. It was the first place she had seen him look as if he belonged. He looked almost calm.

He tossed the ducks another handful of corn, then put the bucket down on the ground and sat beside it. She didn't know whether she was supposed to join him or not. She sat, careful not to get too close. He didn't even seem to notice.

"So, are you going to tell me what 'the thing' is?" she asked, as gently as possible.

He nodded, slightly, and stared at the ducks for a moment before speaking. When he did, his tone was matter-of-fact.

"My mother had this theory that there was a curse on our family," he said.

"Was this theory based on anything?"

"A seventy-five-cent fortune-teller she saw at a county fair when she was nineteen years old." He smiled, remembering, and shook his head.

"Is there a story that goes with this?"

"Yeah, there's a story," he said. "I suppose you want to hear it."

Randa nodded.

"Okay," he said. "Lucy and the Fortune-Teller. Well, she had this friend called Bird, don't ask me why. She and my mother were best friends in school and they hung out until my father started moving us all over creation. So my parents had been married for about a year and they were still living somewhere down near Savannah, where my mother grew up. One night my father and Bird's boyfriend were out somewhere getting drunk, as usual. My mother and Bird didn't have anything to do, and the fair was in town, so they went. Rode rides, played bingo, all that stuff. Just as they were leaving, they saw this cheesy fortune-teller's tent, so they decided it would be fun to have their fortunes told. Bird had this brainstorm: she put on my mother's wedding ring. You know, to test the fortune-teller."

He paused for breath, then continued. "So, they go in and pay their buck and a half to this old woman, who was wearing what my mother described as a tacky gypsy outfit—as opposed to a classy gypsy outfit, I guess—and the old woman looks in her crystal ball for a few minutes, then she looks at Bird and she says, 'Why are you wearing that ring? You're not married and you're going to have a lot of trouble before you're ever married.' Now, Bird's kind of impressed with the ring thing, except that she's engaged and getting married in a month. She decides the old woman must have seen her take Mother's ring. Meanwhile, the old woman turns to my mother. She looks at her, she looks into her crystal ball, she looks back at my mother. Then she gets this look on her face like she's just seen a ghost, and she says to my mother, 'You'll have to leave.' My mother says, 'What are you talking about?' The old woman says, 'When I see this, I don't go near it. That's my one rule.' My mother says, 'When you see *what*?' But the old woman just keeps telling her to leave. Well, Mother's not about to leave now. Finally the old woman says she'll say one thing, but then Mother has to leave. She says, 'You've taken on a debt you don't know about. You'll pay, your children will pay, a lot of people will pay, for a long time.' That's all she would say, and she wouldn't explain what it meant. She just kept saying 'I don't go near this,' and practically shoved my mother and Bird out of her tent.

"So my mother and Bird decided the old woman was a nutcase. Then, a couple of weeks later, Bird's fiancé got drunk and wrapped his car around a tree. Died instantly. Whereupon my mother decided the fortune-teller was the real McCoy, and there was a curse on our family. Everything that went wrong after that, she blamed it on the curse. When we were kids, we believed it. Then we got older and started using it. Told her we had this strange compulsion to get into trouble. We tried hard to resist, but it was just bigger than we were."

"Did she buy it?"

"Of course. It was a hell of a lot easier than believing she was raising a bunch of sociopaths."

"Where did she think this curse came from?"

"That was the big question. She spent the rest of her life trying to figure it out. She imported mediums from five counties and held séances in our house constantly. They consulted Ouija boards, they threw tarot cards, you name it."

"And?"

"Pick a theory. My personal favorite was that my father's father was a direct descendent of Genghis Khan and his spirit was haunting us. Mediums loved the fact that my father was illegitimate, because it left them wide open for the evil ancestors stories . . ."

"What did your mother believe?"

"Whatever was the last story she'd been told. Although I think she liked the Genghis Khan one, too."

"And that's the thing?"

He nodded. "We used to call it Mother's thing, or the curse thing."

"Then that's it."

"What?"

"Ryland and Tallen are trying to tell you that there really is a curse."

"Oh, please."

"I know it's crazy, but it's happening."

"Give me a break." He shook his head. "My family was cursed, all right. It started when my mother married Will Landry, and there was nothing supernatural about it."

"Then how do you explain me seeing Ryland?"

"He's still alive, he's turned on me for some reason, and the family is after Cam's money. They think if they scare the hell out of me, I'll stay away."

"What about the phone call?"

"I imagined it. I'm being taken over by the family insanity."

Randa thought about it. She supposed it made a lot more sense than the alternatives, but it still didn't feel right.

"So, you'd rather believe you're losing your mind than entertain the notion of an afterlife?"

He looked at her, a bit taken aback. "Do you believe in that crap?"

"I don't know. I guess I think it's arrogant to believe there's nothing in the universe that we don't know about."

He shook his head. "It just seems so stupid to me."

"What?" she asked.

"The idea that if you survive this quagmire—not that

you're going to *survive* it, because there's only one way out of here—but if you endure it, and stay reasonably good-humored about it, surprise, there's all sorts of meaning and order in store for you after you die. What kind of sense does that make?"

"I didn't say I thought it made sense."

He picked up a small stone and skipped it, effortlessly, across the pond. He didn't even seem to realize he'd done it.

"So, what's *your* theory?" she asked.

"Theory?"

"Of how it all works."

"I don't have one." He smiled, a sad smile. "I made a deal with the universe. I'll leave it alone if it'll leave me alone."

"Does that work?"

"It did until recently." He smiled again. She was growing fond of that smile, as much as she hated to admit it to herself. Under the jean jacket, he was wearing a pale olive corduroy shirt, the same color as his eyes. Like the denim, it was old and faded. It softened him somehow. *Why do you have to be such a good-looking asshole?*

"What about you?" he asked. "Do you have a theory?"

Randa nodded. "It's simple. God is a sadist."

Jack laughed. "Sold."

She became serious. "I guess I have my own version of a deal with the universe."

"What's that?"

"I've agreed to be okay with the mess."

"What do you get in return?"

"I don't know. I'm spared the pain of hope, I guess."

Not true. She didn't really feel spared much of any-thing, and being "okay with the mess" was only some-thing she aspired to.

"That's not it," she admitted, quietly. "Maybe I don't get anything." She looked away from him. "How much of anything we believe is a choice, anyway?"

"I'd like to think that all of it is."

"Yeah. I'd *like* to think that. I'd *like* to think that Cybill Shepherd really colors her hair with stuff she buys at the grocery store, too, but there's the small matter of the truth."

"And what is the truth?"

"I don't know what it is. I just know what it isn't. Look, you're into control and definitions, and if that works for you, I guess that's fine."

"What are you into? Being a victim?"

"I prefer to think of it as acceptance. Refusing to tilt at windmills. That's why I detest all that New Age crap— everything's all goodness and light if you just look at it the right way. I mean, maybe it is, but I can't get myself interested in remaining in the 'light' for any length of time. It never feels real. It just feels like a lot of work to prop up a façade, and, ultimately, it always lets you down. But the dark is very trustworthy. It's always as dark as you thought it was. And you don't have to work at staying there. All you have to do is survive it. And I've been doing that forever."

"You've got it all figured out. Why aren't you a Zen master?" He smiled when he said it, so apparently he wasn't trying to be hostile. Maybe it was another trait he shared with Cam, who'd always loved nothing better than a good, convoluted philosophical argument. At any rate, she didn't feel self-conscious about answering.

"Because I still wind up with this ache for something better. Something that would feel *right* even if it didn't make sense. But I don't know what that something is, or if it even exists."

Jack nodded. "Yeah, well . . ." He spoke softly. "I think that's the choice you make."

"What?"

"Whether you want to live your life a hostage to that ache."

He stared off at the horizon for a moment and didn't speak. Randa managed to resist the urge to ask the obvious question. (*So what* ARE *you living your life a hostage to?*) Suddenly, Jack stood up.

"Come on, I'll show you the house."

Where the hell did that come from?

A few steps from the back door, he stopped. He turned and looked at her; stared into her eyes for a long moment, unflinching. Was there something he was waiting for her to say or do? Was there something he was trying to get up the nerve to say? She got no sense of either. He seemed perfectly comfortable staring into her eyes.

"I love your eyes," he said, finally.

"Thanks." It sounded incredibly stupid, but she couldn't think of anything else to say. "I love yours, too" would have sounded twice as insipid, even though it was true. She could have lapsed into total codependence and given him fifteen reasons why he *shouldn't* love her eyes, but she could hear her therapist's voice (" *'Thank you' is a complete sentence*"). She stopped there.

He was still staring at her. She felt something shift. Was he moving closer to her? Jesus, was he going to kiss her? How had this happened? He *was* going to kiss her, although he was taking his damned good time about it. Should she protest, or turn away and start walking as if she hadn't noticed?

And then, whatever she'd felt was gone. He stepped away from her. "I'll be right back," he said, and headed for the barn, to return the bucket, she assumed.

She watched him go, wondering what the hell had just

happened. Had she gotten all worked up over something that she had only imagined? She strained, trying to remember what she'd sensed, and why. Nothing came to her. Dammit. When had reality become so slippery, so fucking subjective? It was like trying to fish a piece of eggshell out of a bowl of raw eggs. Every time she thought she had it, it would scoot away, propelled, in fact, by her own effort to close in on it.

He returned from the barn with a key in his hand and, with no further comment, unlocked the back door. He motioned her inside.

"After you."

She brushed past him and stepped across the threshold, into their house.

The back door opened into the kitchen—an old farm kitchen with beaded-board walls, covered in yellow-white paint that was flaking in random and somehow sinister patterns. The appliances were all several decades old, and the floor was a hideous gray-and-maroon marbled linoleum, rippled by time and curled in the corners. Jack turned on a light, which she knew only from the sound of the switch; the room didn't get any brighter.

There was nothing "ghostly," per se, about the place. The eerie feeling had nothing to do with the threat of diaphanous apparitions or a sudden drop in room temperature. It was something much more insidious. Something blacker.

Evil.

That was it. There was something downright evil here. She didn't know what that meant, or if she even believed in such a thing. Still, the word was flashing through her head like a neon sign.

Randa stood and looked around at the room, taking it all in. Jack seemed to understand (or at least be willing to indulge) her need to do that. He stood in silent patience. He followed her when she moved on.

The living room was even drearier than the kitchen. The same beaded-board in a worse state of peeling. The sofa and chairs were covered with dingy sheets. Randa couldn't imagine why Jack would feel the need to protect the furniture, or that there was anything under the sheets that was worth protecting. The end tables were probably halfway decent antiques, under about twenty coats of black varnish. There were a couple of fringed Victorian lamps and even framed photos on the tables—mostly various school pictures of the boys. (Randa cringed as she spotted a gap-toothed six-year-old Cam grinning up at her.) Overall, the room looked as if the family had just gone out of town for an unknown period and simply never come back.

There was a hallway on the other side of the room. Randa glanced down it and could see an open door and a little bit of a bedroom that seemed to have a similarly depressing decor.

"My parents' room," Jack said, answering her unspoken question. "Our rooms are upstairs."

"I can see why you never come in here. No offense, but I can't believe this was a better option than any of the rented places."

"The rented places were nicer, but my father liked it here. My mother thought that would make a difference."

"He *liked* it?"

"He wasn't exactly a cheery guy. Cam may have mentioned that. I think he was attracted to the house's history, too."

"The man who murdered his family?"

Jack nodded. "His name was Bennett Reece. I think he was Will's hero."

"*Because* he murdered his family?"

Jack nodded. "I think Will admired him for having the guts to do the full job."

Jack opened the front door and stepped onto the porch. Randa decided to leave him alone, and took the opportunity to check out the bedroom. She stood in the doorway and stared at a double bed with a wrought-iron head-board, and wondered how on earth a woman could lie down and go to sleep beside a man who routinely sent her children to the emergency room. What sickness had bound the two of them? She knew it was too late for questions like that to be answered. It was too late for them to even matter.

When Randa returned to the living room, Jack was still outside. She could see him in the front yard, walking aimlessly, gazing out at the land. He obviously did not want to be in the house. She opted to finish the tour without him.

The old wood of the stairs creaked in protest under her weight. They were sunken in the middle from too many years of use, and the entire stairway, wall included, listed toward the left side of the house. It was almost as though the house was tilted from the burden of what had gone on within it.

About halfway up the stairs, the beaded-board ended, and Randa was amazed to find that the remaining walls were unfinished. The planks were gray-brown and weathered like the side of a barn, and there were cracks between them on the inside walls. There were three tiny rooms; all still had small beds and dressers. There were twin beds in the middle room, which left space for little else. Randa assumed this was the room that Jack and Tallen had shared.

She felt a lump rise in her throat as she thought of Cam and Jack, and even the ones she didn't know, living up here in what was barely more than an attic. She thought of them lying in bed, listening to their parents try to kill each other in the rooms below. Cam had told her that he was the only one of the four who'd ever ventured downstairs to try to break up the fight. The rest of them had either put their heads under their pillows, or climbed out windows and gone off into the night, looking for trouble that they could control.

She made her way back down the stairs, slowly, formulating an explanation in case she needed one. She stopped when she saw Jack. He was standing just inside the front door, staring at an empty spot in the far corner of the room. He didn't show any sign of noticing her.

"Jack?"

He didn't answer.

"Jack?"

"What?" He broke out of his trance and saw her looking at him. "Sorry. I just . . . flashed on something."

"What?" She eased down the last two stairs, hoping he wouldn't notice she'd been up there without him. She needn't have worried. His mind was somewhere far away.

"The day they killed Tallen," he said, in a quiet voice. He breathed deeply, collecting himself before he continued. "He didn't want any of us there, so my mother and Cam and I were sitting here the next morning. . . ." He nodded toward the corner. "There used to be a TV over there, and we were watching the news. This sports . . ."

He stopped; laughed to himself, a bitter laugh. "I almost said sportscaster." He shook his head; took another moment.

"This reporter was interviewing people on the street about the execution . . . and there was this woman . . . she had on this *hat*. I don't know why it matters, but something about that hat just irked the hell out of me. Anyway, the reporter asked her if the execution made her feel like justice had been served, and she said that it did, then she said, 'Some people are just animals, and you kill rabid animals, so what's the difference?' "

He stopped again and took yet another breath, upset by the memory.

"My mother had this antique iron she used as a doorstop. I grabbed it and . . . kind of . . . hurled it through the TV screen." He smiled sadly.

"That couldn't have been good for the TV," Randa said, trying to lighten the mood.

"No, but it sure felt great." He chuckled, looking at the corner again. "Glass flew everywhere. Smoke, sparks, the works. My mother screamed."

"What did Cam do?"

Jack's face clouded over. "Jesus was not pleased. He just picked up his suitcase and walked out the door. Went back to LA. I didn't see him again until my mother's funeral, about a year later." Jack looked out the window, as if he were watching Cam go.

"What happened then? After Cam left?"

He looked back at her, a bit startled. The story was over, as far as he was concerned.

"What do you mean?"

"Was your mother angry?"

"With me? No."

"With Cam?"

He snorted. "Are you kidding?" He paused for a second, letting the anger pass.

"My mother," he continued, "was so far gone by that point Tallen's death was really the last straw."

He took a few steps away from Randa, as if he needed the distance. She could see his face go taut with pain.

"Have you ever read a detailed account of what happens when someone is electrocuted?" he asked.

"No," Randa answered, without admitting that she'd tried to and couldn't get through it.

"I read every one I could get my hands on. I hunted for them. It was like a compulsion. I just had to know."

Randa prayed he wasn't going to share any of it with her, but she knew what was coming.

"They shave the person's head, you know, so they can attach the electrodes. And then they have to rub this gel in—something that helps conduct the electricity. The gel has to be rubbed in really well; takes about forty-five minutes. Imagine sitting there for forty-five minutes while someone rubs gel into your head so they can kill you easier. But that's really nothing compared to the rest of it."

Randa wanted desperately not to hear the rest of it, but she sensed he needed to tell her. She braced herself.

"You know, they have to wear a diaper because their bowels and bladder let go. Tallen was so dignified, in his own way—he must have hated that, having to die in a fucking diaper . . ." He paused, thinking about it, then went on. "They also vomit blood. The body reaches a temperature of about nineteen hundred degrees—there have been cases where a body was so hot it melted the electrodes. The skin turns bright red and stretches, almost to the point of breaking. The brain reaches the boiling point of water. The eyes pop out of the sockets and end up resting on their cheeks. Witnesses say there's this loud sound, like bacon frying, and it smells—I don't know, like however it smells when you cook a person. Smoke comes out of the person's head; sometimes flames. And this is all if everything goes *well*. I read about this one where something went wrong and it took twenty minutes and three separate jolts of electricity to kill the guy. He stayed conscious for a while, and in between jolts, he was begging them to hurry. By the time he was finally pronounced dead, the body was so hot they had to wait an hour before they could even touch him to move him out of the room." He stopped for a moment, but he wasn't done. "In one of the articles I read, a doctor described it as 'setting a person on fire from the inside.' "

He stopped, closed his eyes for a moment, working to steady himself. Randa could see him shaking.

"Everybody tries to justify it with this eye-for-an-eye shit. Well, Tallen didn't set anybody on fire from the inside. In fact, I read a lot of true crime, and I've never read about a murder that was as cruel as what happened to Tallen."

Randa nodded. She wanted to tell him that he was preaching to the converted, but there'd be time for that later.

"Anyway . . . can you *imagine* having all of that happen to someone you love? Your brother? Your *child*?"

"No," Randa said, quietly. There was no way she could imagine it.

"Well, if it does, there's no way you can *avoid* imagining it."

His voice cracked and he couldn't go on. He closed his eyes and took a deep breath. Randa could feel tears welling in her own eyes; she blinked them back. After a moment, Jack opened his eyes. He had summoned a bit of strength from somewhere.

"So . . . if you want to know how my mother was . . . that's how she was. The warden might as well have strapped her in next to Tallen. When she finally killed herself, it was just a formality."

Randa didn't know what to say, yet the silence was too sensitive to bear. Jack stared at the floor, unable to meet her eyes. Randa doubted he'd opened up like that in a long time—maybe not even since Tallen's death. She

ached for him. She had a strong urge to go over and put
her arms around him, just hold him for a long time, but
she couldn't imagine him letting her (or anyone) do that.

"Jack."

He looked up. His eyes were red.

"I'm really, really sorry." It sounded ridiculously
lame, but she didn't know what else to say.

"You didn't do anything."

"You know what I mean. I'm sorry for you."

He just stared at her, not knowing what to make of it.

"Why don't we go," she suggested. She was uncomfortable under his stare, and he needed to get out of the
place, whether he knew it or not.

He nodded, looking enormously relieved. He turned
and headed back through the kitchen. Randa followed.
She reached up and put her hand on his back. She felt
him flinch under her touch; she pulled her hand away.

Outside, he locked the door behind her and then
returned the key to its place in the barn. When he came
back, he had an odd look on his face. He stopped in front
of Randa and stared at her, the way he had done before.
There was something in his eyes that looked like desperation on a tight rein. It was hard not to look away, but
Randa was determined to hold her own in whatever this
was. Her resolve seemed to calm him. He reached for her
hand. Randa wouldn't have been any more surprised if
he'd slapped her, and she doubted she was doing a good
job of hiding that fact. He led her back toward the car,
gripping her hand tightly, as if they'd come to some kind
of an understanding.

Suddenly, he stopped walking. In one motion that didn't
leave her time to think, he pulled her to him and kissed
her. There wasn't a trace of first-kiss awkwardness; his
lips met hers as if they'd rehearsed. She knew instantly
that no one had ever kissed her like this, although she

couldn't have defined the difference with a gun to her head. He kissed her the way she'd always wanted to be kissed—the way she always imagined it would be, in those seconds before someone kissed her, those seconds that were always followed by mild-to-moderate disappointment, and a mental analysis of what wasn't working. *This* was working. It literally took her breath.

Still, she could feel him holding back. She could feel the desperation she'd seen in his eyes, but it was under unyielding control. Something wild in her wanted to cut loose and break through his wall. Something else was afraid to move. She ended up, like him, in some ill-defined area in between.

Out of nowhere, he broke away. He turned and looked behind him.

"What was that?"

"What?"

He cocked his head and squinted, as if reacting to a sound.

"That!" He looked at her. "You didn't hear that?" She shook her head.

He took a few steps toward the house, listening. After a moment, he turned and hurried back to her.

"Let's get out of here," he said, and got into the car. Randa, left with no option, followed.

"What is going on?" she asked, slamming her door.

"Nothing. It must have been the wind." He was gone again, back inside his shell. And there was no wind, but Randa knew it would do no good to point that out.

Neither of them spoke on the ride back into town. Randa didn't know what to say, and Jack just stared out the window. He asked if she would drop him off at his place, and she pulled up in front of the boardinghouse and turned the engine off.

"Now," she said firmly, lest he try to make a run for it, "do you want to talk about it?"

"There's nothing to talk about. It was just the wind."

"I meant before that."

"Oh." He stared at the dashboard. "Should I apologize?"

"Only for stopping."

He smiled a little at that, which encouraged her.

"What happened? Scare yourself?"

"Something like that." He finally looked at her. He was still smiling, but it was a nervous smile.

"Look, why don't we go out to dinner tonight?" she said, pressing her luck. "We can relax, talk some more." She stopped. A look had come over his face, as if she'd just told him the tumor was inoperable.

"Dinner? You mean, at Tillie's or something?"

"No. Someplace nice. Someplace with dim lighting and a liquor license."

He looked out the window. "I don't know."

A thought occurred to her. "Is it that you don't have anything to wear?"

He looked at her. "Did you go through my closet, too?"

"That's not an answer," she said, avoiding the accusation.

"Neither is that," he said.

"Jack . . ."

"No, it isn't because I don't have anything to wear. You can't belong to my family without owning a suit, there's a funeral every five minutes."

"Then what is it?"

"You know. I don't do things like that."

"Yeah, it seems to work, too. You're obviously deliriously happy."

"It's not about being happy."

"Then what is it about?"

He shook his head, but didn't answer. She tried again. "One night isn't going to kill you. It'll be good for you. You might even have fun. Or is 'fun' something else you don't do?"

"All right," he said. "Call off the hounds."

"You'll go?"

"If it'll shut you up. But I'm not drinking, and you're not getting anything out of me in dim lighting that you wouldn't get out of me at Wal-Mart."

"We'll see."

He leaned over and kissed her; a quick peck on the cheek, as if it were no big deal.

"I'll be back here at six to pick you up," she said.

"Whatever," he said, either resigned or feigning resignation. He held the door open, but didn't make a move to get out.

Uh-oh . . . he's coming up with an excuse . . .

He leaned over and kissed her again. Like he meant it. Like the first time.

He pulled away, smiled at her.

"*Did* you go through my closet?"

"Don't worry. I didn't touch a single skeleton."

"I don't understand why I don't hate you," he said, and got out of the car. As Randa drove away, she could see him in her rearview mirror, standing at the curb, watching her until she was out of sight.

Well, Randa, you've done it. You've managed to find someone even weirder than Cam.

She soaked in the antique claw-foot tub in her bathroom at the guest house, and took stock of her life.

She'd been valedictorian of her high school class. Graduated magna cum laude (fifteenth in a class of 929) from a college that prided itself on an impossible curriculum and a high suicide rate. She'd moved to Los

Angeles to set the world on fire, win a Pulitzer, and
marry some fascinating man who adored her—preferably
another writer. They'd buy a Green & Green bungalow
in Pasadena, just off the parade route, and every year
they'd throw a New Year's Eve party people lived in
terror of not being invited to. She and Mr. Perfect would
both have offices at home, on opposite sides of the house,
and they'd write all day. On those rare nights when, for
some reason, they could stand to keep their hands off
each other, they would sit in front of a fire and drink
brandy and read poetry aloud, or talk about their work.
(Mr. Perfect, of course, would be far too secure to be
jealous of her accomplishments.) Eventually, they'd have
a couple of gorgeous kids and a politically correct dog,
and in between carpooling and trips to the vet, she'd
write the Great American Novel.

Now here she was, all these years later, without one
thing that even resembled the life she'd dreamed of.
Instead, she lived alone in a tiny, overpriced apartment
with no air-conditioning and lousy plumbing; she was
welded to a low-paying, dead-end job, the politics of
which were taking years off her life. Mr. Perfect, who
wasn't all that perfect to begin with, had ridden off into
the sunset with her best friend; and then, just for spite, had
invited Randa to his suicide. Now, for reasons unknown
to her, she was spending her trust fund on a lovely vacation in Hicksville, after she'd sworn it would take the
Second Coming or her mother's funeral to get her back
here. She was sitting in a strange tub, in a strange room, in
a strange town, thrilled to death because Mr. Perfect's
estranged brother—an antisocial day laborer with a prison
record—had grudgingly accepted her dinner invitation.

Back home in LA, Randa belonged to a small therapy
group, all women. For the most part, the group had been
a lifeline, but there was one woman who had grated on

Randa's nerves from day one. Bernadette. There wasn't an addiction on the planet that Bernadette didn't claim to be recovering from, and she had a twelve-step quip for every occasion. Right now, one of Bernadette's favorite maxims was reverberating in Randa's head, over and over, without mercy (and in Bernadette's whiny, nasal voice): "If you want to make God laugh," Bernadette would say, "tell Him your plans."

CHAPTER 9

She hadn't heard it. How was that possible? It had been so close; so clear. He'd tried to figure out where it was coming from, but it seemed to be coming from everywhere.

"Jack..."

A man's voice, whispering; a loud whisper that wanted to be heard. Eerie, in some way he couldn't define. At first it had just called his name. After he'd moved away from her, it had said something else . . .

"I know who you are."

What the hell did that mean? And where had it come from?

Your brain, idiot. Where else could it have come from?

Why couldn't he shake the feeling that she was somehow responsible?

How could she be responsible?

From the moment he'd first seen her, he'd been torn in two. Half of him was drawn to her as if he'd been waiting for her all his life. The other half wanted to turn and run in the opposite direction, as far and as fast as possible. That panic had tripled the moment he kissed her, even though it had felt better than anything he could remember in his life. Why did she scare him so much?

She's dangerous.

She's not dangerous. She's honest and good. I can feel it.

Really? Where exactly can you feel it? Hell, she could have pushed Cam out that window, for all you know. She could be here for you now.

Oh, for Christ's sake...

Losing his mind was so much more lucid than he ever would have guessed. He would have imagined it as all of reality starting to blur and fade, like a watercolor left out in the rain until nothing was recognizable; or else the colors would form new shapes and images that made sense only to him. But it wasn't like that at all. Reality remained in place, as relentless as ever. *He* was the only thing blurring and fading, and no one else could see it.

Why did you say you'd go out to dinner? Why didn't you get rid of her while you had the chance?

What do you mean, get rid of her? I don't want to be rid of her.

What if the voice wasn't in your head? What if it's real?

Don't be ridiculous.

He was standing in the shower, lost in a spray of hot water and steam. The water felt good, but he hadn't taken his eyes off the shower curtain, vigilantly watching for shadows or signs of movement. (Damned paranoid crap. Damned Alfred Hitchcock.) He was afraid to turn the water off—the silence was somehow worse than any noise, and he didn't want to do anything to upset the delicate equilibrium. But he couldn't stay in the shower forever, and he was starting to lose the hot water.

He forced his hand to turn the water off. The spray became a trickle; the last few drops hit the tile in angry little splats, gurgled down the drain, then the room was quiet.

Deathly quiet. He slid the shower curtain back slowly, wishing he'd brought some kind of weapon into the shower with him.

Do you hear yourself? What are you going to do, stab disembodied voices with a kitchen knife?

Still, he looked around the small room before stepping out. He felt as if he were looking at his bathroom for the first time. Nothing seemed familiar. Had that crack in the tile been there all along? Why had he never noticed all the rust on the chrome of the medicine cabinet? Why did he feel someone was watching him?

He dried off quickly, twice startled by the sound of the towel hitting the sink. He hung the towel over the shower rod to dry. He was compulsively neat. He'd always been compulsive about anything he could control. (There were so few things in that category, they were almost sacred to him.) He shaved quickly, then replaced the razor and shaving cream in the medicine cabinet. The sound of the magnetic catch made him jump, even though he'd expected it.

"Jesus, get a grip," he said out loud. The words dissolved into the air, and didn't prompt any unearthly response.

Would you stop! There's no fucking voice!

When they were young, Tallen used to say he could hear a voice.

"What kind of a voice?"

"Just a voice."

"What does it say?"

"I'm not supposed to tell anybody."

"You're so full of shit."

"It's the truth! I swear!"

Around the same time, Tallen started to have night terrors. He'd wake the entire house, screaming. He'd be hysterical for half an hour, babbling about some kind of winged monster with red eyes that would fly into his room and hover, staring at him. God himself couldn't have convinced Tallen it was a nightmare. Tallen said the flapping of the wings always woke him up.

This went on for a couple of years, then Tallen had been packed off to reform school, and Jack had no idea what ever became of the red-eyed, wing-flapping monster. After Tallen came home from reform school, he was a different person. When he'd get mad, there was a look in his eyes that no monster would have messed with.

Jack took a deep breath and headed to the other room to dress. He'd lied about having a suit. He'd given it to Goodwill two days after his mother's funeral. But he had a nice jacket, slacks, tie, the whole deal. He'd bought it all a couple of years ago, when he'd gone with Cathy to her son's junior high school graduation. Jack could still feel the stares he'd gotten that night. He'd actually enjoyed it, in a perverse way. *(Yeah, I clean up pretty nice, don't I, you shitheads? What are you gonna do with that?)* He'd made a lot of people uncomfortable that evening. It's one thing to have executed the brother of a lowlife misfit, but another to have executed the brother of a guy in a camel-hair coat and a Perry Ellis tie. The reaction he'd drawn caused him to instigate a new routine. Every once in a while he'd put on the nice clothes and go to the coffee shop for breakfast, as if he were on his way to an appointment. Once he'd even asked Tillie, in a voice loud enough to be overheard, "What's the exit to Buckhead? Buford Highway or Druid Hills?" Tillie had been forced to admit that she didn't make it to Buckhead (the Beverly Hills of Atlanta) all that often.

He liked making them squirm. That was exactly why he'd stayed in Barton all these years, instead of changing his name and vanishing into the anonymity of some distant city. He wanted to be there every time they looked up—a constant reminder, for whatever small degree of discomfort that might cause them.

He could barely remember how to tie the tie, but it gradually came back to him. After a half a dozen attempts, he decided it looked good enough for "dim lighting."

Don't do it. Call her and cancel.

No. She was right, one night out wasn't going to kill him. And he wanted to show up somewhere—anywhere— with her on his arm. He wanted that feeling back—the rush that came from her lips on his. How could anything legal feel so good?

What about the voice?

There was no voice.

There was, and you know it.

How?

It doesn't have to make sense to be there.

Like Tallen's voice on the answering machine. Had he imagined that? Had there been something else on the tape? Had he imagined Tallen's voice because that was what he wanted to hear? And if so, why had he imagined a warning? Was his subconscious trying to tell him something? Then what about Cam? Why had he told people he'd seen Tallen? Why would Cam have imagined Tallen? He didn't even know Tallen. And what about Ryland? They'd always been so close, if Ryland were still alive, why wouldn't he come to Jack? Why would he be sending messages from 3,000 miles away by a total stranger? And why would Ryland have let Jack go years thinking he was dead? But what was the alternative? That Randa really had a conversation with a ghost? Then why wouldn't the *ghost* of Ryland come to see him? There was no scenario in any of this that made any sense.

He checked the mirror. Not bad. Not bad for a delusional paranoid schizophrenic.

He should tell Randa tonight. About what happened at Cathy's. About the voice. She deserved to know the extent of his insanity, if she were going to get involved with him.

It's not "involved." It's one dinner. She's got a life on the other side of the country. She's going back there any day . . .

There's something in here.

He looked around. Nothing. Why did the room suddenly feel different? Like the air was heavier?

He looked around again. The room was still.

Is it cold in here? Isn't it colder, all of a sudden?

The ticking of the alarm clock broke the silence in a steady rhythm. Usually it was a calming sound. Now it sounded threatening, like something closing in on him.

"Jack . . ."

The same voice as before. He whirled around, looked in the opposite direction. Nothing.

"Jack . . ."

It wasn't in his head. It was outside. *Where? How?*

There was another sound. A scratchy sound, like wind against dry leaves. He looked around.

Do I really hear something?

He held his breath. The sound was growing louder. Deliberate.

Oh, Jesus . . .

The sound formed a word. It took him a moment to make it out.

"Away . . . away . . ."

What did that mean? Why was it always talking non-sense?

What "it"? Why do you keep saying "it"? There is no "it."

Oh, yeah? Then why can't I move?

Why *couldn't* he move? He was straining, but his limbs didn't seem to be connected to his brain anymore.

"Away . . ."

A woman's voice. A breathy whisper, meant to terrify him. Working beautifully.

"Leave me alone, goddammit!" he screamed, at nothing.

Another voice. Male. Laughing; a smug laugh. *An evil laugh.* The woman's voice was saying something else. A sentence. He couldn't make it out, but he could hear his name in it.

Get out of here. Get to the door.

His legs began to move, slowly. There was something bearing down on him, trying to stop him. Pressure, like the centrifugal force of a carnival ride.

Do I really feel it? Is any of this happening?

Under the man's laughter, the woman's voice became more distinct. By the time he made it to the door, it was chillingly clear.

"*This is the house they built for Jack. . . .*" A mocking cadence, like a nursery rhyme. "*Away . . . away . . .*"

With a desperate burst of energy, he grabbed the door-knob and flung the door open. Randa was standing there, about to knock. She jumped back, just in time to avoid being hit by the door. They both gasped.

"Jesus!" Jack said breathlessly. "Give me some warning."

"That I'm about to knock? How would that work?"

"Oh" was all he could say. He gasped for breath.

"Are you okay?"

"Yeah," he lied. "You just scared me."

He turned and looked back at his apartment. The sounds were gone. Whatever had been there was gone.

"Did you need something?" she asked.

"No," he said, turning back to her quickly.

This is not in my mind. Something is really happening.

"Look . . ." he said.

Maybe dinner's a bad idea. Maybe you should just drive me straight to the psych ward . . .

"What?"

His train of thought was suddenly derailed, as he got a good look at her. She was wearing a short black cocktail dress, which revealed the fact that the sweaters and jeans had been hiding a world-class figure.

Damn the ghosts.

"What?" she asked again.

"Nothing." He closed the door. "Let's go."

They sat at a table in the dining room of the Ritz-Carlton Buckhead, where she had made a reservation.

"You're kidding. I used to work there."

"I know. That's one of the few things Cam ever told me about you."

"He told you that? In what context?"

"The context that you're a classic underachiever."

"Yeah, well. He's a classic asshole."

"Not anymore."

"Sorry."

He didn't like being reminded that he'd inherited her from Cam. He couldn't help wondering what would have happened if he'd met her while Cam was still alive. Would she have even looked at him twice, or would she have written him off as Cam's weird hermit brother? She could have done that anyway. What could she possibly see in him? Like everything else in his life right now, it made no sense.

He was grateful she'd brought him here, of all the places they could have gone. The hotel had hardly changed in the ten years he'd been away, and he felt perfectly at home. He'd served enough people dinner here to know how it worked. (He could even order a martini—*"Bombay gin, dry, straight up with an olive"*—with the right attitude: I-do-this-so-often-I-get-tired-of-hearing-myself-say-it.) He wished there were still people working here that he knew, so he could have the pleasure of introducing Randa, but no such luck. He'd have to settle for the envy of strangers.

Her face was bathed in the flickering light of the candle in the center of the table. It gave her a soft, golden glow. She was talking about her father and his political ambitions, how they had superseded any code of ethics he might have possessed, although she'd never seen any sign that he'd possessed one. And something about him intentionally losing a court-appointed capital case when he was in private practice—in return for which, he'd been awarded a well-positioned job in the DA's office. Jack had nodded in all the right places and let her do most of the talking, because it gave him an excuse to stare at her without being obvious.

He wondered how long he would have to stare at her face before he'd be tired of it. It wasn't flawless, which was what made it interesting. He'd never been drawn to women who looked like models or movie stars. Since they all had to meet the same standard, they all looked alike to him. If you've seen one perfect nose, you've seen them all. Randa's face was complex; her features were somehow unexpected, and required work to memorize. Her dark brown eyes always seemed to be on the verge of tears, even when she laughed. There was a deep sadness in them that she never quite managed to hide. To him, it was seductive as hell. Her mouth was full and soft. She had a habit of biting her bottom lip when she was thinking—a gesture that always went straight to his groin. All he could think about was how much *he* wanted to be the one biting that lip.

Dinner was over and they were waiting for coffee. He was amazed at how smoothly it had gone—no awkward moments, no searching for topics of conversation. On the surface, they had absolutely nothing in common; and yet, he'd never felt so comfortable around another person. Talking to her was like dancing with a partner whose steps he already knew. He found himself wishing the evening weren't drawing to a close. He dreaded the moment when he'd have to leave her, but he told himself he'd worry about it later. He didn't want anything to spoil the remaining time they'd have together.

The waiter appeared with their coffee, and then was gone.

"Okay," Randa said, "here's something I've always wondered."

"What?"

"Coffee. How did anyone ever come up with the idea for coffee? Who said, 'I know what! Let's take these little beans and dry them in the sun. Then we'll grind them up and pour hot water over them and make a drink. But it'll taste like hell, so we'll mix it with cream and sugar until we can stand to drink it . . . of course, we'll have to wait for it to cool off first . . .' "

Jack laughed.

"You like that? I've got a million. Who looked at an artichoke and decided there was anything inside worth the trouble it would take to get to it? And why is it we put a man on the moon before anyone ever thought of squeeze-bottle ketchup?"

"Are all your existential dilemmas food-related?"

"No. I'd like to know why everyone in LA forgets how to drive the moment a drop of rain hits their windshield. And what God has against famous musicians in small airplanes. And why do people think pushing the elevator button again will make the elevator show up faster."

"You mean it doesn't?" he said, still laughing. He could tell she was enjoying his laughter and didn't want it to stop. Neither did he. It had been a long time since he'd really laughed. It felt good.

"Here's my personal favorite," she said. "Why will people only elect a president who's never had therapy? 'We're sorry, you've explored your emotions, you're disqualified. We only allow a repressed individual with a lot of internalized rage to have his finger on the button.' "

"Okay," he said, surrendering to the urge to chime in. "Here's one I've always wondered about. 'Four out of five dentists surveyed recommend sugarless gum . . .' What did that fifth guy say? 'Rot your teeth out, what the hell do I care?' "

That cracked her up. When she laughed, her entire face lit up, and the light in her eyes danced mischievously. On impulse, he reached down and took her hand. It startled her so much, she stopped laughing. She let her eyes meet his, and they sat like that for a moment without speaking.

"Will you tell me now?" she asked, suddenly serious.

"Tell you what?"

"About the armed robbery."

Reality came crashing down on him.

"Why?" he asked. "Were we having too much fun?"

"I just can't imagine it, that's all. You just don't seem . . ."

"What?"

"I don't know. Like the armed-robbery type."

"Known a lot of armed robbers, have you?"

"All right. Never mind."

"No, I'll tell you. It's just . . . a stupid story. It's embarrassing."

She leaned closer, which amused him. He hadn't meant he was embarrassed for the *waiter* to hear it.

"My brothers and I used to rob convenience stores . . . recreationally. You know. Some guys play football. Anyway, this was one night, about a year or so after Ethan died. I don't know where Tallen was, but I was alone and I was just driving around, and I found this two-pump gas station and general store out in the middle of nowhere. I was bored, so . . ."

"And you just happened to have a gun in the car?"

"As fate would have it," he said, smiling. "Nothing major. Something in the Saturday Night Special family. I stuck it in my pocket and ambled in. There was absolutely nobody there except me and the cashier. I got kind of depressed right away because the cashier was this girl, about my age. Long blond hair. Really cute. But it's kind of hard to flirt with someone and point a gun at her at the same time."

Randa laughed.

"No," he said, becoming serious. "I looked at her and I felt bad because I knew I was going to scare her. But I also knew I wasn't going to hurt her, so I figured she'd be scared for a few minutes and then have a great story to tell for the rest of her life, it wasn't really a bad deal. Anyway, I told her to give me whatever was in the cash register, and she said all the money was in a cash box under the counter. I said fine, I didn't care where it came from. She reached under the counter and came up with a sawed-off shotgun."

Randa laughed. "What did you do?"

"What could I do? I wasn't going to shoot her, and she damned well was going to shoot me."

He laughed, remembering. He'd never told this story to anyone. It wasn't really such a bad story, now that he heard it.

"She made me go to the pay phone and call the cops and tell them to come get me. Made me use my own dime."

"And then?"

He shrugged. "Then I did ten years for it. That part's not funny."

Her smile faded.

"Don't," he said.

"Don't what?"

"Don't stop smiling. I love your smile."

She smiled again.

He leaned over and kissed her, and wondered again why it felt so incredible. There were only so many variables in kissing a person. Cathy was the only woman he'd kissed in ten years, but he remembered how it used to feel, and it never felt like this. Did she feel it, too? Was there any subtle way he could ask her?

She pulled away from him. She had a serious look on her face.

"Jack, what's going on?" she asked, in a quiet voice.

"What do you mean?"

"You know. Between us."

"I don't know." Not much of an answer, but it was the truth.

"But there's something, right? You're not just kissing me because you need the practice?"

He smiled. "No, I'm not." He kissed her hand, then held it up to his cheek.

"Well, for the record, you don't need the practice."

He smiled again. "Neither do you," he said.

She was quiet for a moment, studying his face.

"It terrifies you, doesn't it?" she asked.

"Yes. That much I know."

"So . . . what about it? What do we do?"

"I'm not sure what you're asking me," he said.

"Neither am I. I just know—" she shook her head, but didn't finish.

"What?"

"I don't want to go back to LA."

"I don't want you to." *But how can I ask you to stay here and watch me sinking further and further into God knows what?* "What *do* you want to do?" he asked, letting himself temporarily off the hook.

"Honestly?"

"Yes."

"I want to go to the front desk, take out my American Express card, get a nice suite on the twenty-second floor, and stay here tonight. With you."

Even sitting, he felt his knees go weak.

"Does that scare you to death?" she asked, though he was sure she already knew the answer.

"Yes."

"Okay. What do *you* want?"

"Honestly?"

"Yes."

"I want you to hurry back with the key."

The door unlocked with a gentle click, and he followed her inside. He was trying to keep a cool exterior, but his heart was racing. He was slightly comforted by the fact that Randa's hand had been shaking when she put the key in the door. Among other things, it assured him that inviting a man she barely knew to spend the night in a hotel was not something she did routinely.

Once inside, he shed the tie and jacket, mumbling something about them making him feel claustrophobic. He laid them across the back of a chair, taking a moment to survey his surroundings. He'd put in some time working room service when he'd been an employee, but he'd never made it past the seventh floor. The guys with seniority always duked it out for the big tippers in the suites. He'd often fantasized about staying here, but never in his wildest dreams would he have envisioned himself in one of the most expensive rooms, courtesy of a beautiful blond with great legs and dishonorable intentions.

He tried to fake a certain amount of nonchalance, but it wasn't easy. It was as if the suite had been designed with intimidation as its major objective. The sitting room alone was the size of his apartment. It was filled with French Provincial reproductions upholstered in sky-blue brocade, sitting atop matching sky-blue carpet. The heavy curtains across the back wall were open, revealing a panorama of the midtown skyline, glittering against the night sky like rhinestones on black velvet. He glanced (inconspicuously, he hoped) into the bedroom. The maid had turned down the king-size bed and left mints and room-service menus on the pillows. (As if he could think about what he would want for breakfast.) He looked at Randa. She had been looking at the bed, too. Their eyes met, and she ducked her head and blushed. Something in that small gesture broke the tension. For him, anyway. She might be used to living like this, but she was still self-conscious about the circumstances.

"So . . ." he said, smiling at her. "Should we see if there's anything good on TV?"

She laughed. She had taken off her shoes and without the heels she looked tiny and, for the first time since he'd met her, vulnerable.

"Come here." She did. He put his arms around her and held her close to him.

"Tell you what," he said. "Why don't we just skip the

part where we make awkward conversation and wonder who's going to make the first move."

"Are you volunteering?"

"I'm always happy to make a martyr of myself for a good cause."

She smiled and was silent; waiting. He kissed her. Gently, at first. He didn't want to do anything drastic without a clue from her. He didn't have to wait long. She put her hand behind his head and pulled his face closer, her mouth seeking his urgently; zero to sixty in under ten seconds. He took it as permission to override his own restraint. He cupped her face in his hands and kissed her forcefully. He could feel his breath speeding up, his blood rushing to all the pertinent destinations. She kissed him with the abandon of someone who'd been waiting a long time for the opportunity. Strangely, that was how it felt to him, too. Like he'd been anticipating this moment for years, and couldn't contain himself now that it was finally here.

"Oh, God . . . Jack . . ." she whispered, between kisses. The lustful, breathy sound of his name on her lips made him shudder, and reinforced the already severe urge to rip her dress down the middle. Instead, he found the zipper and unzipped it. She let it drop to the floor, never taking her mouth off his in the process. He peeled out of his own clothes as if they were on fire, then helped her out of hers with equal intensity. The instant the clothes were gone, he pulled her to him. He felt what he'd been longing for—her soft skin against his, everywhere. Beneath his rough hands, her back felt as smooth as a new bar of soap. A part of him wanted to stand there for the rest of his life and hold her, savoring the feeling of her body against his. Another part of him was aching to move on. That part won. He picked her up and, still kissing her, carried her to the bed. He laid her down gently, trying to catch his breath, trying to regain some sort of control. She was having none of that. With a strength that surprised him, she pulled him down on top of her. "Don't wait," she pleaded, breathlessly. Before he'd had time to wonder what she meant, he felt her hand on his thigh, slipping between his body and hers, groping for ground zero. He felt her take hold of him firmly, and guide him into a warmth he'd swear he'd never felt before. She moaned as if she were in pain; the sound almost sent him over the edge. He took deep breaths and tried to remember the Gettysburg Address.

Oh, God . . . Oh, God . . .

It was too good. He didn't deserve anything that felt so good.

Too damned bad, I've got it.

He could feel her breath against his neck. Rapid. Hot. He was breathing with her, just as desperate. She bit his ear and whispered, "Hard!" It was an order, not a request, but he was all too happy to oblige. She groaned her approval and moved faster beneath him.

"Hurt me," she whispered.

Christ, don't say things like that.

Was she reading his mind? He was fighting an inexplicable urge to cause her pain. He had an equally strong feeling that if he did anything even as slight as close his teeth on her earlobe, it would unleash something he couldn't control. He'd never had a thought like that during sex. It scared him. He whispered her name to drive it out of his mind. Even so, its passing through had driven him to a fever pitch. He started to slow down, determined to wait for her.

"No, don't!" she said, sharply. He didn't.

He heard her gasp—a sharp gasp, followed by something inaudible that sounded like "yes." The gasp turned into a low, desperate moan, which turned into a hoarse unbridled cry, followed at once by his own, which was wild and raw; too long pent-up, too long denied. He made no attempt to stifle it. He didn't care if people in another room heard them. He didn't care if people in another *state* heard them. His mind exploded with colors: blues, purples, reds, one bursting into another. He wondered insanely if she could see them, too.

Far too soon, the colors began to fade, and he felt himself falling, like a leaf caught on a breeze, grasping for every last second of flight. He held Randa in a death grip, as if she might dissolve and vanish with the rest of it. He could hear her gasping. The sound reassured him. She was still there.

He drew deep breaths and tried to parry the depression he always felt at this point—the depression of having traveled to some euphoric realm for twenty seconds, only to return to the hellhole of reality. It wasn't so bad this time, though. Not when he was returning to . . .

To what?

To something worth living for? Jesus, what a thought.

He wanted to look at her, but he felt too exposed. Laid bare, as it were. He opened his eyes and turned his head, so he could at least stare at the side of her face. She turned toward him. He felt her soft cheek against his, as intimate a feeling as anything that had just happened, which made him realize there was no place to hide. He rolled over slowly, regretfully, pulling her over to face him. He brushed a loose strand of hair out of her eyes.

"Hi," he whispered, smiling at her.

"Hi," she answered, suddenly shy again. Her face was beautifully flushed, and the look on it brought a lump to his throat, though he didn't know why. Maybe it was just the thought that he'd made someone as happy as she looked. She averted her gaze for a moment. When she looked back, some cloud had moved in. She started to say something, then thought better of it.

"What?" he asked.

"Nothing," she said, barely above a whisper. "Never mind."

"What?" he insisted.

"Really, it's nothing. It's just . . . something I'm afraid of."

"Tell me."

She looked down for a long moment. Finally she answered him, in a strained whisper. "I know how crazy this is, but—I love you."

He had to remind himself to breathe. How could she even *think* that she loved him? It took him a moment to find his voice.

"God, Randa—" He felt his throat closing up. "You shouldn't."

Her eyes welled with tears and she nodded slightly, as if she were sorry she'd bothered him with such an unwelcome disclosure and wanted him to know that she wouldn't mention it again. It sent a pain clear through him. The pain triggered something deeper. He felt dizzy. He closed his eyes as it hit him—a flash flood of banished emotions, sweeping over him in a rushing torrent. He buried his face and tried to will it away. He wanted to cry. He couldn't let himself. If he let himself start to cry, God only knew when he would stop.

"I'm sorry," he heard her say, mistakenly thinking she had caused this anguish.

God, no. Don't be sorry.

"Randa, no . . ." He looked up again. The tears had spilled down her cheeks and her lip was quivering. He couldn't stand it. He had to tell her the truth. Damn the cost.

"I love you, too," he whispered. He saw the shock of it register on her face.

"You do?"

He nodded. "I'm just . . . so scared . . ." It was all he could get out.

"Of what?" she asked, barely able to talk herself.

Of having something I'm this afraid of losing.

He just shook his head. She kissed him and pulled him closer. "It's okay," she whispered.

He lay still in her arms, reliving it, making sure he'd heard her right. God, was it possible? Was there any chance that she really meant it?

No. And besides, how much is she going to love you when she finds out you're psychotic?

Well, she's not going to find out tonight, so shut the fuck up.

He felt her fingers on his back. Light, like a feather. Gently tracing a lazy pattern; meant to calm him. Damn near working. She kept it up for what felt like hours, until he finally fell asleep in her arms, huddled like a refugee, safe for the night.

CHAPTER 10

There was a warm wind blowing, gentle against his face. He and Randa were lying on a blanket on a beach, watching the sunset, a bottle of champagne between them. They took turns drinking from the bottle, giggling. He kissed her.

"AWAY..."

He pulled back. The damned voice again.

"AWAY..." The woman's voice; a throaty whisper that traveled on the breeze.

"AWAY..."

He stood up, looking around. Beyond the beach, the sand disappeared into a thick forest. He knew, somehow, that the voice was coming from there.

"AWAY... AWAY..."

He got up and followed it, determined to confront his tormentor. The woods were dense. The sun was blocked by the trees, and it was as dark as night.

He stopped short as he saw her, up ahead. She was sitting on a tree stump, waiting for him. It was the blond girl—the one from before. She was laughing at him now, a hollow, evil laugh.

"This is the house they built for Jack..." she said, with scornful glee.

"I'm sick of this!" he screamed. "Go play your fucking games with someone else!"

She just kept laughing. His anger amused her. Her laughter infuriated him.

"I mean it!" he yelled. "I've got a life, finally, and I want you to get the hell out of it!"

She stopped laughing, but retained a taunting smirk.

"What life?" she asked. "Your girlfriend? The one who's sleeping with you because she was in love with your brother?"

He reached for the first thing he could find—a thick branch that had fallen off a tree—and started for her. She watched him coming, and began laughing again. Her laughter and her lack of fear fueled his anger until he was lost in it. He lifted the branch and brought it down on her head with all his strength. The force of it knocked her off the log. She staggered a couple of steps; he brought the log down on the back of her head, knocking her to the ground, her face buried in the dirt and pine needles. Consumed by his anger, he continued to pummel her until his fury was spent and he was too tired to go on. He dropped to the ground and gasped for air. He looked at her still form on the ground beside him, and didn't feel any remorse. She deserved it for making him think he was crazy all this time. It took him a moment to realize that he was covered in blood, and then the enormity of what he had done started to sink in.

Christ. How was he going to explain this to Randa? How was he going to tell her that he'd beaten this girl's head to a pulp because she'd been torturing him, in a voice that Randa could never hear? Jesus, how was he going to tell Randa that he'd **killed** someone? She'd never understand. The girl would just look innocent and he'd look like a crazy person.

He reached for the girl. He took her by the shoulder and turned her over.

The bloodied, lifeless face in front of him was Randa's.

"NOOOO!"

"Jack!" A voice in the distance. Whose?

Hands on him. "Jack, it's okay! Jack!"

He woke up.

"Jack, it's okay! Jack! Jack!"

The fact that she kept calling his name made him realize he was still screaming. He forced himself to stop.

"Oh, God . . . Randa . . ." She's alive! She's here!

"Jack, it's okay. You just had a bad dream."

He could feel her arms around him. He was still breathing hard and he could barely control his trembling, but he took her face in his hands and looked at her.

"Randa, you're okay . . ."

"I'm fine. You were dreaming."

He pulled her to him and held her as close as he could without hurting her. He rocked her and kissed her on the forehead, and murmured her name, over and over. He could feel her arms on his back, hugging him. It was okay. It was okay.

"Was it one of those dreams?"

"I thought you . . . were hurt."

"Well, I'm not." She kissed him on the cheek. "Here, lie back down."

He obeyed. She pulled him close to her and held him. She stroked his cheek with her hand and whispered, "It's okay."

There was no way he could explain. It wasn't even the dream that had scared him so badly. It was that feeling, when he was lost in that homicidal fury. It was the familiarity of that feeling. He'd been there before, and not in a dream. But he couldn't tell her that.

He felt her kissing his shoulder.

"I'm okay," he whispered, lying again. "I'm sorry."

"Don't be."

She put her head on his shoulder and snuggled closer. She continued to touch him—his cheek, his arm, his chest—reassuring him; calming him like before. Except the job was too big for her this time.

She fell asleep after a few minutes. He stared at the ceiling and waited for the sun to come up.

He dressed in the sitting room, where his clothes were still lying in a pile on the floor. Tied his tie in front of the mirror over the wet bar. Nothing he could do about shaving, but the hair on his face was so blond it took him days to look unkempt. He didn't know why he was so concerned about his appearance, except that he felt so horrible about what he was doing, he didn't want anyone to look at him and suspect anything close to the truth.

There was a MARTA station on Lennox Road, within easy walking distance. He could take the MARTA downtown, then catch a bus back to Barton. Maybe when she woke up and found him gone, she'd be angry enough to give up without a fight.

What if I'm blowing this all out of proportion? What if I'm leaving her for no good reason?

You can't risk it. You can't gamble with her life.

He stuck his head in the door to the bedroom to look at her one more time. The room was darkened by the heavy hotel drapes, and the light from the doorway fell across her like a pale spotlight. Her face was partly covered by her hair, but he could see how peaceful she looked. There was a tiny smile that only showed up on the corners of her lips. Her arm was still bent upward beside her, where he'd slipped out from under it.

God, she's beautiful . . . she's so fucking beautiful . . .

It came back to him in a rush, the memory of her skin against his, the smell of her hair, the safety he'd felt in her arms. But *his* safety wasn't the issue.

He forced himself to turn away from her, closing the door softly behind him. When he left the suite, he hung the DO NOT DISTURB sign on the door. By the time she woke up, there'd be a safe distance between them. He'd make sure that distance remained, no matter what.

Making his way down Lennox Road, it was all he could do not to relive the night in his mind. The good part. The part that, up until the nightmare, was easily the best night of his life. *Why, goddammit?* Why did she have to show up at the exact moment that he was disintegrating? Just one of God's practical jokes, he supposed. One more in the endless series that made up his life.

Maybe he should have told her. Maybe he should have

let *her* decide whether or not she wanted to be in love with a lunatic. They could just enjoy his sane periods while they lasted, then she could come and visit him in the asylum.

It's too dangerous.

What? He looked around, then realized the "voice" was clearly internal this time, although it was as obvious and as intrusive as the "outside" voice.

You know who you are.

What was that supposed to mean?

You know what it means.

It was true. He'd known last night, even before the dream. He'd known in that chilling moment when he'd wanted to hurt her. He hadn't wanted to hurt her in any malicious way . . .

Not this time . . .

. . . but it was too similar. He hadn't even been angry. What would happen the first time something triggered one of those lethal moments that crop up in any relationship? The first time he wanted to strangle her for something. *Would* he?

It's not like you don't have it in you.

Yeah, thanks. I'd almost forgotten.

He didn't need to be reminded of the incident that had ruled his every waking moment for the last decade. The night that had, for all intents and purposes, ended his life. Provoked by what? Anything worth throwing his life away? Hardly. One mouth-breathing hillbilly yelling at a TV screen. One drunk, ignorant asshole exercising his constitutional right to free speech.

"Oh, shut that ACLU bitch up and fry the fucker!"

And then an unaccountable lapse of time, until he was suddenly aware of people pulling on him, shouting, and the drunk on the floor, his face a strange purplish red, his eyes bulging, and Jack's hands around his throat. The strength in those hands when people had tried to pry them off. The fury into which his consciousness had dissolved, in that unknown moment when he had unleashed whatever was inside him and then just stood out of its way. And the most frightening part—that even after he'd realized what he was doing, he'd still wanted to kill the guy. And if the others hadn't been there to stop him . . .

I WOULD have.

At Cathy's trailer later, in the early hours before dawn, holding on to her like a drowning man clinging to a buoy.

"Jack, you didn't kill the guy."

"But I would have."

"You don't know that."

He knew it. Knew it then, knew it now. And every minute in between, even though he rarely let himself think about it head-on. He couldn't. It was excruciating. That's what people never realized—what you could never explain to the "they're-just-animals" crowd. The pain of hurting someone that way. (And the pain that made you *want* to.) He could only imagine what that pain would be like if he'd actually killed the guy . . .

Was that what had happened to Tallen? Had something snapped inside him and called forth some uncontrollable rage? How long could such a thing last? Long enough, after the initial impulse, for Tallen to find the gun, drive to Alabama (a two-hour drive even if he was going ninety), park the car, go into the church (why a church? And why *that* church, as opposed to all the others he must have driven past?)? Long enough to climb the stairs to the balcony and (from what witnesses had described) sit there waiting for the right moment—when everyone stood up to sing, unwittingly lining themselves up like beer cans on a fence rail? (Had Tallen specifically waited for them to sing "Joy to the World"? Something in that logic made a strange kind of sense to Jack—not that any of it made any *real* sense.)

If he'd been in some kind of wild fury, why wouldn't he have opened fire on the local Dairy Queen? Or a local church, if it had to be a church? It was Christmas Eve, it wasn't like he had to drive far to find a church that was holding services. Why did he drive almost two hundred miles? Was he trying to outrun it somehow, whatever "it" was? Then why did he give up?

No, it wasn't possible. No one could have sustained a blind rage for that length of time. He had to have known what he was doing. Still, that wasn't the way Tallen had described it, the one time they'd talked about it.

Jack had spent the entire year trying to get Tallen to talk about it. The only thing Tallen would ever say was, "I'll tell you someday. I don't want to talk about it now." Finally, the night before Tallen's execution, Jack had pressed the point.

"Tal, I need to know what happened."

"No, you don't. How's that gonna change anything?"

"I don't want to spend my life wondering."

"Then don't."

"Oh, for Christ's sake, since when is there something that you can't tell me?"

"Since last Christmas Eve."

"Why? Do you think it would change how I feel about you?"

"I just don't see the point."

"The point is that I'M the one who's gonna have to live with this for the rest of my life, so at least do me the fucking courtesy of telling me what it is that I'm living with!"

Tallen had been quiet for a long time, staring at the floor. Then, finally, he sighed—a long sigh, as if he were exhaling something more than air. The macho façade melted away before Jack's eyes, and when Tallen looked up, Jack had seen a flash of the guy he used to know.

"Okay. If I tell you this, you'd better swear to me you're not gonna tell the fucking ACLU or the fucking Atlanta Constitution or anybody else. You don't even tell Mom."

"All right. I swear."

"I haven't told you because . . . I don't remember."

"What do you mean?"

"I don't remember. Driving there, going into the church, any of it. I don't even know where I got the damned gun."

"Are you serious?"

"No, it's a joke. Of course I'm serious. I remember calling Mom that night, looking for you. She said you had to work and you wouldn't get there until after midnight. Cam was there and the two of them were going out to eat, did I want to come? I said yes, just because I knew how much it would piss Cam off. I remember getting into the car and starting to drive to the house. The next thing I remember, I was lying in the church parking lot with a cop pushing my face into the gravel with one hand and pointing a gun at me with the other, saying if I moved, he'd blow me to hell where I belonged."

"Jesus, Tallen . . . were you . . ."

"No, I wasn't on anything. And you know I'd tell you if I was."

"Did you tell any of this to the shrink?"

"No."

"Your lawyer?"

"No."

"Why the hell not? Are you crazy? It might have made a difference."

"I know."

Their eyes had locked, and Tallen hadn't taken it any farther. He didn't have to. Jack knew. Now it made sense, why Tallen had been so insistent about dropping all his appeals. Tallen didn't want to live, because he didn't want to live with what he had done. Especially since he had no memory of it, because he'd never be able to understand it, and it would never get any easier. Somehow, all of that was conveyed in the look that passed between them. No more was ever said about the crime. They'd spent the rest of their time together reliving some of their escapades, and talking about Lucy and what Jack was going to do about her, and going over the disposition of Tallen's few worldly goods.

Jack had never planned to stop on the way home. He certainly hadn't planned to stop at a bar. He'd made up his mind he wasn't going to drink until after Tallen was dead. But he had underestimated how hard it was going to be to leave Tallen. (*"Tell Mom . . . just tell her I love her. Tell Cam to take care of himself, not that he won't anyway. And, you . . . you just . . . [his voice cracking] . . . God, Jack . . ."*) That was as far as Tallen could get— as close as he could come to saying good-bye to Jack. The guards had let Tallen hug Jack. Hadn't even told him when to stop. Jack had prayed that they would. It was the most agonizing decision he'd ever made: at what moment to let go of his brother, knowing he'd never touch him—never see him—again. When he'd finally pulled himself away, all he could do was look Tallen in the eye and nod. If he'd tried to say anything, he would have started sobbing and embarrassed them both. He'd managed to mouth a silent "I love you, Tal," and then turned and walked away without looking back.

He'd underestimated how hard that was going to be, even though he'd expected it to be devastating. He hadn't thought about having to walk through that parking lot, through the carnival of TV news crews and cameras and weeping protesters and festive revelers. The fucking tailgate parties. High school kids with six-packs and buckets of fried chicken. (They'd come with *dates,* for Christ's sake. *"So, we could go to a movie, or we could go over to*

Huntsville and have a picnic while they kill that guy. . . .")
One comedian dressed like the Grim Reaper and carrying
a handmade sign that said, BURN, BABY, BURN, with a
lighting bolt through it and a happy face in the corner. By
the time he somehow made it to his car and got out of
there (after almost cold-cocking a reporter who wouldn't
stop shoving a microphone in his face), he'd been in such
agony, he couldn't think about anything *but* finding a bar,
and getting drunk as fast as he could.

Maybe if he hadn't been so upset by the last-minute
knowledge that Tallen might have saved himself, but
chose not to . . . Maybe if he'd been mentally prepared
for the scene in the parking lot . . . Maybe if the asshole
in the bar had shot his mouth off *before* Jack had time to
get so drunk . . . Maybe if even one element of it had
happened differently . . . he might be back at the hotel
right now, asleep in Randa's arms.

But it did happen.

Ever since that night, he'd asked himself how much
difference there was between his deed and Tallen's. The
difference was one of degree and circumstance. Fundamentally, they were the same. Jack had wanted to kill the
guy. Had *tried* to. Someone had stopped him; no one had
stopped Tallen. Jack was alive and free because a couple
of redneck truck drivers had pried him off his victim. But
what was the difference between what was in his heart
and what was in Tallen's?

Precious little.

Could he live the rest of his life without acting on it
again? He'd fought it all these years with rigid control,
convinced that the only way to keep from doing something horrible was to keep from doing anything. Cathy
had been right; he did sit on a volcano of rage, all the
time. What would happen if his mind slipped into someplace where he wasn't aware of the danger?

You know what would happen.
I don't know for sure.
If Cam couldn't escape it, what makes you think you can?

Jesus. Cam. He'd almost forgotten. When Randa told him about Cam and the liquor store, he'd immediately written it off as a case of mistaken identity and his-brother-was-a-criminal-so-he-must-be-too. But what if it wasn't? What if Cam, who didn't even cheat on his income taxes, really did kill someone? Was it possible?

Look at the facts. Your father probably killed Ethan. He could have killed other people you don't know about, given all the time he spent away from the house. Tallen went nuts and killed five people. Now Cam's friends say he went nuts, the cops say he killed someone. What does logic say will happen next?

It was true. Everyone in his family went insane, sooner or later. The men went insane and killed people. Whether it made sense or not, it was undeniably the pattern.

Up ahead, through the heavy morning fog, he saw the dark stairwell of the MARTA entrance, beckoning him underground. He walked faster, eager to accept the offer. He thought of Randa, waking up in the hotel room to find him gone. He hoped she'd be too angry to be hurt. He couldn't stand the thought of causing her pain. Still, it was better than what he might cause her if he stayed.

He would return to his life, just the way it was. Working, eating, sleeping, reading. No human contact. A danger to no one but himself, and free from any ridiculous hope for the future.

You can't hide from it forever.

No, probably not. But he'd hide as long as he could. And if he took anyone down with him in the end, it wasn't going to be Randa.

If you had the guts to kill yourself, you wouldn't have to worry about taking anyone down with you.

It was true. He wasn't sure whether it was because he was gutless *(yes, you chickenshit coward)* or just that he wasn't convinced it was the only answer.

When WILL you be convinced? When you're standing next to a corpse?

Shut up! Just shut the hell up! I need time to think.

You mean rationalize.

He reached the stairs and descended, stopping at a machine to buy a token. In his coat and tie, he blended easily into the morning commuters. He could be any one of them—an accountant, a salesman, a computer programmer—on his way to the same world as everyone else.

But you're not one of them.

No, he wasn't. He knew that much. He just wasn't sure how far it went in the other direction.

Don't kid yourself. You know.

For a fleeting moment, the voice in his head was Randa's. *"I know how crazy this is but . . . I love you."* He felt her hand on his face; heard her whispering, *"It's okay."*

But it wasn't okay. It would never be okay.

The train was coming. He could hear the wind whistling through the tunnel. It slid into view and squealed to a halt. The doors hissed open and Jack climbed on board, flowing with the sea of humanity. He sat and waited for the train to move. Away from her.

"The doors are about to close . . ."

The metallic warning evaporated into the air above the indifferent commuters; the doors closed and the train pulled out.

Jack stared blankly at the people surrounding him. The fact that the train was packed was a mocking irony—a cruel wink from a vindictive God. Wherever Jack was headed, he was going alone.

BOOK TWO

Look around; there is someone else, always someone else.
What he breathes is your suffocation;
What he eats is your hunger;
Dying, he takes with him the purest half of your own death.

Rosario Castellanos, from "The Other"

THE OTHER

CHAPTER 1

"Father, can I get you a cup of coffee?"

Michael shook his head. "No, thank you."

"Are you sure?"

"I'm sure." He offered the best smile he could muster. The plump stormtrooper-with-a-heart-of-gold nurse had been offering him coffee about every thirty minutes. (He almost never wore the collar for exactly this reason: it made people so solicitous he wanted to strangle them.) He'd thought about accepting the coffee, just to make her stop asking, but he really didn't want it, and she seemed to be the type who would check to see if he was drinking it and give him grief if he wasn't. She gave up easily this time and headed back to her station. He breathed a small sigh of relief. All he wanted was to be left alone with his thoughts.

He looked at the clock. His grandfather had been in the operating room for two and a half hours now. The doctor had said it would be between five and eight. Michael wondered how it could take so long, just to take out one organ. The doctor had explained it all in a vocabulary that meant nothing to Michael:

"The operative death percentage is high. For someone your grandfather's age, as high as thirty percent. And you should keep in mind, it's only a palliative procedure."

"A what?"

"Its purpose is to prolong life and reduce pain. My best educated guess is that it would give him a couple more months."

That day the words had been horrifying. Today, a couple of months seemed like an extra lifetime.

Vincent was the only "parent" Michael had ever known. Both of his parents had died when he was a toddler, and Vincent had raised him until he'd left home, at seventeen, to join the Jesuits. After that, Vincent had been an adviser, a mentor, a friend. Michael couldn't imagine his life without Vincent in it. He tried not to. The reality of it would be here soon enough.

"How about a homemade honey bun?"

She was back. He smiled again and shook his head.

"I don't think so."

"You need to eat something. You don't have a bit of color in your face."

"I don't think it's from hunger."

She sat down in the chair next to him.

"How about a hug from a fat old lady?"

She put her arms around him without waiting for a reply. She smelled like a mixture of roses and cheap hand cream. She pulled herself away and looked at him. The pain in her eyes was not forced; it touched him.

"My father was a Methodist minister," she said. "I used to think, everyone cries on his shoulder, but whose does he cry on?"

Michael could only nod.

"Let me know if you change your mind about the honey bun."

"I will," he said, through a tight throat. She smiled and was gone.

He stood up and made his way down the stark hospital corridor. He couldn't stand another minute of fluorescent light.

* * *

The tiny chapel was dimly lit, which in and of itself was a great relief. He sat in the back pew. There was no place to kneel, as 99 percent of the chapel's visitors were Protestant. He sat for a while and stared at the cross on the stained-glass window above the altar, and wondered what to pray for. For Vincent to survive the operation? Why? To die a slow and torturous death, spending his last days helpless and in unimaginable pain? For Vincent to die now and be spared all of that? For God's will? Wouldn't that happen anyway?

For the strength to handle whatever lies ahead.

That was it. All he could really hope for.

And considerably more than I deserve.

All day he'd been thinking about something he and Vincent used to do—an old routine, from as far back as he could remember. Every Friday, as soon as they sat down to dinner, Vincent would announce the date, and then ask Michael, "Where are you today?" Michael would give an assessment, recounting the highlights of the week and working them into the context of his life. Vincent would never comment, except for an occasional nod or smile. Scrutiny was unnecessary. The point was to make Michael take a focused look at the big picture. After he'd moved away from home, Michael had continued the practice mentally, by force of habit. For a long time, it had been a comfort—a psychological deep breath. Lately, it seemed more like a type of self-inflicted torture.

How would he answer that question, if Vincent were to ask him today?

I'm a parish priest—the last thing I ever wanted to be—in rural Georgia—the last PLACE I ever wanted to be—because I was stupid enough to take on a vindictive bishop. And I'm mourning things you don't even know about.

It had been a year of losses. Vincent would be the greatest loss by far, but there were a slew of close seconds. New York was a huge loss, encompassing many smaller ones. He missed everything about the city—even the things he hadn't particularly liked: the crowds, the subway, the ill-tempered cabdrivers. Waking every morning to the familiar sound of the Con Ed "Dig-We-Must" jackhammers. He missed his work, his friends, his sense of purpose and belonging. The Jesuits had always been more than a community to him. They had been his family—the family he'd never had.

The intensity with which Michael had loved New York was paralleled by the intensity with which he hated Barton. He hated the isolation—both the isolation of being the only priest in a tiny parish, and the isolation of being an hour's drive from a decent bookstore. He didn't like the work at all. In fact, it was hard to think of what he did as work: marrying nineteen-year-olds who had no business being married but weren't about to be told so. Listening for hours on end to people confessing to the exact number of *damn*s and *hell*s they'd uttered that week. And then there was the wide assortment of for-this-I-took-advanced-Greek crap that should have been handled by the staff that the parish couldn't afford.

Most of his time this week had been eaten up by a plumbing problem, in the form of a John Candy look-alike in bib overalls, who wanted $3,500 to hook the rectory's septic tank up to the county sewer line. Inflamed by Michael's uncalled-for comment (*"That sounds a little steep"*), Plumber Bubba had accused Michael of trying to "Jew" him down. Delivered with the appropriate "that ain't how we do things 'round here" tone, lest Michael should forget for one second that he was an outsider. Topped off by:

"Maybe y'all can find a Catholic plumber in this county who'll do the job for free."

(A snort)

"Hell, if y'all find a Catholic plumber in this county, I'LL do the job for free."

Even when he managed to block out the surroundings, it was impossible to ignore the fact that there was no one to talk to, no one to have dinner with, no one who might drop by unannounced with an existential crisis and a bottle of twelve-year-old scotch. At the Jesuit residence in Manhattan, all he had to do was step into the hall and yell "Deli run!" and he'd have all the company he needed. Then they'd sit around the living room until late into the night, draped haphazardly over armchairs, arguing heatedly over some arcane theological point. These days, he'd be happy to find one person who didn't think that monotheism was something one needed to be vaccinated against.

Supposedly this torment was only going to last for another month, but he didn't have a lot of hope that the next assignment would be any better. The powers that be were just keeping him quiet temporarily until they could find a way to keep him quiet permanently. They knew Michael wasn't going to make a career out of one flaky issue, but there was no assurance that his next attack wouldn't be launched against something more serious—birth control, mandatory celibacy, the exclusion of women from the power structure, or any of the other sacred cows with which he took issue. His editorial column had developed something of a cult following among disenfranchised Catholics, which was not winning him any points in the chancery office. Michael was the status quo's worst nightmare: a loose cannon with a deadly pen and unlimited access to volatile ears. As one auxiliary bishop had put it (or, at least, as it had filtered back to Michael), "The last thing we need now is a rock-and-roll Jesuit with a fan club."

Michael hadn't set out to be a crusader. He just couldn't help writing about things that bothered him, and nothing bothered him more than the current state of the Catholic Church in America. It was a subject that alternated between frightening him, depressing him, and breaking his heart. Church attendance might be up and baby-boomers might be flocking back in droves, but none of that mattered in the face of what was happening to the priesthood. The statistics alone told the story. Parishes were closing left and right, or remaining open, with one Mass a week by an itinerant priest. Priests were resigning by the thousands and being ordained by the dozens. It didn't take a genius to do the math.

Michael didn't see any hope for improvement on the horizon. The rumor, according to friends and spies in Rome, was that the Vatican had simply decided they could live without the United States, which was why none of the realities of life in the nineties were being addressed (and were, in fact, being militantly ignored). The unspoken undercurrent on this side of the fence seemed to be "Yeah, well, we can live without you, too." The American Church was in business for itself, creating a growing gap between what was being said publicly and what was being said (and lived) behind closed doors. It was a survival technique, Michael knew, but the entire energy of it made him feel hypocritical.

But then, there was plenty else making him feel hypocritical these days.

Tess.

The fact that she wasn't first on his list of losses only proved how brutal the list was. He missed her so much, it made every muscle in his body ache. He felt as if he'd had the flu for the last three months. He wasn't sure whether that was from missing her, or from hating himself for missing her.

With the clarity of hindsight, he knew now he should never have agreed to work with her. He'd told himself it would be okay because it was a short-term assignment. When the assignment had turned into a friendship, he ignored the warning voice in the back of his head in favor of the voice in the foreground—the one that said "nothing will happen." The one that kept saying "nothing will happen" until the morning he woke up in her bed.

When inclined to give himself a break, he remembered that there was no coincidence in the timing that connected his fall off the celibacy wagon to the aftermath of the article. The first night he'd stayed at Tess's apartment was the night he'd found out he was being sent to Deep-in-the-Sticks, Georgia. Anger piled on top of disillusionment did not make for cheerful compliance, even in a carefully brainwashed Jesuit. Besides which, the anger was further fueled by the fact that, by that time, he'd fallen out of his rational-Jesuit-mind in love with her.

His last days in New York had not been pleasant. He and Tess had bickered incessantly. There was so much she couldn't understand: how he could remain loyal to the Church when they were clearly punishing him for telling the truth; why he felt so guilty about his relationship with her, since he'd told her that he thought celibacy was a stupid and antiquated concept that was destroying the Church; why he couldn't accomplish anything he wanted to just as easily in a secular context. Michael hadn't done a very good job of explaining it to her. They weren't things he could explain on some logical level. They weren't things he understood himself.

"You know what it is, Michael? You just have zero interest in living in the real world."

"Maybe that's true. Is that so horrible?"

"No. But as we know, I'm not allowed on your lofty plane. So you tell me, how is this going to work?"

When he'd left for Georgia, they'd agreed to three months with no contact, to give him some time and space in which to make a decision. Since then, he'd only talked to her once. He'd called her when Vincent was diagnosed. After the initial awkwardness, she'd been sympathetic and concerned about him. She offered to come down for a few days, but he told her it probably wasn't a good idea. He didn't tell her how much he would have loved it, how badly he wanted her there. Like everything else he was feeling, it was best left unspoken.

He'd been tempted to tell Vincent about Tess, but he'd decided against it. Vincent considered his grandson the Jesuit to be the greatest accomplishment of his own life. In fact, no matter what he decided, Michael knew he could never resign while Vincent was still alive. He'd been coasting on that rationalization for months now, but it wouldn't be available much longer.

God, You know where I am. I'm lost. I'm scared. Please help.

God must be sick of hearing that refrain by now, Michael thought. Fine. Maybe soon God would get sick enough of hearing it and answer.

He sighed, from somewhere deeper than bone marrow, and willed himself to his feet, to return to the waiting room.

He'd begun to have second thoughts about coffee and a honey bun, but the nurse wasn't at her station. He walked out into the hallway and looked down it. He saw her, in front of the door to the operating room, talking to someone . . . the doctor . . . why was the doctor in the hallway, when the operation wasn't supposed to be over until . . .

Oh, God, no . . . not yet . . .

The doctor looked up and saw him . . . said something to the nurse. She looked at him, too, and the look on her face told him everything. . . . He nodded to them slightly, reached into his pocket for the vial of holy oil he'd brought with him, just in case. He felt himself shift into autopilot. Things to do. Rituals to hide behind.

It was early afternoon by the time he was done with all the hospital paperwork and necessary phone calls. He'd gone through it in a daze. Even though he'd known the odds, it had never really hit him that he might be doing all of this today. By the time everything was wrapped up, the doctors and nurses had moved on to other priorities. He left the hospital alone, unceremoniously.

He was already in the parking lot when he heard the nurse behind him.

"Father Kinney!"

He stopped, turned to her. She was hurrying toward him with an envelope in her hand. Surely there weren't more papers to sign.

"I promised your grandfather I'd give you this if . . . if he didn't make it . . ."

"What is it?"

"I don't know. I didn't open it."

He took the envelope and thanked her, then accepted her condolences one last time. He waited until she was gone and he was encased in the relative privacy of his car before he opened the envelope. There was no paper, but something solid in the bottom. He turned it over and a microcassette player spilled out. No note, so he assumed the tape inside would explain itself.

So typical of Vincent. He couldn't leave a note or, God forbid, have an actual conversation. Michael knew what the tape was: Vincent's assurance that he'd have the last word. A few last pearls of wisdom. Advice. Admonitions (for things it was probably too late to avoid). Michael put the recorder back in the envelope and laid it on the passenger seat. He wasn't about to listen to it right now. The drive to Vincent's house already felt like an insurmountable task.

Vincent still owned the house where Michael had grown up. Vincent had designed it himself, in 1945—a year or two before he became the most sought-after architect in the city. He had designed almost a third of the houses in their neighborhood, Branwyn Park, a suburb due north of downtown Atlanta. By now Vincent had restored most of the houses he hadn't built. In fact, anyone who lived in Branwyn Park and had not had their house restored by Vincent Kinney was announcing the fact that they couldn't afford it—not the kind of announcement people who lived in Branwyn Park liked to make. Vincent had also designed several of the buildings prominent on the downtown skyline, a couple of churches, and a gorgeous retreat center in the north Georgia mountains. His name was well known and highly respected in the state, the region, and even the country, among people who knew anything about architecture.

Vincent's style was clean-lined and no-nonsense, just like Vincent. His buildings were an eclectic mix, though all classically inspired. His houses were all variations of his basic prototype, which was a pared-down Victorian. There was a minimal amount of spindle work, and Vincent would only allow the houses to be painted in basic colors (white, gray, tan) with subtle shutters (black, brown, dark green). Vincent's theory was that Victorian houses had beautiful lines, which were betrayed by "curlicues and jelly-bean colors" that kept them from being taken seriously. Vincent always said he built Victorian houses that didn't look as if Hansel and Gretel lived in them.

A couple of years back, a retired college professor from Emory had painted his Vincent Kinney house bright pink with white trim, and Michael had thought Vincent was going to take to his bed. Instead, Vincent went over to the house one night and left a case of Pepto-Bismol on the front porch. There was a note taped to the box that said "In honor of your new decor." Vincent didn't sign the note; he knew he didn't have to.

Vincent's house was white with black shutters. There were white Brumby rockers on the front porch, and flower boxes, which Vincent kept filled with red begonias; the overall effect was classic and dignified. Michael used to joke that the house looked as if it had been designed by Calvin Klein. Vincent couldn't decide whether to take it as a compliment or an insult, so he'd just give Michael his best ambiguous "hmph" and change the subject.

Vincent had begun construction of the house in 1945. It had taken almost two years to build because Vincent had to scrutinize every nail that went into it. It was supposed to have been finished in time for Christmas 1946, but Vincent had made some last-minute structural changes that had thrown everything off schedule. Since he'd sold the house that he and his wife, Claire, had owned for the duration of their twenty-year marriage, and since he'd promised the buyers that they could have *his* house in time for Christmas, Vincent and Claire found themselves homeless for the month of December. There was an additional problem: Michael's parents (Vincent's son, Matthew, and daughter-in-law, Laura) had planned to come up from Savannah to spend all of December in Vincent and Claire's new house, so that Michael—who had just turned one—could spend some time with his grandparents. Since Vincent's perfectionism had thoroughly upset the December applecart, he came up with a new plan: they would all check into adjoining rooms at a nice hotel downtown. It wouldn't be as comfortable as Christmas in the new house, but in those days, downtown Atlanta was an exciting place to be during the Christmas season. The plan was agreed upon, and on the fifth of December, they'd all checked into two rooms on the eleventh floor of the Winecoff Hotel.

At the time, the Winecoff was one of the city's nicest hotels, located in the heart of the shopping/theater/restaurant district. It was right across the street from Davison-Paxon's, the largest department store in Atlanta, where the women could shop and Michael could visit with Santa. Though Vincent would never admit it, Michael had always suspected that Vincent had chosen the Winecoff as much for its architecture as for its location. It was a beautiful building: red brick, Beaux-Arts–inspired, crowned by a white concrete facing that covered the bricks on the first three and upper two floors. Elegant and simple. Vincent could have designed it himself.

On the afternoon of Friday, December 6, Laura and Claire had taken Michael across the street to the Paramount Theater to see *Song of the South,* while the men drove around the city, critiquing arches, columns, and patterned masonry. They'd all met back at the hotel for dinner, and then retired to their rooms. The plan was to get up early Saturday and go back to Davison's, so that Michael could ride on the four banks of escalators scheduled to begin operating that morning.

Somewhere around 3:45 A.M., the hotel caught fire. With *Titanic*-style arrogance, the hotel's builders had declared it fireproof, and therefore had not included sprinklers, fire escapes, or fire doors. The elevator in the center of the hotel was surrounded by an open stairwell that became a funnel, quickly sucking the fire through every floor of the hotel. By the time the fire was extinguished, near dawn, 119 people were dead. Among them were Michael's parents and grandmother.

Vincent had told him the story so many times it was almost as if Michael could remember being there. He'd heard how the five of them had huddled in the corner of Vincent's room, under blankets they'd soaked with water from the bathtub; how the room had filled with smoke and the mattress on the bed had begun to smolder and the water they'd spilled on the floor had begun to boil. He'd heard about the screams of the people who leaped to their deaths, the matching screams of the people who were watching on the streets below. He'd heard all the stories of how the dead had died and how the living had managed to survive.

Vincent and Matthew had made a rope out of bedsheets, hoping they could all climb down to the aerial fire ladders, which only reached to the eighth floor. Vincent had insisted on going first—not because he was trying to save himself, but so that if the rope didn't hold, he'd be the sacrificial guinea pig. He had made it safely to a fire ladder, and was climbing down to the street when Claire started down the sheet rope. When she reached the top of the ladder, Michael's mother started down. Laura was three months pregnant with what would have been Michael's younger sibling, and she wasn't strong enough to hold on to the rope. She had fallen, knocking Claire off the ladder on her way down. Vincent had watched it all in helpless horror. Instead of rushing toward the women, though, he waited for Matthew and Michael. He had thought they would make it. They were halfway to the fire ladder when there was a flashover explosion inside the hotel—a combustion of the gases produced by the fire. Flames shot through windows on all floors. The sheet rope holding Matthew and Michael was burned in two, sending them plummeting toward the ground. As Matthew fell, he tossed Michael toward the hotel's awning. Michael hit it, rolled off and was caught by Vincent, who had seen what was happening and was waiting. Matthew fell onto the hotel marquee and was impaled on one of the wires holding it up; he died instantly. His father's dying act had saved Michael's life.

Michael had no memory of the fire, yet he'd had nightmares about it all his life. The nightmares were so real and so terrifying, he felt as if the memory were locked somewhere, deep in the cells of his body. Other than his being an orphan, it was what made him feel most like an outsider—the fact that an event he couldn't remember, except in some dark pocket of his subconscious, had directly determined the entire course of his life.

Somehow Michael managed to survive the drive from the hospital to Vincent's house. He was met at the front door by Barbara Berryhill, Vincent's secretary for almost twenty years. (Vincent, in a typical act of defiance, had hired her just before his sixty-fifth birthday.) Michael had called her from the hospital, so that she could get started on all the preparations for the funeral.

Barbara, who was a year or two younger than Michael, was not given to displays of emotion; at this moment, Michael was deeply grateful for that. Her eyes were a little red, but otherwise she was as composed as ever.

"Hi," she said, softly, and stepped aside to let him enter. Her hand on his back was all the consolation she would offer. She knew him well enough to know he wouldn't want anything more. She launched straight into business.

"I spoke with the funeral director. Vincent left him written instructions down to the tiniest detail."

"Good."

"Apparently he also gave a copy to Monsignor Graham."

"Even better."

When they'd discussed the memorial service, weeks ago, Michael had told Vincent there was no way on earth he could officiate. He'd promised to do a short eulogy, and right now even that was a daunting thought.

"I think this guy is General Patton come back as a funeral director," Barbara continued. "I'm just going to stay out of his way. He and the monsignor can duke it out for King of the Hill."

Michael nodded. Tom Graham was someone's spinster aunt come back as a priest.

"I've been calling people," Barbara said.

Michael had noticed a portable phone on the coffee table, and a list of names and numbers that he was sure Vincent himself had made. There was also a hand-drawn map, with directions to the church, written in Vincent's flawless draftsman's hand, still steady at eighty-three. Michael knew Barbara was faxing the map to people who needed it. Vincent and Barbara together were a machine of frightening efficiency.

Michael collapsed into a love seat, took his glasses off, and rubbed his eyes.

"How tacky would it be if I made you call everyone?" he asked.

"It's fine. They'll all think we split the list and they're on my half. Don't worry, I'll spare you everything I can. However . . ." She paused, giving him time to brace himself.

"Why do I suspect I'm about to hear Tom Graham's name again?"

"He's called half a dozen times already."

"I thought he had the instructions."

"Michael, you know how he is. When he comes over here, he makes an ordeal out of deciding where to sit. Now he's got a genuine drama."

"I'm granting you power of attorney."

"I tried that. He said all the decisions have to come from you."

"Okay. Next time he calls, tell him you'll check with me. Then call him back in fifteen minutes and tell him anything you want to."

She smiled. "I applaud your lack of integrity. He also wants you to let him know if you change your mind about saying the Mass."

"I haven't and I'm not going to." He felt lousy enough about the Masses he couldn't avoid saying.

"I told him that, he said he has to hear it from you."

"I'll send him a telegram. Is the heat on? It's freezing in here."

"Michael, it's stuffy in here. You're not getting sick, are you?"

"No." He felt fine, physically. At least, no worse than usual, these days. He just felt like he was sitting in a crypt.

The last time you felt like this . . .

Stop it. You've got enough to deal with without adding paranoia to the list.

"All right," Barbara said. "The only thing left is that you have to decide when you want everyone to come over here."

"Here? I don't want anyone to come here."

"I know, but they're going to come anyway, and if you don't give them a time, they'll be traipsing through here constantly. If you give them a time, at least you can get it all over with at once."

She was right. There was no way to avoid the onslaught of casseroles and banana bread.

"What about Wednesday night, after the wake service?" Barbara asked.

"Fine," Michael said. "Just promise me you'll hire a bouncer to get rid of anyone who's still here at ten," he added, "including and especially Monsignor Graham."

"Easily solved. Close the bar at nine-forty-five. That'll get rid of everyone, including and especially Monsignor Graham."

Michael nodded his approval.

"Listen," Barbara said, "if there's one thing I have down to a science, it's throwing a party in this house. And Vincent told me it had to be a party. He didn't want a bunch of long-faced people standing around being miserable on his account."

That was Vincent, Michael thought. Running the show from the grave.

"Maybe we shouldn't have it here, then," he said. "Maybe we should rent a bus and take everyone to Six Flags. Or Underground Atlanta. Or the Cheetah Club, I'll bet Monsignor Graham would love that."

"How do *you* know anything about the Cheetah Club?"

"I went in there by accident once. I thought it was a wildlife conservation society."

She gave him a look. "I don't even know if you're kidding."

He smiled. "And you never will."

"Michael, you're bad." Barbara laughed.

I know that. Believe me.

"Okay," he said, relenting, "give me my half of the phone list."

"No, no, no. You go lie down. I know you didn't get any sleep last night."

"How do you know that?"

"Because I know you. You spent half the night bargaining with God and the other half convincing yourself that it's your fault Vincent got cancer in the first place."

He pulled himself to his feet. "You do know me," he said, patting her on the shoulder as he started away.

"Michael?" she called behind him.

He stopped.

"Are you okay?" she asked.

He groped for a truthful answer.

"I'm as okay as I can be, under the circumstances."

"You've had a rough year."

He nodded. *You could say that.*

"If you need anything . . ." She stopped; tried again. "I worry that you aren't going to have anyone to talk to now."

"Don't worry."

"Don't worry, you'll be fine; or don't worry, you have someone to talk to?"

He looked at her. He knew how Barbara's mind worked. She was fishing.

"Barbara, don't do the subtext thing."

"Well, it's really none of my business."

"What isn't?"

"I've always had this feeling that you left more than your job in New York."

He felt himself stop breathing. *How does she know?*

"Like what?" he asked, trying to stay calm. "My dry cleaning?"

She stared at him for a moment before she spoke. "Forget it. I shouldn't have said anything."

"You *haven't* said anything."

She sighed. "A couple of months ago, right after you moved to Barton, a woman called here looking for you."

"It was probably my editor from *The New Yorker* article."

"Yeah. That's who she said she was."

"So?"

"I don't know. Just . . . something in her voice . . ."

He stared at her and didn't speak. Barbara had an uncanny knack for figuring things out based on very little information.

"Barbara—" He didn't know what to say. There was no way he could lie to her, chiefly because he was a notoriously lousy liar, and she'd see through it in an instant.

"I'm not being judgmental," she said. "I'm just worried about you."

"Well, be worried about something that needs to be worried about. It's not like there's a shortage."

It came out harsher than he'd intended, but he couldn't care. He started to leave again, then stopped. He looked at her.

"Tell me you never said anything like that to Vincent."

"Of course I didn't."

He nodded, reassured, but knowing he'd probably just confirmed her suspicions. He couldn't worry about it now. He didn't have the strength. He'd rest for a while, come back and crack a few jokes, and everything would return to the façade of normality.

At the top of the stairs, he stood and stared at the closed door of the room that had been his. For a moment he fantasized about going through that door and back in time. Back to a moment when life had made sense, and he'd never heard of such a thing as committing a sin by loving someone too much.

CHAPTER 2

He stretched out on the twin bed in the room that had been his. The bed was far too small to accommodate his six feet three inches with any degree of comfort, but he felt a strong need to be there. He pulled a blanket over him, but it barely took the edge off the chill. He pulled it up to his chin and continued to shiver.

He never felt like he was alone anymore. He felt . . .

Something (someone?) . . .

It was like the intangible heaviness that wakes a person when someone is watching him sleep. Michael couldn't shake the feeling that something was hovering over him.

Why?

Waiting.

For what?

A clear shot.

He turned onto his side and stared out at the room, hoping to distract himself.

Vincent had not changed a thing in the room since Michael had moved out. There were model airplanes hanging from the ceiling that the two of them had made together. Michael had never had the heart to take them down, even in high school (opting, instead, to make the room off-limits to anyone who might tease him about it). The bookshelves still held all his favorite books from high school—*The Great Gatsby, The Sound and the Fury*, a collection of Flannery O'Connor short stories . . . funny, his taste had never changed, in books or anything else. He still loved everything he'd always loved, just on an ever-deepening level.

Over his desk there was a bulletin board covered with layers of mementos: ancient baseball cards, a charcoal sketch of himself and Vincent, done by a stringy-haired blond girl, whose face he could still see, on the boardwalk at Myrtle Beach, summer of 1951. Ticket stubs from sporting events and concerts. A picture of himself and Donna Padera: St. Pius Senior Prom, 1962. Poor Donna had been convinced that the two of them would become "pre-engaged" that night, whatever the hell that meant. (One of those terms teenage girls used to throw around in those days, just to give their boyfriends heart failure.) Instead, he'd broken the news to her that he was going into the seminary. She hadn't taken it well. She'd thrown her corsage on the floor, stomped on it, called her mother to come get her, and had never spoken to him again. Even now, over three decades later, she refused to speak to him when they occasionally ran into each other, despite the fact that she was married to a radiologist and had three kids in private schools. So far, he'd resisted the urge to tell her to grow up, but just barely. He could only imagine how she would react if she knew about Tess. Probably hire someone to have him shot.

You should be thinking about Vincent. (And Life and Death and Resurrection . . .) Why are you thinking about your neurotic high school girlfriend?

There were a number of reasons—good reasons—not to think about Vincent. The most obvious was that it hurt too much to remind himself that Vincent was gone.

Not gone. You know he's not GONE.

All right. But Vincent was somewhere beyond

communication, on any level that Michael understood. He couldn't pick up the phone and call Vincent. He couldn't turn around and see Vincent standing there, or reach out and touch him. Any contact he had with Vincent from now on would be subject to scrutiny and suspicion; there had been several moments already when he'd thought he *felt* Vincent around him, and immediately told himself that he was just making it up out of the need for comfort. It was a sad, frightening feeling to know that he'd never again be *sure* that Vincent was with him.

He told himself to stop focusing on the things he couldn't know. He should be grateful for things he *did* know. Like the fact that Vincent was safe and sound, and out of pain. And happy. If Vincent Kinney wasn't in whatever constituted "Heaven," there was no hope for a soul on the planet. For all his stubbornness and his crotchety demeanor, Vincent was, without a doubt, the best person Michael had ever known. Religious without being pious. Moral without being judgmental or self-righteous. Most of all, Michael had admired Vincent's vehement refusal to claim his own goodness. God only knew (literally) how much money Vincent had given away. He would go out of his way to keep people from finding out. Among other things, he'd built a church and a retreat center with his own money, on the condition that the funds used were identified as gifts from an anonymous benefactor. He would only admit to having donated the plans. (Vincent's humility came to an abrupt halt at the edge of his drafting table.) Vincent would allow his name to be used by charities on their literature only because it might inspire others to be generous, or because its absence might inspire them to be stingy. Still, he would grumble if his name was too prominent. *"I've seen my name till I'M sick of the sight of it, so I know everybody else is."* Vincent had no interest in proving what a saint he was. He did what he did for one reason: to serve God. Vincent had constantly admonished Michael to live a good life with a low profile. *"God knows everything you do. If you need to crow about it, you must be doing it for someone else."*

Vincent was happy now. Happy and out of pain.

What if he isn't? What if he is just GONE?

You know better than that.

Do I? How?

You know how.

In the winter of 1954, when Michael was nine, he'd almost died in this room. A couple of weeks before Christmas he'd become very ill, with what the doctors had finally diagnosed as rheumatic fever. That night, he had a fever of 105 degrees and was in and out of consciousness. The doctor and Vincent were with him; he remembered trying to hear what they were saying, but their voices sounded garbled, like a record set on a slow speed. He couldn't read the looks on their faces, either. Everything was a blur, as if he were underwater. Whatever they were saying, he could tell it wasn't good.

He fell asleep for a while. When he woke up, Father Donahue was there, so he knew he was in trouble. Vincent, the doctor, and Father Donahue were in a huddle across the room, speaking in low voices. Michael knew Vincent well enough to know what was going on. Vincent was trying to delay the inevitable. Once he broke down and told Father Donahue to administer Last Rites, he'd be admitting that Michael was going to die, and Vincent wasn't going to make such an admission until there was no way to avoid it.

The doctor came over to the bed and checked Michael's pulse. Michael could open his eyes for seconds at a time, and his focus was a bit clearer. He could see the grave expressions on all their faces. He saw the doctor look over at Vincent. He saw Vincent read the look, then pass it on to Father Donahue. Father Donahue moved to the bed and uncapped a vial of holy oil. Behind him, Michael could see Vincent put his face in his hands. He could see Vincent's shoulders moving up and down as he wept silently. Then Michael heard Father Donahue speak, in a solemn, hushed tone.

"Per istam sanctam Unctio nem, indulgeat tibi Dominus . . ."

Michael didn't feel anything when Father Donahue touched his forehead. Suddenly, he realized he was above everything, looking down. He could see the top of Father Donahue's head. He could see Vincent and the doctor, his own body—even his face. He didn't feel frightened; merely confused. He knew he wasn't asleep and dreaming. On the contrary, he felt keenly alert. He wondered if he was dead, and if so, why he hadn't gone anywhere. He was still wondering what he should do when he heard someone call his name. He looked toward the voice. There, in the corner of the room, stood a beautiful woman in a maroon velvet dress with ivory lace around the collar. She was smiling at him, her eyes full of kindness and love. He recognized her from photos he'd seen. It was his mother.

He opened his mouth to speak, but found he couldn't. Instead, she spoke to him.

"It's all right, sweetheart. You're going to be fine." Her voice was gentle and it calmed him immediately. "You're going to be around for a long time," she said, "because there's something you have to do."

A million questions raced through his head at once. She seemed to know what he was wondering.

"Don't worry. You'll know what it is when the time comes. It's not important right now. I want you to listen carefully to what I have to tell you."

He nodded. (At least, he thought he did.) She went on.

"It's going to be a constant struggle for you to see the world the way you need to see it. Don't get too caught up with what's in front of you, what you can see and touch. None of it is very important. You won't be able to see and touch the things that really count, but you'll always be able to *feel* them. If this doesn't make sense to you now, don't worry. It will later, when you need it, as long as you don't forget." She smiled at him again, then added: "Always go inside, to the place where you know the truth."

Then as suddenly as she'd appeared she was gone, fading before his eyes. He wanted to run toward her, to stop her from leaving, but he couldn't move. He felt himself being pulled back toward the bed, as if by a strong undertow. He had a sensation of dizziness and for a brief moment lost all sense of being anywhere. Then he felt himself open his eyes and look up at Father Donahue, who looked back at him, surprised.

"Grandpa," he said to Vincent, "I saw my mom."

Ignoring that, Vincent asked him how he felt. Michael kept trying to tell them what had happened, but they wouldn't listen. They were preoccupied with the sudden improvement in his condition. Two days later, he was strong enough to get out of bed, and a week later he was back at school.

No matter how hard Michael tried, he couldn't get a rise out of Vincent. It wasn't that Vincent didn't believe him; it was that Vincent acted like Michael was casually reporting something he'd seen on TV.

"Grandpa, I'm serious. I saw my mom!"

"I believe you."

"But . . . she's dead."

"I know."

"Well . . . dead people can't just show up and talk to you."

"Sure they can."

"Then why don't they do it all the time?"

"That would get a little confusing, don't you think?"

"THIS is confusing!"

"Look, Michael . . . you're right. It doesn't happen often. My hunch is that they can't show up without it costing them something."

"Like what?"

"I don't know. But every time I've ever heard a story like this happening, it was because they had something important to say."

"What is the thing I'm supposed to do?"

"I don't know. You're going to have to figure that out yourself."

"But what if I miss it—"

"She said you would know. You will know. Meanwhile, stop worrying about it and live your life."

"But—"

"Michael, what was the one thing Jesus told every person He cured?"

"Not to sin anymore."

"Besides that?"

"I don't know."

"He told them not to mention it to anyone. Which they all promptly ignored, but that's not the point. Why did He try to keep the miracles quiet?"

"I don't know."

"Because He knew that faith based on magic tricks is a shallow faith. He didn't want them all to get so caught up in the supernatural that they didn't hear what He was saying to them. All you need to worry about is the message. Stop worrying about how the message came to you."

The logic made sense, but Michael had never been able to follow the advice. The vision changed his entire personality. Up to that point, he'd been outgoing and gregarious, and loved running around the neighborhood and hanging out with his friends. Afterward, he felt too removed from them to be very interested. He spent a lot of time alone in his room—reading, writing, thinking. Wondering about the other reality . . . this realm that was out there, somewhere just beyond his reach.

Because of his experience and the way it changed his life, Michael had never been afraid of death. He was afraid of other things—of not living his life the way he was supposed to; of somehow not seeing this thing he was meant to see. He had decided, within weeks of the vision, that he wanted to become a priest. It hadn't felt like much of a decision—just something he suddenly knew, without any question. Nothing else would have made any sense. He could help the world by lending his faith to people who needed it. And he'd be ready, whenever this thing he was supposed to do came along.

Michael had been convinced that Danny Ingram was the thing. It still could be. Maybe he'd blown it. Obviously he'd blown it. A tragedy with that much forewarning should have been averted, and he should have been the one to avert it. He asked himself, for the billionth time, if it would have ended differently if he had taken it more seriously, before it was too late. He'd never know the answer, but it didn't really matter. It certainly didn't matter to the Ingrams.

He finally fell into a ragged sleep.

It was almost dark when he woke. He changed clothes and went downstairs. Barbara was on the phone. He could tell by her forced-patient tone that she was talking to Monsignor Graham, even before she looked over and rolled her eyes.

"Mortuary," Michael mouthed, and she nodded.

He left a note in the kitchen, telling her to lock up and turn on the alarm when she went home. He had no intention of being back any time soon.

He drove slowly through the neighborhood, looking at all of Vincent's houses and wondering what to do with himself. He'd lied about the mortuary—he'd already called from the hospital and been told there was no reason for him to go there. Vincent had already picked out and paid for everything. Michael was glad about that. Faith or no faith, rooms full of coffins gave him the creeps.

After weighing the options, he got onto I-85 South and headed downtown. He'd decided that a trip to The Varsity, his favorite fast-food restaurant, would solve both his problems: hunger and the need for a religious experience.

The Varsity, an Atlanta institution, was a glorified hot-dog stand on the outskirts of Georgia Tech. Michael wasn't sure exactly how old it was, but everyone in Atlanta acted as if it predated the Civil War. Tradition and atmosphere were probably larger draws than the actual food, although the latter left nothing to be desired. Michael had loved the place all his life. So had Vincent. It had been "their" place. Vincent used to say that when he died and before he went to heaven he was going to stop by The Varsity for a fried peach pie. Remembering that, Michael smiled to himself and wondered if he was going to The Varsity just to make sure Vincent wasn't there.

His timing proved perfect; the lunch crowd had thinned out and it was too early for dinner. He made his way up to the mile-long counter. There was no system for standing in line. The next person to get the attention of one of the surly, red-shirted cashiers, by whatever means, was the next person to be served. Right now that posed no great challenge, but after a Georgia Tech game it was an awesome undertaking, to be risked only by the bravest or most foolhardy.

Michael got a couple of hot dogs and fries and sat in his usual place, an upstairs corner that overlooked Spring Street. He felt somewhat guilty about having an appetite, even though he'd had nothing but coffee in the last forty-eight hours. He was also sad to realize the place wasn't as much of a comfort as he'd thought it would be. He tried to think about all the good times he and Vincent had had here, but he couldn't get his mind off the fact that they'd never come here together again.

The man at the next table was disregarding the NO SMOKING sign, and the smoke from his cigarette was drifting straight into Michael's face. Michael waved it away, and looked over. He was planning to ask the guy to put the cigarette out or move, but the words stopped in his throat the minute he got a good look. The man was in his mid-thirties, wearing an obviously expensive black leather jacket that did nothing to offset some intangible smarminess. He was staring at Michael intently, with a look that said he was *hoping* Michael would say something, so he'd have an excuse to vent a lot of pent-up rage. Michael quickly turned his attention back to his food. After a second, he glanced over. The guy was still staring.

Oh, for Pete's sake . . . like I need this . . .

Michael picked up his tray, and moved to the other side of the room. When he glanced up, a few minutes later, the guy had turned in his chair so he could continue to stare at Michael.

He has that "look."

Did he, or was Michael just imagining it? No. It was a real thing, regardless of its meaning. It showed up in the eyes, as if they were glazed over by a film of something very nearly colorless, like the thinnest possible coating of milk. No sign of life underneath, they were like the eyes of a deer head mounted on a wall. Soulless eyes.

Or worse.

Michael had seen the look before—in fact, had noticed it often in the course of his travels, even though he didn't know what it meant. The first time he'd noticed it was when Vincent had shown him the Winecoff Fire scrapbook. One of the clippings showed a photo of a man who had been suspected of starting the fire. The alleged arsonist, a career criminal named Roy "Candy" McCullough, was the son of a well-known murderer who was executed in Georgia in 1933. McCullough had the "look," so blatantly it seemed as if someone had tampered with the photo. (In fact, Michael had always half-suspected that this was what had happened, until he got out into the world and noticed the look over and over again.) Michael had always been fascinated by McCullough, since he had no one else to blame for his own parents' death. (Certainly more comfortable to blame an ex-con than to blame God.) The rumor was that McCullough had gotten into a heated argument with another participant in a big card game that had been taking place on the third floor. He had stormed out, threatening to get even, and had returned a couple of hours later and set the place on fire. Apparently McCullough had bragged about it to several of his friends, but the authorities had never been able to come up with enough proof to make an arrest. In the meantime, McCullough was convicted of another crime and sentenced to life in prison, and the police let it go at that.

Of the many things he'd read about McCullough, there

was one description that had returned, during the Danny
Ingram episode, to haunt Michael. It came from a book
written by a man who had known McCullough in prison:
*"Nobody could be better to you than Candy, if he liked
you, and nobody was more dangerous than he was if he
hated you. . . . I don't know that I'll ever understand how
Candy could be a warm friend one minute and totally
heartless the next, void of any basic human emotions."*
Michael could never understand such a thing either,
before he met Danny. Now he understood, all too well.
These days, he had too many answers. Answers to questions he wished he'd never asked.

The Danny Ingram affair had started simply enough. In
the middle of an ordinary day, he had received a phone
call from Kevin Ingram, an old St. Pius classmate whom
Michael barely remembered. Kevin, who now lived on
Long Island, had tracked Michael down through the
magazine; he needed advice. He was having a horrible
time with his oldest son, and the priest at his parish had
been very little help and, in fact, was now becoming
annoyed by Kevin's continued pleas for assistance.

"What kind of problem is your son having?" Michael
had asked.

"I think he's possessed."

Michael had laughed. Not because he didn't believe in
possession (though at the time he didn't) but because he
thought Kevin was joking. Most parents of eighteen-
year-olds were convinced that their kids were possessed.
When there was no laughter on the other end of the
phone, the realization had hit Michael—the guy wasn't
kidding.

Michael had asked why Kevin thought such a thing,
but Kevin's answers were vague: *"Weird things happen
around him. And he's not himself anymore. Plus there's*

this thing . . . I can't describe it, it's a feeling . . . the air in the room gets thick and it bears down on you, like gravity has suddenly doubled or something . . . I know this doesn't make any sense. You have to come feel it for yourself." Michael had agreed to go over to the house and feel it for himself.

The Ingrams lived in a beautiful Cape Cod solidly upper-middle-class house in the suburb of Plandome, on the north shore of Long Island. Kevin was an investment banker and his wife, Maureen, was an attorney in private practice. Their house was decorated in perfectly coordinated fabrics and expensive antiques. A little too heavy on the hunt prints for Michael's personal taste, but it definitely reflected careful attention to detail and two sizable incomes.

Danny was in his room, where, according to his parents, he'd been all day. He'd been told that Michael was coming and apparently was not thrilled about it; he'd been in a morose stupor for hours. Still, the way things had been going, Kevin said, they preferred catatonia to the other options.

"What's been going on?" Michael asked.

"A lot of weird stuff," Kevin said. "Things happen . . . lights go on and off . . . the toilet flushes itself . . . one night I was in the den, paying bills, and the TV just came on by itself. When I pushed the button, it wouldn't go off. I finally had to unplug it."

"Things fall off shelves," Maureen chimed in. "A couple of times, the gas flame on the stove shot up about a foot high, for no reason."

"What makes you think Danny's responsible for all that?"

"It didn't start happening until a few months ago," Kevin said. "About the same time that Danny started behaving strangely."

"And how has he been behaving?"

"He has these bizarre mood swings," Kevin said. "Before all of this, he was a pretty normal kid. A little shy, but nothing to worry about. All of a sudden, he starts flying into these fits of rage, without any warning or provocation."

Maureen nodded. "He throws things, screams—and he says the most vile things you can possibly imagine."

"The rest of the time, he's just kind of sullen and morose, hardly talks to us anymore," Kevin said. The pain of it was obvious in his voice. "Every now and then he's his old self, but not very often, not anymore." He shook his head, then added: "And there's that feeling, you know, like I told you. Sometimes it's a lot stronger than other times, but it's around all the time."

"Father, I know my kids," Maureen said, in a mildly defensive tone. "When Danny was little, he would get ear infections, but he didn't react to the pain, so there was no way to tell. But I always knew. I'd take him to the doctor and tell him Danny had an ear infection, and Danny would be running around like a wild man, and the doctor would stare at me like I was a lunatic . . . until he looked in Danny's ear and saw that I was right. I'm not saying I'm psychic. But I know when something is wrong, and there is something in Danny that is not Danny." There were tears in her eyes and she could barely talk. "I don't care how crazy you think I am, I know I'm right."

"I didn't say I thought you were crazy."

"Well, I know you think it."

"I promise you, I haven't had a thought one way or the other. I'm just listening. The minute I think you're crazy, I'll tell you, okay?"

Maureen nodded and even smiled a little. Kevin reached across the table and squeezed her hand.

"We're both pretty wrung out," he said.

"How long has this been going on?" Michael asked.

"Six months, more or less."

"And you haven't been able to get anyone to do anything?"

Kevin shook his head. "Father Garra came over one night and blessed the house, but Danny started screaming obscenities at him and he got mad and left. I think he writes Danny off as a spoiled, obnoxious rich kid who resents authority."

"Father Garra grew up in Brooklyn, in a very poor family," Maureen added. "I think he was done with us the minute he saw the house."

"Well," Michael said, smiling, "Kevin probably told you that I grew up a spoiled obnoxious rich kid. And I *still* resent authority."

Maureen and Kevin both laughed, but their eyes were filled with fear.

After talking with them a little longer, Michael met with Danny alone, in Danny's room, the walls of which were covered with posters of heavy-metal bands and pictures of skeletons and winged demons—drawn, apparently, by Danny. The furniture was draped in clothing, mostly jeans and black T-shirts, also sporting heavy-metal logos. Any good Republican would have hit the door, saying "I told you so," but Michael could still remember, too clearly, Vincent's horror during Michael's celebrated Elvis period. (During that time, Vincent had probably thought Michael was possessed, too.) Danny was a thin, pale-skinned boy with shoulder-length blond hair and watery blue eyes. He sat on the bed and stared into space, answering Michael's questions with shrugs and two-word sentences. None of which was a sign of anything other than youth. He did seem to be more depressed than the average teenager. His eyes had a peculiar unstable quality, as if he couldn't see anything in the room, but saw something else in its place. And the air *did* seem heavy, somehow, although Michael couldn't be sure if he really felt it, or just felt it because he'd been told that he would.

"Who the fuck invited you here?" Danny suddenly asked, in a voice surly beyond his years.

"Your parents."

"And what do you think you're gonna do?"

"I don't know yet."

"Just couldn't pass up the chance to get into a teenage boy's bedroom?"

Michael forced a smile. "Wrong number, pal. Don't believe everything Geraldo tells you."

"What then? Little girls?"

"Sheep. I grew up in Georgia. Why don't we talk about *you* for a while?"

Danny stared at him and said nothing.

"You wanna tell me what's going on?"

No answer.

"Your folks say you've been having a rough time."

No answer.

"Look, I'm arrogant enough to think I might be able to do something for you, but you're going to have to give me a hint."

"FUCK OFF!" Danny screamed. He picked up the lamp by his bed and hurled it across the room; it crashed against the wall and fell to the floor in a thousand pieces. Michael tried to stay calm. Danny was breathing hard and still trying to stare Michael down.

"Well, Danny," Michael said softly, "we'll talk again when you're in a better mood."

Michael headed for the door; was about to open it when he heard Danny speak.

"Father Kinney?"

Michael turned around. What he saw stunned him.

Danny had collapsed on the bed. He was sitting slumped
over, tired. The murderous stare was gone, replaced by a
look of fright and complete helplessness. He was barely
recognizable as the same kid. Danny didn't speak or look
up. For a moment, Michael thought he'd imagined
hearing his name called.

"Father Kinney," Danny whispered. It was a statement, as if Danny were somehow introducing the thought
of Michael to his brain. Absorbing it.

"What, Danny?"

Danny still didn't look up.

"Do you really think you can help me?" he asked, in a
small voice.

Michael couldn't speak for a moment, he was so
shocked by the transformation. The kid on the bed was a
portrait of humility.

"I'm going to do my best," Michael finally said.

Danny nodded. He stared at his hands, which were in
his lap, trembling. At that moment, Michael swore to
himself that no matter what it took, he was going to find a
way to help Danny Ingram.

Kevin and Maureen were waiting for him in the
kitchen, eager to have their suspicions solidly confirmed.
Michael knew he couldn't do that, but he was not going
to be one more priest who wouldn't take them seriously.

"I don't know what's going on," he said to them, "but
there's obviously something and it's obviously serious.
What I'd like to do, as soon as possible, is get someone
in here who knows a lot more about this kind of thing
than I do."

"How long would that take?" Kevin asked, ready for
another runaround.

"How's tomorrow?" Michael had no idea how he was
going to pull it off, but the outpouring of gratitude and
relief that followed was enough to cement his promise.

He'd called his secretary, Linda, from the first pay phone he could find. "I need to find someone who has a lot of experience with exorcisms, and I need to find him fast."

"Exorcisms?" she asked, in her usual charmingly patronizing tone. (No one on the staff could pour a cup of coffee without an editorial comment from Linda.)

"I'm not joking and I'm pressed for time. You can give me crap about it later."

"Where are you?"

"Plandome. Long Island. First thing you'd better do is check and see if there's an official exorcist for the Rockville Center diocese. I seriously doubt it, but I don't want to get anyone's nose out of joint."

"And if there isn't?"

"I don't know, try the Yellow Pages. Figure it out. I'll be back there in about half an hour."

"I'll find someone by the time you get here."

Linda was true to her word, and when Michael got back to his office there was a list of names and phone numbers waiting. Michael looked at the local names and, flying by instinct, called one Father Robert Curso, a parish priest in the South Bronx. According to Linda's note, he worked at a soup kitchen on 124th Street during the week; there was a number, Michael could probably reach him there. It took a little effort to get in touch with him, since the person who answered the phone at the mission spoke no recognizable language. (Michael tried three and gave up.) He finally got through to Father Curso (*"Call me Bob," he said, not warmly, more let's-cut-through-the-formal-bullshit*), who had a brusque smoker's voice and sounded like a former drill sergeant. Michael explained who he was and why he was calling, then started a brief summary of the case. Halfway through Michael's spiel, Bob cut him off.

"Has he shown any signs of abnormal strength?"

"Not that I know of."

"Spoken any foreign language he's never studied? Exhibited telepathic ability or aversion to religious symbols?"

"They didn't mention anything like that. Just these minor disturbances and fits of temper."

"So what makes you think he's possessed?"

"I didn't say I thought that," Michael said, losing patience. "I don't know anything about possession. I'm trying to find someone who has some experience with it, so *they* can tell *me* whether he's possessed or not, whatever that means. If you're not interested, just say so and I'll call someone else, but somebody has got to do something, because *whatever* is wrong with this kid, these people are going through hell and no one is doing a damned thing to help them!"

There was silence on the other end of the phone for a moment, then Bob asked, "How old are you?"

"What the hell does that have to do with anything?"

"Nothing, really. I'm just surprised."

"At what?"

"You got a lot of spunk for a Jesuit."

"What is *that* supposed to mean?" Michael asked, though he knew exactly what it meant. Curso, like most parish priests, thought of himself as in-the-trenches and therefore superior to the order priests. To him, a priest who belonged to a religious order was someone who sat in an ivory tower and wasted time writing his latest PhD thesis on some obscure, esoteric, and irrelevant subject. Secular priests resented the Jesuits in particular, because they thought the Jesuits considered themselves better than anyone else. Which, of course, they did. (The truest description Michael had ever read was a quote from Denis Diderot: "You may find every imaginable kind of

Jesuit, including an atheist, but you will never find one who is humble.")

"Give me the address," Curso said.

Michael gave him the address and detailed directions.

"What's that," he asked, "forty-five minutes on the expressway?"

"About that."

"Okay. I'll meet you there."

"When?" Michael asked.

"In forty-five minutes."

"Are you kidding? This time of day, it'd take me forty-five minutes to get to the midtown tunnel, not counting the forty-five minutes it would take me to get a cab. I was thinking maybe first thing tomorrow morning . . ."

Bob chuckled. "There you go. *Now* you sound like a Jesuit."

"I'll get there as soon as I can," Michael said, and hung up, already hating Bob Curso and wondering what the hell he'd gotten himself into.

At the house, Kevin and Maureen had their lists of incidents and witnesses spread out on the table, ready for Bob's perusal. He ignored it all and asked to see Danny, alone. Michael waited with the Ingrams in the kitchen, telling them what he knew about Bob, which wasn't a lot. Bob hadn't been in Danny's room ten minutes when he returned to the kitchen.

"Father, we've been writing everything down," Maureen said, "in case you have any questions."

"I don't have any questions," Bob said. "Keep all that garbage for the skeptics, though. We're going to need all the help we can get."

"Then . . . you think we're right?" Kevin asked, afraid to hope.

"No," Bob said. "I know you're right."

At that moment, Michael concluded that Father Bob

was, in the kindest estimate, some sort of occult-obsessed drama junkie. (But then, it probably wasn't easy to find a calm, rational person with a strong exorcism-conducting résumé.) Michael didn't see how Bob could hurt anything, though, and there was still the outside chance that he could help. Kevin and Maureen were so thoroughly convinced that Danny was possessed, they'd probably convinced *Danny* that he was possessed. For all Michael knew, the theatrics of an exorcism might be enough to convince Danny he was cured.

The bureaucrats had given them the runaround Bob had expected, and then some. They put Danny through weeks of psychological tests, physiological tests, interviews, and various other forms of torment. When the bishop finally exhausted every stalling method he could think of, he sent Michael and Bob to the cardinal. They did the whole dog-and-pony show and left over a hundred pages of test results and documented incidents. The cardinal promised to get back to them as soon as possible, and reminded them how busy he was.

Bob, who'd been through it all before, was frustrated but not surprised. Michael was dumbfounded. What on earth could it possibly hurt for him and Bob to dress up and throw around a little holy water? "The guys in the red hats don't like to be bothered by thoughts of the supernatural," Bob said. "They're afraid it'll make people think they're not serious politicians."

Another week went by. Danny's fits were becoming more violent and lasting longer. It was clear that if he wasn't already, he would soon be a threat both to himself and to everyone around him. It was also clear that Kevin and Maureen weren't planning on doing anything other than waiting. There was no point in suggesting they move on to another potential remedy.

At the end of the week, Michael called the cardinal. It took two days to get him on the phone, for which he did not apologize or offer an explanation. He did explain that he had sent the reports to an independent psychologist for "further evaluation." Dr. Brennan was on vacation for a couple of weeks, but he'd look at them as soon as he got back.

Michael had gone ballistic. "We don't have a couple of weeks! We don't have a couple of *days*! Something has got to happen *now*!"

He might as well have been talking to concrete. The cardinal just kept repeating his refrain, showing no sign of even hearing Michael, much less taking him seriously.

The next morning, Michael got a call from Maureen. The night before, Danny had attacked Kevin with a fireplace tool, leaving a gash in Kevin's forehead that had taken eleven stitches to close. Danny fled the house. When he returned, in the early hours, he claimed he didn't remember doing it. He'd been in his room ever since, but Maureen was afraid to even be in the house with him. Michael hung up and called the bishop.

"Michael, I have been as clear as I know how to be. There is a very definite way a thing like this is handled and it's being handled. It will proceed at its own pace."

"Yeah, well my thing's got *its* own pace, and it's not waiting for you! I'm telling you, if we don't do something *right now*, something serious is going to happen! Someone is going to end up dead!"

"Then take him to a psychiatrist."

"He's been to a *hundred* shrinks! If there's one thing that's obvious, it's that he doesn't need another damned shrink!" *And if you'd get off your royal ass long enough to go sit in a room with him, you'd know that . . .*

"The experts will make that determination. Meanwhile,

I've heard all I want to hear about it, and I'm sure you have more than enough work at the magazine to keep yourself occupied."

Late that afternoon, Michael and Bob had a long talk over a pitcher of beer. Bob knew what he was going to do. He was going to proceed without the Church's authorization. He wanted, and needed, Michael's help. At that point in his life, other than the occasional dicey article and a bad habit of running his mouth too much, Michael had never been anything but a good soldier. The thought of being involved in an illicit undertaking did not appeal to him. But there was a prospect that was much worse: the way he would feel if he said no and something awful happened. He agreed.

Michael had been naïve enough to assume that "yes" meant "give-me-the-text-and-I'll-read-the-responses." To Bob, it was a license to begin indoctrination procedures.

They took a cab to Bob's church. Bob led Michael to a classroom just off of the fellowship hall. He instructed Michael to have a seat in one of the chairs, then Bob went to the green chalkboard up front. He picked up a new piece of chalk and broke it in half.

"Remember Venn diagrams?" he asked.

"I remember being horrible at them," Michael answered, his mind flashing on connecting circles with shaded areas and letters, and identities like "all attorneys named Sam who drive Mazdas."

"This isn't complicated," Bob said, drawing a small circle on the board. "And it will help you to have a mental image."

He drew an *M* inside the circle.

"Mind," he said, as if that was supposed to make sense to Michael. He drew a larger circle around the *M* circle. He labeled that circle *B*.

"Body," Bob said. "Home of the mind."

He drew another circle, intersecting the *B* circle, and labeled it *W*.

"Will," he said.

"Whose theory are you diagramming?" Michael asked.

"Mine," Bob said. He drew a larger circle around "will" and "body" and labeled it *S*.

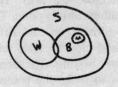

"Soul," Michael said, getting the direction if not the point. Bob nodded.

"Now," he said, "Father Bob's Crash Course on Possession Theory." He smiled; he was enjoying this.

"Is there going to be a quiz?" Michael asked.

"The final exam is tomorrow morning, and this is the only chance you've got, so pay attention."

Michael smiled and nodded. Bob's face became deadly serious.

"Most people think there are four stages to possession."

Most people? Most people would have you committed . . .

"I see the actual possession stage as a couple of phases, although it's all a continuous process," Bob continued, returning to the board. "The first stage is *infestation*," he said, as he wrote the word on the board, then began to draw another diagram.

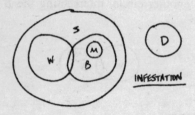

"*D* for demon. Don't worry about what he is or how he came to be there, we don't have the time, and it's not important right now. During the infestation phase, he hovers here, on the periphery, looking for an entry into the body and therefore the will. There are a lot of physical manifestations at this point. Things the Ingrams described: lights turning on and off, toilets flushing, drawers opening and closing. Also unidentified sounds: scratching, banging, hissing. The demon is stalking its prey. The point is to make the potential victim disoriented, off-balance . . ."

Bob went to the board and drew again. "The next stage is *obsession*," he said.

"The victim having been weakened, the demon starts to move in. Invades the spirit, weakens the body and the will. Physical manifestations decrease, usually. Most of what is going on at this point is now going on inside. The victim feels agitated, anxious, ill-tempered, has trouble

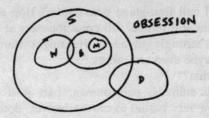

sleeping. People around him will notice a personality change, often a drastic one. The demon's influence starts to manifest itself in the actions of the victim. Danny's mood swings, outbursts. Older victims lose their defenses against old vices or pick up new ones—various addictions, mainly, which weaken the consciousness and consequently the will. All of which helps the demon accomplish its goal—to weaken the victim; mind, body, and soul."

Michael nodded. He couldn't believe he was sitting here with a straight face, listening to a lecture on the operating patterns of demons. Part of him—in fact, the vast majority of him—had never believed any of this, even when he was begging the bishop to let them proceed with the exorcism. There was another part of Michael, though, to whom all this hocus-pocus made some kind of sense, even rang true—as if it were something he remembered from another time, another place.

At the board, Bob was drawing again.

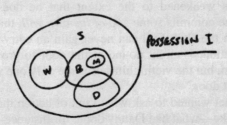

"What I call first-stage possession," Bob explained. "The victim still retains full consciousness at all times, but he is strongly invaded. He might start to hear voices, maybe even see things."

"Like what?"

"Bizarre animals, part human, part goat or pig—demons are very partial to cloven hooves, don't ask me why. Sometimes they're winged. Sometimes they're reptilian. Sometimes there's nothing but a vague black cloud. People who've seen it describe it as blacker than any earthly black."

People who've seen it?

Michael's mind flashed on a commercial he'd seen for some reality-based *(yeah, sure)* mystery show: two men in overalls, with thick Ozark accents, describing the crashed UFO and dead aliens they'd chanced upon in the woods: *"Four were layin' on the grah-yund."*

Bob was still talking.

". . . more sound. Smells. The victim is assaulted in all of his senses, even in his dreams. Dreams become violent and deeply disturbing; they cast a pall over the victim's waking hours, as well. The point of all of this is to exhaust the victim and weaken his will, until the demon finds what is known as an 'entry point.' " He stopped for a moment, giving Michael time to take it all in; then he went on. "We'd be here all night," he said, "if I tried to explain that to you. The simplest way to put it is that the victim is weakened to the extent that he does something—he commits some act, *of his own will*, that aligns him with the Evil. Evil can never gain an entry without an invitation. It might pound at the door to provoke an invitation, but the victim himself is the only one who can open that door."

Michael wanted to ask what kind of action the victim had to take—what had Danny done, for instance—but he

had a feeling it was another "we'd be here all night"
question.

"Then," Bob said, solemnly, "there's stage two. That's
where we are now." He stopped to draw it.

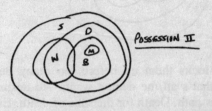

Whether this was a lot of medieval hogwash or not,
Michael felt an involuntary shiver as he watched Bob
draw the "demon" circle to encompass the circles of
body, mind, and most of the will.

"Now the demon has full access to the victim's body
and will. The victim will suffer blackouts, because the
demon can move in and go into business for himself.
That's what happened to Danny last night."

"He said he didn't remember it," Michael said, putting
it together.

"He *didn't* remember it," Bob said. "He could have
passed a polygraph saying he didn't do it, because *he*
didn't do it."

Michael sat back in his seat. This was starting to make
sense, which didn't make him feel better.

"This little sliver"—Bob tapped a crescent-shaped
area of the "will" that remained free of the "demon"
circle—"we'll come back to that." He began to draw
again. "Last diagram," he said.

"*Perfect possession*. What we're trying to save Danny
from. The demon, having invaded the victim's body and
will, takes complete control. Once that happens—" He
shook his head. "There's nothing you can do but hope

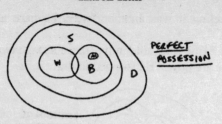

someone locks them up before too many people die. Because that's all the demon wants—to destroy everything in its path. Death for the sake of death. Evil for the sake of Evil. What is it you Jebbies say? 'For the greater glory of God?' Whatever is the exact opposite, that's what the demon wants. To spit in God's face. To destroy humanity, God's creation. To destroy life."

Michael felt a chill and had to remind himself to breathe. Bob walked back over to Danny's diagram.

"Here's what's vital," he said. He pointed to the "free" sliver of "will." He shaded it in with the chalk, drew an arrow to it, wrote "will" on the board, and underlined it three times.

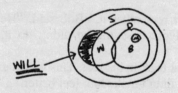

Bob tapped the shaded crescent with this chalk.

"Will," he said. "Will is the heartbeat of the soul. Through will, we can choose to align our souls with Good or with Evil. Danny's will is still alive in there, but it's weak. An exorcism is like a quadruple bypass of the will. We're the surgeons. We have to get in there and make the will strong enough to fight back. Ultimately, there is nothing we can do but strengthen the will. The choice is Danny's. Danny, with his own will, must choose to deny Evil and realign himself with Good. The important thing is, it's through the will that we can save Danny."

He shook his head, disagreeing with himself. "No. *God* can save Danny. We're just there to do a job."

Bob put the chalk down and dusted his hands. The room was agonizingly quiet. After a moment, Michael spoke.

"I'm still a long way from believing any of this," Michael said.

Bob nodded, apparently unfazed. "You know the thing the recovery groups say, about taking the action and letting the feelings follow? 'Act as if,' they say."

"Yeah . . ." Michael replied hesitantly, not sure how it applied.

"Just promise me you'll 'act as if' you believe it between now and tomorrow morning. By the time you find out you *do* believe it, it'll be too late for shoring up."

"You sound pretty confident that I'm *going* to find out."

Bob nodded, with a self-satisfied chuckle. "That's the easy part," he said.

Michael let it go. He could tell there was no point in offering an alternative hypothesis.

"Go home, Michael," Bob said. His tone was different; solemn. "Go home and pray. Say Mass. Do whatever you do—just make sure you're as strong as you've ever been when you walk into that room tomorrow morning. Give yourself enough time to sleep, too. Get as much sleep as you need to feel good. In fact, sleep like a baby." He smiled, a sad smile. "It's the last chance you'll ever have."

Michael kept a straight face and nodded, "acting as if"

he didn't think Bob was a certified fruit loop. He went home, put himself through the motions of "shoring up" ritual, as promised, and went to sleep. Though he tossed and turned and woke up frequently, he slept more peacefully than he knew. In fact, he slept just like Bob had ordered. Like a baby, he slept unaware of the full extent of lurking danger. Like a baby, he did not suspect any vulnerability in the forces protecting him.

Bob had been right. Michael would never sleep like that again.

CHAPTER 3

"God, Father of Our Lord, Jesus Christ . . ."

Michael stood over Danny's bed, dressed in his official exorcism attire (why the devil should care what color stole he had on, he couldn't begin to fathom, but Bob had been adamant about it). He had *The Roman Ritual* open in front of him; he listened to Bob's voice and waited for his cue to respond.

Bob was on the other side of the bed, tirelessly reading the text, as he had been for hours now. Danny was lying on the bed, staring at the ceiling, showing no sign of reacting; he seemed to be in some trancelike state. Early on, he'd yawned a few times, but he hadn't moved at all in the last hour. It made the straps restraining his arms seem even more ridiculous than they already had.

". . . give me strength against this and every unclean spirit tormenting this creature of yours . . ."

Maureen, Kevin, and Danny's younger brother, Chris, were waiting in another part of the house. Michael wondered what Bob was going to tell them, once he finally admitted the futility of the alleged exorcism.

". . . through the same Lord Jesus . . ."

"Amen," Michael answered, hoping Bob wouldn't hear the lack of conviction in his voice. It was obvious to him now that there was nothing tormenting Danny except Danny. Possibly a controlled substance or two. At any rate, if the hocus-pocus placebo were going to work, they'd have seen some sign of it by now.

"I exorcise you, most unclean spirit!" Bob went on. "Invading enemy . . ."

"Oh, give it a rest," Danny said, suddenly.

Bob looked up. Michael looked up. The voice had come from Danny, but, in some way Michael couldn't pinpoint, it wasn't his.

"It's too late for this one, Padre," Danny said. "You waited too long."

Something in Danny's eyes made Michael shiver.

"Here you are wasting time, when you could be downtown feeding the schizos. Noble work, isn't it? Keeping wretched people alive so they can live to see another miserable day. I wholeheartedly approve, for what it's worth."

Danny had a grin on his face that was somehow obscene. He didn't even look like himself.

Would you stop! There's no such thing as a demon!

Danny turned his head to look at Michael, as if noticing him for the first time.

"Well, if it isn't Father Rock-and-Roll." He smiled. "I'd hold off on any big proclamations if I were you."

Michael felt himself stop breathing. How was Danny

reading his mind? And why was it that he couldn't even make himself think of this . . . thing . . . on the bed as Danny anymore?

Bob returned to the text. "I exorcise all evil spirits! Every one of you!"

Danny was still staring at Michael, in a way that made Michael feel as if someone were pouring a coat of slime over him. He felt a strange pressure weighing down on him. He glanced around. Bob was still reading. There was no one else in the room. There was nothing to explain the feeling. It must be the feeling Kevin talked about. *But how . . . ?*

"Too bad you couldn't be at your office today," Danny said to Michael. "Linda wore that red dress. You know. The one with the scoop neck. If she leans over just right—"

Michael looked at Danny, stunned. Danny smiled at what must have been a puzzled look on Michael's face.

He heard his parents talking to Linda on the phone, that's how he knows her name. And every woman in America has a red dress. There's no such thing as a demon. . . .

". . . in the name of Our Lord Jesus Christ," Bob said, making the sign of the cross over Danny. "Be uprooted and expelled from this creature of God."

Danny didn't react, or take his eyes off of Michael.

"She just wears it for spite, you know. She gets off on being leered at by professed eunuchs. She likes proving what hypocrites you all are."

". . . He who commands you is He who ordered you thrown down from highest Heaven . . ."

"Last time she wore it, you went home and dreamed about her all night, didn't you?" Danny said, still smiling. "This Boy Scout routine of yours is such a fucking puppet show."

". . . He who commands you dominated the sea, the winds and the storms . . ."

"But I'm behind the curtain. I know what's under that bullshit choirboy act. You know it, too, don't you? You know who you really are—the liar, the hypocrite, the coward—the weak, spoiled shit who wakes up hard in the middle of the night from dreaming about fucking his secretary . . ."

"Stop it," Michael said.

"Michael!" Bob's tone left no room for argument. Michael turned back to the text, praying it was over. It wasn't.

"Dreaming about licking her clit! Ramming her cunt until she's too weak to move! Any of that ring a bell?"

Michael closed his eyes. He felt his knees go weak, his stomach turn hollow.

". . . Hear, therefore, and fear, Satan!" Bob's voice was growing louder. "Enemy of the faith!"

Danny raised his voice over Bob's. "But that's just a *dream*, right, Father? You can't help what you *dream*, right? That's out of your hands."

". . . Source of death! Robber of life!"

"What about after you wake up?" Danny asked. "At first light, in the dark, when you think you're all alone? It's not out of your hands then, is it?"

Oh, God. Make him stop.

". . . Twister of justice!" Bob snarled. "Root of evil!"

"Quite the opposite, right?" Danny said, still staring intently at Michael. "You rub it and roll on it and *make* it come, don't you? With full knowledge and free consent of will . . ."

MAKE HIM STOP!

"You never quite mention that in confession, do you? You confess your temper and your ego and all your noble sins, but you don't confess the mornings when you take your wet sheets downstairs and wash them yourself, now do you?"

Michael couldn't breathe. The invisible pressure had intensified until he felt he might suffocate. (At this moment, it was hard to think of that possibility as a bad thing.)

"Michael?"

Bob was waiting for a response. Michael stared at the swimming text in front of him. He couldn't force himself to function. His body was paralyzed and his thoughts were scurrying like terrified ants, fleeing poison in useless panic. Running in circles. Colliding.

How can he know that? He can't know. But he does. Danny doesn't know. He does. (What does that mean?) And now Bob knows. I can't breathe. Why did You let him do that? I told You I'd answer for my own . . . What? Sins? Decisions? Failures? You can't possibly expect me to be a saint. Yes, You can. It's me. I cop out. I rationalize. I'm horrible. I'm everything he said . . .

"Michael!" Bob was firm, trying to bring him back.

Michael squinted, trying to make the words come into focus. After a moment, he shook his head. "I can't," he said, in a whisper. He put the book down on the nightstand and left the room. Behind him, he could hear Danny howl with laughter.

By the time Michael had recovered enough to continue, Danny had reverted to his catatonic trance. Eventually he fell into what seemed to be a normal sleep, at which point Bob declared it a day. He told Maureen, Kevin, and Chris not to feel discouraged. (*"The shortest exorcism I've ever heard of lasted three days. It's not as easy as it looks in the movies."*) He promised that he and Michael would return first thing in the morning, and left them his beeper number in case anything drastic happened in the night.

On the train back to the city, Michael couldn't stop shaking. He was nauseated; his body ached, and he went back and forth from chills to feeling feverish. He told Bob he was coming down with the flu. Bob shook his head.

"It happens," he said.

"Do you feel like this?"

"Not as bad as times before. Try not to think about it."

"Fine," Michael said. "If I throw up on your feet, try not to think about that, either."

"Wouldn't be anything new," Bob answered, with a familiar smirk.

"Yeah, yeah, I know. And you're right. Very few Jesuit feet are thrown up upon in a day's work." Michael leaned his head against the window, closed his eyes, and tried to fend off the looming migraine.

"Jesus," Michael muttered to himself. Or maybe to Jesus.

"You did fine," Bob answered.

Michael opened his eyes. "I wasn't having performance anxiety," he said, instantly regretting his choice of words.

Bob didn't show any sign of making the connection. For all his purported calmness, he looked ashen, and about ten years older than he had that morning.

"Doesn't take long in a room with it to make you a believer, does it?" Bob asked.

Michael shook his head. "I just—"

"What?"

"I know I believe something right now that I didn't believe when I woke up this morning. I just don't know *what* it is that I believe."

"Tell me what you're sure of."

Michael waited a moment before he spoke. "There was *something* in that room." He said it quietly, as if voicing it aloud would make things worse. He didn't even like admitting it to himself, but there was no way around it.

Bob nodded.

"It's in Danny," Michael continued. "It can take him over." *I can't believe it, and it makes no sense to me, but I saw it. I heard it. And besides . . .*

Bob waited.

"Everything he said about me is true," Michael said quietly. He hadn't known he was going to say it until it was out.

Are you crazy? You could have told him it was a lie and he would have believed you.

"Don't let it get to you," Bob said. "That's what he wants."

Michael stared at Bob, amazed.

"But . . ."

"No *but*. If you want to talk about it when this is all over, fine. Beating yourself up right now isn't going to help anyone, least of all Danny."

Michael shook his head. "I'm not the person who should be doing this."

"Yes, you are," Bob said, firmly. "You're the perfect person to be doing this. Subjective moral judgments aside, your faith is unshakable, and that's what I need."

Michael looked at him, surprised. Bob smiled.

"I can see it in your eyes," he said, answering the unspoken question. "I can hear it in your voice. When I'm standing next to you, I can *feel* it."

Michael looked away, out the window. Compliments felt abrasive to him at this point. Not to mention undeserved.

Bob leaned forward, closer to Michael, unwilling to let him escape. "Tell me how I can help you," he said, in a tone far gentler than anything Michael had heard from him yet.

Michael looked back at him; sighed. "Make it make sense," he said.

Bob nodded, undaunted by what seemed, to Michael, an impossible request. He thought for a moment before he spoke.

"Obviously you believe in the concept of spirit," he said. "You believe in God."

"Yes." That was the only thing he still felt sure of.

"So, tell me. If you believe in a *benevolent* spirit, why do you have trouble believing in an *evil* spirit? There's just as much evidence in the universe to support its existence as there is to support the existence of God. The cynic in me thinks there's more."

"I don't know," Michael said, shaking his head. "I mean, I throw words around like everyone else: Satan, Lucifer, Christ casting out demons—but I've always thought of those words as symbols. Metaphors."

Bob started to speak; Michael cut him off.

"Don't crank up your anti-Jesuit spiel. Historically, we've been as into the mystic as anyone else."

"Historically, yeah. Have you looked at a copy of your own magazine lately? It's about as spiritual as an ACLU newsletter."

"Spirituality takes on a lot of forms."

"Yeah, well—when we go back in there tomorrow, try reading it the Miranda warning and see how far you get."

Michael didn't know where Bob thought he'd gotten with *The Roman Ritual*, but he let it go.

"All right, you tell me," Michael said. "You really believe in the devil?"

"I don't believe in a little red guy with horns and a pitchfork."

"What, then?"

"I think it's all very complex; interwoven. I believe there's more than one level of evil. At least two that I'm sure of: the evil of man himself, and something larger. I think of it as capital-*E* evil. I think it parallels the hierarchy of Heaven. God, saints, angels—Satan, demons, lesser demons—they are all beings. I know that. Whether there's any logic—any *human* logic—in it or not, my experience has reinforced that belief time and again. I don't know what form it all takes. I don't know what Satan looks like any more than I know what God looks like. What I *do* know is that when big-*E* Evil finds a doorway into the human realm and can communicate on a level we understand, it's not some vague, nebulous force. It's right there, in the room, in your face. It's individual. Personal. I swear to you, these things have *personalities*."

He gave Michael a second to digest this, then continued.

"It's like everything else in life, Michael. You hit a point where it stops making sense, and there's no place left to look for answers."

Michael thought about it. He had no argument for that.

"What did you believe before this morning?" Bob asked. "How did you think of evil?"

"I told you, it was all very abstract," Michael said. "This . . . stuff . . . floating out there, like radioactivity. We could get off course and veer into it, it could corrupt our thinking, pull us farther out, like an undertow. We lose ourselves. We lose God."

"And where did this *stuff* come from?"

"Maybe some by-product of our wrong decisions. Action creates energy, right? Maybe our wrongdoings create some universal cesspool of negative energy."

"And why would an all-powerful and benevolent God let that happen?" Bob asked.

"If He gives us free will, He has no choice. There's no way life can be as wonderful as it is unless the ability to *destroy* life is as horrible as *it* is, and if we have free will, we're going to have that ability."

"Natural disaster?"

"God's way of reminding us not to put our hearts and souls into material possessions," Michael said. "Although I doubt He ever accomplishes much more than making people update their homeowners' policies."

"So you had it all figured out. Now what?"

"You know what. Whatever was in that room today . . ." Michael shook his head. "It wasn't some cloud of New Age negative energy. It was . . ."

"What?"

"Old Age Hell," Michael answered, shivering. He wrapped his arms around himself and wished for a stadium blanket. He was freezing.

Bob nodded. "We rational modern people don't like to think about anything we can't understand. Floods and famines and plagues. We think we can *explain* everything, and if we can't, it's because we haven't isolated the right gene just yet; but a little more money, a little more research . . ." Bob shook his head. "Wrong."

Michael could see Bob shifting into his Professor Bob mode, but that was okay. In fact, he welcomed it.

"It's like this," Bob went on. "There's the literal and there's the metaphor, and the truth is neither, and the truth is not somewhere in the middle. The truth is *beyond* the metaphor. What people don't understand is that a metaphor isn't just a way to *illustrate* the literal. Jesus didn't speak in parables just so we'd have cute little stories to help us remember the rules. That moves us not one inch. Metaphors, symbols, parables—they speak to another level of consciousness, to the subconscious, which, I believe, is the meeting ground for life on this plane and life on the next. I think it's the *only* meeting ground. I think there's a lot we don't understand because there's a lot we *can't* understand in conscious, daily life. But I think that somewhere, deep inside, we understand it completely. Now, what does this mean?"

"I have no idea," Michael said, answering honestly.

"It means we are lying to ourselves when we try to bring it down to a level we can understand. When Christ talked about demons, He wasn't speaking literally and He wasn't speaking metaphorically. He was talking about something we can't understand. But just because we can't understand it doesn't mean it's not *true*. The fact that people in every culture, in every time, have believed in the Devil can't be written off as myth." He shook his head. "*Myth*. The new catchall word for why we shouldn't believe in anything. Joseph Campbell can trace every syllable of Christianity back to some parallel myth, so we must have simply stolen it all. But if the same story is being told over and over in every time, every culture, what about the possibility that the story is true? True, and timeless. True, and so pervasive we can't escape its truth?" He shook his head. "We didn't steal each other's myths, Michael. Myths are like stereotypes. Whether you want to keep perpetuating them or not, whether they're pleasant or not, they exist because somewhere, at the root of it all, someone noticed a pattern. A truth. We didn't start believing in the Devil because we saw evil all around us and we needed a way to explain it. We started believing in the devil because we saw *the Devil*. And . . . we don't know what that means."

Bob stopped. He seemed to be waiting for Michael to speak, but Michael couldn't make his head stop spinning long enough. Bob went on.

"Now, what's a rational, modern Jesuit to do with the thought that when Jesus talked about demons, He *meant* demons?"

"I don't know," Michael answered. "I don't know how to make myself suddenly believe things I don't believe."

"You mean you don't know how to allow yourself to believe things you don't *like*. You can't deny what you saw and heard in that room today. You know what it was. Evil. Individual, personal, intelligent Evil. With a staggering amount of power."

Michael put his face in his hands. *God, help me. I believe it. How can I believe it? What does it mean?*

"The good news," Bob said, "is that the minute you believe that, you become a lot safer. The best thing Satan has going for him is people's refusal to believe in him. You don't arm yourself against something you don't think is there."

Michael looked at Bob. There was something in his eyes. A milder version of something that had been there all day. A vague uncertainty. No. More than that. What, then?

Fear?

A horror of a thought was creeping into the back of Michael's mind.

"Safer?" he asked.

Bob nodded.

"But not *safe*?" It wasn't really a question. Michael could already see the answer in Bob's face.

"What are you telling me?" Michael asked. It took everything he had to speak at all. "When I walk into that room, *God* can't protect me?"

"I don't know."

"You don't *know*?"

"People have died during exorcism. *Priests* have died." He sighed. "I've met a few who may as well have. Others don't seem too worse for wear. I don't know what makes the difference."

"But you're okay."

"So far. Though I wouldn't say I've been the same. No one can go one-on-one with that kind of Evil and come out of it unchanged. I feel it."

"Feel what?"

Bob took a moment, then spoke, softly. "It's taken a plug out of my soul. I can't tell you what that's like. I hope to God you never know."

Bob's voice was filled with pain.

"Why do it, then?" Michael asked. "Why risk your life?"

Bob smiled, sadly. "Back when you guys were 'into the mystic,' you would have known the answer to that."

"*What* would I have known?"

"It's all about who you work for," Bob said, ignoring Michael's tone. "God or Satan. Good or Evil. If you love one, you have to hate the other. If you love one, you have to do battle with the other. It doesn't get any simpler than that."

Michael didn't answer. Nothing felt simple to him right now.

Back in his room, Michael got undressed and set the alarm clock for 5:00 A.M. He wanted plenty of time to pray before leaving for Long Island. He was so tired he knew he wouldn't be able to focus for very long tonight.

He got into bed and pulled the blanket around him as if he were four years old and trying to protect himself from the under-the-bed monsters. He could see Danny's face as if it were still in front of him. Not the real face. The other one. The evil one. Contorted. Hideous. Utterly inhuman.

Utterly not Danny.

He turned off the light; the room was dark.

Dear God . . .

Dear God, what? Dear God, what the hell is going on?

Why would You create something so vile? And if You didn't . . .

*If there really **is** a devil, one of two things **has** to be true: (1) God is not all-powerful or (2) God is not all-good.*

The first thought was merely deeply disturbing. The second thought was too frightening to even go near. Not so much because it was blasphemous, but because it scared the ever-living hell out of him.

Dear God . . .

I'm scared. I'm scared, and I don't even know what I'm scared of . . . except I'm scared of going back into that room. I'm terrified of all the stuff about myself that I can't even bear to look at, and he's going to keep trotting it out . . .

How weird, Michael suddenly thought. The Devil doesn't need any special powers, other than clairvoyance. After that, he can destroy you with your own stuff.

That's what You can't protect me from. You can't protect me from me.

His head was suddenly full of voices. He couldn't make out any words, but the din kept him from being able to hear his own thoughts. In his mind, he could still see Danny's face, and all the voices seemed to be coming from it.

It doesn't make sense.

IT DOESN'T HAVE TO!

He told himself to try something simple. Something he could say in his sleep. What was permanently ingrained?

Our Father . . .

More chatter. Louder. Voices. Laughter. He couldn't think. He couldn't remember the words. A line then. Anything!

DELIVER US FROM EVIL . . .

He could feel himself trembling. He pulled the blanket closer, but he knew it was useless.

Deliver us from evil . . .

He closed his eyes, tightly, but it didn't make Danny's face go away.

Deliver us from evil . . .

"Danny" started to laugh—a depraved howl, rising above all the "voices," so loud in Michael's head he couldn't believe he was doing it to himself. Then Danny stopped laughing and the sounds ended, abruptly. Perfect silence. Danny opened his contorted mouth and spoke: *"Deliver us from evil . . ."* He laughed again. The laughter died down to a sick grin. *"If You can."* More laughter.

It *couldn't* be true . . .

"IF YOU CAN."

Oh, God . . . tell me there's no chance that You can't . . .

A light rain had begun to fall; he could hear it on the fire escape outside his window. Thunder rumbled, somewhere far away.

Please tell me . . .

For the rest of the night, the only voice in his head was Danny's.

Michael picked Bob up at seven o'clock the next morning (having decided the train was more contact with his fellow man than he'd be up for at the end of the day he knew it was going to be). The morning traffic wasn't overly miserable, and they made it to Plandome in an hour and fifteen minutes.

When he turned the car onto the Ingrams' street, Michael immediately stopped. The street was filled with police cars. The Ingrams' house was cordoned off by yellow tape and uniformed officers. There were two ambulances parked in front, but their lights were off and no one seemed to be in a hurry. There was a station wagon from the coroner's office.

Bob and Michael looked at each other. They knew.

It took them about five minutes to find an Irish cop who was happy to supply the details. Around five o'clock in the morning, Danny had taken a shotgun he'd stolen from a neighbor's house and shot his parents and brother while they slept. Neighbors had heard the shots and called the police. The Ingrams had been found in their beds, lying in pools of blood, all dead.

When the cops had arrived, Danny was sitting on the front porch, waiting, with a smile on his face. He laughed the whole time they were reading him his rights.

For Michael, the circus was only beginning.

Danny's court-appointed attorneys found out about the Ingrams' belief that their son was possessed, and they decided it was as good a defense as they were going to come by. They contacted Bob and Michael, who both agreed to testify. They were both ill (not to mention furious) over what had happened, and they wanted to help any way they could. Bob could corroborate facts, but he wasn't going to be an impeccable witness. He'd performed too many exorcisms; the jury would figure he was obsessed with demons and saw them everywhere he looked. Michael, on the other hand, was a highly educated, levelheaded magazine editor, who hadn't even believed in possession until Danny Ingram had made him a believer. He was the defense team's star witness.

When Danny's attorneys made their strategy known, the story became instant national news. The press launched into their feeding-frenzy mode, and Michael couldn't walk out of the front door to the residence without tripping over reporters. He waved them off with "no comment" until he felt as if someone should be briefing him on foreign policy.

A week before the trial began, Michael received a call to meet with his provincial. Michael had expected it; he knew those on high would want him to be careful about the way he worded certain things. But he had not been expecting what happened. Frank Worland informed him that he was not to testify at the trial. He was to maintain complete confidentiality about the Church's involvement in the Danny Ingram affair. Michael couldn't believe what he was hearing.

"Frank, even if I agreed, they would subpoena me. What am I supposed to do, lie?"

"You're supposed to maintain confidentiality. How you do that is up to you."

"This is insane!"

"Whether it is or it isn't, Michael, I'm just the messenger. This is coming from higher up."

"Higher up than what? God?"

"All I can tell you is, it's coming from higher up."

"How high?"

"High."

"As in, we'd need a passport to go there?"

Frank nodded.

"You're kidding."

"No."

"What, they don't have enough to worry about?"

"Look at it, Michael. You were denied permission to perform an exorcism on a kid you claim was genuinely possessed. What do you think the press is going to do with that?"

"The press? Frank, three people are dead and a *child* is on trial for something he doesn't even remember, and they're worried about being *embarrassed*?"

"Michael, there's really nothing I can tell you."

"Well, you can tell *them* that if they're determined to shut me up, they're going to have to shoot me. And if someone finds out they did it and tells *People* magazine, they might be *embarrassed*."

"You're going to get yourself into a world of trouble, Michael, and for what?"

Michael stood up. "For a kid who asked me for help. Against something that is supposedly our mortal enemy."

"Well," Frank said. It was the clipped, condescending "well" of an authority figure who has tired of a conversation unworthy of his attention. The kind of "well" that always launched Michael into full-scale defiance.

"Well what?"

"You can't help him now."

"If I can't, it's not going to be because I didn't give a damn enough to try."

"All you're going to do is stir up trouble and make a fool of yourself."

"Well," Michael said, pointedly. He left the office, slamming the door behind him as hard as he could.

Two days later, he was hauled before the cardinal to repeat the entire charade. He was also given a refresher course on obedience and warned that there would be "consequences" if he chose to testify anyway.

He testified anyway. He told the truth, every crumb of it he could remember. He also went into great detail about the Church's attempt to shut him up. Danny got a twenty-five-year sentence, with a chance for parole after fifteen. His attorneys assured Michael that his testimony had a lot to do with keeping Danny from getting a life sentence. Michael was grateful for that, but he was still fuming.

The press had the predicted field day. Michael's picture was everywhere, from *Newsweek* to *Christianity Today*, along with sidebar stories on other Satan-related murder cases and surveys on people's beliefs about the devil. All of which was met by a deafening silence from the bishop. Michael knew he was waiting for everything to die down. If he were to do anything to Michael so soon, it might invite further criticism, more bad publicity.

It was *The New Yorker* article that had sealed Michael's fate. Those on high couldn't punish Michael for articles written *about* him, but they had no problem nailing him for something that he'd written himself. Two days after the article hit the newsstands, Frank Worland received an irate phone call from the bishop. Michael had "disregarded authority, created a scandal, and publicly humiliated him, the cardinal, and, in fact, the entire diocese." Frank was ordered to do something about it immediately. The next thing Michael knew, he was on his way to Butcher Holler.

Before leaving New York, Michael had gone to the prison to visit Danny. The kid in the visitation room was the same lost kid who had asked Michael for help, the first day they'd met. Danny could barely talk about his family for crying, but he managed to reconfirm everything he'd said at the trial—that he didn't remember a thing about the night of the crime, and that there were large holes in his memory in the six months before it. He did remember hearing voices in his head. The voices told him to hurt people, that they deserved it, that it was what God wanted him to do. The voices became louder and more insistent as time went on. They drove him crazy, and he couldn't get them to shut up. He also said he didn't hear the voices anymore. He hadn't heard them since the night of the crime.

Danny Ingram's face haunted Michael's dreams. So did the faces of Kevin, Maureen, and Chris, who had once confided to Michael that he was afraid Danny was going to kill them all in their sleep. Michael had told Chris not to worry. *"No one is going to let it go that far."* At least once a week, Michael woke up in the middle of the night in a cold sweat, with those words pounding in his brain, those faces tearing at his heart.

The Varsity was beginning to fill up with the early dinner crowd, and the noise brought Michael back to the present. Someone behind him dropped a tray and he jumped. He looked up to see the smarmy guy chuckle at him, which sent him spiraling into even more shame. He told himself to knock it off. The next couple of days were going to be difficult enough. He collected his trash and dumped it, then headed outside.

As he walked through the parking lot, Michael had a mental image of the creepy guy pulling a nine-caliber semiautomatic out from behind the leather jacket and blowing him away through the window of The Varsity. He could see it across the front page of the *Atlanta Constitution*: PRIEST GUNNED DOWN IN VARSITY PARKING LOT. *Neighbors say the gunman, an unemployed postal worker, was a quiet man who kept to himself...*

But Michael realized how exposed and vulnerable he felt, and he knew it had to do with Vincent's death. Even though they hadn't been able to spend a lot of time together in the last few years, just knowing Vincent was alive in the world had made Michael feel somehow protected. He realized, already, how much of a shield Vincent had been for him. Vincent and the Church. One gone, the other teetering on the brink.

And something vile lurking in the wings.

You're making that up. You're turning into a theological hypochondriac.

He heard the vague sound of thunder in the distance,

even though none of the clouds he could see looked threatening.

Look at the bright side. Maybe you'll be struck by lightning.

As he drove out of the parking lot, the thought came to him that he should go to Emory and pick up a grad school catalogue. Maybe he could talk the Royals into letting him go back to school for a year or two.

The standard Jesuit answer to an emotional crisis: get another doctorate. Learn one more language, everything will fall into place.

What else am I supposed to do?

How about the radical concept of dealing with the actual problem?

I will deal with the problem. As soon as I can figure out what the hell the problem is!

You know what the problem is.

No. He knew the symptoms. He had no idea what was really at the bottom of it all. Maybe nothing more than your basic midlife crisis. Maybe he'd become a living cliché. If he were a doctor, he'd be pricing red convertibles.

It was an appealing thought. If this was a midlife crisis, at least it would eventually pass. In his heart, though, he feared that whatever was happening to him was nothing so harmless. And nothing so temporary.

He drove aimlessly around the city for almost an hour. He didn't know what to do with himself. He didn't want to go home until he was sure Barbara was gone. For some reason, he felt compelled to make her believe that he was all right, and he didn't have the energy for any more of that today.

Something Danny had said to him, that day at the prison, was ringing in Michael's head.

"I'm so tired, Father Kinney . . . and there's no rest."

Danny was right. There was no rest. There would never be any rest again, for either of them.

Every time he tried to take his mind off Danny Ingram, it headed for another danger zone. Tess. He kept thinking about the safety he felt in her arms. Even if it was an illusion, it was a desperately comforting illusion.

He'd packed a bag to stay with Vincent for a few days, after the operation. It was still in the trunk of the car. Delta had a seven o'clock flight to La Guardia. He could catch it easily. With a little luck, he could be at Tess's door by nine-thirty. Ten, at the latest.

He told himself he should be ashamed for even thinking such a thing, at a time like this.

He told himself that all the way to the airport.

CHAPTER 4

Tess looked through the peephole, then unlocked the door and jerked it open.

"I don't believe this," she said.

"I should have called, but I didn't want to give you a chance to say no."

She moved aside to let him in. He closed the door behind him and locked it, as Tess was still too stunned to move. He tossed his bag to the floor.

"I really can't believe this," she said again. "I mean . . ." She didn't try to go on. She was wearing a soft pink bathrobe and had her hair tied loosely back with a strip of white chiffon. She looked more relaxed than he'd ever seen her. Tess usually looked as if she were in charge of a state dinner and no one could find the president.

"Can I hug you," she asked, "or am I supposed to keep a safe distance?"

Michael reached for her and pulled her into his arms. "I didn't fly all the way up here and risk my life in a cab for you to keep a safe distance," he said. He held her tightly, for a long time. The familiar smell of her hair was a welcome comfort.

"Vincent died," he finally whispered.

"Oh, Michael." She held him tighter. "I'm so sorry."

"The man was eighty-three years old and I still feel it wasn't fair for him to die. It's crazy."

"It's not crazy." She stepped back and looked at him. "It doesn't matter how old he was, you're still going to miss him."

"I already do."

"I know," Tess said, rubbing his arm. "And I know what it's like to miss someone so much you think you're going to come apart."

He nodded, hoping his look would communicate everything he couldn't find the voice to say. The empathy in her eyes was making it hard for him to keep from crying, and he didn't want to cry. He glanced away from her, toward the back of the apartment.

"Is Krissy here?" Kristen was Tess's twenty-year-old daughter, whom Michael had missed almost as much as he'd missed Tess.

"Are you kidding? If she comes home before midnight, I take her temperature," she said. "You can see her—" She stopped. "Well, when do you have to go back?"

"In the morning. I have a ten-thirty flight."

"And—were you going to stay here?" Her voice had the tentative tone the situation merited.

"If it's okay."

"Of course it's okay," Tess said immediately, but still sounded hesitant. "It's just . . ."

"What?"

"Well, you know. I mean—am I supposed to make up the sofa?"

When he tried to answer, he felt himself start to cry. Tess was there at once, in his arms. He held her as if letting go would kill him, which was exactly how he felt.

"Please don't" was all he could manage to say.

At two-thirty in the morning Michael put on his sweats and went out into the living room. Failing to find any reading material that appealed to him, he settled on the sofa to listen to Ray Charles through the stereo headphones. He was just getting comfortable when the front door opened and Kristen spilled into the room, a human collage of schoolbooks and oversized canvas bags. She was dressed, as always, as if she couldn't decide between three outfits and had therefore worn them all. (It was called "layering," she'd informed him once when he'd given her a hard time about it. He'd suggested she sit in front of the building with a plastic cup and see how much money she could collect.) She was currently too busy grappling with the door locks to notice Michael. He took the headphones off and laid them aside.

"Well, young lady, just where have you been?"

She whirled around, startled. "Oh, my God. I don't believe it."

"Sorry, that reaction's been taken."

She piled all her stuff on a chair, using the time to recover her nothing-fazes-me façade.

"So," she said, with a slow grin, "the Thorn Birds have returned to Capistrano."

He smiled and let her have that one. He and Tess had decided early on that they weren't going to sneak around behind Kristen's back. They sat her down one morning and told her what was going on. She just looked at them and said, "You think I didn't know that?" Michael had asked her how she felt about it. She'd said, "I don't know. Do you have anything I could extort?" That had been the tone of their relationship ever since. He loved her irreverence. At least she talked to him like he was a normal human—a pleasure few people allowed him.

"What are you doing here?" she asked, still smiling.

"It's a long story," he said. "Actually, it's a short story. My grandfather died this afternoon."

"Oh, no . . ." she said, drawing it out like she really meant it, which, he knew, she did. "I'm sorry."

"Well, you know—it wasn't exactly unexpected."

"But still—"

"Yeah. But still."

She came over and sat in the chair next to him.

"That doesn't explain why you're here," she said.

"I'm here because I'm a wimp and I didn't want to spend the night alone in Vincent's house."

"Wouldn't it have been cheaper and less complicated to go sit in a bus station?"

"See," he said, "this is what I hate about you."

"What? That I call you on all your crap?"

"That you're too damned smart for a twenty-year-old." He sighed. "All right. I'm here because I wanted desperately to see your mother."

"Did you tell her that?" (Kristen considered herself hall monitor of the relationship.)

"Of course not."

She was about to lecture him, but he cut her off with a smile. "Yes, I told her."

"What did she say?"

"She said, 'Sure you do. For one night.' "

Kristen smiled. "See? I come by it honestly."

"Oh, I know."

"So after that, did you talk about it?"

"No. After that, I came out here to sulk."

"And she didn't follow you?"

He shook his head.

"Ooh." Kristen winced. "Bad sign."

"I know."

"Michael, if you came back here and nothing has changed, she's really gonna be pissed."

"I know."

"So?"

"She's really gonna be pissed."

"Michael." She shook her head. "Michael, Michael." She stood up. "I'm gonna make some tea, you want some?"

He shook his head. "No, thanks."

She disappeared through the small breakfast nook, into the kitchen, where he heard her banging around.

"Don't you ever sleep?" he called to her, not caring if he woke Tess. (In fact, hoping that he would.)

"I'll sleep when I'm dead," she called back.

He smiled. "Warren Zevon's debut album. 1976. You're *much* too young to know that."

"I have a forty-year-old boyfriend with a great CD collection."

"Kristen!"

She returned, beaming with the knowledge that she'd gotten to him.

"Geez, you're gullible. No wonder you're a priest."

"I'm ignoring that."

"I know it because I listen to Mom's stuff. I love all that dinosaur music."

"Ouch." He grimaced. "Kick a guy when he's down."

"God, that's right. You're gonna be fifty in a couple of months."

"Forty-nine, thank you very much."

"Excuse me. You're right. It makes a big difference."

"Don't you want to point out that I'm losing my hair while you're at it?"

"You're not."

He grinned. "I know."

"You're getting a lot of gray, though."

He picked up a pillow from the couch and flung it at her. She deflected it with her hands and giggled like a kid.

"Why don't you just go in the kitchen and get a butcher knife and finish me off?"

"No way. This is fun."

"For you, maybe," he said, pulling himself to his feet. "I'm going back where I'm loved and wanted."

"Can you get a flight out this late?"

"You know, I'm starting to get some insight into your trouble with guys."

"Yeah, well. You better worry about your own love life."

"Good night, Krissy."

"So, Michael?"

"What?"

"When I get to heaven, am I going to get special privileges because my mom's sleeping with a priest?"

"You'll get first crack at Guns N' Roses tickets. I'll see to it."

"You're assuming Axl Rose is going to be in heaven?"

"Why not? You're assuming *you* are."

"Yeah, I'm also counting on you to have some clout, so I guess it's a shaky premise all around."

He threw his hands up. "I surrender. I abdicate the smart-ass throne. I'm going to sleep."

He started down the hall.

"Michael?"

He stopped, turned. "Krissy?"

Her attitude had vanished, replaced by a shy smile.

"I'm really glad you're back. Even for one night."

"Thanks," he said, then turned quickly away, before she could see the tears that had instantly welled in his eyes.

"I'm awake," Tess said, as Michael closed the bedroom door behind him. She turned on the lamp.

"Don't you worry about her, running around Manhattan till two-thirty in the morning?"

"Of course I worry. But she's twenty years old, what am I going to do?"

He sat down on the bed beside her. "Lock her in her room."

She reached up and rubbed his back.

"Can't sleep?" she asked.

He shook his head.

"Do you want a Xanax?" she asked.

"I don't know. Maybe." He pulled off the sweats and tossed them in the general direction of his duffel bag, then climbed under the covers and pulled Tess as close to him as she could get. He found the curve of her hip with his palm; let it rest there; wondered how many years it would take before such a simple thing didn't stop his heart. He kissed the side of her face.

"I'm sorry you snapped at me," he said.

She turned her face toward his. She wasn't smiling.

"I'm sorry I snapped at you, too," she said. "I'm a bitch when I'm scared."

He felt his throat close up again. "I'm sorry you have to be scared," he said.

He raised up on an elbow and studied her face. Her eyes were cat-green and her hair was the color of Georgia clay after a hard rain. No matter what she did to it, there were always loose wisps that curled around her face. That, combined with the sprinkle of Irish freckles across her nose, gave her an eternally childlike quality, until she opened her mouth to speak. Then it was impossible to ignore the mature edge in her voice—the cynicism of a brilliant woman who'd never fully recovered from the initial realization that the world considered her a second-class citizen.

He brushed a loose strand of hair out of her eyes. "What were you thinking about?"

"When?"

"Right before I came in."

She thought for a second. Remembered. "Joel Wallerstein."

"Who?"

"A guy I was engaged to when I was in graduate school. He was a rabbinical student. I was just lying here wondering, what is it about me and you men of the cloth?"

Michael feigned hurt. "I'm out there pining away for you, and you're in here thinking about former lovers?"

"You were out there flirting with my daughter."

"Well, I'll bring you the head of John the Baptist and we'll call it even."

She stared into his eyes for a long moment. It didn't bother him. In fact, it reminded him that one of the first things he'd ever noticed about the energy between them was that she was a woman whose gaze he could hold without any discomfort whatsoever. In five seconds she had broken through decades of deeply ingrained guilt. He also remembered wondering, at the time, whether that was the good news or the bad news. He was still wondering.

"Are you okay?" she asked.

"Why? Am I acting weirder than normal?"

"Michael, this is too much for you to stuff and cover with wisecracks."

"Really? I thought I was doing a pretty good job."

She gave him a warning-shot look.

"Okay," he said. He looked away for a moment; stared at a Winslow Homer print on the wall by her window and wondered if it was new. He had to force himself to focus his thoughts and go deep enough to give her an honest answer.

"I'm . . . not okay. Or did you want something less poetic?"

"Keep going."

He sighed. "I don't know. Maybe it's because Vincent's death came on top of so many other things. I knew this wasn't going to be easy, even with all the time I had to brace myself, but I'm a lot shakier than I thought I'd be."

Tess nodded, didn't speak, kept staring into his eyes. She wanted more.

He went on. "Death—being around death—is usually not that difficult for me. I haven't been around it a lot, not like most priests. The magazine really was the oasis everyone accused us of being. But I've been around death enough to know how it feels to me, and that it always feels the same."

He gave himself a minute to think. She waited.

"There's always this strange peace that . . . I feel it

around me, then I feel myself slip into it . . . and it's just . . . the greatest thing."

He saw something flash in her eyes; it wasn't at all what she'd expected to hear.

"It's like I'm drugged. And everything makes perfect sense to me."

"What's everything?"

"Death. Loss. Pain. The transcendent sadness of life. The comfort of letting that be. The realization that if you stop fighting it or trying to explain it or understand it—if you just surrender to that deep part of you that knows how it all works—it's just the most bizarre, senseless, beautiful . . . calm."

Tess smiled, but it was a sad smile. "I've never felt anything like that. I envy you." She ran a slender hand across his cheek; let it rest there.

"Is that where you are now?" she asked. "In the calm?"

"No," he answered, without hesitation. "I can't find it this time."

"Why not?"

"Maybe this time I just don't have the strength that it takes to surrender," he said. "Or maybe I think I'd betray Vincent if I were to be calm about his death."

Or maybe I don't have the ability to be calm about anything anymore.

"Can we change the subject?" he asked.

"To what?"

He closed his eyes. "Actually, I'm tired of talking."

"Do you think you can sleep?"

"No."

"Want that Xanax?"

"No."

"Want me to sing you a lullaby?"

"No," he said, opening his eyes; grinning. "But you're on the right track."

"Oh, really?" she said, smiling. "Again?"

"I've got a lot of years to make up for."

"I know. It's one of my favorite things about you."

He knew she meant it. He'd decide later how to take it.

She wrapped an arm and a leg around him and pulled him to her. He felt the soothing warmth of her skin; the heat of her lips on his neck. He lifted her face and kissed her. It took him no time to lose himself. The guilt vanished as quickly as it would return.

He awoke to the smell of coffee brewing. The room was light and he was alone. He'd left his glasses on the dresser across the room, and the numbers on the digital clock were a red blur, but there was a strong chance that the first one was an eight. He forced himself out of bed and staggered to the bathroom.

He showered, shaved, and dressed, donning his standard jeans and a concession-to-New-York-City oxford cloth shirt, white with blue pinstripes. With his glasses on, he probably looked like a Columbia law professor. He studied himself in the mirror and wondered why, if he really loved being a priest as much as he thought he did, he hated looking like one.

He ventured out and found Tess in the kitchen, cooking breakfast. She was wearing a large gray T-shirt that fit like a dress and advertised some kind of ACLU-sponsored walkathon. He leaned against the doorjamb and watched her.

"You'd be lynched if you wore that in Georgia."

She smiled. "They don't lynch white people."

"They make an exception for the ACLU, take my word for it."

He glanced back toward Kristen's room.

"Is Krissy still asleep, or is that a stupid question?"

"Yes and yes."

She stirred eggs in the frying pan with one hand and poured a glass of orange juice with the other. He watched her, thinking of all the people in the world who took such a scene for granted. For him, it was a forbidden form of poetry.

He pulled a chair back from the small table in the breakfast nook and sat down. "I don't have a lot of time," he said.

"I'm keenly aware of that. You're eating breakfast anyway. You've lost too much weight." She brought a plate over and put it down in front of him. "Don't they feed you down there?"

"I've turned into a vegetarian. Vegetables are the only thing they don't deep-fry. And if Krissy were awake, she'd tell you that at my advanced age, I need to worry about such things."

Tess sat down across from him, with nothing but a cup of coffee. She had no business criticizing *his* eating habits. He didn't know how she stayed alive, as little as she ate. But he wasn't going to get into that one this morning. The air was already thick with undercurrents.

"Tell me about the rabbi," he said.

"What about him?"

"Why didn't you marry him?"

"He wanted me to convert. Which wasn't really a big deal, but I realized that what he was after was someone who'd do the whole Mrs. Rabbi thing, and that was never going to be me."

"What do you mean, it wasn't a big deal?"

"It wasn't. My parents would never have lived through it, but I didn't care."

Michael stared at her, not believing what he was hearing. They had spent a lot of time arguing over

Catholicism; but, he suddenly realized, they'd never really had a conversation about what Tess believed.

"Why are you looking at me like that?" Tess asked. "You knew I was a heathen."

"I knew you were opposed to organized religion and rabidly down on the Catholic Church."

"But what? You thought I was a closet Christian?"

Michael couldn't speak. As surprised as he was at the discovery, he was even more surprised at his reaction. Why did he feel like someone had just kicked him in the gut?

Tess smiled. "What, Michael? God is going to be even more disappointed when He finds out you're sleeping with an agnostic?"

"I'm just surprised, that's all."

He felt like he was ten years old. What the hell difference did it make what Tess believed? Didn't she have a right to believe anything she wanted? Why should it affect his life at all? Why was he reacting like a threatened Fundamentalist? Had he been in Georgia that long?

"So . . ." He couldn't leave it alone.

"What?"

"Are you one of those people who thinks Jesus was just a better-than-average rabbi?"

"No. I'm one of those people who thinks He probably didn't exist."

He put his fork down and stopped trying to be open-minded.

"Are you serious?" he asked.

"I read a book; this guy made a very intelligent case."

"What guy?"

"Some Harvard professor."

"Well, that settles it, then. Great. Think how much money we'll save next December."

"Why do you care so much what *I* believe?"

"I don't understand how you can be in love with me when you don't like anything I stand for."

"And I don't understand your stubborn loyalty to the Church, when they've exiled you to Siberia as *punishment* for being a moral human being. And as long as we're playing this game, how can *you* claim to love *me* and work for people who go against everything I believe in?"

"I thought you didn't believe in anything."

She ignored that. "I'm talking about what you and your cronies so charmingly refer to as 'the women thing.' In which area, you work for the Devil."

"I hardly think that's true."

"Which part?"

"I don't work for the Devil," he said. He was trying, without much success, to stay calm.

"The hell you don't, Michael. And you're too smart not to see it. You just put on your Vatican-issued blinders—"

"I do *not*."

"Michael, you're in so much denial, you're in denial *about* your denial!"

"Can we have *one* argument without the psychobabble?"

"Fine. You want it plainer? Explain to me how you can go on for hours on end about how Ronald Reagan corrupted the soul of a decade, and then turn around and defend the pope, who is the same damned person!"

"*What?*" His voice went up an octave.

"It's the truth! The same ego, the same arrogance, the same misogyny, the same lack of empathy . . ."

"Look, it's not like the guy's my personal hero, but you can't ignore—"

"If you say Eastern Europe to me, I will throw something at you!" She slammed her coffee cup down. Coffee splashed onto the table, but she was too worked up to notice. "It's just like the fucking Kennedys!"

"How the hell did we get to the Kennedys?"

"It's that attitude. 'Yeah, they treat women like shit, but look at all the good they've done!' I am *sick to death* of being the shrugged-off side issue! It doesn't matter if the pope is sending women back to the Stone Age, he freed Eastern Europe. In the first place, he freed Eastern Europe about as much as Reagan got rid of the Berlin Wall! In the second place, the *men* of Eastern Europe might be in better shape, but how damned *free* do you think the women are? And in the third place, if men could get pregnant, I'd like to see how long anyone would put up with a bunch of celibate geezers sitting around pontificating on the finer points of Aristotelian causation theory and I'd like to see how long *anyone* gave a *damn* about Eastern Europe!"

She stormed out of the room. He gave her a few minutes to calm down before following her. He needed a few minutes to calm down himself.

He found her sitting on the bed, crying. He leaned in the doorway and waited.

"This is insane," she said. "This isn't about the pope or the Kennedys or Eastern Europe."

"I know," he said.

She took a breath and dried her eyes with the tissue he'd handed her. Finally she spoke. "It's just that I've been in this tunnel for about as long as I can stand it."

"I know." He sat beside her and held her until she stopped crying.

"It just seems to me, Michael, that if it goes on long enough, avoiding the choice *becomes* the choice." She wiped her eyes again, then looked back at him. "I'm not trying to pressure you or issue an ultimatum," she said. "I just can't keep living in this limbo. . . ." Her voice choked to a whisper. "It hurts too much."

She left the room. Michael felt a crushing sadness descend on him the moment she was gone, reminding him how lonely he was—how lonely he'd been, for the last thirty-two years, or perhaps all his life.

On the way to the airport, he decided to go by the Jesuit residence. He found some perverse form of comfort in the idea of reminding himself that a few short months ago he had been happy.

There was no one in the lobby and Linda wasn't at her desk. Michael was glad. He hadn't been able to look her in the face since the exorcism. He didn't know how, but he was convinced that she knew. She'd worn the damned red dress to his "going away" party.

He walked quietly down the hall, to the office that used to be his. It now belonged to Larry Lantieri, who had been appointed to Michael's old job.

The door was ajar. He tapped on it with his knuckles and pushed it open without waiting.

Larry glanced up from his Macintosh, already irritated by the disruption. It took a second for what he was seeing to register.

"I hope I'm interrupting you," Michael said.

"What the *hell* are you doing here?"

"I found the one-armed man who wrote *The New Yorker* article and signed my name to it."

Larry smiled. "Has anyone notified His Eminence?"

"He's on his way over to personally beg my forgiveness."

"I'll make a fresh pot of coffee."

"No, let's just send out for pizza."

"Really, why didn't you tell me you were going to be in town?"

"Can we move on to an easier question and come back

to that one if there's time? I literally have five minutes. I have a ten-thirty flight."

"Okay. How are you?"

"That's not an easier question."

He'd tell Larry about Vincent later. He didn't want to waste what little time he had assuring Larry that he was okay.

"How's Dogpatch?" Larry tried again.

"I hate it."

"There you go. That was easy."

"I'm miserable beyond their wildest dreams. Unless you happen to chat with Bishop Wilbourne and my name comes up, in which case, I've never been happier."

Larry smiled.

"I don't know what I'm doing in New York," Michael continued. "I didn't call you because I didn't know I was coming until about half an hour before the plane took off."

"How long have you been here?"

"Since last night."

"And you're going back now?"

"Let's not analyze it to death."

"So, how *is* Tess?"

"I think she's about ten minutes from pushing me in front of a train. And I don't blame her."

"What are you going to do?"

"I don't know."

"Do you have time to sit down?"

"No. I just want you to solve my major life crisis, then I'll be on my way," he said. "And you can also explain what you're doing with a tan in New York in January."

"I just got back from a couple of weeks in Mexico."

"Life is hell."

"It was hardly a vacation." Larry leaned back in his chair, suddenly serious. "Among other things, I spent a

lot of time with this family . . . the Alvarez
family . . . mother, father, eight kids. No income. Father
works on the docks whenever he can find something,
which isn't often. They live in a hut made out of palm
fronds, slightly larger than this office. The kids are all
sick and malnourished. Youngest kid has Down's syn-
drome, the one before that was born with no ears,
because the mother is too damned old to be having
babies. I don't know how they stay alive, they all look
like the walking dead." He sighed. "But they're devout as
hell. Got that *Time* magazine cover of the pope tacked to
the wall."

"What were you doing there?" Michael asked, when
he could finally speak.

"Researching an article."

Michael looked at him, shocked. "On birth control?"

"No, on how-to-build-your-own-palm-frond-hut."

"Be careful. You'll end up in Dogpatch with me."

"Better Dogpatch than hell."

"Trust me, the difference is negligible."

"All I'm doing is telling the truth. When the Church
and the truth are a fork in the road, something is seriously
wrong." He gave Michael a moment to think about it,
then went on. "To me, the only valid question anymore is
'where can I do the most good?' I'm going to do it here
until they kick me out, which probably won't be much
longer. Then I'll do it somewhere else."

"Where?"

"I don't know. I'll drive off that bridge when I come
to it."

"I'm at the bridge."

Larry looked at him for a moment, as if he wanted to
say something, then looked down at his desk.

"What?" Michael asked.

Larry shook his head.

"What?"

"Nothing. Just . . . it's hard."

"What is?"

"Resisting the urge to tell you what to do."

"Don't resist on my account."

"In my humble and unsolicited opinion, God has tried every way but Sunday to tell you that you shouldn't be here anymore, so I don't know why you'd listen to me. If the one-way ticket to Mayberry RFD didn't convince you, and Tess threatening to leave doesn't convince you—"

"You make it sound easy. I don't see you packing."

"I'm waiting for God to send *me* a gorgeous redhead."

"What's going to happen to the Church if all the good people just throw up their hands and walk away?"

"What do you think's going to happen if they don't? Could a better crew have saved the *Titanic*?"

Michael relented and sat on Larry's couch. "Well . . . even if it had ever been that simple," he said, "it isn't anymore."

"What do you mean?"

"Over breakfast she informed me that she's an agnostic and she doesn't believe Jesus ever existed."

Larry looked relieved. "Is that all?"

"What do you mean, is that all?"

Larry shrugged. "She's just following the trends. Christianity is very unhip these days."

Michael nodded. "I've been informed that intelligent, educated people no longer believe, and I quote, all that Hellenistic hogwash."

"That's right," Larry agreed. "Intelligent, educated people pay four hundred dollars an hour for a middle-aged housewife to channel a thirty-five-thousand-year-old spirit from the lost continent of Atlantis. But if you tell them you believe Jesus really performed miracles, you're a naïve bumpkin."

"I was in no mood to discover that the gulf is even wider than I thought," Michael said.

"How much does it matter?"

"I don't know. I guess that's what I get to figure out." He looked at his watch. "I'd better go," he said. "She's waiting."

"Maybe I'll come visit sometime," Larry said. "I've always wanted to see Atlanta."

"You can't see it from where I live."

Larry smiled. "I hope you know how much you're missed around here," he said, in a different tone.

"No, but thank you for taking so long to mention it."

"I didn't want to feed your already swollen ego."

"The swelling has gone down, believe me."

Larry smiled. "Call me."

"I will."

They half-hugged, then parted, in the graceless way that male friends do.

Tess drove him to the airport in silence. Michael stared out the window, glancing at her occasionally. For the moment, he didn't care how much she hated the Church and he didn't care if she was a Zen Buddhist. He cared only about the way her hair curled softly around the collar of her jacket, and the memory of his name whispered against the side of his face in the dark.

When they reached the Delta terminal, she didn't get out.

"I don't want to go with you to the gate," she said. "It just depresses me."

He hugged her tightly.

"It's not fair," he heard her mumble.

"What?"

"Any of it."

He kissed her, chasing away the thought that it might

be the last time. Neither of them said good-bye as he got out and slammed the door behind him. He didn't look back as she drove away.

CHAPTER 5

When he got home, there was a message from Krissy on Vincent's answering machine. He'd played the messages back with Barbara in the room, having never thought of the fact that this might happen. He held his breath all the way through the message.

"Michael, it's Krissy. I was gonna talk to you this morning, but I didn't know you were leaving so early. Call me, okay? I don't want to, you know, say anything on your answering machine. Call me in the afternoon, while my mom's at work."

He hit the button to erase the messages. He could feel Barbara's eyes on him. He weighed it for a second and decided to pick up the phone and call Krissy then and there. It was a hell of a lot better than letting Barbara's overactive imagination decide he was having an affair with a twenty-year-old.

Krissy answered on the first ring.

"What's up?" he asked, as informally as possible.

"You're not alone."

"You're very astute, as usual."

"Okay. I wasn't sure whether to call. I wasn't sure

whether to even tell you this or not, but I decided I'd better."

"Tell me what?"

"I have to hurry, because she's gonna be home any minute." She took a breath. "There's this guy . . . he's an attorney. I don't know what kind. He told me, but it was so boring I can't remember. Nothing major is going on, I'm not sure if she even likes him, but I know they've had dinner a couple of times."

Michael let himself sink into the kitchen chair beside him. He couldn't speak. Barbara was watching him. The look of concern on her face must have reflected what she saw on his, but he was powerless to do much about it.

"Are you still there?"

"Yes."

"I feel horrible about telling you this, especially today. But if she broke up with you and I could have stopped it—"

"No. I'm glad you told me. Look, I'll call you later when we both have more time."

"Okay."

"Thanks for calling, Krissy. Really."

"Okay," she said, obviously worried. "Michael, are you all right?"

"I'm fine. Don't worry about me. Worry about school and your boyfriend (*did you hear that, Barbara?*) and the ridiculous hours you keep."

"I'm too young to worry."

"Good-bye."

He hung up the phone. He didn't know how on earth he was going to get past Barbara.

"Who else died?" she asked. She wasn't kidding.

He managed to get to his feet.

"No one you know," he said, and left the room.

* * *

Michael and Barbara spent the day in separate rooms, going through the tedious process of shutting down Vincent's life. Michael spent hours cleaning files out of a couple of computers that were going to be donated to St. Pius. He was initially glad to have something mindless to do, until he realized that it left his mind free to conjure up scenarios starring Tess and the lawyer. Even if the relationship was as harmless as Krissy claimed, knowing it made him feel even more pressured than he'd already felt. That, in turn, made him angry. Angry at Tess, angry at himself, angry at the world.

When Barbara called to him that it was time to leave for the wake service, he wanted to sneak out the back door and hitchhike to Maine. Or New Mexico. Any place where no one knew him and he could hide. Get a job at a gas station, wear a blue jumpsuit with someone else's name stitched on the pocket. The last thing on earth he wanted to do was to throw himself into a throng of people who didn't know him very well but felt obligated to console him. But there was no way out. No way that wouldn't cause more drama than he could handle. He settled for dressing in a suit and tie and hoping no one would recognize him.

At the church, he sat stoically and listened to Monsignor Graham recap Vincent's life, starting at conception. Michael tried not to listen closely, since he knew the monsignor would repeat it all verbatim tomorrow at the funeral. Instead, he stared at the assembled crowd and tried to guess the identities of the people he didn't know. He felt completely detached from all of it. He wasn't ready to let himself feel it, and by this point in his life, blocking his emotions was frighteningly easy. Most of the time.

The service lasted for almost two hours, and the wake itself didn't get under way until almost nine-thirty. The irony, Michael thought, was that what would *really* feel like consolation to him would be for everyone to go home and leave him alone. But since none of them were there for his sake, he knew that he and Barbara would be throwing them out at midnight, bar or no bar.

The gathering was rife with miseries Michael hadn't even anticipated. On top of everything else, Monsignor Graham appointed himself Michael's emotional guardian for the evening and trailed Michael all over the house, droning on and on, telling stories that had been only mildly amusing the first dozen times Michael had heard them. Now he had Michael and a couple of other hapless victims trapped in a corner, with no way out short of flagrant rudeness.

Michael scanned the crowd and found Barbara, who was positioned near the kitchen, directing the flow of incoming food. It took him a few minutes of diligent effort to catch her eye, but he finally succeeded. Using his hand to shield the side of his face, he mouthed "HELP." She nodded, excused herself from the cluster around her, and came over to him. Along the way, she picked up speed and a convincing look of urgency.

"Excuse me," she said, in the general direction of Monsignor Graham. "Michael, your housekeeper's on the phone, she says she has to talk to you. I tried to take a message, but she said it's an emergency."

Bless you, Barbara.

"Okay," he said, and excused himself. He made his way quickly through the crowd and into the sanctuary of the kitchen. Barbara followed and closed the door behind them.

"I have *got* to get out of here," he said, "even if it's just for a few minutes."

"I know. You're starting to get that nailed-to-the-cross look."

"So what do I do?"

"It's not that far from here to Barton, is it?"

"Great idea. Wal-Mart is still open, I can browse in the automotive section."

"I'm not saying go there. But, if you were to get a call that, say, one of your parishioners was threatening suicide and refused to talk to anyone but you, you'd make that drive, right? Even if you had to leave your grandfather's wake."

"I love you," he said, reaching for his car keys. "I'll be back in time to help you clean up."

"You'd better."

"I'll call first to make sure it's safe." He patted her on the shoulder and headed for the back door. "If you still had a job, I'd give you a raise."

"I'll settle for a good letter of recommendation."

"I'll lie my head off," he said, and was gone.

Michael found a parking place on Ellis and walked up the hill to Peachtree. There was a fair amount of traffic; a couple of limos were pulling in and out of the Ritz-Carlton. The glass tower of the Westin Peachtree lit up the sky for seventy-four floors; he could see the glass elevator, currently on its way to the top. The downtown area was putting forth a gallant effort, but between its legitimately respectable crime rate and the equally crippling plague of white paranoia, it was still just an echo of its former self. Michael turned away from the nightlife and walked a few feet, to stand directly across Peachtree from the building that had been the Winecoff Hotel.

(The builders had been right about one thing. The *building* hadn't burned. Just the furniture, the carpet, the drapes, and the guests.)

The building was dark now; deserted, except for a Chinese restaurant on the first floor. Half the windows were broken out and there was a large FOR SALE sign above the door. In spite of the broken windows and peeling paint, the building was still beautiful. Michael felt some strange link to it. Like an abused child gravitating to the offender parent, he returned again and again. And now that Vincent was gone, it seemed, somehow, the right place to remember the dead.

He thought about the first night he had stood on this spot. The night Vincent had told him about the fire. Up until then, Vincent had told him that his parents and grandmother had died in a car wreck while out Christmas shopping, and that Michael had survived because they'd left him at home with Vincent. One warm spring evening, a week before what would have been his First Communion, Vincent drove Michael downtown, parked, and led him down the hill to stand where he was now standing. It was 1953, and the hotel was then the "Peachtree on Peachtree" retirement home. As they stood there and looked at the building, Vincent told Michael the true story for the first time. He said he hadn't wanted to tell him the truth until he felt Michael was old enough to deal with the visions it would inevitably conjure. Michael had been too stunned to feel much of anything at first; he had been embarrassed by his lack of feeling—felt he should be crying or something, and that his reaction would disappoint Vincent. He covered by asking questions: which window had been theirs; how, exactly, had his parents died; how, exactly, had he and Vincent managed to escape. Vincent answered everything, and did not try to sugarcoat it.

Back home, Vincent had taken out a scrapbook he'd made of newspaper clippings about the fire. He'd been waiting to give them to Michael when the time was right. They sat down together and went through the book. It was all overwhelming that night, but Michael had returned to it time and again, and was deeply grateful that Vincent had put the book together. At least he'd had something tangible in front of him—a place to search for answers, even if there were none to be found. He read the names over and over, including several accounts of how his father had saved Michael's life. There was even a picture of Michael—at least, the caption said it was Michael—being carried by a fireman. The baby in the picture was smiling and playing with the fireman's mustache, oblivious to the agony around him. Michael could not connect himself to the photo, no matter how hard he tried.

The tears had come as he and Vincent looked at the book, as Michael read the gruesome details and saw the pictures, and it had all started to become real. Vincent just held Michael in his arms and let Michael cry for as long as he needed to. Vincent cried with him. The night had lived vividly in Michael's memory ever since. It had cemented the bond between them that had never weakened. But it had also created their first rift.

In Vincent's mind, there had been a healing significance to Michael's hearing all of this a week before his First Communion. In Michael's mind, the juxtaposition had been jarring.

"Grandpa, how many people were in the hotel?"

"Two hundred and eighty."

"How many died?"

"One hundred and nineteen. God saved me so that I could save you, Michael. And you were saved for some special purpose, don't ever forget that."

"If God saved us, why couldn't He save everybody?"

It was the first time Michael had ever asked Vincent a question that he couldn't answer. Not only couldn't he answer it—he admitted that he didn't know.

Michael, making his first "adult" decision, had refused

his First Communion. He couldn't go through with it, given this huge question in his mind that no one could answer. He spent the following year asking Father Donahue, over and over. He heard a lot of rambling about God's will and acceptance, but nothing ever made sense. It was just words. Almost a year from the night Vincent told him the real story, he got sick and "saw" his mother, and the questions were answered, on some level that went far beyond words.

Now here he stood again, with more questions that couldn't be answered, dousing himself with a barrage of his own meaningless words.

Okay, run it down. Pretend you're an accountant and you can remove emotion from it. What's the bottom line?

I'm a priest and I've fallen in love with a woman. (That last part being, in fact, the problem. If I'd fallen in love with another priest or a twelve-year-old boy, the Church would be much less horrified—but I'm digressing.)

What are the options?

Stay a priest and leave Tess. Stay with Tess and leave the priesthood. No troublesome gray areas there.

What are the issues?

Vocation. I've always been so thoroughly convinced I had a divine calling. If it's all dissolving before my eyes, what does that mean? I was deluded? God had the wrong number? (Larry's predictably nonchalant answer: "First of all, if you did have a calling, who said it had to be permanent? You've done a lot of good work here, now you'll go do a lot of good work somewhere else. And secondly, there is the possibility that God is and always has been as silently indifferent to your occupation as He is to most people's.")

What about this "real world" thing? Is it true that I don't want to live in the real world?

Yes.

Should I be living in the real world?

Probably.

What does that mean?

I have no idea.

Real-world stuff. A mortgage. (Rent, at least.) Bills. Some kind of a job. Cocktail parties. Car trouble. Income taxes. Friends over for dinner. Quiet nights at home—sitting in front of a cozy fire, arguing with Tess about whether or not Jesus ever existed.

What was the alternative? Spending the rest of his life as a priest, knowing forever what he'd given up. Dying of old age in some home for senile priests. Alone.

And it's not like everything was perfect until Tess showed up. You've been having problems with the Church for a long time.

There were a lot of things that had been bothering him for years. He'd always minimized their importance, tucked them away in the back of his mind, in a file marked "Things to Worry About Later." Over the years, the file had gotten fatter and fatter. When it became too large to ignore entirely, he'd just stepped over it whenever it got in his way. Lately he'd been aware of it as a bundle on the "Tess" side of the scales. The Priesthood vs. Tess-and-P.S.-All-This-Other-Stuff-That's-Been-Bothering-Me-Anyway.

When did it start?

The first seeds of doubt had been planted in his mind in 1967, while he was still in seminary. He'd been working on the school paper and had written a rather blistering antiwar editorial. He was immediately hauled before the school president.

"It is not the university's place to take sides in a political matter."

"It's a moral matter. People are dying in an unjust war."

"Who are you to declare it an unjust war? Has the bishop said it's unjust? Has the pope said it's unjust?"

Michael was then informed that there had been complaints from four members of the Board of Trustees, not to mention several "routinely generous" alumni. While no one disputed the fact that Michael was quite talented and had been making a valuable contribution to the paper, the president was left with no choice but to remove him from the staff. (Thus establishing a lifelong career pattern—people telling him how talented he was while they were getting rid of him.) Furthermore, anything that Michael wrote for publication while he remained a student must first be approved by the president himself.

On the heels of all that came *Humanae vitae*—Pope Paul VI's encyclical on birth control, which had destroyed, in one fell swoop, Michael's hope (and the hope of all liberal Catholics) for reform on that issue. Try as he might, Michael could not come to terms with the idea of a God who would tell half the world's population that they could not have control over their bodies— meaning, in turn, their lives, their destinies, their hearts. Not to mention how much it bothered him that children did not have the right to come into the world to parents who wanted them, and who could feed and protect them. Already unsettled, he'd then discovered that, prior to the encyclical, the pope had appointed a pontifical commission to study the morality of birth control, but had ignored a majority ruling in favor of several forms of birth control. Thus proving (to Michael, anyway) that the commission had only been formed in order to support the pope's existing opinion. Which made Michael wonder: if the pope felt so strongly that he was right, why would he need to appoint a commission to support him?

Celibacy.

His own personal peccadillo. Kind of hard to analyze it with anything approaching objectivity. Maybe it would have been easier if he'd been a virgin going into seminary. If he hadn't known what he was being asked to give up. But he'd had far too much curiosity (not to mention far too many raging hormones) to commit himself to abstinence and ignorance. He'd just see what it was like, he'd thought. So he wouldn't have to spend the rest of his life not knowing. Unfortunately, no one had explained the Lay's potato-chip principle to him at the time. "Just once" hadn't worked. Neither had "just a few times" or "just until I leave for seminary." It had been a battle from the beginning; it was a battle still.

Even if he left himself totally out of the picture, though, he could look around and see that mandatory celibacy was causing people a tremendous amount of pain. He could see all the energy it consumed: at best, coping; at worst, sneaking and lying and covering up. And there was the small matter of the corrupt history of mandatory celibacy, which had absolutely nothing to do with anything holy, and (like most else) everything to do with the distribution of wealth and power. And that was the truth, whether it served to make him feel less guilty or not.

Then there was the not unrelated issue of pedophilia, and what seemed to be emerging as the Church officials' unconscionable pattern of covering it up—shuffling offenders from one parish to another, exposing new victims to a known threat, with cognizance and without warning. Michael had even heard of cases where bishops had destroyed files on repeat offenders in order to avoid lawsuits and, of course, bad publicity. (Given what had happened to him, Michael had no problem believing it.)

Thanks to all the publicity that the Church had not been able to fend off, buy off, or lie its way out of,

pedophilia had become a problem to every priest in the
country, guilty or not. At his own parish, it had taken
Michael two months to get to the point where the altar
boys didn't quake when they had to be in a room alone
with him. One particularly paranoid couple had met with
Michael before he'd finished unpacking, to inform him
that he was never to be in a room with their son unless
one of them was present. None of this had anything to do
with the priest Michael had replaced. He knew that from
asking, and from having grown up in the South. Southerners had only to hear of something once, from any
source of national media, to be convinced they were all
its next victims. And his parishioners' fears were exacer-
bated by the fact that Michael had come to them by way
of a liberal magazine in New York City, which meant
there was no limit to the range of perversion he might be
importing. He realized, thinking about it now, that his
preference for civilian clothes had a lot to do with getting
tired of watching strangers size him up everywhere he
went. He knew the look and he knew what it was about—
people wondering if he was someone with a penchant for
adolescent boys. (A couple of times he'd had to bite his
tongue to keep from saying, "Don't worry, I've got a
girlfriend.")

Whenever he confronted his superiors with any or all
of these issues, the unvarying response was "the Church
isn't perfect." Maybe not, but if it didn't at least *aspire* to
be, it might as well be a bank. He'd spent all these years
telling himself that the bureaucracy and the religion were
two different things; but the bureaucracy controlled him:
where he lived, what he did, what he was allowed to
write. They could keep him from telling people the truth—
and if his life wasn't about telling people the truth, then it
wasn't about anything.

And yet.

And yet ... and yet ... and yet. . . .

He loved being a priest. And, in spite of all his disillusionment and all his gripes and frustrations, he loved the Church. Fiercely.

Maybe blindly?

Maybe. But not completely. It was impossible, these days, not to ask questions. It went far beyond Church issues. Larry was right. The current theological trend was "let's find a way to salvage something from all of this, given the fact that we civilized intellectuals know it can't possibly be true." Since it was no longer respectable to believe in Jesus' divinity, scholars had to convince themselves and everyone else that it really didn't matter. To Michael, this was sheer insanity—to say that it made no difference whether Jesus was God come down to live on earth or simply the greatest hoax ever perpetuated on civilization! And then there were people like Tess, who were convinced that Jesus' entire existence was a fabrication. Which would mean the gospels were all a very elaborate fraud. Not to mention damned good fiction.

Why was it, Michael wondered, that everyone had decided the gospels couldn't be trusted, but any piece of parchment that turned up in a cave somewhere had to be the work of scrupulously truthful historians? He was sick to death of hearing about the Dead Sea Scrolls. He'd read every word of them, and he knew for a fact that there hadn't been so much stink raised about so little since the Judds' farewell tour. The problem with the Dead Sea Scrolls was not what they contained (if anything, they *substantiated* existing scripture)—the problem was all the people who hadn't read them, but had *decided* what they contained. And when that couldn't scare up enough hysteria, they'd announce that the Church was secretly withholding the really good stuff. Michael had even met an alleged theologian who was convinced that Rome had Jesus' skeleton locked in a vault in the Vatican.

Even the people who agreed with him kept his head spinning with their constant commentaries and analysis and insights and new theories and new versions of old theories. All of them convinced they'd happened upon the angle that was going to make sense of the whole mess once and for all. There were more versions of Jesus these days than there were of Barbie. Historical Jesus. Eschatological Jesus. Mythological Jesus. Political Rebel Jesus. New Age Jesus. Jesus Seminar Jesus. Twelve-step Jesus. Apocryphal Jesus, who made clay birds fly and killed a playmate and brought him back to life. Jesus AKA Joshua and/or Jeshua, who was channeling new holy books and starting new cults all over the place in order to explain (to the select few who happened to be in the right bookstore staring at the right shelf at the right time) where it had all gone astray.

We can never know—really know—anything.

And still, people are expected to devise a moral code and make life-altering decisions, based on what they suspect or guess or hope to be true. What sense does that make?

None.

But plain old New Testament Jesus must have lived. Who could have invented such a person? Such a story?

That "person" and that story had owned Michael's heart for as long as he could remember. That was the main reason Tess's proclamation had upset him so much. If Jesus never lived—and even if he lived as a mere mortal—then the foundation of Michael's life was a lie. And if she thought everything Michael stood for was "Hellenistic hogwash," then *who* did she think she was in love with?

They needed to talk about it. Really talk, with no clock

ticking. He needed to give her a chance to answer some of these questions. It wasn't fair for him to go through all the mental gyrations and just announce the verdict to her.

But what if she talks you into something you end up regretting? Your brain goes out the window the minute you get into a room with her. (Some rooms more than others.)

If my faith is so flimsy that I can be "talked out" of it, I have bigger problems than Tess.

He heard a noise and looked toward it. A member of Atlanta's large homeless community was making his way up the street with a shopping cart full of meaningless possessions. The guy was barely recognizable as human. He looked like he hadn't had a bath in decades, and there was a wild, glazed stare in his eyes that led Michael to believe that he was high on something other than life.

Oh, great.

The guy stopped his cart against a bus bench (downwind, mercifully) and looked at Michael. "You got a cigarette?"

"No. I don't smoke," Michael said. "I don't have any money, either," he added, fending off the next question. "I left my wallet at home."

And I don't have a MARTA token or the time and I don't know the bus schedule and even if I had any money, I wouldn't give it to you because I'd be afraid I was subsidizing your addictions, which is why I send checks to organizations that would be happy to help you if you went there, and besides, I didn't vote for the people who're responsible for putting you on the street, so why don't you go bother a Republican?

The guy turned his crazy gaze away, across the street.

"You'd never know it burned, would you?" the bum asked, staring at the hotel.

Michael looked at him, surprised.

"It was a sight," he continued, eyes fixed on the building. "Flames comin' outta the windows, people jumpin', like it was rainin' bodies."

Michael stared at the guy, trying to put it together. It was difficult to tell his age, under the dirt and beard and ravages of alcohol, but even if the guy *was* old enough to have been alive in 1946, he certainly would not have been old enough at the time to remember it in any detail, much less talk about it like it was a week ago.

The bum pointed to Ellis Street. "There was bodies piled up on that street, musta been a dozen. People knockin' each other off of ladders. This one woman jumped and her arm got caught on the cable that held up the sign with the name of the hotel. She just hung there like meat on a hook. 'Nother guy fell on the cable, 'bout cut his head off."

In addition to the fact that he shouldn't possibly have been able to remember the fire that well, there was something else about the guy that gave Michael a bad feeling. Even as he described the horror in vivid detail, his eyes were dead. If anything, he seemed to be trying to suppress a chuckle. And there was something familiar about his voice. Michael couldn't place it, but it wasn't a comforting familiarity. More like something from an old nightmare.

The bum looked back at Michael. The dead eyes came alive for a second, and the face looked a little more human. Then, without warning, the bum broke into a rotten-toothed grin, which turned into a laugh—a brittle, cackling laugh. Michael felt himself jump, startled. He was too confused to move, even though he was starting to get nervous. This guy's insanity was not necessarily harmless. Still, Michael stood transfixed, for reasons he couldn't understand.

The bum stopped laughing, but continued to stare at

Michael. It was a chilling stare. Penetrating. Michael felt the creep was looking into his soul.

It's that look again. Jesus. Is there a full moon, or what?

"I don't have to tell *you* about the fire, do I?" the bum asked.

Michael couldn't speak. How could this lunatic know?

Because you were standing here staring at the building with a forlorn look on your face? It doesn't take a Rhodes Scholar.

"Well—" Michael said, his voice trailing off. He didn't want to divulge anything to this creep and his stroke-of-luck intuition. What he wanted was to get the hell out of there, but somehow he didn't like the idea of turning his back on the guy. And what was he supposed to say to announce his departure? *"Have a nice evening"?*

"Hey, don't let me hang you up," the bum said. "I just run my mouth, I got nothin' else to do."

Michael nodded, again unsettled by the guy's clairvoyance.

"Yes, well—" Michael said. He wondered what Bob Curso would do. Bob stood in unairconditioned buildings in the Bronx and fed throngs of these smelly creatures every day. How did he find some common plane for even the most basic communication? He wished Bob were here, except if Bob were here, he'd be laughing his head off at his friend the pampered Jesuit. (*"You guys are gonna get to heaven and be pissed off that they don't serve two liqueurs after dinner."*)

Still, Michael told himself, there was more going on than his aversion to two years' worth of BO. This guy was bad news.

Evil.

The derelict obviously had no intention of leaving, so Michael was either going to have to walk to his car backward, or turn his back and pray. He decided on the latter.

"Well . . . good night," Michael said.

The bum just nodded, apparently unfazed.

Michael turned and started up the hill, walking as fast as he could without looking as nervous as he was. He listened for the sound of footsteps behind him. None. Thank God.

Now that he felt relatively safe, Michael chided himself for his paranoia, not to mention his lack of compassion. The bum was just a guy who'd fried his brain with drugs or alcohol, for reasons that would probably tear at Michael's heart if he knew them. Or else he was at the mercy of screwed-up brain chemicals, which certainly wasn't his fault.

Would your hero Jesus be hurrying up the hill, greatly relieved to make a getaway?

"Hey, Father?"

Michael stopped, on instinct. Then, almost instantaneously, remembered he wasn't wearing anything remotely clerical.

How the hell . . . ?

He felt a chill go through him, as if someone had thrown a switch. He turned around slowly.

"Bring your wallet next time." The bum was staring at him, smiling.

"What makes you think I'm a priest?" Michael asked, unable to resist.

The smile grew even broader. "Isn't the better question, What makes *you* think you are?"

Michael tried again to place the voice. Did this guy know him? Had they crossed paths, somewhere along the way? He strained to remember, but nothing came to him. He turned around again and headed for his car.

"Hey, Father!" the bum called behind him. Michael didn't stop or look back. "See you around, huh?" The bum laughed, that insane, piercing cackle.

When he was in his car with the doors locked, Michael looked up the hill to where the bum had been standing.

There was no sign of the guy.

Michael was still shaken and uncharacteristically quiet while he and Barbara wrapped casseroles in aluminum foil and loaded the dishwasher. He knew Barbara was coming out of her skin to know what was going on, but she was just going to have to live with it. He worked quickly, eager for her to go home before it was too late for him to call Tess.

He was scanning the living room for discarded dishes when Barbara's self-restraint collapsed.

"Michael?"

He looked at her. She had her jacket on her arm, but she wasn't getting his attention to say good-bye.

"I get it that you don't want to tell me what's going on with you. . . ."

"It's not that I don't want to, Barbara. It's that I can't."

"Okay," she said, resigned. "I just hope you know that I'm your friend. At least, I try to be."

"I do know that."

"So it's hard for me to keep my mouth shut when I see you falling apart in front of my eyes."

It startled him. He thought he'd been doing a good job of camouflaging that fact.

"Listen," he said, buying time, "I really appreciate your concern, but I can't—" *What can I tell her?* "Just let me get through the funeral, okay? Then we can sit down and talk." By then, he'd be a lot clearer about what he should and shouldn't tell her.

She nodded, not thrilled, but appeased.

"Okay. Well. I guess I'll see you tomorrow."

"Thanks again, for tonight."

"You're welcome." She stared at him for a moment,

then came over and hugged him. He felt his defenses go up, automatically. He'd always been afraid that Barbara had a crush on him. He patted her on the back, reinforcing the platonic nature of their relationship. Barbara pulled away and looked at him.

"Michael, if I were interested in seducing you, I would have tried it a long time ago. I'm a human being who loves you and is worried about you. I can't help what gender I was born."

She turned and walked to the door. "I'll see you in the morning," she said, over her shoulder. Then she was out the door and gone.

Michael hated himself. At least he could take comfort in the fact that Barbara and Tess were going to love each other.

He reached for the phone, then stopped himself. What was he going to tell her?

I haven't decided anything but I still want you to ditch the lawyer.

No.

How about:

Come down here and talk me into becoming an Episcopalian and marrying you.

Better.

Come down here and let's spend about three days in bed and kill millions of brain cells and we'll worry about the rest of it later.

Much better. Not very productive, but definitely more appealing.

He picked up the phone and dialed her number, not checking his watch until after it started to ring. It was almost midnight.

What if she's not home?

He held his breath.

Please be home.

The phone rang and rang. There was no answer, and the machine wasn't on.

It took him forever to get to sleep, and when he did, his dreams were chaotic, full of violent disconnected images: the fire, the bum, the skeletons and demons on Danny Ingram's bedroom wall—alive now, and snarling at him like rabid dogs. And all of it punctuated by wails from some unknown depth, mixed with the bum's inhuman cackle.

Around 3:00 A.M. he sat bolt upright, trembling in the dark, gasping for air. In the middle of the dream it had come to him, splitting his consciousness like lightning from Hell.

He knew where he had heard that voice.

CHAPTER 6

Jesus.

How?

How could the voice he'd heard come from Danny, six months ago in Long Island, turn up in a homeless wino in downtown Atlanta?

It couldn't have been the same voice. It was just similar.

No. You knew there was something strange about that guy. He knew all about the fire. He knew all about you.

But there has to be some logical—

Something was wrong. Now. In the room.

He looked around. Everything looked normal, but there was a heaviness. He recognized it: a milder version of what he'd felt in Danny's room.

It's in here.

He turned on the light. The feeling remained. He shivered, then realized that the room was cold. Not ordinary cold. Icy, but stuffy at the same time. He was having trouble breathing. The air was too thick. There was an odd smell, like a smoldering candle.

It's getting stronger.

The air was closing in on him, squeezing from all sides. He tried to move; his body was paralyzed. The air squeezed tighter. He felt as if he were in a pressure chamber. It had never been this strong with Danny.

"Get . . . out . . . of . . . here . . ." he managed to whisper. But the only response was that the pressure became more intense. Michael could almost hear it laugh. He searched his mind for the words Bob Curso had used.

"I . . . command . . . you . . ." He was barely able to force the words out of his mouth, much less sound commanding.

God, help me. It's going to kill me.

". . . in . . . the . . . name . . . of . . . Jesus . . . Christ . . ."

There was a loud sound, like wind through a tunnel. He felt the air reverse direction. The squeezing became pulling. A sucking motion. For a few seconds, he felt he was being pulled apart.

Then it was gone.

The sudden absence of pressure almost threw him to the floor. He steadied himself, then looked around, checking the corners. But he knew it was gone. The air was warm again.

His first impulse was to tell himself he'd imagined it. Or maybe it was something physiological. He'd worked himself into a state because of the bum. He'd convinced himself the demon was after him, and had given himself an anxiety attack.

But he knew better. The same way he'd known during Danny's exorcism. It was on the outside. A Presence. With a will and a fury of its own.

With a trembling hand, he picked up the phone and dialed Bob's private number. Held his breath until he heard Bob answer.

"Hello?" Groggy. Annoyed.

"Bob, it's Michael Kinney. I'm sorry to—"

"Hello?" Bob insisted, angrier.

Michael yelled into the phone. "Bob, it's Michael—"

The line went dead. Michael cursed the phone company and hit the "redial" button. A ring. Another ring. A clicking sound. A sickeningly sweet voice: *"The number you have dialed is not in service at this time. Please check the number and dial again."*

Michael hung up; he tried again, dialing the number carefully. He heard two rings, another clicking sound, and then loud static—crackling, popping, white noise in the background. A final try yielded the same. He gave up.

He put on his sweats and went into Vincent's study. He searched the bookshelves and pulled down all the books he'd accumulated during the Ingram case. He stacked them on Vincent's desk, then began a frantic search of the chapter headings, looking for any reference to a demon stalking a priest who'd participated in an unsuccessful exorcism. Nothing. At the bottom of the stack, he started again, this time combing the indexes. POSSESSION. *In the Bible. Catholic views of. Characteristics of. History of. Legal aspects of. Medical treatment of. See also: Multiple Personality Disorder; Exorcism.* EXORCISM. *Characteristics of. Duration of. History of. See also: Possession.*

A noise in the room. Tapping. He jumped half a mile and slammed the book shut; looked up to see Barbara standing in the doorway, tapping on the door. Dressed in black.

Oh, shit. Vincent's funeral.

"Sorry I scared you."

"It's okay," he said, trying to catch his breath.

"What are you doing?"

"Nothing," he said, too quickly. She came over; looked at the stack of books.

Don't read the titles.

She leaned over; read the titles.

"Demons? Again?"

"Barbara, I don't want to hear it."

"Hear what?"

"Anything. Sarcasm. Jokes. Good-natured ribbing. Just leave it alone."

"I didn't say anything."

"Don't even *think* anything. You don't get to have an opinion about this. I've got enough to worry about. I'm sick to death of having to deal with this thing while people give me a hard time for even believing in it."

"Michael—"

"You think I *want* to believe in this crap? You think I got up one morning and said 'Let's see . . . I love my job . . . I love where I live . . . I love my friends and colleagues . . . I know! I'll tell everyone I believe in demons and see what kind of trouble that'll get me into! Because otherwise life's just too damned good.' Do you think that's what I did?"

"Of course not."

"I'd love to be cynical and sophisticated and smug, but I don't have that luxury anymore!"

"Michael, I don't care if you believe in the damned

tooth fairy. I just came in here to tell you that the limo will be here in half an hour."

It took a moment to register. The limo. The mortuary limo.

He nodded. "I'll be ready," he said, and left her.

The church was packed and people were standing in the aisles, which didn't surprise Michael. He was waiting for the end of Tom Graham's marathon eulogy. Nervously curling the edges of his notes. He was going to have to read his eulogy, otherwise he'd never make it. He'd sweated over it for the last month, wanting it to be perfect. Now he just wanted to get through it.

The old coot finally shut up. Michael took his place. Leaned on the podium for support. Looked at the notes and decided to skip the intro. Anyone who didn't know who he was could ask somebody later.

"When I was about thirteen years old—" His voice was shaky. He cleared his throat and tried again. "—I went through a brief cynical phase and I stopped going to Mass. I'm not sure how I had it worked out in my mind, because I still wanted to be a priest. I guess I was going to find a way to do it without the Church. An ongoing struggle . . ."

(Chuckles from his friends.)

"Vincent sat me down one day and asked me what I thought I was doing. I said, 'Grandpa, there's nothing at that Church but a bunch of hypocrites.' Vincent looked at me and nodded and said, 'Well, there's always room for one more.' "

(Laughter.)

Okay . . . it's going okay . . . keep reading . . .

"If you knew Vincent at all, you knew that side of him. It wasn't my favorite side. Especially when I was thirteen."

He could feel his throat starting to constrict. He forced himself past it; kept reading.

"Vincent always had answers like that. He could always shoot me down. Last year, when I asked him what he wanted for his birthday, he said he wanted me to buy two tickets and go with him to the Atlanta Speedway. I told him I'd rather have gall-bladder surgery. He nodded and said, 'I know. That's what makes it a gift.' "

(More laughter. A moment.)

Breathe. Keep reading. Forget the fucking demon; this is too important . . .

"The stories are endless and, if my voice would hold out, I could talk about him for hours without having to stop and think. But my voice is not going to hold out. So I'll tell you what I loved the most. I loved how *alive* Vincent was. He's been that way for as long as I can remember, and he was like that until the very end.

"Vincent's cancer was diagnosed a little over four months ago. I'd gone with him to the doctor, just because I happened to be in town. Neither of us had expected the news to be as grave as it was. We drove home in silence. I was in shock, I think. Vincent was his usual stoic self. About ten minutes into the drive, he asked me if I minded taking him to Marietta. I asked, 'What's in Marietta?' He said his favorite computer store was there, and he wanted to go by and see if they had a color printer that had just come out. I thought he'd flipped—the news had been too much for him and he'd gone into some kind of bizarre denial. I said, 'Vincent, you know, the doctor said—' 'I heard the doctor,' he said. 'That's why I want to go right now. They may have to order it.' "

(More laughter. Nods of recognition.)

"As most of you know, Vincent put in a lot of volunteer hours, for the Church and a few other organizations. He could have just written them all large checks, and he did that, too. But to stop there would have been too impersonal for him. Vincent was not someone who lived life from a distance. In the last couple of years he'd been spending a lot of time at Grady Memorial, visiting AIDS patients. He'd read to them or just sit and chat and get to know them. When he'd tell me about them, he'd never mention anything about their conditions or their symptoms. Instead, he'd tell me who they were—their names, their ages, their backgrounds. He'd talk about the family members he'd met, or repeat anecdotes they'd told him. He didn't see them as victims of a disease. He saw them as people, as individuals, and as friends.

"I don't know how he did it—how he could allow himself to become so close to people he knew he was going to lose. How he could live through one death after another, and keep showing up with a smile on his face, volunteering for more pain.

"I never asked him those questions. I only asked him one thing. I asked him what he said to them, in those final hours. What could he have possibly found to say that didn't sound empty, in the face of such cruel, senseless circumstances? Without hesitation, he said, 'I tell them that love is a real thing.'

"At the time, I thought 'Oh, please.' It amazed me—it even *frightened* me, that Vincent, who *always* found the right thing to say, had reduced all of life to a Hallmark card, at a time when it really mattered.

"For the last couple of days, that conversation has been haunting me. That insipid little line. I've been in a daze since Wednesday, as I'm sure many of you have noticed. But I haven't been completely unconscious. I've seen the casseroles and the cards and the flowers. I've already received notices from charities. I've watched all of you, hugging each other, hugging me, or maybe just smiling across the room at someone you recognize and haven't seen for a while. I see the sadness in your eyes, but I also see you trying to comfort one another, trying to comfort me. I see that, in one form or another, what you're offering is your love. It's the only thing any of us can offer each other right now, because it's the only thing we have. As I've seen that, it has come crashing home to me that I was wrong when I thought Vincent's answer was shallow. Instead, Vincent had—once again—found the definitive answer."

Home stretch. You've made it.

"We can't look across this room and see Vincent's face right now, but we can still feel his love, as strong as it ever was. I've spent so many years of my life wondering how I would ever live without Vincent. If I'd asked him, he would have told me. I never have to."

Michael sat. The church was quiet. There were a lot of people wiping away tears. In the silence, Michael thought about his own words. Wondered if he really believed a thing he'd just said.

Michael spent the afternoon in Vincent's study, packing books into boxes. He could hear Barbara knocking around in another part of the house, and was grateful for her presence. He dreaded nightfall. He was halfway thinking about going back to Barton for the night.

He heard Barbara's voice from down the hall.

"Michael, I'm on my way to see you. I'm five feet from the door. Don't jump out of your skin."

"Thank you," he said, as she appeared in the doorway. Things had warmed up between them in the course of the day. She'd probably written off his rant this morning as anxiety about the funeral.

"I need you to sign some papers," she said. "Something about putting all of Vincent's money into one trust fund, and they need to do it before the will is read, don't ask me why. All I know is, I was attacked by a swarm of suits at the funeral." She laid the papers on the desk. "All the places are marked with tabs."

"I'm sure they are," Michael said, making his way through the maze of boxes.

"Do you know who Edna Foley is?" she asked.

"No. Should I?"

"I don't know. She lives in Jonesboro, and Vincent has been sending her a check for fifteen hundred dollars every week for almost ten years. I've never had access to his private account before, so this is the first I've heard of it."

"Me, too."

"I can't find a phone number for her, so the only thing I know is to drive to Jonesboro and ask her who she is."

"Give me her address and I'll do it."

"You? Don't be silly."

"I want to."

"You *want* to?"

Anything to keep from sitting in this house by myself.

"I need a break anyway. I wouldn't mind the drive."

"Well . . . okay." She handed him the address. "Is it all right if I go home?"

"Please."

She gave him a quick hug, which he tried his best to return, and then she was gone.

The temperature had dropped considerably since the funeral. Even in a wool sweater and blazer, Michael was chilly. He turned the collar of the jacket up as he climbed the three stairs to the unadorned front stoop and rang the doorbell. Hearing nothing, he followed it with a knock. He waited. The glass on the front door was covered with a lace curtain, so he couldn't see inside. The neighborhood was decidedly working-class—small, one-story houses; a few side porches full of outdoor furniture and hanging baskets. Rocking chairs and painted antique milk cans. People trying to inject a soul into rental property.

He knocked again. He was about to give up when he heard a sound; the door opened and he was confronted by a middle-aged black woman wearing a white uniform and an expression that was anything but welcoming.

"Hi," he said. "I'm looking for an Edna Foley."

"Uh-huh," she said. She folded her arms across her chest and didn't say anything else.

"Does she live here?" he asked.

"Depends on what you're sellin'."

"I'm not selling. My grandfather just passed away and I'm trying to figure out why he's been sending checks to a woman named Edna Foley, at this address."

"Who's your grandfather?"

"Vincent Kinney."

An undefined look replaced the scowl. "Well . . ."

She unlocked the screen door and opened it. She motioned him inside.

"I'm Edna Foley," she said.

Michael hoped the surprise didn't show on his face.

"I got somethin' on the stove," she said, and headed for the kitchen. He followed, assuming that was what she'd intended.

He stopped at the doorway of the small kitchen. Edna was at the stove, stirring a pot of something that looked like navy-bean soup. It smelled wonderful, but somehow he had the feeling she wasn't going to invite him to stay for dinner.

"Mr. Kinney died," she said, to herself. She shook her head. "That's the last news I needed to hear."

"I'm not exactly thrilled about it myself."

"Well, I'll work till the end of the month, then it's gonna be your problem what to do with her."

"With who?"

She didn't seem to hear him.

"I said from the start, I just do my work and cash my check," she huffed. "I don't wanna be mixed up in nothin' . . ."

"Listen," Michael said, interrupting, "let's start at the beginning. Why was Vincent sending you money?"

"It's my salary, plus some extra to pay the rent. He said it was easier for me to do that than him." She picked up a large saltshaker and shook it, liberally, into the pot. "And if you think I don't earn it, you stay here a couple of days."

"I don't doubt that you earn it. I just need to know what it's for."

"I cook and clean and do the laundry and buy the groceries. And I do 'bout everything for her. She can't do much for herself anymore."

"Who?" Michael asked, restraining himself.

Edna stopped stirring and looked at him; she seemed to put it together. "You don't know?"

"No. Whatever is going on here, I don't know anything about it."

"Well," she said. She shook her head. "I don't know much myself. Just what Mr. Kinney told me when he hired me. He said she was a friend of the family and he wanted to get her out of that county hospital. I don't blame him. I've seen that hole."

"Does this woman have a name?"

"Rebecca. I usually call her Becky or Miss Becky, but he called her Rebecca. When he talked to me, I mean. He didn't never talk to her. He wouldn't even let me tell her that he was payin' her keep. He sent some priest over here to tell her the rent was bein' donated by somebody anonymous, and to this day she thinks I'm a volunteer from the Red Cross. I told her that they had a program for shut-ins and . . ."

"Let me get this straight," Michael said, cutting her off. "This woman—Rebecca—was in a county institution. My grandfather took her out—"

"The priest took her out. Mr. Kinney said she wouldn't accept nothing if she knew it was from him."

"Okay. He had a priest take her out. He hired you and he's been paying you and paying her rent for ten years. Is that it?"

"That's it."

"And Vincent didn't tell you why he was doing this?"

"Just what I told you."

"What about the priest? Do you remember his name?"

"Yeah. It was Father something."

"That's very helpful," Michael said, matching her sarcasm. "Do you remember what he looked like?"

"Yeah. Like a white man in black clothes. It was ten years ago. I don't remember what I had for lunch yesterday."

"Was he from around here?"

"I don't know. I told you, I just do my job. I don't ask questions."

"And that's absolutely all you know?"

"That's it."

"Then why do I have the feeling there's more?"

She bristled. "Who are you? Matlock?"

"I'm the person who's got your paycheck in his back pocket," he said. It got her attention.

"All right."

"What?"

"I didn't hear this from him. She told me this, years ago, back when she used to talk a lot more than she does now. And she didn't know how much she was tellin' me, 'cause she didn't know I knew Mr. Kinney. But if there's one thing I can do in this world, it's put two and two together, you know what I mean?"

Michael nodded. He had no idea what she meant.

"She told me she got pregnant when she was fourteen, and she had to run away from home," Edna continued. "She's been on her own ever since. So I asked about the baby's daddy and she got all upset and said she didn't want to talk about it. So I figured it must have been Mr. Kinney."

WHAT!?

He struggled to keep his composure. "Why?"

"Why else would he be payin' her rent and payin' for me?"

Damned good question.

"Maybe he's a friend of hers. Or a friend of the family, like he said."

"Then why would he tell me not to mention his name to her? And why didn't he never come to visit?"

Two more damned good questions.

No way! Not Vincent!

"Like I said," Edna continued, "she didn't want to talk about the father. She said she didn't even want to think about it."

"How old is she?"

Edna shrugged. "I don't know. Old."

Was Vincent fourteen when it happened? Or was he twenty-five? It makes a hell of a lot of difference! Assuming any of this is true. But it can't be true!

"What happened to the child?" he asked, with forced steadiness.

"What do you mean?"

"Is he still alive? Do you know where he is?"

Edna shook her head. "She said he killed hisself, years ago."

Jesus. Did Vincent know? Did he ever meet his son?

Edna returned her attention to the soup. "Now, that's all I know."

Why didn't he tell me? How could he keep it a secret, all these years?

"Everything's paid for till the end of the month," she added. "You better call County and warn them she's comin' back."

"No," Michael said, almost automatically. "Vincent wouldn't want that."

Vincent knew he was dying. He knew I'd end up here. Why didn't he tell me?

"Don't worry," he said. "I'll set something up . . ." Robot voice. He couldn't force an inflection. ". . . so you'll keep getting checks for as long as she's alive. A trust fund or something."

She stopped stirring the soup and looked at him. "You mean it?"

Michael nodded. "Just keep doing what you're doing."

Suddenly Edna saw him in a new light. "Bless your heart! 'Cause I ain't in *no* mood to be job huntin' right now."

Maybe it's not true. This is all based on Edna's math. No one involved has said that it's true.

"Could I talk to her?" he asked, trying not to sound like his life depended on it.

Edna shook her head. "She's takin' her nap, and if I wake her up she'll make my life hell for a month. Besides, it wouldn't do no good. She don't hardly talk to me, and I know she ain't gonna talk to no stranger. And if I told her who you was, she'd throw your tail out and mine right behind it."

"Then maybe I could come back later. You could set it up."

"What am I supposed to say?"

"I'm your Red Cross supervisor and I need to talk to her to make sure you're doing a good job."

"Uh-huh. And why does my Red Cross supervisor need to talk about something that happened sixty-some years ago?"

She was right. It needed work.

They exchanged phone numbers, and she started to walk him out. He stopped in the living room, having noticed a crucifix hanging on the wall by the door. Impossible not to notice it; it was at least a foot high. A severe-looking cross, made of some kind of dark wood. It sported a full-color Jesus wearing a crown of vicious black thorns; eyes rolled heavenward in agony, blood everywhere the "artist" could find an excuse to paint blood.

"Is she Catholic?" Michael asked. He already knew the answer. No Protestant on earth would have that thing hanging in the living room.

"Hmph," Edna said, rolling her eyes. "She makes the pope look like a Presbyterian."

"Really?" Michael said, though he didn't know why it would matter.

"I tried to get her to put it in her room," Edna said, making no effort to conceal her distaste, "but she said it had to go by the door. I don't know, maybe they got some rule that it's gotta be by the door. I hang my dust rag over it when I'm in here watching my stories. She'd have a hissy fit if she knew that."

It felt somehow very odd to Michael that Edna didn't even know he was Catholic, much less that he was a priest. He just nodded and let it go, gave her the paycheck and left. He'd call tomorrow and start working on wearing her down.

* * *

Barton was only another fifteen minutes along I-75, and Michael felt obligated to put in an appearance at the church. A priest from the nearest town had been covering for him, but he was starting to feel guilty about not having checked in.

He drove on autopilot and replayed the conversation with Edna, trying to make some sense of it. Too many holes. No place to look for answers, unless he could talk to Rebecca. Even then, Edna didn't make her sound like someone who'd be at all forthcoming, especially given her strong negative feelings about Vincent. But if he hadn't inherited another thing from Vincent, Michael certainly possessed Vincent's tenacity. He had complete faith in his ability to break through whatever information remained available.

He reached Barton and pulled into the church's small parking lot. It was empty except for an ancient Buick owned by his ancient volunteer secretary, Annie Poteet. Annie put in four hours a day, five days a week, if her rheumatism wasn't bothering her and she didn't get a better offer. The fact that Annie was holding down the fort did not comfort him, since Annie generally caused more problems than she solved.

He opened the door to find the rectory filled with flower arrangements and sympathy cards from parishioners, which caught him off guard. It hadn't dawned on him that they'd have any reaction to his grandfather's death. He stopped to take it in, and to fend off another wave of guilt.

Annie fairly leapt from her chair the minute she saw him and made a tremendous fuss over him, calling him "Father" about fifteen times in three sentences. Then she went to work giving him the rundown on each flower arrangement and planted basket: who'd sent what; which of the town's two florists was responsible for each; a couple of editorial comments regarding the sexual persuasion of one of the town's two florists; and a couple of editorial comments about flowers that did not properly reflect the income brackets of the families from which they'd come. From there, she moved on to other late-breaking developments.

"The toilets are backed up again," she said, in a tone that said "this is the blow that's gonna sink us." "I called the plumber and he said he's on his way, but you know how they are. He said we're just going to keep having this problem if we don't hook up to the county. I know you think it's too expensive, I'm just repeating what he told me. And Father Hennessey called and said he can take the two morning Masses on Sunday, but not the five o'clock because he's got the five o'clock at his own church—"

Annie continued, rattling off a list of problems that went on for ten minutes. Michael flipped through a stack of mail and hoped she'd take the hint, but she just prattled on. He heard about half of it.

"—and that charismatic group, whatever they call themselves, wants to know when you can come to one of their meetings."

"Twelve years after I'm dead," Michael said, handing her a stack of bills.

Annie stared blankly at him. Decoding sarcasm wasn't in her job description. Michael tried again.

"Tell them I appreciate the invitation and I'd go to war for their right to exist, but I'm wholeheartedly uninterested in participating."

Not knowing what to do with that, Annie mumbled something about needing to water the flowers and left the room.

Michael went upstairs and threw some clothes into what used to be his gym bag. (He could still remember the look he'd gotten from Annie when he'd asked her if there was a racquetball court in Barton.) When he came back downstairs, the plumber was there. He and Annie were intensely bemoaning the rectory's bleak plumbing prognosis. Michael snuck out the back door, unnoticed.

Before heading back to Atlanta, he decided to duck into Tillie's Good Food Coffee Shop. He was starting to feel the effects of too many sleepless nights, and he needed caffeine if he was going to survive the drive home. He went to the takeout counter and ordered a large coffee from the perky redheaded waitress, who addressed him with the tentative tone she reserved just for him: *"I-know-I'm-not-supposed-to-flirt-with-you-but-I-don't-know-any-other-way-to-talk-to-men."*

He looked around to make sure he wasn't snubbing any parishioners. The place was packed with the usual dinner crowd, but he didn't see anyone from his flock. He was thankful for that. He was completely out of "everything is fine" energy.

The waitress returned to tell him a new pot was brewing and would be ready in a few minutes. He paid her, then sat at the counter, stared at the napkin holder, and resumed his attempt to make some sense out of Edna's story.

Why hadn't Vincent told him? How could he have kept such a huge secret, all those years?

The same way you kept your secret from him.

It's not the same thing.

It's pretty damned close.

What else didn't he tell me? Was all that saintliness just an act?

No. He spent all those years tracking her down. That means something, doesn't it? At least he felt guilty. And maybe there was more to it than that. Maybe she was the one true love of his life. Maybe he spent his whole life pining for them—the woman who'd rejected him and the child he wasn't allowed to raise. So he made a mistake? He spent his entire life trying to make it right. That's not so far from the Vincent you knew, is it?

I don't know.

What if you had died, and Vincent had found out about Tess? Would he have wondered if he'd ever known you? Would it have made him suspect hypocrisy of your entire life?

I don't know.

The irony of it. The two of them, suffering in silence, each determined not to disillusion the other. Faking the intimacy they were actually shutting out. It was sad. Sad, and stupid.

He emerged from his reverie to notice someone sitting down on the only empty stool, the one beside him. He glanced over, then wished he hadn't. It was the weird guy. The hermit. Michael turned away from him without speaking. He'd made that mistake before, and the paranoid idiot had decided Michael was trying to pick him up. But then, he'd probably brought that on himself, by spending too much time staring at the guy, trying to figure him out. Michael had heard enough coffee-shop gossip to know the guy lived alone in a boardinghouse and worked as a day laborer. Michael had seen him standing in front of Western Auto, looking out of place among the blacks and Hispanics competing for unskilled employment. It wasn't just his ethnicity that made him stand out. There was also the look on his face—a look of sharp, angry intelligence. There was something in that look that called out to Michael. Maybe just the fact that he saw the same look every day, every time he looked in the mirror.

Michael had also heard incoherent bits and pieces of

chatter that had to do with the guy's family. Apparently there had been some sort of scandal years ago, but the locals only spoke of it in shorthand now. Something about the guy's father; something about his brother. Someone had murdered someone, from what he could tell, but Michael hadn't been able to figure out anything more specific. He'd thought about asking Annie, but it didn't feel right. The guy was obviously obsessed with his privacy; Michael wouldn't have felt clean about trying to tunnel under the wall.

The waitress finally appeared with Michael's coffee. She was gone again before he could ask her for cream. He saw a small pitcher on the counter, an arm's reach in front of the weird guy. The waitress was at the other end of the counter, flirting with a cop. He knew from previous experience that at Tillie's once you've paid the bill you're as good as dead.

"I'm not making a pass," he said, as he leaned over the guy. "I need the cream."

The guy shoved the pitcher over; then, to Michael's surprise, he handed him a spoon.

"Need this?"

"Thanks."

Michael was careful not to say anything else, although he did detect a subtle change in the energy. At least the guy wasn't sending the usual death vibes. As had always been the case, Michael felt a strange compulsion to talk to him. Even now, when he knew what a waste of time it was.

Michael stirred his coffee, then handed the spoon back. On impulse, he leaned over and spoke quietly.

"For the record, I'm not gay and I'm not interested in saving you. I don't believe in that."

"Which?"

Michael was amazed. He hadn't expected a response, let alone a response that invited further conversation.

"Saving people," he said, trying to hide his shock.

"You don't think people can be saved?"

"Not by other people."

"Then what's your job?"

"These days, I'm not very sure."

The guy was completely thrown by that and didn't speak. Michael felt a sense of victory far beyond the accomplishment.

"As soon as I get it figured out, I'll get back to you. If you're still interested." Michael picked up his coffee and left. Quickly, while he still had the advantage.

He found a note from Barbara lying on the kitchen counter.

Michael—
I left a list of messages by the phone. Apparently
Vincent's obit came out in The New York Times
today, so all your New York pals are worried
about you. Some guy named Larry said to tell you that
you're a jerk for not telling him.

Michael had forgotten that Vincent had been famous enough to rate such an honor. He'd also forgotten Larry's perverse habit of reading the obituary column out loud during staff meetings, to "put everything in the proper perspective."

Also, you got calls from every Jesuit in North
America. They all send condolences, they all want you
to call them back, and a couple of them volunteered
to move in and do your grieving for you.

*Someone named Luis Estrada called and said to
tell you he lives in Henry County and he's a Catholic
plumber. (What? You don't allow Protestants to
touch your plumbing? I thought no one was
allowed to touch your plumbing. I'm sorry. This
is what happens when I lose too much sleep.)
Let me know what you found out about Edna Foley.
I'm around if you need me.*

Michael crumpled the note and tossed it into the trash.
He didn't even look at the phone list. It would still be
there in the morning.

He went into the den and poured himself a couple of
fingers of Chivas. He stared at the phone for a few minutes, then finally picked it up and dialed Tess's number.
The machine answered on the first ring.

"Hi. We're not here. Leave a message after the beep."

"It's Jesus," he said. "There's some talk going around
that you don't think I exist, so I thought I'd call and set
the record straight. I've heard a few other things about
you, but we can get into all of that later."

He started to hang up, then remembered something.

"Thanks for the wreath from you and Krissy. It was
really pretty. I mean, it's still pretty—" He sighed. "This
has been the day from hell's outhouse. I'm going to drink
heavily and go to sleep. I'll call you tomorrow. I love
you."

He hung up, chased pictures of Tess and an attorney in
a dark restaurant out of his mind, and retired all related
concerns for the night. He sipped the scotch and flipped
through an issue of *Commonweal*, until he realized he
couldn't care less about the future of Northern Ireland or
the interpretation of the Catholic vote in the '92 election.
It was hard to believe he'd ever care about anything like

that again. Such musings were a luxury for people to whom life made some degree of sense.

He put the magazine down. He was going to have to find some way to pass the time.

He noticed something in the pile of junk that had been accumulating on the coffee table: the tape recorder Vincent had left him. He'd put it there when he came home from the hospital and hadn't thought about it since. He was going to have to listen to it sooner or later, but the thought of hearing Vincent's voice was not inviting. Especially tonight.

But . . .

But what if the tape was a confession, of sorts? Was that how Vincent had decided to tell him about Rebecca? Michael picked up the recorder, rewound the tape, and let it play. He braced himself.

"Well . . . if you're listening to this, it means I've moved on to the Big Time. Pour yourself a stiff drink, if you haven't already."

Michael smiled at that, even though the sound of Vincent's voice stung like an icy wind; it was frail, and groggy with pain medication.

"Michael . . . you've been the joy of my life, and I can leave here knowing I did at least one thing right. It might be the only thing. I'm proud of you. I'm proud of what you've done, and I'm proud of what I know you'll go on to do. God got Himself a priceless ally the day you signed up."

Michael turned the tape off. He took a few deep breaths, then turned it on again.

"I have to tell you . . . bad things, Michael. Horrible. Dreadful things. I didn't want you to ever have to hear this story, but there's no way to avoid it now . . . because . . . things are happening . . . I thought it was

all over, but I saw something this morning . . . read something . . . (A PAUSE. A SIGH.) Michael, I think I know what it is . . . that you have to do. The thing your mother was talking about."

(A LONG PAUSE. VINCENT BREATHING. MAYBE CRYING.)

"I don't know how to tell you this . . . I don't want you to hate me, but you should. (A SIGH.) Let's start with something easy. You're in Barton because of me. I know you're too smart to think that the shortage of priests is so extreme that they have to start pulling Jesuits out of the order, so you must think you're there because Bishop Wilbourne was being a vindictive SOB. Not that he isn't, but that's not the reason. You're there because I wanted you there. I called the archbishop and cashed in a few chips. He talked to Frank Worland and they worked it out. I know how unhappy you are there, and I'm sorry about that. Deeply sorry. (A SIGH. A TONE SHIFT.) Michael . . . you're never going to be able to forgive me . . . but you have to do what I ask anyway . . ."

There was a sound in the background. Banging. Rattling. A woman's voice.

"Okay . . . well . . . my chariot has arrived. I'll have to finish this later. . . ."

There was the sound of Vincent turning off the recorder, and then the tape went dead. Michael stared at it in disbelief. The sounds must have been the nurse coming to take Vincent into the operating room. Michael had stayed with him until about fifteen minutes before that, when Vincent had asked to have some time alone. Michael had thought Vincent wanted to pray; now he realized Vincent had wanted to make the tape.

He rewound the tape and listened to all of it again. The second listening told him no more than the first. He turned it off again, and resisted the urge to fling the machine across the room.

Great. Terrific. Thank you, God. Things weren't quite strange enough.

Whatever Vincent had been about to disclose, it was more than the fact that he'd an illegitimate son over sixty years ago. Vincent was not prone to dramatics. If Vincent said the news was dreadful, then the news *was* dreadful. But what? And how the hell was Michael supposed to find out now?

Rebecca was the only person who might have the answers, but how was he going to get them from her? If she wouldn't let Edna talk about Vincent, what would make her agree to talk to Vincent's grandson? He had a strong feeling Rebecca wasn't someone who'd respond to calm reasoning.

He closed his eyes and tried to think. Almost immediately, he saw Edna's face in his mind; heard her voice: *". . . she makes the pope look like a Presbyterian."*

Of course! He reached into his pocket and found the piece of paper with Edna's phone number on it. He picked up the phone and dialed.

"Hello?"

"Edna, this is Michael Kinney. I'm on my way back down there. I'll be there in forty-five minutes. You'd better let me in and she'd better be awake, because I'm *going* to talk to her."

He hung up before Edna had time to argue. He opened the closet and started searching for a clean black shirt.

Edna opened the door with a speech prepared. She stopped midbreath when she got a look at Michael.

"Did you tell her I was coming?" he asked.

Edna's eyes were fixed on the Roman collar. Finally she found her voice.

"Did you rent that?" she asked.

"No."

"You mean . . . that's what you was, when you was here before?"

"Open the door."

She did. She watched him enter, still trying to recover. Probably rehashing their earlier conversation, wondering if she'd used any profanity.

"Did you tell her I was coming?" he repeated.

"No. I was gonna turn your . . . you . . . around at the door. But I didn't know 'bout all this . . ."

"Is she awake?"

"Yeah. But I ain't supposed to disturb her."

"You don't have to," Michael said. He headed for the hallway. In front of him were two closed doors.

"Which one?" he asked.

"Don't ask me," Edna said. "I didn't even see you come in the house." She waved both hands at him, dismissing it all, then disappeared into the kitchen.

Michael knocked on the first door. No answer. He moved to the other door and knocked. Still no answer, but he could hear the faint sound of music on the other side. He turned the knob; the door was unlocked. He pushed it open slowly.

He was immediately aware of the flickering light, which came from dozens of votive candles placed around the room. His eyes were drawn to an antique dresser on the back wall, the top of which was covered with more candles and icons of every saint known to man. Above the dresser hung a dime-store painting of the Crucifixion in a gold plastic frame. He detected the familiar scent of incense, though he couldn't tell where it was coming from.

Rebecca was sitting in a wheelchair to the left of him, facing an old mahogany vanity table upon which she'd fashioned a shrine to the Blessed Mother that made Lourdes look subtle. She was speaking in a low, steady mumble. He recognized the rhythm before he saw the pearl rosary in her hands. Her eyes were closed.

Michael took a moment to survey the rest of the room. It was too much to take in at once: the antique bed with a canopy and spool posts, which he remembered from having once been in a guest room at Vincent's house; a curio cabinet filled with icons, rosaries, relics, an entire shelf of crucifixes; by the bed, a hideous statue of St. Michael—a good three feet tall, ceramic, painted in vivid jewel tones, with gold wings that glittered in the candle-light. St. Michael was standing with one foot on top of a red-and-black-winged Satan, who was lying on his back and staring up in horror at St. Michael's lance, which was pointed straight between his horns. All of it was bizarre, but it was all made more eerie by the music, which was coming from a ghetto blaster on the floor by the dresser. Gregorian chant would have made sense. Rebecca was listening to the soundtrack from *Damn Yankees.* (*"Whatever Lola wants . . . Lola gets . . . And little man . . . little Lola . . . wants you . . ."*)

Michael closed the door, purposefully making noise. It startled Rebecca; she jumped, then turned to look at him.

"I knocked," he said. "I guess you didn't hear me."

"You scared me," she said, simply. Her voice was soft; childlike.

"I'm sorry."

"Do I know you?" she asked. She looked to be in her late seventies, but her voice sounded like that of a twelve-year-old.

"No, you don't," Michael said. He took a moment to refresh his memory on the lie he'd concocted on the drive down. "I'm Father Riley," he continued, borrowing his mother's maiden name. "I'm new here." *(Vague enough to pass muster.)* "I was asked to stop by and check in on you."

He smiled and waited, hoping her response would provide some information he could work with. He got his wish.

"Do you work with Father Graham?"

Michael felt his breath catch in his throat.

"Tom Graham?" he asked.

"Yes."

Jesus. GRAHAM? *Vincent told Tom Graham about this, but he didn't tell* ME?

He took a breath. "Yes, I do," he said, trying to sound matter-of-fact. "He knew I was going to be in the neighborhood and he asked me to stop by."

"He hasn't been here in so long, I thought he'd forgotten me," she said. Her tone was plaintive; pitiful.

"He hasn't forgotten you. He's been very busy. And he's slowing down a little, I think. Cutting back. That's why he thought you and I should get to know each other."

She nodded, but was staring at him like she didn't quite believe it.

"You look familiar," she said.

"I don't know why," Michael said, suddenly remembering that he bore a striking resemblance to photos he'd seen of Vincent as a young man—which was how Rebecca would remember him. "May I sit?" he asked, hoping to distract her.

She nodded. "I'm sorry. I don't get much company. I forget my manners."

Michael sat in a rocking chair next to her.

"You like musicals?" he asked, nodding toward the ghetto blaster.

"No," she said.

"Just this one?"

"None of them."

She laid the rosary down on the dresser; it hit the wood

with a brittle staccato rattle that for some reason made Michael shiver. Rebecca didn't seem to notice.

"I play them because the devil doesn't like show tunes."

Michael didn't flinch. He'd been a parish priest just long enough to have developed a good poker face.

"Really?" he asked, with no patronizing tone whatsoever.

Rebecca nodded.

"How do you know that?" he asked.

"Jesus told me."

"I see," Michael said. "Has He . . . been here recently?"

"He's always here. You know that."

"Yes, but . . . how did He tell you that?"

"In my head."

"Oh," he said, nodding as if it made perfect sense.

He took a moment to study her face. Her eyes were a clear, pale green; her white hair was tied in a loose bun at the nape of her neck. Even behind the wrinkles and the weariness, it was easy to see that she had once been a beauty.

"You look so familiar," she said. Something in her tone made him feel terribly guilty. Since she wasn't the shrew Edna had made her out to be, Michael wondered how much it could hurt if he leveled with her. Besides, if he told her who he was, it would take a lot less time to get the information he needed.

"Rebecca," he said, calmly, as if speaking to a frightened child, "I wasn't honest with you. My name isn't Riley. That was my mother's name." He gave her a second to take that in, then continued. "I'm Father Kinney. Michael Kinney. I'm Vincent Kinney's grandson."

In less than a second, the expression on Rebecca's face changed to pure terror.

"Edna!" she screamed. "Edna!" She reached for a bell that was sitting on the vanity and started to ring it with all her might.

"Wait," Michael said, trying to grab the bell. Rebecca threw it at the door and screamed louder. "Edna!"

"Calm down," Michael said. He put his hand on her shoulder, trying to reassure her.

"Don't touch me!" she screamed. "Don't touch me! Get out of my house!"

"Rebecca, I'm not—"

"Edna!" she screamed again.

The door opened and Edna flew in. She hurried to Rebecca.

"What did you do?" she asked, flinging a look at Michael.

"Nothing, she just—"

"Get him out of here! Get him out!" Rebecca was completely hysterical; having trouble catching her breath.

"You heard her!" Edna said, loud enough to drown out Rebecca and the music. "Get out!"

Michael wanted to argue, but he was worried about Rebecca. Edna was opening a prescription bottle she'd snatched off the vanity.

"Should I call someone?" Michael asked.

"No, dammit!" Edna screamed. "Just get out!"

Michael didn't move.

"GET OUT!" Rebecca screamed, with every ounce of her strength. With a parting look at Edna, Michael turned and left. He ran to the car, got in, and peeled away. He drove to the first service station he could find, dialed 911, and asked for an ambulance to be sent to Rebecca's address. If Edna didn't need it, she could tell them when they got there.

He returned to the car, sat down, and tried to stop shaking.

It was a little after ten o'clock when he rang the doorbell at the rectory at Sacred Heart. He waited. He heard shuffling, then the door opened.

"Michael?" Graham was wearing a navy silk smoking jacket and bifocals and had a paperback in his hand.

"We have to talk," Michael said.

"Of course." Graham nodded, as if this were no unusual request. "Come in."

Michael followed him down the hall to his study. The light was on. Graham sat behind his desk and motioned for Michael to sit on the sofa.

"Have you read this?" Graham asked, holding up the paperback. Michael shook his head without looking at it.

"It's fascinating. A collection of essays from MDs analyzing the Crucifixion. The one I was just reading is by a member of the faculty of the medical school at Duke University. He's talking about this rare phenomenon called hematidrosis, caused when severe anxiety is followed by sudden calm. Evidently the abrupt restriction of the dilated capillaries forces blood into the sweat glands, which results in a person actually sweating blood—"

"Tom," Michael interrupted, "I'm not here to talk about the Crucifixion and sweat glands."

"I'm sorry," Graham said, putting the book down and adopting his best grandfatherly pose. "Of course you aren't. I was presuming you wouldn't mind a brief distraction."

"I already have a hell of a distraction. I just left Rebecca's house." He realized he had no idea what her last name was, but the look on Graham's face told him he didn't need it.

"Oh," Graham said quietly.

"Obviously you've known about this for a long time."

Graham didn't reply.

"Would you mind telling me what the hell is going on?"

"I don't think I'm the person to answer that question."

"No, but you're the person who's alive." It was an unnecessarily sharp reply, but Michael didn't care.

"And that is very much to the point," Graham said, in a paternal tone that made Michael want to throw a lamp at him.

"Meaning what?"

"Your grandfather is dead. Why dig up his past?"

"What am I supposed to do, keep paying this woman's room and board and ignore the fact that no one will tell me who the hell she is?"

"Michael, if Vincent had wanted you to know, he would have told you."

"He tried to," Michael said. "He was explaining it on a tape that he was making right before the operation, but he didn't get very far."

"Maybe he changed his mind."

"He didn't change his mind! He died! And stop talking to me like I'm a fucking ten-year-old!"

"I'm sorry," Graham said, in the same syrupy tone. "I didn't realize I was doing that."

Michael counted to ten and waited for visions of homicide to pass.

"Look," he said, forcing himself to stay calm, "Vincent left me this tape with a fifteen-minute incoherent preamble about some god-awful thing he did. I went to try to get the rest of the story from Rebecca, and she became foaming-at-the-mouth hysterical the minute I told her who I was. You're the only person who can tell me what the hell is going on, and dammit, I deserve to know!"

Graham waited a moment, letting Michael's anger hang in the air and dissolve into a strange silence. Then he spoke, calmly and evenly.

"Michael, I have complete confidence that everything you need to know will be made known to you, but it can't be through me."

The look on Graham's face told Michael that further pleas would be a waste of time. He knew he should leave now, while he still had an ounce of dignity intact.

"Fine," he said, his cool voice matching Graham's. He stood up. Graham didn't.

"Then I guess there's no point in asking you why Vincent might have pulled strings to get me to Barton?" Michael asked, unable to resist one final attempt. Graham just stared at him.

"Which means you know," Michael said, and headed for the door in a huff.

"Michael?"

Michael stopped.

"When was the last time you went on a retreat?"

Michael could feel his blood pressure rising. He stared at Graham, pondering all the ways in which one could say "none of your fucking business."

"You don't have to answer," Graham continued. "Just something to think about."

Right. My entire life has just been blown to smithereens, I have no future in a career I seem to be addicted to, I'm in love with a woman who's about to dump me for some slimeball lawyer, the only relative I had in the world just died and left some deep dark secret that I may never know, and you know the answer and refuse to tell me . . . but you're right. A couple of weeks in the woods with the "Spiritual Exercises" ought to fix me right up.

Graham opened a desk drawer and took something out, Michael couldn't tell what it was. Then he walked over and handed Michael a business card.

"You might want to call this person," he said.

"Who is it? The retreat director who could save my misguided life?"

"Just take it."

Michael took the card and stuffed it in his pocket, though he didn't know why.

"Thanks for all your help," he said; he turned, without waiting for a response, and was gone.

Michael was in his car before he took the card out of his pocket. He would have torn it up on the spot, except he couldn't help wondering who Tom Graham thought might be wily enough to save even Michael.

He turned on the map light, held the card under it, and read it.

> *Charlotte Dunning*
> *210 Shorter Avenue*
> *Rome, Georgia 30125*
> *(706) 555-9212*

The first surprise was that it was a woman. He'd been convinced Graham had in mind some wizened priest who'd come out of retirement long enough to whip Michael into shape. It was hard to believe that Graham even *knew* a woman.

Below the name, in the left corner, was a job description that left Michael equally puzzled: *Author/Lecturer.* What could that mean? Was this one of those housewives who'd become famous for writing a book with a title like *Heal Your Inner Child Through Aromatherapy*? Or maybe a layperson expert on how blood got into Jesus' sweat glands? Knowing Graham, it could be anything.

He was about to toss out the card when his eyes finally registered the word in the right-hand corner: across from Charlotte Dunning's job description was a more specific title. He stared in disbelief. All by itself, stark and chilling in its simplicity, was the word that had stopped Michael's heart:

Demonologist

CHAPTER 7

Michael called Charlotte Dunning shortly after sunrise. She told him she'd been expecting his call for "years," offering no explanation. She said she had a full schedule for the day, but could see him any time after 5:00 P.M. At 5:05 he was sitting in her living room.

He hadn't expected Laura Ashley and needlepoint, but Charlotte Dunning's living room was like something from a childhood nightmare. The walls were adorned by an assortment of African tribal masks and other less recognizable but equally sinister items. Grimacing gargoyles peered out from every nook and cranny; tables and shelves displayed everything from statues of winged demons to a collection of genuine Haitian voodoo dolls. Michael expected a Santerian priestess to step out of the shadows at any moment.

Charlotte herself seemed reasonably normal. She was in her mid-sixties, with weathered skin and silver-gray hair. She wore faded jeans and a Duke sweatshirt and chain-smoked without apology. She was currently rummaging through an oak filing cabinet on the other side of the room. She'd left him sitting on the sofa, with a cup of coffee that would kill a horse and a copy of her latest book, *Hell on Earth: Real-Life Encounters with the Demonic.* Under normal circumstances he would have been interested, but he couldn't concentrate on anything right now except to wonder why Tom had sent him here. (He'd posed that question immediately upon crossing the threshold, but Charlotte had just laughed and said, *"Patience, Father. The Baptists tell me we've got at least three more years until the Rapture."*)

She closed the file drawer she'd been searching through and opened another one.

"My father's filing system," she said. "Sheesh. He died ten years ago and I have yet to figure it out. From what I can tell, the alphabet was in no way involved." She smiled. "I know I could refile it all, but I seldom need any of it. I keep it around mostly out of sentiment."

"Was your father . . . in the demon business, too?" Michael asked.

She laughed. "You're uncomfortable with the term 'demonologist,' Father?"

"I'm not uncomfortable. I'm just not sure what it means."

"It's not complicated. A person who studies demons."

"Does that mean you believe in demons?"

"If I didn't, I'd be wasting time studying them, wouldn't I?"

"You could study other people's beliefs," he said, trying to sound as condescending as she had.

"That's true," she admitted. "That's how my father

became a demonologist, actually. He began his career as an anthropologist. He went all over the world, studying various cultures' concepts of Evil, until he started to realize there was a lot more to it than just legends and superstitions."

"What happened to convince him?"

"The same thing that happened to all the near-death scholars. He kept hearing identical stories from people all over the world who'd never laid eyes on each other."

"I had a near-death experience when I was a kid and I didn't see a tunnel or a light or any of that." Which had nothing to do with anything, but Michael felt the need to announce it.

"Did you see anything unusual at all?"

"Yes," he said. If she wanted details, she was going to have to fish for them.

"Did it have a dramatic impact on your life?" she asked.

"Yes."

"Then you saw exactly what you needed to see, didn't you?"

He hated her.

She laughed. "Jesus is a very economical guy. He doesn't waste special effects on people who don't need them."

He loved it. The demonologist was going to explain Jesus to him.

"Did He tell you that Himself?" he asked.

She nodded. "He makes an appearance in one of my bathroom tiles on the thirteenth of every month."

Michael laughed in spite of himself. Charlotte laughed, too.

"I knew I could win you over," she said.

"One laugh doesn't prove anything. I'm not that easy."

"We'll see."

"So tell me. What are the universal demon stories?"

"Everything you described in your *New Yorker* article. The voice, the presence, the smell, the ESP—that's all textbook stuff."

"Yeah. I've read a few of those textbooks myself."

"Here it is," she said, pulling a folder out of the drawer. "Filed under *G*, for reasons known only to a dead man." She opened the folder and looked at the contents as she made her way back over to the sofa.

"I know the story very well," she said. "I just wanted to have the details in front of me, in case you needed them."

She sat in an upholstered chair across from him and placed the closed folder in her lap.

"Did you know Vincent?" Michael asked.

She nodded. "I met him through my father, initially. Tom hooked the two of them up when Vincent started having problems. It was strictly professional at first, but they became friends. After my father died, Vincent and I kept in touch. We'd have dinner about once a year."

"What kind of problems was Vincent having?"

"This was eons ago. Before you were born. First it was a series of physical ailments. Nightmares, headaches, anxiety attacks. Then it moved into sensory assaults. Smells, sounds."

"And Tom told him a demon was causing it?"

"No, actually it was Vincent who told Tom what was causing it."

"Why did he think—?"

"We'll get to that," she said.

She reached for her cigarettes; took one out, lit it, stuffed the matchbook under the cellophane, and tossed the pack back onto the coffee table.

"Tom tells me you and Vincent were very close," she said.

"Yes."

"I can understand that. Vincent was a real character."

Michael nodded, unable to speak for the lump that had risen in his throat.

"I feel for you," Charlotte said. "None of this is going to be easy for you to hear."

"I want to know the truth."

Charlotte nodded. She took another drag on the cigarette, then continued.

"A few months after the sounds and smells and whatnot, Vincent started having these . . . spells, I guess you'd say. He'd black out, and wake up somewhere hours later, with no memory of the intervening time. And he wasn't waking up in church, if you get my drift."

"Where was he waking up?"

"Bars—speakeasies, I guess—brothels . . . places like that. He didn't tell anyone. Just kept hoping it would stop. Then one night he woke up in a room with a prostitute who was cowering in a corner with a recently acquired black eye and a bleeding lip, and there was no one there but the two of them." She paused to let him digest this.

"*Vincent?*" Michael asked.

She nodded, tapping ashes into an ashtray. "That was what prompted him to go to Tom."

"No way," Michael said. Still, in the back of his mind he could hear Vincent's voice from the tape. "*I did a horrible thing. . . .*"

"My father and Tom worked with him," Charlotte said. "Blessings. Prayers. Never a full-scale exorcism. He didn't need it. He threw himself into the Church so completely, it was obvious his choice had been made and his mind wasn't going to change. But your father—he was never very religious, you know."

Michael nodded. His father had apparently been an avowed agnostic—a major source of agony for Vincent.

"So," Charlotte went on, "that left the entire family vulnerable, and the demon damn near wiped you out."

"Wait a minute," Michael said. "You think a *demon* was responsible for the Winecoff fire?"

"I can't prove it, obviously. But yes. I do."

"That fire was set by an arsonist."

Charlotte chuckled.

"What?" Michael asked, annoyed.

"You know the Eskimo story?"

"What Eskimo story?"

"It's an old joke. A guy goes up to the priest after Mass and says, 'This God thing is a bunch of crap. I just got back from Alaska and while I was there, I got stranded in a snowstorm and I got down on my knees and begged God to help me, and He didn't do a damned thing.' The priest says, 'Then how is it that you're standing here talking to me now?' The guy says, 'Well, luckily for me, this Eskimo just happened to be walking by—' "

She stopped to give Michael time to digest it, then continued.

"God works through people. The Devil works through people. We're all soldiers, for one side or the other. Didn't St. Ignatius teach you that?"

"But you're saying all those people died because of Vincent's demon?"

"What do you think? The Devil's gonna make sure he doesn't hurt any innocent bystanders?"

Michael had no answer, but it still sounded insane.

"Tell me something," Charlotte said. "How much do you know about Vincent's childhood?"

"Not a lot."

"What, exactly?"

Michael thought about it. "I know his mother died when he was born. His father was a mortician. Owned a couple of funeral homes. They had a fair amount of money. His father wanted Vincent to take over the business."

She chuckled. "Yeah. You could say that."

"What's funny?"

"Your grandfather grew up in Charleston, South Carolina," she said, ignoring his question.

"Yes."

"Have you ever been there?"

"No."

"Beautiful place. All those antebellum homes and huge old trees with Spanish moss hanging down. So peaceful looking, you'd never suspect the things that go on . . ."

"What do you mean?"

"They don't mention it in the Chamber of Commerce brochures, but Charleston has a long history as a hotbed of Satanism. There are cults there now that go back to the *Mayflower* and beyond. Transgenerational cults, passed down in families for centuries."

Michael nodded as if he believed her. He had some vague memory of Vincent talking about Charleston and Satanic cults and Freemasonry and other related issues. Vincent had always been paranoid about cults and secret societies—convinced they were highly organized and poised to take over the world. It was a side of Vincent that Michael hadn't liked very much. A pocket of unsophisticated weirdness.

"Do you know anything about Satanists?" she asked.

"I saw *Rosemary's Baby*."

Charlotte didn't smile. He tried again.

"I know as much as the average person, I guess. They've been getting a lot of press lately—"

Charlotte rolled her eyes. "Let me give you a clue," she said. "One way to tell a die-hard Satanist is that you'll never see him on *Oprah* with the word *Satanist* superimposed on his chest while he chats it up with the housewives."

She stubbed out her latest cigarette, reached for another. She lit it, took a slow drag.

"The word *Satanist* is misleading to begin with. There are all kinds of Satanists—"

Michael shifted in his seat, annoyed by the digression. Charlotte plowed ahead, unfazed.

"You've got your self-styled individual weirdos. You usually hear about them when they get arrested. That 'nightstalker' character, for example. They make it up as they go along and then blame the Devil. Not that the Devil isn't involved. But Satanism, like Christianity, was always meant to be a group activity.

"Then you've got the dabblers. People who think it's cute. I've seen more than a few heavy-metal teenagers who've conjured up something they don't know what to do with. I'd be willing to bet that's what happened to your Danny Ingram.

"Then you've got your 'Pop' Satanists. The Anton LeVay crowd. They're just slightly more sophisticated dabblers.

"The gang to worry about are the traditional Satanists. You'll rarely hear about them, and very little has been written. But they're out there. They've been out there for a long time. They're very quiet and very careful. They have to be, or they'd all be in jail."

"So you're one of those people who believes they're out there in organized droves, killing people and throwing them into portable incinerators?" Michael asked. Vincent had been one of those people, too. They'd had several fierce arguments about it.

"Michael, I've been studying this stuff for longer than you've been alive. And things are becoming clearer lately. The baby-boomers are starting to remember, and a lot of them are starting to talk."

"And a lot of people with impressive degrees think this recovered-memory thing is a lot of bunk."

"Yeah, well . . . You asked me to tell you what I know."

"I meant what you know about Vincent."

"I *am* talking about Vincent."

Michael chuckled. "What? Are you going to tell me Vincent was a Satanist?"

"Not exactly." Her face didn't change.

"What does that mean?"

"Your great-grandfather, Andrew Kinney, was a Satanist. He was the high priest of a Satanic cult."

Michael stared at her. She might as well have said his great-grandfather was a hyena.

"A traditional, transgenerational cult. The real McCoy."

"That's absolutely insane."

"Why?"

"For one thing, Andrew Kinney was a militant Catholic. Vincent told me he went to Mass every day of his life."

Charlotte nodded. "They do that. They go out of their way to look like pillars of society. It diverts suspicion. I've even heard of *priests* who were Satan worshipers. The cults love infiltrating the Church, because then they can steal relics and consecrated hosts and defile them in every way imaginable."

Michael didn't know what to say. It was all too incredible to take in.

"Vincent was raised in the cult," Charlotte continued. "He received the standard treatment of children raised in

Satanic cults—he was ritually abused, emotionally blackmailed, made to participate in all sorts of atrocities, and then they convinced him that he'd be killed if he told anyone. Meanwhile, he was being groomed to take Andrew's place. If it makes you feel any better, he hated it from day one. He went along because he thought he had no choice. He thought they'd kill him if he resisted. He was probably right."

Michael shook his head. "It's just not possible."

"Michael, why are you sitting in my living room?"

"What do you mean?"

"Who sent you to me?"

Michael thought about it. She was right. Tom Graham was not only Vincent's friend. He was also Vincent's confessor. There was nothing about Vincent that Tom wouldn't know, which was why Michael had gone to Tom in the first place.

"Monsignor has been known to embellish the truth," Michael offered.

"I didn't hear the story from Tom, for the same reason you didn't."

Of course not. She had to have heard it from Vincent. *Jesus . . .*

He sat back, bracing himself. "What else did Vincent tell you? Is Rebecca a part of all of this?"

"Yes."

"How?"

"Rebecca lived in Charleston. I don't know whether Vincent knew her before it all happened or not. They were in such different social classes that I seriously doubt it. She was one of about thirteen children, her parents were sharecroppers. She was apparently very beautiful, but in a fragile way. And she was only thirteen when it happened."

"When *what* happened?"

"Rebecca was abducted by a couple of the men from

the cult. They took her into the woods behind Andrew's house. Andrew had built a barn way back in the woods, which was where they held all their rituals. The two men locked her in a room of the barn and waited until around three in the morning, when they all convened for the ritual. There's a specific ceremony for the purpose of consecrating to Satan the heir to the throne—to Andrew's throne, so that meant Vincent. They do all the usual stuff. Black Mass, animal sacrifices, they drink and eat things you don't even want to know about. The rest of the ritual involves a mock wedding between the chosen heir and an unwilling virgin. In this case, Rebecca. Drugs and alcohol are often involved, and between that and the ritual itself it's a very frenzied thing. At the end of which, the marriage is consummated."

It took Michael a moment to recover enough to speak.

"You're telling me . . . Vincent raped a thirteen-year-old girl?"

"Well, he was only a couple of years older than that himself, if that makes any difference."

"Hell, no, it doesn't make any difference."

"Then, yes. That's what I'm telling you."

Michael looked at her. She was dead serious. She was real. He wasn't going to wake up, and no one was going to tell him that this was someone's idea of a sick joke.

He stood up. "I need some air," he said, and made his way out the front door.

After a moment, Charlotte came out onto the porch and sat on the stoop beside him.

"I realize this is horrible for you," she said, "but there's more. You need to know why Tom sent you here."

"I don't care."

"You'd better care, Michael. This is all a lot more personal to you than you realize."

"It feels pretty damned personal."

"I mean, there are consequences for you. More than just having to live with the knowledge of what happened."

He looked at her. She went on.

"Rebecca got pregnant—"

"I figured that much."

"—and Vincent helped her escape the cult and the two of them ran away. Vincent wanted to marry her and try to start a decent life. But she ran away from him, the first chance she got. It took him years to find her again. Meanwhile, he married your grandmother, settled down, tried to leave it all behind him. Except he didn't have that luxury. And neither do you."

"He ran away with Rebecca?"

"Yes."

"So he could have run away before that."

"Michael, he was right about the danger involved. These people don't kid around. But there was finally something that scared him more than what they might do to him."

"Which was?"

"He knew what they'd do to the baby when it was born."

He looked at her. "They'd kill it?"

She nodded. "As a sacrifice to Satan. They probably would have made Rebecca kill it, as these things go. And then they would cut it open, take out its heart—"

"Stop," Michael said.

"—chop it up and eat it."

"Stop."

"The reason Vincent knew they'd do that is he'd seen them do it before. He'd been forced to participate—"

Michael stood up. "I can't hear any more of this—"

"You have to hear it."

"No, I don't."

She grabbed his arm. "Yes, you do. You have to know that you're in danger."

"What are you talking about?"

"The reason Vincent knew what was happening to him is he'd seen Andrew do it before. He'd seen the consequences."

"Of what?"

"Andrew's cult had a ritual where they would conjure a demon and attach it to someone. The demon's job was to destroy the bloodline."

"Oh, please," Michael said, turning to walk away.

"Michael, think about it. Do you think it's just a coincidence that you ended up involved in the Danny Ingram thing? He was trying to get you then. He wanted you when you were unprepared—before you knew the story. You saved yourself by calling Bob in, because as long as Bob was the exorcist, you were sheltered. But he's not going to give up."

"I have to go," Michael said. She was still saying something to him as he made his way to his car, but he didn't hear her. He refused to hear another word.

He tried to take a shortcut and ended up lost on a country road that might have worked, had he wanted to get to Atlanta by way of Egypt. The fuel tank and his nerves were both on empty by the time he finally saw the light of a two-pump gas station/convenience store.

When he got out to pump gas, he could hear the sound of the interstate, so he figured he should be able to find it without compromising his manhood and asking for directions. He listened to the ticking of the pump and tried to calm down.

Why was he having such a hard time believing what was happening to him? He was a priest, for God's sake, it wasn't like the Devil was a new concept. And as for

Andrew Kinney and his cult—look at Nazi Germany. If people can throw women and children into gas chambers and then skin them and use their skin for lampshades, why was it unthinkable that they'd kill a baby and chop up its heart and eat it? People were capable of doing inconceivably despicable things, and in an organized and ritualized manner.

But Vincent... not Vincent... not even Vincent at seventeen...

He heard a noise and looked up to see a lanky kid in a blue uniform with RUSTY stitched on the pocket. He had matching coffee and tobacco stains down the front of the shirt and looked like he hadn't drawn a breath through his nose since the third grade.

"Need me to check the hood?" he asked.

"I've got it, thanks." *See, the reason I pulled up to the self-serve pump is that I wanted to serve myself....*

The kid looked disappointed, but didn't argue. Didn't leave, either. He stood there, staring at Michael.

"You're Ricky Reynolds's cousin, ain't you?"

"No."

"I know you from somewhere."

"I don't think so."

"You kin to any of them Reynolds?"

"No."

"You know who I'm talkin' about?"

"Yeah," Michael lied. "But I'm not related to them."

"Oh."

"Listen, am I anywhere close to I-75?"

The kid grinned like he'd just laid down a royal flush. "Depends on what you call close, I reckon."

A comedian. Thanks, God.

"Are you kin to Jackie Brumfield?" the kid asked.

"No," Michael said, starting to get testy. "I'm not kin to anyone left on the planet."

"I must have you mixed up with somebody else, then."

"Evidently." *Now crawl back into the swamp and leave me alone.*

The kid leaned toward Michael and spoke in a voice that was lower, deeper than before.

"People don't always turn out to be who they look like they are, right?"

"I don't know."

The kid grinned. "I think you know," he said. "I think you know 'bout as well as anybody."

He gave a rattling chuckle and walked away.

It landed on Michael like someone had spit on him from a nearby window. For a moment, he was too stunned to move. Then he moved fast. Shoving the gas nozzle back into its niche in the pump, he took off after the kid. He'd be damned if he was going to let another of these encounters go unchallenged. The kid was walking fast now. Michael quickened his pace, but so did the kid, who reached the men's room and disappeared inside. A few steps later, Michael grabbed the doorknob and found it locked. He pounded on the door with his fist.

"Open this door! Now!"

An elderly attendant was passing by, staring at Michael.

"You need the key?" he asked.

Michael looked up. "Yes. Thank you."

The old man shuffled over, reached into his overall pocket, and came out with a key attached to a lime green rabbit's foot. He handed it to Michael.

"Just bring it inside when you're done."

Michael nodded, took the key, gave the old man a few seconds to shuffle off, then unlocked the door and pushed it open.

The room was dark. He found the light switch and turned it on. A single small room. A toilet. A sink. An

empty towel dispenser. No window. No other door. No
Rusty.

With the most normal stance he could fake, Michael
returned the key to the old man, and was informed there
was no employee by Rusty's name or fitting his description. The only people working were the old man and his
son, who was in his mid-forties. They had both watched
Michael fill his tank. Alone.

The minute he got home, Michael called Bob Curso. He
got a machine.

"Bob, it's Michael Kinney . . ."

There was a loud snap, followed by a lot of static.

"I have a bad connection," Michael said. "I don't
know if you can hear."

The static got worse.

"Damn," Michael said. He hung up and tried again.

Bob's outgoing message was perfectly clear, but as
soon as Michael started to speak, the static returned.

"Bob, I need to talk to you," he said. "Call me."

He left Vincent's number, but seriously doubted Bob
would be able to understand it over all the noise.

Michael put his face in his hands. He couldn't think.

Danny.

A voice in his head. Out of nowhere.

What do you mean, Danny?

The voice was silent, having returned to the recesses
from which it had emanated. Michael thought about it.
There were a couple of things he'd like to ask Danny, but
he knew from experience that getting Danny on the
phone required something just short of an act of Congress. He felt compelled, just the same. At least it would
give him the illusion he was doing something. He hunted
for the number; found it; dialed.

He talked to three Officer Somebodys, a Coordinating

Officer Somebody, the prison chaplain, and, finally, the assistant warden, who assured him that Inmate Ingram would be allowed to return Michael's call within the hour. Ten minutes later, the phone rang.

They exchanged amenities for a couple of minutes, then Michael's tone shifted.

"Listen, Danny. I need your help with something."

"Sure. With what?"

"Can I just ask you a couple of questions?"

"Sure."

"Okay." Michael sighed, not sure how to proceed. "When this all started . . . you know, the way you described it to me . . . when you first began to hear the voice . . ."

"Yeah?"

"Did you . . . was there anything before that? Something that might have triggered it."

"What do you mean?"

"Well, you know—when I was reading about all this stuff, during the trial, I remember reading about how . . . how demons attach themselves to people."

There. He'd voiced the preposterous.

"Uh-huh." Danny's tone was as flat as if he were responding to a perfectly normal statement. But then, Michael reminded himself, Danny would be the last person to laugh.

"I need to know if there was anything you did. Anything that might have brought this thing on."

Silence on the other end. Michael had never asked before, because it wouldn't have made any difference. He wasn't sure what difference it made now. But if he was being haunted now for something Vincent did sixty-seven years ago, he wanted to know all he could about how such a process worked.

"Danny?" Michael prompted.

"Yeah?"

"I'm not asking because of anything that has to do with you."

"Then what's it got to do with?"

"I'll tell you all about it when I understand it better. I'm still trying to put it together myself. Just tell me, was there anything? Ouija board? Séance?"

"Okay, there was something." Danny's voice was softer.

"What?"

A pause; then: "This friend of mine had this book. He bought it at some weird bookstore in Chelsea. Anyway, it had these—spells—you know, like black magic—"

"Rituals?"

"Yeah. Like devil worship."

Danny didn't go on.

"And?"

"A bunch of us . . . four guys, counting me, and a couple of girls . . . we got together one night at midnight and, you know, acted out one of the rituals. It was just supposed to be a joke, though. I mean, we were giggling all through it."

Rituals. Again.

"How soon after that did you start to hear the voice?"

"Pretty soon. A couple of days."

Rituals as a doorway. That made some sort of sense. If there was one thing on earth he knew he believed in, it was the power of ritual. He didn't understand the mechanics, but he'd felt it, time and again. And if one person could conjure Jesus, what would stop another person from conjuring Satan?

"Why didn't any of this come up at the trial?" Michael asked, more to fill in the dead space than because it mattered.

Danny sighed. "I don't know. I just . . . I knew I

wasn't going to get off anyway, and I didn't want to sound so . . . stupid. Besides, I might have gotten the rest of them in trouble."

The rest of them. What about the rest of them?

"Here's what I don't understand, though," Danny went on. "If that's what caused it, how come nothing happened to anybody else?"

The answer shot through Michael. *Because Danny was the one with a connection to me.*

"You know?" Danny's voice sounded cloudy.

Michael didn't answer.

"Father?"

"Yeah. I'm here." Michael fought to regain his composure. "Okay. There's just one more thing. When you were hearing this voice . . . and it was telling you things . . ."

"Yeah?"

"Did the voice ever say anything about me? Specifically?"

A long pause. Michael could feel all his muscles tighten.

"Danny?"

"Yeah."

" 'Yeah' it did say something about me?"

"Yeah."

"What did it say?"

Another pause.

"Danny, you're not going to help me by withholding anything."

The room was suddenly filled with an odor. Putrid. Like someone had just smashed a carton of rotten eggs. Michael covered the phone receiver to stifle his gagging. He looked around, though he already knew he wouldn't see anything.

"Danny . . ." He forced himself to remain calm. "I need to know." Michael could feel the air bearing down on him, just like before. He shoved a window open, but it didn't help.

"It told me not to hurt you."

Michael had his nose against the window screen, fighting for fresh air. "Not to hurt me?" That was as far as possible from what he'd expected.

"It said 'Don't ever hurt the priest.' I said, 'Which one?' It said, 'The young one. Don't ever hurt the young one.'"

"That doesn't make any sense," Michael said, more to himself than to Danny.

"Well, then it said something else."

"What?"

Danny sighed.

"*What*, Danny?"

"It said, 'He's mine.'"

The line went dead. The smell began to fade. To recede. Michael's senses seemed to go berserk. Somehow, he could *feel* the sound of unvoiced laughter.

CHAPTER 8

He'd gone to bed around 2:00 A.M. He knew he wouldn't be able to sleep, but he was so exhausted he needed to at least lie down. He stared at the ceiling and took stock.

Okay. There's a demon after me. It sounds insane, but that doesn't change the fact that it's also true. "His body isn't in the tomb" probably sounded pretty insane to the first person who heard it, too.

Unless no one ever heard it . . .

Shut up!

No one ever heard it . . . no one ever said it . . .

"Stop!" he said, out loud, embarrassing himself. He rolled over and went back to reliving the conversation with Charlotte, trying to fit all the insanity into some sort of context. He wondered if this information might explain a lot of things that had always puzzled him—chiefly, the fact that he'd always felt like a bad person without knowing why. He'd always felt that something was fundamentally wrong with him. At the same time, he'd always liked himself, which made him feel guilty for liking a bad person.

What was the truth? Never mind what had been summoned and attached to him; what was in his blood? What was there in Andrew that had made him such a vile person? Whatever it was, had any of it filtered down to Michael? Did that explain his restlessness? His anger? His pervasive sense of disquiet? Did it explain his inability to function from a place of serenity and kindness and charity? His tendency to put up walls, even with the people he loved?

In a very real way, Vincent had been Michael's spiritual lifeline. He'd told himself that there was enough goodness in Vincent for both of them. He'd told himself that, ultimately, the blood that ran in his veins was Vincent's, so all the negativity must be superficial garbage that he'd eventually work his way out from under. Now he realized that Vincent's blood was not going to save him. He couldn't even be sure he'd ever known Vincent. Hell, for all Michael knew, Vincent could have still been meeting in the woods with fellow Satan worshipers, doing God only knew what horrible things. The exterior

Vincent could have been a façade, just like Andrew Kinney, the friendly town mortician and devout Catholic. Or maybe Vincent had just hidden in the Church, building a fortress out of icons and rituals and charitable works. Maybe his goodness had been nothing more than a torch to ward off the circling wolves.

The fire. Was Charlotte right about the fire? He knew Vincent had harbored a lot of guilt about it, but he'd always thought it was because it had been Vincent's idea for them to stay at the hotel. Had Vincent known he was responsible in an even more direct way? Had there been a supernatural component to the fire? Michael remembered quotes from arson investigators he'd read in the newspaper clippings: "... the flammable materials in the hallway (carpet, wainscoting, a folding mattress left out on the third floor) absolutely would not account for the effects produced by this fire... the speed with which the blaze spread has baffled officials..." Maybe the fire had spread unnaturally because it was an unnatural fire. Because it had unnatural help.

Michael continued to pummel himself with unanswerable questions until finally, somewhere in the hours before dawn, he fell into a haunted sleep.

He dreamed he was running through a thick forest. Briars were scratching his arms, his legs, his face. He knew he was being chased by something odious, and that he had to escape it at all costs.

He saw a cave up ahead and ran into it, seeking shelter and a place to rest. He found neither. Inside the cave were sinister-looking men in black robes, standing in a circle around a small fire. The leader looked at Michael and his mouth formed a smile, but it was devoid of any warmth or humanity.

"Welcome home," he said.

Another man, who'd had his back to Michael, turned around. It was Vincent. He smiled, too, but his eyes were cold and dead.

"I told them you'd be here," he said.

"No," Michael said. "Nooooo!"

The men all started to howl with laughter. Michael turned and ran out of the cave. He ran back through the forest, stumbling and picking himself up over and over. Ahead he could see a light. It was a brilliant green. He couldn't tell what it was, but he felt compelled to run to it anyway. By the time he got close, he was out of breath. He collapsed into the light. When he was able to look up, he found himself in a large meadow. The soft spring grass was dotted with orange and yellow poppies.

There was a lone Georgia pine in the middle of the field. There was a guy leaning against the tree. He was wearing jeans, a flannel shirt, and work boots. His shoulder-length hair was a reddish-gold and slightly windblown. His eyes were a strange gray-blue, startlingly clear, and fixed on Michael in a gaze that was unsettling in its intensity. He smiled. It was the warmest smile Michael had ever seen on a human. If this was indeed a human. There was something beyond ethereal about him. A sense of calm, and a transcendent sadness the smile couldn't mask.

"Hi," he said.

"Do I know you?" Michael asked.

The smile turned into a bemused expression. "That's a tough call," he said.

Michael searched his memory, but nothing came to him, even though the face in front of him was vaguely familiar.

"Michael..." the guy said. He paused as if he were giving Michael time to shift gears, then went on. "You aren't a bad person. But until you're able to accept that, you might as well be. Because you're denying your own strength, and you're cutting yourself off from your access to mine."

And then Michael knew. He couldn't breathe. He opened his mouth to speak, but nothing would come out.

The guy smiled again. A different smile this time. It seemed to say, "Yes?" It calmed Michael to the point that he could speak.

"All right," Michael said. He took a breath. Then another. Then unleashed the mental floodwaters: "All right. If it's really you, and you're really here, then I don't know how long you'll be here and I don't want to waste the time being paralyzed by the scope of it . . . I have too many questions."

"What questions?"

"Everything. Anything. I don't know where to start."

"Start with one."

Michael forced himself to focus, and a question came easily.

"Okay. Vincent."

"What about him?"

"Did I ever know him at all?"

"What kind of a life did you see Vincent live?"

"But now I know about his past. What am I supposed to do with that?"

"You could remind yourself that you believe in redemption," the guy said.

Suddenly he was gone, fading like a whisper. Michael felt a cool breeze blow by his face. And then nothing.

He woke, trembling. Aching. Smothering in an unbearable sense of loss.

He lay awake for hours, waiting for the sun to come up. Trying desperately, without success, to remember the guy's face. His mercurial smile. His steady voice. His strange demeanor. Tender, but strong. Warm, but demanding as hell. A thousand times more frightening than anything in the dark forest.

When Michael went down to breakfast, Barbara was sitting at the table, reading the paper.

"Good morning," she said, glancing up at him. "You look like hell."

"Good. That's what I was shooting for."

"Did you sleep at all?"

"Yes."

"You don't look like it."

Well, maybe that's because my great-grandfather was a Satan worshiper and Vincent was a teenage Satanic ritual rapist, there's a demon with a vendetta against me, and I spent five minutes in a dream with Jesus, got scolded, and woke up wanting to throw myself off a fucking cliff.

"What are we doing today?" he asked, hoping to change the subject.

"This morning we're going through the rest of the stuff in Vincent's office. This afternoon the truck from the St. Vincent de Paul Society is coming to pick up the stuff we've decided to give to them. And in between those two events, we're going bungee jumping with the pope and the artist formerly known as Prince."

"You're very ill," Michael said.

"Maybe, but I look a lot better than you do early in the morning."

"That's the beauty of my life. I don't have to look good for anyone early in the morning." He got a mug out of the cabinet and headed for the coffeepot. "Tell me this isn't some weird esoteric decaffeinated crap."

"It's high octane. It'll keep you going until at least lunchtime."

He filled the mug with as much coffee as it could hold.

He looked out the window. The sky was a pale pewter and he could hear thunder rumbling in the distance. It had been storming off and on all week. Even one thunderstorm would have been strange for this time of year.

Barbara suddenly put the paper down and looked at him. "Michael, are you not sleeping because of Vincent, or is it more than that?"

Come on, Barbara. Don't do this to me again. Especially not right now.

"Isn't that enough?"

"It would be. But whatever is radiating from you feels like more than grief."

He didn't respond, hoping she'd let it go. She didn't.

"Does it have something to do with that woman in New York we're pretending I don't know about?" she asked.

He sighed. "Would you also like to know when I stopped beating my wife?"

"Michael, *is* there a woman in New York?"

"There are a lot of women in New York."

"Yes, but how many of them are you fucking?"

Michael almost dropped his coffee mug.

"Barbara!"

"Well, at least I got your attention."

"Jesus." Michael put his coffee down on the counter and tried to imagine the path of least resistance.

"If you're trying to figure out how to get out of this," she said, "I offer the suggestion that the truth is a wonderful fall-back position."

"All right, for God's sake." He took a breath, then: "Yes. There is a woman in New York." It hardly seemed to matter, at this point, what she or anyone else thought of him.

Barbara actually looked surprised.

"Really?"

"What do you mean 'really'? You knew it."

"Yeah, but it's still a shock."

"That doesn't make any sense."

"I know."

He tried to read the look on her face. He couldn't.

"We're in the process of breaking up," he offered. "If that makes you feel any better."

"Does it make *you* feel any better?"

He shook his head, not trusting himself to speak. Somehow he forced a quiet "no."

Barbara gave it a respectful nanosecond of silence, then lobbed the next round.

"So, was she the first?"

"Would you like me to fire up the Macintosh and give you spreadsheets and graphs?"

"Just tell me it's in the single digits."

"This year, or since seminary?"

"Forget it," she said, and returned her attention to the newspaper.

He started out of the room, happy to oblige.

"Is that what's been wrong with you?" she asked.

He stopped. "That's a big part of it."

"What's the rest of it?"

"Everything. Every possible thing."

"What about God?"

"What about Him?"

"You two aren't breaking up, are you?"

He shook his head. "I don't know. Maybe we'll just agree to see other people."

He left her to ponder it.

He stood in the living room and wondered what to do with himself. He didn't want to spend the morning sorting through Vincent's possessions. That had been hard enough before he'd known about Vincent's past.

Now he couldn't even stand the thought of going into Vincent's study. He couldn't think of anywhere he *could* stand the thought of being right now. He just wanted to curl up into a ball and dissolve.

Barbara wandered in, carrying the newspaper and still reading it. She stopped; looked up.

"Michael, do you know a guy in Barton named Jackson Landry?"

Michael shook his head. "He must be Protestant. I don't fraternize with the heretics." He sipped his coffee. "Why? What about him?"

"You really should read this."

"What?"

"It's an article about this weird family. It's just bizarre. These parents had four sons. One committed suicide at age fifteen. One was a psycho who opened fire on a Christmas Eve service and killed four people. He was eventually executed. The youngest one became a successful novelist; then, last week, for no known reason, he robbed a liquor store and killed the clerk, then threw himself out of a fifteenth-story window. And the parents both committed suicide. The father blew his brains out about a year after the first son died, and the mother slit her wrists on the anniversary of the other son's execution."

Michael didn't know how to respond, since he had only heard about every third word. He sipped coffee and pretended to be contemplating it.

"This Jackson Landry is the oldest son, who seems to have remained unscathed so far. Wonder what his secret is." She shook her head. "I can't believe you haven't heard of these people. I'd think they'd be the talk of the town."

"They might be. I'm not exactly up on the local gossip."

"Oh, wow," she said, still reading. "You're going to

love this. The guy who wrote this story interviewed the mother right after her son's Christmas Eve killing spree. She told him that the family had a curse on it and was being haunted by a demon."

Michael stopped breathing.

"She said the reason it happened on Christmas Eve was that Satan was pissed off about it being Jesus' birthday."

"Are you serious?" he asked. Now she had his attention.

"Well, she didn't say *pissed off*. She said *angry*."

"Where did she come up with this theory?"

"A fortune-teller told her she had, quote, 'inherited a horrible debt.' And she also had a recurring dream that she was surrounded by a bunch of men in long black robes and the leader told her he had conjured a demon and attached it to her husband's bloodline and they were all going to die. I love how she puts it off on the husband—"

Michael took the paper out of Barbara's hands.

"Hey, I wasn't finished . . ."

"Why is this story being printed now?" he asked.

"Because the novelist-son-who-shot-the-liquor-store-cashier-and-then-jumped-out-a-window-thing just happened a few days ago. I remember seeing a little blurb about it. GEORGIA-BORN NOVELIST ROBS LIQUOR STORE, KILLS SELF. It didn't seem like much of a—"

"When did you see that?"

"I don't know. A couple of days ago."

"Before Vincent died?"

She thought about it. "Oh, yeah. It was the *day* Vincent died. I was sitting here reading the paper and waiting for you to call."

Michael heard Vincent's voice on the tape: "*. . . this morning I saw something . . . read something . . .*" And Vincent had been reading the paper when Michael had arrived at the hospital that morning. Was it the story of the novelist he'd seen? Was it just that he was obsessed with another demon-infested family? Possibly. But on the tape, he'd made it sound like whatever he'd seen was connected to the horrible thing he'd done. How could Vincent have had any connection to the novelist-turned-murderer and the family from hell?

"Holy shit," Michael said, as the answer dawned on him.

"What?"

Michael went to the kitchen, found the piece of paper with Edna Foley's phone number, picked up the phone and dialed. Barbara was not far behind.

"Who are you calling?" she asked.

"In a minute," he said, waving her off.

The phone rang twice, then Edna picked it up.

"Hello?"

"Edna, it's Father Kinney. I'm sorry to bother you. I need to know Rebecca's last name."

Edna snorted. "You got a lot of nerve calling here. She been sick ever since you left. They put her in the hospital last night, said she's in a coma. And if she dies, I consider you owe me a job."

"If you want to keep the one you have, you'd better tell me her name."

"It's Landry," Edna said. "L-A-N—"

"I know how it's spelled," he said, quietly.

Jesus God, I was right.

"Edna, do you know the name of the baby?"

"What baby?"

"Rebecca's baby. The one you told me about."

"Why are you asking me?"

Michael decided to take a shot. "Because I read the article."

Silence on the other end of the phone. Beside him, Barbara was whispering.

"You found Edna Foley? Why didn't you tell me? Who is she?"

Michael ignored Barbara and continued to drill Edna.

"The father of the Landry family was Rebecca's son, wasn't he?" Michael asked.

Still no answer.

"Wasn't he, Edna?" Michael pressed.

"I don't have to answer that."

You just did.

He hung up. "Holy shit," he said again.

"Michael, would you please tell me what is going on?" Barbara asked.

Vincent must have wanted me in Barton because this Jackson Landry was there. His last living grandson from the demonic side of the family. The only one who hasn't spilled any blood. Yet.

"Michael?" Barbara asked again.

"What the hell did he think I could do?" Michael asked, out loud.

"What did *who* think?"

"Barbara, just . . . stop asking me," he said. He handed the newspaper back to her and left.

He went into his room and started shoving things into his duffel bag. His mind was racing, pasting the story together.

Vincent's illegitimate son, conceived during a Black Mass, became the father of the family from hell . . . he had four sons of his own . . . two killed themselves, one was executed . . . two sons took other people's lives . . . one son left . . . Vincent's other grandson, what a thought . . . only the two of us left . . . the two of us and the demon . . .

Outside it had begun to rain hard. Hail was beating on the window like the cracking of hundreds of tiny whips.

A loud clap of thunder made the house shudder; Michael shuddered with it.

The smell returned. Stronger than ever. Michael gagged so hard he had to hold on to the bedpost. With his free hand, he fished a handkerchief out of the duffel bag and held it to his nose. It helped enough so that he could draw small breaths.

"Get . . . out of . . . here," he managed to say.

Fuck you.

The bum's voice. Danny's demon voice. Michael couldn't tell whether it was in his head or actually in the room.

"I . . . command . . . you . . ."

You don't command shit.

Michael's sides were aching from trying to breathe in the foul air. He searched the duffel bag for a crucifix, though he didn't know why he thought it would help.

And then, as suddenly as it had appeared, the smell was gone. The voice was gone. Even the sound of the hail was gone. The room was still.

Michael dropped to his knees, leaned his arms on the bed.

Jesus . . . I can't do this. He's right. I can't fight him. And You know that. What do You expect me to do?

Pack.

Michael looked up. The voice was nowhere, and everywhere.

Pack? What kind of an answer is "pack"?

Silence.

Look, if this is about Good and Evil, You'd better find someone else for this side of the fence.

IT ISN'T ABOUT GOODNESS, MICHAEL. IT'S ABOUT FAITH.

What is that supposed to mean?

Dead silence.

What does it mean?

Exasperating silence.

"Why?" Michael asked, out loud. "Why can't You ever *once* in the history of humanity just *say* what You fucking *mean*?"

"Michael?"

Barbara's voice, at the door. He couldn't look at her.

"Who are you yelling at?" she asked.

"No one," he said quietly.

She walked over to him, tentatively, like she was trying to keep from frightening a wild animal. She knelt on the floor beside him. When he didn't resist that, she put her arm around him.

"Michael," she said.

He was crying. He let his head drop onto the bed. He could feel Barbara's hand on the back of his head.

"It's okay. You can cry. You *should* cry."

He reached behind him, found her hand. He held on to it as if she could tow him in.

"I can't sit here," he said, when he was able to speak.

"Shhh," Barbara said. "Sure you can."

"No," he said, pulling himself to his feet. "I have to . . . pack."

"For what?"

I wish I could tell you.

"I have to go back to Barton. Whatever is left to do here, you'll have to do it without me."

"Fine. If you'll tell me what the hell is going on."

The wind had begun to howl around the side of the house. The air in the room was thick again, and Michael felt a presence, but for the life of him he couldn't tell which one of them it was.

He listened intently to the sound of the mournful wind, as if the sound might yield a clue.

As if it mattered.

As if the wind could change a thing.

BOOK THREE

They are what saves the world: who choose to grow
Thin to a starting point beyond this squalor.
Mary Oliver, "On Winter's Margin"

THE CHOICE

CHAPTER 1

"What are you in such a funk about?" Randa's mother asked. Randa had lost count of how many times Jane had asked some version of that question since she'd arrived. But it had been three times since they'd sat down to dinner, and this was her second night home. But Jane would keep asking, until Randa gave her an answer she could sink her fangs into.

"I told you, Mom. I'm just tired."

"Well, if you're gonna fly across the country to sit and mope, I don't need any more surprises."

Don't worry.

Randa speared a broccoli floret and let most of the Velveeta drip off before she put it in her mouth.

"You oughta be on your knees, thanking God you're still alive," Jane said.

Now what is this about?

"You think I don't read the papers?" Jane asked, her charm bracelet clinking against the Corelle dinnerware. "I know you think I'm dumb, but I do read the papers."

"Mom, I don't think you're dumb."

"I read what happened to your boyfriend."

Oh, hell.

There must have been something in the *Atlanta Constitution* about Cam, Randa realized. Why hadn't she thought of that? Because apparently she was incapable of rational thought these days. If she'd thought, she'd still be in LA. If she'd thought, she wouldn't have spent the night with yet another Landry. If she'd thought, she wouldn't have been surprised to wake up and discover he'd walked out on her. And if she'd thought, she certainly wouldn't have decided that the cure for her latest broken heart was to come running to a woman who made her want to throw herself into a concrete mixer just to get some relief.

"I *told* you," Jane said. "Back when you were telling me how wonderful he was and he wasn't like the rest of his family. I said, 'Randa, he's trash. You can dress trash up and put perfume on it and give it all the money in the world, it's still gonna be trash.' "

"Well, Mom, he's dead now, so you can relax."

"And so is that poor store clerk. You think he didn't have a family that loved him? Why don't you feel sorry for *his* family, if you want to feel sorry for somebody's family?"

"What makes you think I don't?"

"Hmph."

Randa got up and headed for her room. The only thing that had changed since high school was that her father wasn't there to yell at the two of them about their inability to get along.

"You can get mad at me all you want," Jane called behind her.

Randa sat on her bed and stared at her suitcase. She'd left everything packed in case she needed to flee on a moment's notice. She could even leave right now. She wondered if the relief of leaving would be worth hearing about it for the rest of her life, and decided probably not. And besides, it wasn't like she had somewhere to go.

She had two choices, as she saw them. She could get on a plane and go back to LA, return to her low-paying, dead-end job (assuming Tom hadn't successfully lobbied to have her fired by now), and when people asked where she'd been, she could say she'd gone to Santa Barbara for a few days of rest. And that would be the end of the entire sorry Landry saga. Three or four or twenty years from now, she might even stop feeling like a fool.

Or she could go back to Barton. She could knock on his door and demand an explanation. If she sounded angry enough, her groveling might even disguise itself as self-righteous indignation—a display of strength and courage. And he might offer an explanation that resembled the truth. That way, when she went home to get on with her life she'd have one more piece of the puzzle with which to torment herself.

One scenario sounded about as appealing as the other.

"Randa?" Jane knocked on the door. "You're missing a good movie."

Randa didn't answer, hoping Jane would think she was asleep.

"It's a true story about that teacher that got fired for hanging a picture of Jesus in her classroom."

Well, good. Now she could spend a relaxing evening arguing with Jane about the First Amendment.

"No, thanks. I have a headache."

"Well, you might as well have it out here. At least you won't be bored. You know who plays in it? That woman who played on that show you used to like . . ."

Randa relented, since she knew from prior experience that it was the path of least resistance. She lay on the sofa and pretended to watch the movie, while Jane provided political color commentary. (*"Pretty soon the government's gonna make it so you can't even pray in church."*)

"Mom?" Randa asked, her voice rising over a tampon commercial, "why do you believe in God?"

"What kind of a question is that?"

A direct one. The unpardonable sin.

"I just wondered."

"Well . . . because I've read the Bible," Jane said, as if nothing could be more simple or more obvious.

"How do you know it's true?" Randa asked.

"Because," Jane said, firmly, "I just do." She furrowed her eyebrows and fixed her gaze on the television screen.

"That's not a reason," Randa said.

"Randa, don't you come into *my* house with your California atheist shit."

"I just asked a question."

"Well, I gave you my answer and you didn't like it."

Randa opened her mouth to speak again; she was cut off by a harsh "Shhhh!" Jane picked up the remote control and turned the volume up a couple of notches.

Randa set her clock for 5:00 A.M. She got up, wrote a note to Jane saying she'd decided to take an earlier flight, and drove off into the dark. She headed for the airport, but when she got to the exit, she could not make herself turn. She kept driving. She stopped in McDonough for gas and in Griffin for a peach milk shake. Neither pause weakened her resolve, now that it had a life of its own. It was a little past nine o'clock when she drove into Barton.

She didn't give herself time to think about what she was doing. She parked in front of the boardinghouse, walked determinedly straight to his door, and knocked. She prayed to anyone who might be listening that he was there. She didn't want to have this confrontation at Tillie's—though why she cared what the good citizens of Barton thought about her was beyond her comprehension.

The door opened and Jack stared at her; his eyes had a glazed look and she wondered if he was on something. He didn't speak, forcing her to take the offensive.

"What did you think?" she asked. "That I'd wake up,

see you were gone, and just nonchalantly hop a plane back to LA?"

"Who says I thought anything?"

His voice was different now, in some way she couldn't pinpoint. He turned and walked back inside, leaving her at the door. She followed.

Everything in the formerly immaculate apartment was askew. The air was stale and smelled of cigarettes and cheap whiskey. There were dirty clothes lying across the unmade bed. His nice clothes from the Ritz-Carlton night were thrown haphazardly across the back of the sofa.

Jack looked worse than the apartment. He obviously hadn't shaved since she'd last seen him. His eyes were bloodshot. He was wearing khaki pants and a denim shirt, the latter unbuttoned and both as wrinkled as if he'd slept in them. Which couldn't be true, since he looked like he hadn't slept in a decade.

He picked up a pack of cigarettes from the desk; lit one; blew smoke toward the kitchen.

"Jack, the James Dean act is cute, but can we cut the crap—"

"Look, you knew who I was!"

It was loud. Randa felt herself jump.

"I didn't want to go in the first place!" he said. "It was your brainstorm!"

"Well, that night you seemed to think it was a good brainstorm," Randa offered, feebly, trying to maintain what little composure she still possessed.

"Yeah? So what? When have you ever met a guy who complained about getting laid? You think that proves something? Is that your big accomplishment?"

Randa felt as if someone were scraping her throat with hot sandpaper. She didn't even try to speak.

He walked into the kitchen and dumped ashes in the sink. She watched and wondered what to do. He came back, looking no less angry. Stood and stared at her. She searched his eyes for any sign of compassion; found none.

"Randa, go home," he said. "You're all out of brothers."

As soon as she could force her legs to move, she turned and left. He was standing in the same spot when she slammed the door.

CHAPTER 2

Michael ignored the ringing phone. It was the public line, anyway, and Father was supposed to have a buffer zone between himself and the mere mortals. He was going through the *L*'s in the Barton phone book one more time, as if *Landry* might have been misfiled somehow. He couldn't imagine why else he was unable to find a *Jackson,* a *Jack,* or even a *J Landry.* No one in a small hick town (not even the brother of a mass murderer) would have an unlisted number; it wasn't like a person could hide, even if he wanted to. Still, there was no *Landry,* and no amount of staring at the page was going to make one appear.

Realizing that Annie Poteet wasn't going to answer the phone, and that the person on the other end wasn't going to give up, he reluctantly lifted the receiver.

"St. Bernadette's," he mumbled, hoping it was a wrong number.

"Michael?"

Tess.

He closed the book and put it down. He felt his defenses kick into macho.

"I thought maybe your machine wasn't working. Does this mean you got my messages and chose not to call me back?"

"Yes," she said calmly. "That's what it means."

He hadn't expected her to be so unfazed, and it threw him. He recovered quickly.

"So, to what do I owe the current honor?"

"I have something to say, and I hope you'll be a grown-up and hear it."

His mind auditioned possible responses, all lame.

"Go ahead," he said.

There was a pause.

Well, how hard could it be? I'm sure you've rehearsed it with your boyfriend.

"I don't want to see you anymore," she said.

"Well, I'm shocked."

"Excuse me. Would you like to explain to me how *I* became the bad guy?"

He took a breath. He couldn't tell her. The last thing he wanted to do was get Krissy in trouble.

"Sorry." He leaned back in the chair. She was right. Even the lawyer was, ultimately, his fault.

"Tess . . ." His voice was not going to make it past three or four words. He closed his eyes and tried to get it back.

"Michael, we've talked it to death. I don't see any reason to make it harder—" Her voice was going, too, but she pushed through it. "Any harder on ourselves than it has to be."

He grasped for options and found none. He couldn't

ask her for more time. There were exactly two ways this phone call could end.

"Good-bye, Michael," he heard her whisper. "I love you."

"Tess!" he yelled, as if he'd have no chance to ever talk to her again if she hung up.

"What?"

He took a deep breath.

"What would you say—" Another breath. "If I told you I've been thinking very seriously about resigning?"

It was true, even if he'd only been thinking it for the last thirty seconds. It took her an eternity to speak.

"Really?"

"Yes. Really."

"I don't know what to say."

He sighed. Bullet dodged. For now.

"Listen. Why don't you come down here this weekend. We can stay at Vincent's. We can talk."

"Michael, I told you—"

"We can talk about what the hell I'm going to do with the rest of my life. I'm not going to make a decision without having that conversation with you."

"Oh. I'm sorry. Okay."

It was the first time he'd ever heard her flustered.

"Book a flight and call me back," he said. "Let me know when to pick you up."

"Okay."

"I love you," he said.

"I love you, too."

He hung up, feeling like he'd just been granted a stay of execution on a bogus appeal.

Why did I do that?

You know why.

No, I don't.

The intercom on the phone buzzed. He stared at it for a

moment before picking it up. Annie probably had a doctor's appointment for one of her many ailments.

"Yes?"

"Father, I have company coming over for dinner. If it's okay, I thought—"

"Sure, Annie. Turn on the answering machine and go home. And why don't you take one of those flower arrangements with you?"

He couldn't believe the tone of his voice. Why would lying to Tess make him feel warmer toward Annie?

I wasn't lying. I was buying time until I know what the truth is.

"Oh. Okay. Thank you, Father." Annie was obviously surprised as well.

"Good-bye," he said, and was about to hang up when he remembered.

"Oh, Annie!"

"Yes, Father?"

Stop calling me that!

"Do you happen to know anyone named Jackson Landry?"

Dead silence.

"Annie?"

"Well, I don't *know* him. I know who he is. Why?"

"I need to talk to him about something and I don't know who he is or how to find him."

"Yes, you do, Father."

"Excuse me?"

"I've seen you talking to him at the coffee shop. Because I was thinking I should tell you that you shouldn't do that. People will talk. It's bad enough being Catholic in a small town."

"You've seen me talking to him? When?"

"At the coffee shop, Father. You know who he is. The one that always wears those blue-jean clothes and sits by himself at the counter." She lowered her voice. "He's the one whose brother killed all those people at that church in Alabama on Christmas Eve—"

The hermit? The hermit is Jackson Landry?

"—none of my business, but I think you should just leave him alone, like everybody else does. How do you know *he* won't kill somebody before it's over with? I don't know why he stays here. I wish he'd just move."

Michael sighed and tuned Annie out. Well, here was another stellar development.

Excuse me, I know you hate my guts, but I'm actually your second cousin and we need to have a conversation about our Satanic heritage, because evidently Great-grandpa Kinney put a curse on us. Has anything strange been happening to you lately?

He had a vague awareness of Annie's voice, droning on through the receiver. He had a much stronger awareness that the odor was starting to return. He mumbled something and hung up the phone.

The odor wasn't as fierce as before, and the air wasn't as heavy.

Maybe it's getting weaker. Maybe this whole thing will die if I just leave it alone. Maybe it feeds off my fear.

The phone rang again. He picked it up.

"St. Bernadette's."

"Salsipuedes."

The demon's voice. He knew it now.

"What?" he asked.

The familiar cackle, loud and long.

"Look, if you have something to say to me, just fucking say it!"

The cackle faded out. The phone line popped and hissed, a sound that resembled static, but wasn't.

"Michael . . ." the demon's voice said, in a whisper.

Somehow hearing the vile thing use his name made it worse.

"What?" Michael demanded. "What do you *want*?"

"Salsipuedes," it said, then cackled again. The line went dead. Michael put the receiver down, and sat. The smell remained, and Michael knew he was not alone.

Salsipuedes. It sounded like Spanish, but Michael didn't recognize the word.

Maybe it's not a word, Padre. The voice again, but now it was in his head.

Michael fumed. This was all bad enough without having to play games. But demons loved games. Bob had told him that. They especially loved word games.

It's not a word? Then why is he saying it?

I didn't say it's not a word. I said maybe it's not A word.

Not a word. More than one word?

"Salsipuedes," Michael said, out loud. "Salsi puedes."

He got it.

Sal si puedes.

Get out if you can.

The cackle filled the room again; rose, fell, and finally receded, its echo trailing it. Michael felt no relief in its retreat.

CHAPTER 3

Randa found a pay phone right outside Tillie's Good Food Coffee Shop, affixed to the wall of the neighboring establishment, which billed itself as Stephen's Quality Food Grocery. (Evidently there was some bad food in town that the local food merchants felt the need to distance themselves from.) She dialed Delta's reservations number from memory and booked the next flight to LA. It left in two hours. She could make it if she left now.

She bought a soft drink from the vending machine outside Stephen's. It was lukewarm, but she didn't care. She was buying it mainly to hear the angry sound of the bottle sliding down the chute. She'd turned toward her car, thinking how glad she'd be to see Barton in her rearview mirror, when she saw Jack.

He was standing by her car, waiting for her. The cold anger from a few minutes ago was gone, as was the glazed look. He'd shaved and changed into a clean work shirt and painter's pants. He looked like the version of himself she'd fallen in love with, which made his presence all the more cloying.

"Hi," he said.

"You're in my way," Randa answered.

"I don't blame you for being angry."

"Well, that's very magnanimous of you. Move." She said it like she meant it, since she knew her façade was likely to crash at any moment, without warning.

"It's good to see you," he said.

What the hell are you talking about?

"Well, it's not good to see you, and I have a plane to catch."

"I thought you'd gone back a couple of days ago."

"You thought, or you hoped?"

"Both."

She hadn't seen that one coming.

"Excuse me?"

"Randa, I was just trying to protect you," he said. Now he sounded angry.

"Protect me? From what?"

He stepped closer to her and spoke quietly.

"Look, let's face it. Whatever it is, it's in my blood. Everyone in my family goes insane, and the men go criminally insane. If *Cam* wasn't immune to it, I'm sure as hell not gonna be."

"Fine," Randa said. "So you stay here and rob liquor stores and I'll go back to LA. What's the problem?"

"I don't think you're hearing me," he said.

"I hear you. I also heard the part about pretending to like me so you could get laid." She said it loudly enough to be overheard. She could embarrass him if nothing else.

"What?" He sounded surprised.

"You heard me."

"Half the town heard you, but I don't know what you're talking about."

"I'm talking about 'is that your big accomplishment?' " She did the best job she could of imitating him. "I'm talking about, 'Randa, go home. You're all out of brothers.' "

"When did I say that?"

"Half an hour ago, Jack. At your apartment. What the hell is your problem?"

"You came to my house? Today?"

"Jack, if you're going to blame amnesia for the ass you made of yourself, you should go all the way back. Tell me you don't remember the Ritz-Carlton either."

"I remember that," he said. "But that's the last time I saw you, until now."

"Well, was that your evil twin I ran into at your apartment?"

"I didn't . . . you weren't . . . I was alone, and then I came to Tillie's to eat, and I saw you on the phone. I thought you were in LA."

She looked at him. The confusion in his eyes was real.

"Jack—"

"Oh, shit," he said, rubbing his forehead.

"You really don't remember?"

He shook his head.

"How can that be?" she asked.

"Shit," he said again. Then he mumbled something she couldn't understand, although she caught the last word.

"What about Tallen?"

Jack shook his head. "Go," he said. "You'll miss your plane."

He seemed to be totally disoriented. She took him by the arm. "Jack, I came here to help you. I'm not going home with you like this."

He looked at her; she could see his focus returning.

"You came here to see your family," he said.

"No. That was a lie. And don't ask me to explain, because I don't understand what's happening to me any more than you understand what's happening to you."

That seemed to register. At least he couldn't find an instant way to argue with it.

"Things have been happening that you haven't told me about, haven't they?" She didn't know how she knew that, but she would have bet family heirlooms on it.

He nodded.

She took his arm. "Okay. Let's go sit down."

He didn't offer any resistance as she led him away.

They were greeted by the usual stares and whispers from the Tillie's regulars as they settled into the booth. Jack had regained his stoic mask and ordered a couple of Cokes as they sat.

"I can't tell you much more than I've told you. I've been coming apart. I've been hearing voices and seeing things—now I'm blacking out. I don't know. Maybe it's some kind of genetic schizophrenia . . . ."

"No."

"No?"

"You're way too old to be showing first signs of schizophrenia."

He smiled. "Oh really, Doctor?"

Randa wanted to hit him, more for the smile than for the remark.

"I am a highly educated hypochondriac, especially when it comes to mental disorders. And people develop schizophrenia in their early twenties. Besides, schizophrenia doesn't explain my conversation with your dead uncle."

"I told you, he's obviously not really dead. Or that wasn't him you talked to. You aren't going to start with the demon crap, are you?"

"Why are you so touchy about it?"

"Because there's no such thing as a fucking demon. That was just my mother's way of shirking responsibility."

"Oh? Does that mean *you're* responsible for what's happening to you?"

He started to answer, but was cut off by the appearance of the waitress and the Cokes. She plunked them down and was gone, but so was Jack's inclination to speak, apparently. He sat in a mute funk.

"Jack, Cam knew what was happening to him," Randa said, trying another approach. "At the end, I mean. He had some weird reason for calling me the night he died, because we hadn't spoken to each other in a year. He could have called a lot of other people. But he said he had to talk to someone, and I was the only person he knew who might believe what he had to say. And then he said, 'I'm in trouble that I didn't even know existed.' "

"And then what? The demon took him over and he jumped out the window?"

"Doesn't it make sense?"

Jack laughed and sipped his Coke. "Yeah. Sounds like a perfectly logical thing for a demon to do."

Randa fumed. "Jack, there are colleges with parapsychology departments. Duke has one. There are educated people who believe in this stuff enough to specialize in it."

Jack was watching a woman at the takeout counter. The woman, who looked like someone who had lived forty-some years the hard way, smiled and waved at him. He smiled and waved back.

"Friend of yours?" Randa asked, trying not to sound catty.

"Yes. I actually have a friend." He smiled at Randa. "You almost sound jealous."

"I almost am."

The woman at the counter picked up her takeout bag and started to leave. She mouthed something to Jack that Randa couldn't understand. He immediately looked injured. He nodded to the woman.

"Damn. I told her I'd come fix her gutters when it stopped raining and I forgot all about it."

"I'm sure she'll live," Randa said. Jack smiled at her, warmly.

"I like this," he said. "I haven't had anyone jealous over me in a long time."

"Well, good," Randa said. "Bask in it."

For a moment, Randa could almost imagine that they were a normal couple, doing the normal beginning-of-the-relationship dance. She felt comforted by the mundane thoughts of ex-girlfriends and leaky gutters. It was all so concrete and familiar. How could demons be lurking in a world where gutters needed mending?

She saw Jack's expression change again, his wall going back up. She followed his gaze and saw a man walking toward them. The man was about Jack's age, dressed in a plaid shirt and jeans. Nice looking, to put it mildly. Staring intently at Jack.

Jack spoke before the other man had a chance. "Whatever it is, I don't want to hear it."

"Oh, I know. You've made that very clear."

"Apparently not clear enough," Jack said.

"May I sit?"

Randa slid over to give him room just as Jack said no. The man sat.

"Look," the man said, in a low voice, "before I was trying to be friendly. Now we really have to talk."

"Am I stopping you?" Jack asked.

The man looked at Randa. "I'm Michael Kinney," he said.

"Randa Phillips," she said, shaking the hand he offered. His handshake was as firm as the look in his dark blue eyes.

"*Father* Kinney," Jack said pointedly. Now Randa heard a note of jealousy, and it amazed her. Almost as much as it amazed her that the guy sitting next to her was a priest. She was about to comment on the latter, but Father Kinney had already returned his attention to Jack.

"We need to go somewhere private," he said. "You can bring Randa if you'd like. But this will take a lot of explaining, and I don't think it's anything you want repeated all over town."

"God knows there's nothing anybody can say about me that hasn't already been said."

Father Mike nodded, resigned to the fact. "Suit yourself," he said. He took a breath, then: "I know something that you don't know, and I think you—"

"Something about what?"

"Your family."

Jack stood up.

"Now I *know* I don't want to hear it," he said. He looked at Randa.

"I'm going over to fix Cathy's gutters. I'll be back by dinner. You can wait at my place."

"Okay," she said, but he was gone before it was out of her mouth. She suddenly felt very self-conscious about sitting on the same side of the booth with the good-looking priest, but he stood before she had to worry about it.

"Okay," he said, under his breath. "Nice meeting you." It was a perfunctory exit line, and he was gone.

Randa felt the weight of every eye in the place. She watched through the window as the priest and Jack walked off in opposite directions. She kept her seat for a few more minutes, trying to understand why such a slight encounter had left her with such a huge sense of foreboding. It was like the low rumble at the beginning of an earthquake. A useless warning of something that is coming, but cannot be escaped.

CHAPTER 4

To hell with it, Michael thought. If the asshole didn't want help, why should he put himself out? He'd come home to a zillion phone messages, committee meetings—the parish's big fund-raising fiesta was less than a month away—not to mention the ever-present plague of plumbing disasters. And while he'd been gone, apparently every person in the parish had suffered some major life crisis that needed immediate attention.

He made it through his eleven o'clock appointment only minimally distracted. A couple who wanted to get married on Valentine's Day and were incensed to be told that the church was booked. They'd already had their invitations printed. Michael tried to point out that since they had printed the invitations and booked the reception before checking on the availability of the church, maybe the three of them needed to discuss the order of their priorities. The couple wasn't interested in discussing anything except alternate places where Michael could perform the ceremony. They'd thought about a neighboring parish, but the priest there was old, and the bride thought Michael would look better in the pictures. Michael suggested they meet again in a week.

Back in his room, he played it all in his head one more time. He knew he couldn't forget about Jack; knew it would haunt him. Even if Jack was a waste of time, Michael had to see past that. Given Jack's family history, there were potential innocent victims to consider. And then, there was the fact that, to all intents and purposes, it was Vincent's deathbed request.

His throat constricted immediately when he thought of Vincent. He was simultaneously angry with Vincent and sick with grief from the loss. He couldn't think of a thing he wouldn't trade to be able to talk to Vincent right now. To get the truth, if nothing else.

The truth. Even if he could get near it, he wasn't sure what that would accomplish. It would take more than knowledge to free him at this point.

He sighed and told himself to lighten up. He'd been through six months that would have institutionalized a weaker man. He just needed time. Maybe Tom Graham was right. Maybe he *did* need four weeks in the woods with St. Ignatius. Some time to recharge. Time to focus on something besides the darkness.

No. It's bigger than that.

That was what scared him the most. The fact that everything he was going through was bringing to the surface serious questions about his theology. The demon, whatever he was, was forcing him into a corner, where he had to look at things he'd shoved aside for too long.

Something about Evil. Something about all of it. The math had never added up for him. He'd always been abstract—used to drive Vincent crazy quoting Descartes and Pierre Teilhard de Chardin—at first because he thought it made him cool and sophisticated; then, as he got older, because he genuinely thought that the truth had to be more complex and more logical than meat-'n'-taters Catholicism. The Bible was lovely poetry, but the picture it painted was one of total chaos. A vengeful God, exasperated with His fallen children (who had fallen either by design or by design flaw, neither a comforting thought), patiently pleading with them while sending massive destruction at regular intervals. Finally deciding that the only way to redeem them was to send His son for them to torture and kill. Then He'd call it even. And for the rest of history, all anyone had to do was to believe this nonsensical tale, and they'd be "saved." He'd scoop them up ahead of time at the last minute, to spare them the final and total destruction, which would wipe out anyone who had problems with the story.

It had never made any sense to Michael. He'd only been able to believe it by declaring it misinterpreted and incomplete. Basically, by believing the stuff he liked and concocting his own theories to fill in the gaps.

He poured himself a glass of scotch, at the same time chastising himself for drinking so much lately. But what the hell else was he supposed to do? Sit calmly and wait for the next demonic attack?

Bob Curso suddenly came into his thoughts. Bob and his simple, black-and-white universe, where the Devil was bad and God was good and everyone got to decide whose team they wanted to play on.

To what end? What would the winner get? And why did the Devil waste his time in a battle that he surely knew he couldn't win? And why . . . and why . . . and why . . .

Michael found the number and dialed Bob's soup kitchen. He was amazed when the phone was answered on the third ring, and by a person with more than a passing knowledge of the English language. Michael asked for Bob.

"He's not here anymore."

"Oh. Well, where is he?"

"He retired."

"Retired?"

Bob?

"Health reasons. He had a heart attack or a stroke or something. I'm not sure."

Michael took the number of the retirement home. When he tried it, he got the same static and disconnected lines as before. Exasperated, he sat down at the computer and wrote Bob a letter. He could FedEx it in the morning, and maybe Bob would call him over the weekend and help him figure out what to do about Jack.

Dear Bob,

I was deeply sorry to hear about your health problems. I hope you're feeling better. I can't imagine you in a retirement home; hopefully this is just a "time out" until your heart promises to behave!

I've been trying to reach you, with no success. I need your help on a case. Can you try calling me at any or all of my numbers? Failing that, try getting a message to Larry Lantieri at the magazine, and he can call me.

I look forward to hearing from you, as soon as possible. Warm regards,

He proofed the note and told the computer to print it, then searched for a FedEx envelope while he was waiting. He realized how tightly he was wound when the sound of the printer made him jump. That was the main reason he wanted to talk to Bob, he knew. He was really getting sick of being in this thing by himself.

He filled out the address form, stuck it into the clear plastic pocket, and went to get the letter. He sat down at his desk to sign it. Something looked wrong. He squinted, then took his glasses off. It took him a moment to realize what the printed letter looked like; when he got it, it took his breath.

Dear Michael,
Sal si puedes. Sal si puedes. Sal si puedes.
Sal si puedes. Sal si puedes. Sal si puedes.
Sal si puedes. Sal si puedes. Sal si puedes.
Sal si puedes. Sal si puedes. Sal si puedes.
Sal si puedes. Sal si puedes. Sal si puedes.
Sal si puedes. Sal si puedes. Sal si puedes.

The room filled with the sound of hideous diabolical laughter, and the smell returned. Michael balled the letter up and threw it across the room. More angry now than frightened, he grabbed his jacket and wallet and stormed out of the room. He got into his car and took off. He headed north. He'd like to see how the damned thing planned to stop him from getting on a plane.

He landed at Newark just in time for the worst traffic; called Tess from the airport and left a message that he'd be showing up at her door in a few hours (last thing he needed was to catch her with the lawyer); called Bob's retirement home, managed to get through to the office and get directions. He rented a car and joined the gridlock.

Two hours later he arrived at the retirement home, which seemed a nice enough place. A two-story brick building, set off the road in a small grove of trees. He got the usual "Yeah, sure you're a priest" looks from the staff until he flashed several IDs that began with "Archdiocese of . . ." He was led to Bob's room by a young priest who called Michael "Father" and treated him as if he'd be a resident here in less than five years. Seeing Bob's door ajar, Michael thanked the young twerp and sent him back from whence he'd come.

Bob was sitting in his room with the drapes drawn. The only light came from a small lamp by the bed. Bob stared at the curtains blankly, as if they were open and he was gazing out the window. He didn't respond to Michael's slight rap on the door, so Michael stepped into the room.

"Are you growing mushrooms in here?"

Bob turned slowly toward the voice. Michael hoped his surprise didn't show. Bob looked years older than he had six months ago. He also looked as if he'd lost twenty pounds. His formerly round face was thin and hollow, and his formerly soulful eyes were lifeless. He stared blankly at Michael for a few seconds, then recognition set in and he offered a frail smile.

"Michael," he said, in an unsteady voice that should have belonged to an old man, "what are you doing here?"

"I was going to ask you the same thing."

"Sit down." Bob motioned to the bed and Michael sat. He hadn't expected a bear hug, but Michael was disappointed in Bob's detached reaction to his appearance. Then again, Bob seemed to be detached from the planet.

"How did you find me?" he asked.

"I called the mission and they told me. I hope you weren't hiding from me."

"No," Bob answered, as if it had been a serious question. "Not from you."

"How long have you been here?"

"Three months, they tell me. I don't remember much about the first two."

"How are you feeling?"

Bob just shook his head.

"Did you have a history of heart trouble, or was this out of the blue?" Michael asked.

Bob looked at him for a moment, as if it were a difficult question. Finally he answered.

"Is that what they told you? A heart attack?"

"Or a stroke. The guy said he wasn't sure."

Bob looked back at the drapes.

"No," he said quietly.

Michael waited. When it became clear that Bob wasn't going to speak again, he pressed it.

"What, then?"

Bob looked at Michael. For a long time he didn't say anything. Then, softly: "I got into something that was over my head." He nodded to himself, sadly. "And I'm paying for it."

"Got into what?"

There was another long pause, and Michael wondered if Bob had heard him. Then Bob spoke.

"Are you happy where you are?" Bob asked.

"No," Michael answered easily, then changed the subject so he wouldn't have to explain. "I've been trying to call you. I think I've got a problem."

"With?"

Michael told him the entire story. Bob listened intently, with no verbal response, although his eyes widened at the part about Vincent's past, and again at "sal si puedes." When Michael was done, Bob spoke immediately.

"Get away from it," he said.

Michael looked at him, confused.

"Michael, the thing I got into was just a more powerful demon than I could handle, and look at me. You're in deeper than I was. It's not after whoever happens to take it on. It's after *you*. And it's been waiting a long time."

Bob stopped, winded. He took a couple of breaths, wheezing as if he'd just climbed a long flight of stairs.

"That's why I was trying to call you," Michael said. "I wanted your help, but I'd settle for advice."

"I just gave you my advice."

"To run from it?"

Bob leaned forward. "You're not going to do anything but get yourself killed. Or end up like me, which is worse." He stopped again to breathe. "Michael, this is probably the same demon that was in Danny."

Michael nodded. "That's what the demonologist said."

"Every time they win one, they get that much stronger. And you were no match for this one before."

"Well, what am I supposed to do? Vincent started all of this. It's my debt."

"To hell with your debt. You're going to end up with a worse debt than you can imagine."

"How am I—"

Bob was angry. "You said you wanted my advice. Get

the Jebbies to send you to some unheard-of village in Central America. Or resign, and let it have what it wants. Let them have the whole damned planet."

Michael was too stunned to speak. Bob apparently took this as a sign that he was getting through, and lightened up.

"I hope I'm not wasting my breath. I don't have any to spare."

"Well, look," Michael said, "this is a lot to take in at once. Why don't you sleep on it and we can talk again in the morning. If you still feel the same way—"

"I will still feel the same way."

The look in Bob's eyes was a steel door. After a moment, Michael nodded.

"Okay. Suit yourself." He stood up; patted Bob on the shoulder. "Take care," Michael said. Bob nodded.

Michael had reached the door when Bob spoke again.

"He wasn't there, Michael. When I needed Him. I know what it feels like when He's there, and He wasn't there."

Michael felt a chill go through him. He didn't have to wonder who Bob was talking about.

"Take my word for it. That's not something you want to have to live with for the rest of your life."

There was nothing Michael could say. He nodded as if it had registered, and slowly turned and made his way out of the building.

He could barely remember the way back to the city. Bob's appearance haunted him, and Bob's last words hung in his mind like a bad radio jingle, taunting him.

The first wave of nausea hit him halfway through the Lincoln Tunnel, and by the time he reached midtown Manhattan it was all he could do to drive. The closest garage was five blocks from Tess's apartment, and he had to take a cab from there. He was too weak to walk.

The doorman, Deneb, recognized Michael and quickly opened the door for him. Michael walked past him and headed for the elevator.

"Hurry," Michael said.

Deneb followed without question. Closed the old elevator gate behind them and headed for the sixth floor.

"I'm not well," Michael managed to say.

"I can see that," Deneb answered in his thick Ukrainian accent. He opened the door again to let Michael out. "I should wait?"

Michael shook his head no. He knocked loudly on Tess's door, at the same time searching for his own key. The door opened and he brushed by Tess.

"Michael?"

He was able to mumble "bathroom" and headed for it, slamming the door behind him.

He made it without a second to spare, and was convinced he was going to throw up internal organs before it was over. It didn't make any sense, as he hadn't eaten anything all day, except for a bag of peanuts on the airplane.

He heard Tess outside the door.

"Michael? Are you okay?"

He flushed the toilet; leaned back against the wall. He knew he didn't have the strength to stand.

"I'm okay," he called to her. He doubted it sounded convincing. "I'll be okay in a minute."

"All right," Tess said, obviously unconvinced. "Well—I'll be out here—yell if you need me."

"Thanks."

As soon as he could stand, he turned on the water, ditched his clothes, and got into the shower. The water felt cool against his skin, and he realized he must have a fever.

In his head, the babel started again. First the demon's cackle, followed by what sounded like the soundtrack from the bar scene in *Star Wars*—garbled, unearthly voices with cocktail-party inflections. Over it, he could hear a voice similar to the demon's, only more effeminate, singing "salsipuedes" to the tune of some annoying kid's song. All of it was way more than his pounding head could stand.

Shut up. Just shut up!

Instead, it became louder. Michael thought he was going to have to scream.

Please . . . God . . . help . . . me . . .

A tune came to him; he didn't recognize it, but it was clear and lovely and he could hum it. He hummed with what little strength he had, and slowly the babel began to fade. So did the heaviness in the air.

He breathed a sigh of relief. He made the water cooler and let it fall over him, until finally he felt some of his life returning.

By the time he got out and dried off, he felt light-years better. A bit dizzy, and certainly not strong, but he didn't feel sick anymore. He dried his hair with the towel, threw his shirt into Tess's hamper, and put his jeans back on. He found his toothbrush in the medicine cabinet and brushed his teeth until he couldn't taste anything but Crest. He looked at himself in the mirror. He was several shades paler than normal, and there were purple caverns under his eyes.

Dear God . . . this thing can do anything it wants to me, whenever it wants to. Wherever it wants to. How am I supposed to fight that?

Maybe Bob was right. Maybe I shouldn't fight it.

Tess knocked again.

"Michael?"

He opened the door. Forced a smile. "Hi, honey. I'm home."

"Are you okay?"

He nodded. "I guess it was something I ate," he lied. There was no reason to get her involved and worried. "Do I still have any shirts here?"

"I'll get you one," she said.

He followed her into the bedroom. She rummaged in the back of her closet and came out with a Loyola sweatshirt.

"Don't I have anything secular?" he asked.

She gave him a look and stuffed the sweatshirt back in the drawer. "Do you have a color preference?"

"Anything but black."

She found a gray sweatshirt and tossed it to him.

"So how's that for a romantic entrance?" he asked, pulling the shirt on.

"Well, the throwing up didn't bother me, but I can't deal with the fact that you sing the Kyrie in the shower."

"What?"

"You heard me."

"I wasn't singing."

"Yes, you were. Maybe you do it unconsciously. In which case, I might be able to live with it."

"You heard me singing?"

"Yes. At the top of your lungs. You were singing the Kyrie, to some tune I'd never heard before. It was lovely, though."

"You heard actual words coming from me? Not humming, but actual words?"

"Yes, Michael. How else would I have known what you were singing?"

God. Was I singing without realizing it? Or was I humming with someone else who was singing . . . a voice I didn't even know I heard?

"I want to lie down for a while," he said, suddenly realizing how tired he was.

"Okay." She kissed him on the cheek. Stared at him for a moment. "You know, you really don't look good. Maybe I should call a doctor . . ."

"No," he answered, too quickly. "I'll be okay."

"How about a glass of ginger ale?"

He nodded.

As soon as she was gone, he lay down on her bed and pulled the comforter over him, clothes and all. His teeth were chattering, and his muscles ached. He would have thought it was the flu, but he recognized it. It was the same way he'd felt on the train home from Danny Ingram's exorcism. It was that, only ten times worse.

"*. . . you were no match for it the first time . . .*"

Tess came in with the ginger ale and set it down on the nightstand. She sat on the bed beside him.

"Why are you in New York?" she asked.

"Long story," he said, shivering. "Do you have another blanket?"

"You're still cold? I can bring you Krissy's."

"Where is she?"

"On Long Island, with her boyfriend and his parents. She's going to be sorry she missed you."

"I'm sorry I missed her, too. If I die, please say good-bye for me."

"Michael, don't make jokes like that."

He tried to smile. "I'm not sure I'm joking."

Tess left to get the blanket. Michael closed his eyes and tried to block out the pain and the image of Bob's sullen face.

The next time he opened his eyes, it was dark. The digital clock said 3:47, and Tess was asleep beside him. He got up long enough to take his clothes off, slid back under the covers, and fell asleep right away.

* * *

He came into the dream as if it had been going on without him. Joined himself in progress. He was in the meadow, sitting on the ground. The guy in the flannel shirt was sitting opposite him, leaning back against the same tree as before. His jean-clad legs were stretched out in front of him, crossed at the ankles. His eyes seemed darker than before—more gray than blue. The look in them was the same. Steady. Calm. Uncompromising.

Michael was already talking when he became aware of being there. Somehow he fell into the flow of it.

"I know this is the thing," he said. "This is what I'm supposed to do. And Vincent set everything up so I could be near Jack. That's why he wanted me in Barton."

The guy in the flannel shirt nodded slightly, but didn't speak. He was twirling a long piece of grass between his thumb and index finger. His skin was brown, as if from the sun. His hands were somehow sturdy and delicate at the same time. Michael had to work not to stare at them.

"So that's it?" Michael asked. "This is what my whole life has been building up to?"

"You're not happy about that."

It wasn't a statement or a question. More like, "Admit it so we can get on with this conversation."

"Well—I'd just like to think that I came to the planet for something more than to save someone else."

The guy looked down at the piece of grass in his hand; he chuckled. He had an odd look on his face.

"What?" Michael asked.

The guy looked up. He was smiling.

"You'll forgive me if I don't get all choked up," he said.

It took Michael a moment to understand. Then he realized what he'd said, and to whom he'd said it.

"Well, that's different."

"Why?" he asked, pulling himself to his feet.

Michael realized he'd been backed solidly into a corner. What was he supposed to say? My life is more important than yours?.

Before he could figure out how to answer, the guy turned and was walking away. Michael got up and followed him, eager to hear more.

Suddenly, the meadow dissolved before his eyes; the guy went with it.

Michael felt himself fall, then hit the ground running. He didn't know where he was, or why he was running. He just ran. The terrain under his feet was hard and uneven, and there was a fog so thick he couldn't see anything around him. He caught a glimpse of something up ahead. A movement. A shadow. He ran faster, toward it. The fog grew slightly thinner, and he could see the shadow clearer. A person. Moving ahead, in a steady pace that seemed unhurried, yet running as fast as he could, Michael couldn't catch up. He didn't know why he felt so driven to catch up, except that everything in front of him felt safe.

The person up ahead stopped, and now Michael could see him. It was the same guy. Dressed differently now, in something loose and light colored. He didn't smile this time. He had a stern look on his face. He motioned for Michael to follow him.

"I'm trying!" Michael called. "Slow down!"

The guy didn't answer; turned and moved forward again, in the same steady pace that Michael couldn't keep up with.

Michael suddenly stopped, his heart pounding, as he saw that he was about a foot from falling into a deep gorge.

"Hey!" he called to the guy. "Wait!"

He could see the figure in the fog stop again; turn toward him.

"How am I supposed to get across this?" Michael asked, pointing to the ravine. It was a good twenty feet wide, and when Michael looked down into it, there was nothing but a darkness that seemed to have no end.

"Jump," came the answer, in a rather matter-of-fact tone. The guy was looking at Michael, waiting. As if what he was asking was not clearly insane.

Michael looked at the crevasse. Moved closer to it. Stared down into the darkness. A clear impression came to him. Something down there he couldn't afford to ignore. He needed to be in there, not jumping over it. The truth, he thought. The truth is down there, in that darkness. The only way to find the answers to all his questions. Without the answers, there was no truth.

"No," the guy called to Michael.

Michael looked at him.

"Even if you found the answers, you wouldn't find the truth."

"But . . . the truth is in there," Michael argued, sure of it.

The guy shook his head. "No," he said. "The truth is in the jump."

Michael woke up shivering, but not from cold. He sat up. Looked around the room, as if he might see something. He felt consumed by a gut-wrenching emptiness. Much worse than before.

Tess lay beside him, breathing peacefully. No hallowed convictions tormenting her. No enigmatic messiah haunting her sleep.

CHAPTER 5

Jack opened his eyes and had no idea where he was. It was dark and cold, and he was lying on the ground. He looked around. As his eyes began to focus, he could see that he was surrounded by woods.

Oh, shit. I did it again.

He sat up; pulled a couple of dead leaves off his face and threw them down. The night was quiet except for the sound of a train in the distance.

He smelled whiskey and looked down to see a pint bottle of Jack Daniel's on the ground beside him. It was half empty. Trying to stand left no doubt as to where the other half had gone.

He steadied himself against a tree. He looked at his watch. It was nine-thirty. Randa would be frantic. Either that, or on her way back to LA.

Shit.

His jacket was a few feet away. He crawled to it, managed to get one arm in a sleeve on the third attempt, and left it at that.

The last thing he remembered was sitting on Cathy's sofa, drinking a Coke. He'd finished the gutters and was in the process of telling Cathy the Randa story. The last thing he remembered was Cathy going to answer the phone. It had given him an opportunity to look at his watch. It had been 4:35.

Where the hell have I been for five hours?

Where the hell was he now, for that matter? He surveyed the landscape; started to move slowly in the direction of the most light.

It didn't take him long to clear the trees, and then he realized where he was. He was in the woods just down the road from Cathy's. He could go back there and use the phone to call Randa. And maybe Cathy could shed some light on the missing block of time. Maybe she could do that while he worked on an explanation for why he smelled like a still.

The road was deserted, which made everything feel even creepier. He walked to Cathy's as fast as his unsteady legs would carry him.

When he got within sight of her trailer, he froze. From between the trailers, he could see a reflection of blue light traveling in a circular pattern that was all too familiar.

He slowed down and edged closer. He made his way behind a dark trailer, then crept along the side of it until he had an unobstructed view of Cathy's.

His embryonic fears were instantly confirmed. There were two cop cars and an ambulance in front of Cathy's trailer. The door was open and there was a cop standing there, barking at someone inside. There was a semicircle of neighbors gathered around, as close as the cops would let them stand.

Jack's breath left in one acid rip.

Oh, no . . . please God . . .

The cop in the doorway stepped aside to let two attendants bring a stretcher through the door.

Oh, God . . .

The body (*it has to be Cathy there was no one else there*) on the stretcher was covered with a blanket, but Jack couldn't see all of it. The cop was blocking Cathy's head.

Please be alive . . . oh dear God, how could I have hurt Cathy, even if I'm crazy, how could I have hurt Cathy?

He heard a noise nearby, the static of a two-way radio. Cops in the woods. Searching for a suspect. Searching for him.

Maybe it wasn't me . . . maybe it was someone else . . .

It was you. Don't be a naïve jackass.

I don't know for sure.

You know. You know who you are.

He saw the beam of a flashlight, far too close to him. Whether he had done it or not, a Landry lurking in the woods near a crime scene was all it would take for the sheriff to consider the case closed. He had to get the hell out of there.

He moved away from the sound of the radio, grateful for all the years he'd spent hunting, which had taught him as much as could be learned about moving through dead leaves with a minimum of noise, even given his current alcohol level. He also knew, from younger years, that the woods ran behind the Haskins' dairy farm and came out just north of town. If he could make it to the other side, he could make it home.

Home. And then what?

Worry about that when you get there.

He could hear the cops, moving in his direction. They had the advantage of not needing to be quiet, so they could move at twice his speed. They'd be on him in a minute if he didn't do something.

He looked down at the ground. Found the right-sized rock. The moon gave him just enough light to see how to aim, though dodging the trees would have been a near-impossible task stone sober. He found the clearest spot, aimed, and sailed the rock directly in front of him. It cleared a good eighteen feet before hitting the trunk of an oak, but the sound was nebulous enough to be anything. He heard the feet and the radio noise begin to move toward it. He used the cops' footsteps to camouflage his own, and got away from them as quickly as he dared.

As had always been true in the course of Jack's criminal career, Barton's finest proved easy to elude. In ten minutes he had emerged on the other side of the woods. He waited until there were no cars coming, then trotted out to the road and picked up a normal pace.

All the while, he knew he was only buying time. Half the trailer court had seen him at Cathy's, he had no way to account for the hours since he'd left there, and his last name was Landry. The trial would probably take an hour. Not that it mattered. Whatever remained of his newfound will to live had disintegrated the second he'd seen Cathy on the stretcher. If she was alive, she'd wake up feeling hideously betrayed, as well she should. If she was dead, he didn't want to live anyway.

But he needed a chance to tell Randa what happened. He needed to tell her to leave quickly, before anyone knew she'd been at his place. She shouldn't even be alone in a room with him, but he had to warn her. And maybe he wanted a chance to say "I told you so." Hell if he knew. Hell if it mattered. He was long past needing to examine the purity of his motives.

In his cloudy and grief-infested mind, he knew one thing. He was going to do what Tallen did. He wasn't going to argue when they came for him. He was going to shut his mouth, drop his appeals, and get this shit over with as fast as possible.

CHAPTER 6

Randa stared at the clock and wondered what to do. By seven, she knew it was too dark for Jack to be fixing gutters, so she'd decided he must be on his way home. By eight, she'd decided he'd stayed to have dinner with his friend and, since he wasn't used to having someone at home waiting for him, had forgotten to call. By nine, she decided he was dead, hit by a truck while walking home in the dark; he was lying flattened on the highway somewhere, human roadkill. She was about to go and look for his remains when she heard him open the door.

"Where have you been?" she asked, instantly sounding like a nagging wife.

He closed the door and locked it. Something was wrong.

"Jack?"

He was pale and shaking, and when she hugged him, she could smell alcohol. He held her so tightly she thought he was going to bruise a rib.

"Jack, what's wrong?"

"Something happened," he said.

"What?"

He shook his head. "I don't know. I blacked out again. I woke up in the woods. When I went back to Cathy's, there was an ambulance—" He had tears in his eyes. "I think I hurt Cathy."

"Are you sure the ambulance was at her place?"

"Yes."

"Well, maybe she got sick—"

"No. There were cops everywhere."

He went and sat on the couch; put his head in his hands. "Oh, God. What if she's dead?"

Randa tried to stay calm. Someone had to, and it clearly wasn't going to be Jack. Maybe he was mistaken. Maybe this was more of the same paranoia that made him leave her at the Ritz-Carlton.

"Jack, do you know anyone who lives near Cathy?"

He didn't answer.

"Jack?"

He looked up. "The old lady who lives next door. Why?"

"Where's your phone book?" Randa asked.

"Closet. But I can't call—"

"I'll call. I won't mention you." She found the book. "What's her name?"

"Hardie. Marie, I think. Or Mary."

Randa searched. "There's an M. Hardie on Chalk Level Road."

"That's it."

The old woman answered the phone on the first ring. Randa identified herself as a neighbor from across the street, and asked what all the commotion was about.

"What did you say your name was?" the old woman asked.

"Randa."

"Amanda?"

"Yes."

"And you live across the street?"

"Yes."

"In that brick house with the wagon wheel in the yard?"

"Yes."

"I thought that was Rufus Turner's house."

"No. He's next door," Randa said. Marie sounded too old to run across the street and find out Randa was lying.

"In the yellow house?"

"Yes," Randa said. She looked at Jack and rolled her eyes.

"Well, I hope you have your doors locked," Marie said. "Because they haven't caught whoever done it."

"Yes, I was trying to find out—"

"And I'm here by myself," Marie went on. "I called my son, but I guess he already left for work. His wife won't answer the phone at night because she knows it might be me and she's too stuck up to talk to me, ever since she started working for the school board. Jeanette Hardie. Do you know her? She used to be a Weatherford—"

"No, I don't know her. But—"

"She thinks I'm tryin' to move in with them, but I wouldn't ask them for a biscuit if I was at death's door starving—"

"Mrs. Hardie, I'm a friend of Cathy's and I need to know—"

"Poor Cathy, I told her last week to be careful because we haven't had nothing but problems since they built that apartment complex behind us. It's just full of blacks, and I knew it was just a matter of time before something like this happened."

"Mrs. Hardie, is Cathy dead?" Maybe the direct approach would work.

"Yes, she's dead."

Randa tried to keep it from registering on her face, so Jack wouldn't know until she could tell him. Marie was still going.

"I know it's true because the policeman was Billy Thomas and I asked him and he said she'd been dead for a couple of hours when they found her. And I was sitting right here by myself, it could just as easy have been me . . ."

"Thank you. I have to go lock my doors now." Randa hung up; looked at Jack. She'd rather die than tell him, but no one was going to offer her the option.

"Cathy's dead?" he asked.

Randa nodded. "I'm sorry," she said.

Jack was quiet for a moment. Randa was about to go over and put her arms around him when he stood up. He walked to the door. He walked back to the sofa. He picked up a glass from the coffee table and hurled it against the wall.

"Goddammit!" he yelled.

"Jack, be quiet!" Randa grabbed his arm as he reached for an ashtray. "Jack! The last thing you need is the neighbors calling the cops."

He jerked his arm away. He sat on the sofa again, buried his face in his hands, and sobbed.

Randa went to sit beside him. She hugged him. He didn't respond, but he didn't knock her away, either. He just kept sobbing—deep, gut-wrenching sobs. Randa had never heard a man cry that way.

"Jack?" She shook his shoulder gently. "Jack?"

He didn't answer. But then, she had no idea what she'd say if he did.

"It's okay." (It's not okay.)

"Don't take it so hard." (He killed a woman. He should take it hard.)

"You weren't conscious, it isn't your fault." (So what? The fact that he wasn't conscious doesn't make Cathy any less dead.)

"Jack, you have to pull yourself together. We have to figure out what to do."

"There's nothing to do," he said.

"If the cops come—"

"I'll turn myself in."

"No, you will not! You don't even know if you did it."

Jack put his face in his hands again.

"Oh, God . . . how can this be happening?" His tone was plaintive, as if she might have an answer.

"What is the last thing you remember? Were you—"

Randa was interrupted abruptly by the sound of pounding on the door. She gasped.

Jack pulled the curtain back, just enough to see out.

"Oh, hell," he said.

"Cops?"

He nodded.

"What do we do?" Randa asked.

"Let 'em in. What else are we gonna do?"

He reached to unlock the door. Randa took a deep breath, and started to work on her lie.

CHAPTER 7

Michael woke up. The nausea was gone. The dizziness was gone. The headache was gone. The worst of it remained. The feeling of evil that seemed to taint everything around him, as if it were something he was causing, instead of something he was caught up in against his will.

Tess was standing in the doorway, dressed for work, looking at him. He reached for his glasses, so he could see her.

"What?" he asked.

"You're so cute when you're asleep."

"But then I have to wake up and ruin it?"

"Do you feel better?"

He nodded. "Physically," he said.

"What's wrong?"

He sat up. Waited a moment to make sure he wasn't dizzy. Most of his current fog was left over from the dream.

"What, Michael?"

"I don't know." He wanted to tell her. But he wasn't even sure how he'd describe it to himself. "I've been having these dreams that make me feel bad." It sounded sophomoric, but he couldn't think of a more sophisticated way to put it.

"What kind of dreams?" She came over and sat on the bed, appearing genuinely interested.

"I keep dreaming about this guy you think never existed."

She didn't laugh, to his great relief.

"What about Him?"

Michael shook his head. "I don't know, exactly. It's not like I thought it would be. *He's* not who I thought He would be. But, it's just a dream, right? No big deal."

"What's He like in the dream?"

He didn't know why she cared, but he welcomed the chance to talk about it. "Kind of . . . I don't know . . . it's not that He isn't warm, but there's . . . something else. Aloofness. No. I don't know. There's no word for it."

She smiled. "Did you expect Him to have a sappy smile on His face and a robin on His finger, like Snow White? Because that's Saint Francis. People tend to get the two of them confused."

He knew she was trying to cheer him up. Somehow that annoyed him.

"Yeah, I think they mentioned that somewhere in my seventeen years of theology."

"Ooooh. Was that back when you had to walk to seminary, twenty miles in the sleet and snow, uphill both ways, while supporting a family of ten on a paperboy's salary?"

He laughed.

"That's better," she said. "I was about to send out a search party for your sense of humor," she said. "Did I step on a Jesuit nerve?"

"You did, but I've recovered."

She became serious again. "Tell me more about the dream."

He shook his head. "I don't know why I got so upset. I just don't want to think . . ." He sighed. "I'd rather never know Him, than to know Him and realize we'll never be close."

Tess chuckled. "Oh, I see. You wanted to be a peer."

It was one of those statements that was so true, Michael knew instantly it would hound him forever. He got up, without speaking, and headed for the bathroom. He considered it the announcement that he was now officially angry.

Tess came to lean in the open doorway, apparently having missed the message. She stood there, watching him brush his teeth.

He looked up. "Is this fascinating?" he asked.

"I didn't realize the conversation was over."

"There's nothing more to say." He wiped his mouth with a towel. Looked at himself in the mirror and instantly wished he hadn't. He took his glasses back off and laid them on the sink.

"Well," Tess said. "I guess I'll go to work. I left my flight information by your duffel bag, assuming I'm still invited."

"I'm sorry," he said. "I shouldn't have brought it up. It's not something we can talk about."

"I don't mind talking about it."

"Well, I do."

"Why?"

"Because I'm trying to talk about something that means everything to me, and as far as you're concerned, I might as well be discussing my relationship with Captain Kangaroo."

She smiled sadly and shook her head. "You don't get it, do you?"

"What?"

"That I *want* to be wrong," she said. "Almost as much as you want to be right."

He didn't know what to say. He realized he'd projected all manner of smugness and moral superiority onto her that she hadn't been feeling. It had never occurred to him that she was *unhappy* being a cynical agnostic. The thought alone gave him new hope—the first whisper of hope he'd felt for a long time, on any front.

He took a moment to look at her. She was wearing a red suit with a wraparound skirt that hit her a couple of inches above the knee. She was standing so that the opening in the skirt exposed the top of her thigh—just enough to fuel his imagination, and he suddenly lost all interest in anything else.

He moved closer to her, slowly, afraid of injuring the fragile mood. "I'm sorry," he said, pulling her to him, and feeling no resistance.

"For what?"

"Being a self-righteous asshole," he said, and kissed her. Feeling her respond, he slipped his hand beneath the skirt and found the soft inside of her thigh, the spot he knew would buckle her knees. He heard her gasp, then laugh.

"What?" he asked, feigning innocence.

"You came in here to brush your teeth in the middle of an argument."

"So?"

"You were already plotting to seduce me while you were still angry."

"Do you love me?" he asked.

"Very much."

"Then shut up," he said, kissing her neck and reaching for the button on her jacket. "I'll analyze it to death with you afterward." That was a lie, but he didn't have to worry about it now.

She laughed and he knew she thought he was being charming and impatient. She didn't realize he was deflecting her scrutiny. She had no idea how he struggled to keep all of his desires in check, if only within the confines of his own definitions and his improvised code of ethics. She knew nothing of his fear—that if he ever lost his tight grip on this stuff, it would own him. He'd spend his entire life in his current state, swept away by the force of his own need.

This time, as always, he had no trouble losing himself. The guilt was vanquished, replaced in no time by a glorious desperation, until he couldn't care about anything else; couldn't imagine a God who would expect him to. Lifted, mercifully, out of himself, his soul cradled in the arms of someone who loved him—someone he could touch, could cling to; someone who could reassure him that they both existed, and that it mattered. Until the magnificent agony burst into ten seconds of stupefying relief—of which he could only enjoy the first five seconds before he was hit by the inevitable flood of shame that defiled the pleasure, leaving him humiliated, demoralized, defeated. Hopeless. His gasping for breath an ugly reminder of the crudeness he tried to deny. His only source of redemption a God who would forgive him (*"Go, and sin no more"*) only if he made a promise he knew he couldn't keep.

His plane was half an hour late getting into Atlanta, and Annie was leaving for her lunch break by the time he drove up to the rectory. She came to meet him as he was getting out of the car.

"I left your messages on your desk, Father," she said.

"Thanks." She was probably dying to know where he'd been, but she would just have to die.

"I guess you heard what happened to your friend," she said.

"What friend?"

"That Landry." She had a look on her face like she'd just gotten a call from Ed McMahon. "They arrested him for killing a woman out at that trailer court."

Michael felt himself go weak.

Oh, God . . .

"Are they sure he did it?"

She nodded. Lowered her voice. "They say he strangled her with a lamp cord."

Oh Jesus . . . it's my fault . . . I should have made him listen . . . why did I let him walk away?

"Didn't I tell you?" Annie went on. "I knew it would happen sooner or later. At least this oughta get rid of him, and we'll be rid of the last of them . . ."

In his head, Michael could hear the sound of the demon's cackle. Sneering. Triumphant.

"Anyway, that's the news," Annie said. "Oh, and that plumber—"

Michael snapped. "Annie, tell him to get over here and do whatever the hell he wants to do and send me the bill. I'll pay him as soon as my grandfather's estate is settled, and in the meantime, I don't want to hear another damned word about the piddlyshit plumbing problems! Is that clear?"

Annie had turned pale and could barely nod. He could still feel her wide-eyed stare as he turned away, and he was sure she was already planning her letter to the archbishop. He kept walking. Hell if he cared.

The police station was filled with stern faces, hushed tones, and self-satisfied looks. The Barton police department finally had a case worthy of its talent, and they were about to get rid of the final Landry, to boot. No one looked surprised to see Michael. They probably assumed the church had been vandalized again.

"Hi." A sheriff's deputy greeted him awkwardly. The Protestants knew they weren't supposed to call him Reverend and couldn't bring themselves to call him "Father," so he was used to clumsy greetings.

"Is the sheriff here?" Michael asked.

"Yeah, but he's gonna be tied up for a while. Can I help you?"

"I want to talk to him about Jack Landry."

"Is that so?" the deputy asked, with no discernible attitude. "And why's that?"

"I think I might be able to help you guys out." Michael delivered it with subtext and a meaningful look, as if the implications were obvious.

Come on, Deputy, do the math. Every cop show in the history of television and a trillion B movies . . . bad guy kills somebody, confesses to the priest . . . priest has moral dilemma, finally goes to the cops, finds some ingenious way to divulge what he knows . . .

The deputy's face was blank for a second, then slowly brightened.

"Wait right here, Father," the deputy said. Evidently it was okay to address him as Father if he was going to be on their side. The deputy disappeared quickly down the hall.

The receptionist looked up from her desk and smiled at Michael, apparently thrilled and grateful that he'd brought a new dimension to the drama.

"Father?" The deputy was back, motioning for Michael to follow him.

Michael was halfway down the hall when a door opened and the sheriff appeared, looking appropriately grim.

"Father, you wanted to see me?"

Translated: "This better be damned good."

"Actually, Sheriff, I'd like to see Jack Landry."

"And why's that?"

"I assume he's not having a good day."

"Well, I assume that unless you're an alibi witness, you aren't gonna be able to brighten it very much."

"And I assume you aren't getting much out of him, otherwise you'd be in a better mood."

Michael moved on before the sheriff could decide whether or not he was angry. "I might be able to help you," he said.

"How's that? Even if he tells you he did it, you can't tell me."

"No, but I might be able to get him to talk to you."

"How are you gonna do that?"

"I'm not sure. But he trusts me. He'd listen to me a long time before he'd listen to anyone else." *Forgive me, but it seemed that a flaming lie was necessary for the greater good.*

The sheriff weighed it. "Well . . ." He stared at the floor for a long moment. Michael got the feeling he was just waiting until enough time had passed that everyone would assume he'd reasoned it out in his head and decided that Michael had stumbled upon a good idea.

"All right," he said. "I could use a break anyway."

He led Michael back down the hall, to the door he'd come from.

"When was he arrested?" Michael asked.

"He's not under arrest," the sheriff said. "He's being held for questioning."

Michael nodded. Somehow he didn't think the Barton SWAT team was out combing the countryside for the real killer.

The woman who'd been with Jack at the coffee shop was sitting on a bench in the hallway. She looked exhausted, and her eyes were swollen and red. She looked up, justifiably puzzled to see Michael. He searched his mind for her name.

"What's going on?" she asked.

Before Michael could answer, she saw the sheriff reach for the doorknob.

"Hey, wait one minute. I've been asking you all night to let me go in there."

"Are you a priest?" the sheriff asked, with a patronizing glare.

"No. I'm not male, either. What's the third strike against me? My California driver's license?"

"Look, ma'am," the sheriff said. "I don't—"

"Actually, I think it would be a good idea if—is it Randa?" She nodded; Michael went on: "—if Randa came in with me."

"Or do I need to have a sex change first?" Randa asked. "And be ordained?"

"Don't forget the Georgia driver's license," Michael offered.

Randa gave him a look that made him wonder if she realized he was on her side.

"All right, Father. You can have her. Just take her with you when you leave." The sheriff opened the door. "Y'all got fifteen minutes."

Michael wondered where that law was written, but didn't want to push his luck.

"Thank you."

Jack looked up as they came into the room. He didn't seem to have the energy to be surprised. He looked worn out and distraught. Randa hurried over and hugged him. He held her tightly, burying his face in her shoulder. Michael found it impossible to politely turn away. The sight of Jack hugging someone was amazing, yet even in its incongruity, it seemed right. Michael sat; waited for Randa to sit.

"Okay," Michael said, looking straight into Jack's eyes. "You have three choices. You can hope they don't have enough to convict you, and if you're right, you can go free and kill more people until your luck runs out. Or you can let them lock you up and/or execute you for something you have no memory of doing. Or you can listen to me and do what I tell you to do."

"How do you know I don't remember it?" Jack asked, instantly defensive.

"Because, unlike you, I know what's happening to you."

"All right," Jack answered, annoyed. "What's happening to me?"

Michael thought for a second. He had to make it something Jack wouldn't immediately reject. Details.

"Your father was illegitimate, is that correct?"

"Yes."

"His mother was from a poor family. Itinerant workers. She left home when she was very young."

Jack nodded. "I don't know much about her, but that sounds right."

"Okay," Michael said. "Let me tell you a little about my family."

Randa broke in. "Do we really have time for this?"

"We have to have time," Michael said, and went on. "My parents died when I was a year old. I was raised by my grandfather. His name was Vincent Kinney."

"The architect?" Jack asked.

It was Michael's turn to be surprised.

"I read," Jack explained. "The *Atlanta Constitution* did a feature on him a while back."

"Well, what I'm going to tell you wasn't in the article. Vincent Kinney is . . . was . . . the father of Will Landry."

Jack was clearly stunned. He stared at Michael in disbelief.

"You mean . . . your grandfather . . . " Randa looked at Jack, then back at Michael. "Your grandfather was also Jack's grandfather?"

Again, Michael nodded.

"There's more," Michael said, "and it's not good. And it's going to sound insane." He thought for a second. There was no easy way to say it. "My great-grandfather—Vincent's father—was a Satanist. Apparently a pretty heavy-duty one, as these things go."

"Wait a minute," Randa said. "Did Oprah say we could start without her?"

"Believe me," Michael said. "I know how crazy it sounds. But it also happens to be the truth. My grandfather was raised in the cult . . . was a member of the cult until he was seventeen. They—" He took a breath, preparing himself. "The cult kidnapped a thirteen-year-old girl and . . . Vincent . . ." He stopped. He couldn't bring himself to say it. "Your father was conceived during a Black Mass. Ultimately, that's what is wrong with you, and that's what was wrong with your family."

"Let me see if I have this straight," Jack said. "You're saying that this cult kidnapped my grandmother, and your grandfather fucked her during some kind of a devil-worship ceremony, and she got pregnant, and that's how the world was graced with my father's presence?"

Michael winced at the harsh sound of the truth. "Yes," he said. "That's exactly what I'm saying. The cult planned to use the baby—your father—as a sacrifice to Satan. My grandfather helped them escape."

"I hope you don't want me to thank you for that."

"I'm just trying to tell you what happened. I don't care what you thank or blame me or my grandfather for. None of that is important. You need to know this: that your father was a by-product of very dark circumstances, and he carried that darkness with him, and he passed it on."

"Jack's mother always thought there was a curse on the family," Randa said.

Michael nodded. "Jack's mother was right." He looked back at Jack. "The thing that is hounding you and taking you over and making you black out is an evil spirit. Summoned intentionally by my great-grandfather and ordered to destroy our bloodline."

He saw Jack roll his eyes.

"You know what? I think it's stupid, too!" It came out loud, and half an octave higher than his normal voice, but Michael couldn't help it. "I do this for a living and I can barely say the word *demon* with a straight face. You know what else? This thing doesn't give a flying fuck whether we believe in it or not. So much the better if we don't. No one will get in its way."

Randa shook her head. "It sounds so . . . I mean, I believe in Evil, but . . . demons?"

Michael nodded. "I know." He could see a trace of belief in her eyes; he followed it. "We've put a lot of energy and imagination into trying to define and categorize and tame a four-thousand-year-old tradition into submission—into something we can understand and live comfortably with. I'm as guilty of that as anyone. Meanwhile, the fact is that this primitive, archaic crap is somehow true. Whether we're comfortable with it or not—whether we *believe* it or not—there really is a Devil. There really are demons. There really is some sort of war going on between forces of Good and Evil. All around us. All the time. Infecting our lives in ways we don't even dream of."

"I wish I *could* believe it," Jack said. "I'd love to blame everything I've ever done on the Devil."

"Well, you couldn't do that," Michael said.

"Why not? Isn't that what you're saying?"

"No. These things can't get in by themselves."

"What does that mean?" Randa asked.

"It means that somewhere along the way, Jack did something to accept its offer. He took some action, willingly, that unlocked the door."

Jack was staring at the table. Michael thought he saw Jack react, very subtly, to what Michael was saying. He had a feeling that whatever Jack had done, Jack knew what it was. There was no point in exploring it, though. It didn't matter anymore.

"Look, Jack, you don't have to believe it," Michael said. "You don't have to believe anything. Just let me do what needs to be done."

"What's that?" Randa asked.

"He needs an exorcism," Michael said.

Jack laughed sardonically. "Well, I saw the movie and it looked like a lot of fun, but I'm kind of tied up at the moment. In fact, even if all this nonsense is true, you're a little late showing up to tell me about it."

"What have you told the police?" Michael asked.

"The truth. I fixed Cathy's gutters. I woke up in the woods next to a mostly empty bottle of Jack Daniel's. I don't remember anything in between."

"Do they have anything? Witnesses? Evidence?"

Jack shook his head. "I don't know."

"I don't see what they could have," Randa said. "He admits to being in her trailer, so forensics won't prove anything."

"Okay," Michael said. "We have to get you out of here and get them off your back."

"And how are we supposed to do that?" Randa asked.

Michael had already been thinking about it. He remembered something Bob had said to him the day after Danny slashed his father's face.

"... *Danny could have passed a polygraph, because Danny didn't do it.*"

"Offer to take a polygraph," Michael said.

"I can't do that," Jack said.

"Why not?"

Jack was quiet for a moment before he spoke. "Because I'm almost positive I did it," he said, his voice shaky with emotion.

"I'm telling you, *you* didn't do it. Your body did it, that's all. As far as your conscious mind is concerned, you weren't even there at the time."

Jack stared at the table. He looked anything but convinced.

"Did you know this woman?" Michael asked. Jack winced and shut his eyes tightly.

"Yeah," Jack finally said, in a barely audible voice.

"Were you angry with her about anything?"

"No," Jack said quickly. "Cathy was my ..." He stopped. Took a breath. Tried again. "Cathy's the last person I'd ever want to hurt," he said, his voice trembling.

Randa put her arm around him. She had tears in her eyes. Michael worried that his line of questioning had triggered Jack into further self-hate, which was the last thing he'd wanted to do.

"Jack, you have a right to try to save yourself," Michael said.

"Yeah? And what will I have saved?"

"Your life."

"You've gotta do better than that," Jack said.

"I don't agree," Michael said. "I think life is always worth saving."

"Oh, please," Jack said, and looked away.

Michael gave it a moment, then asked, "Do you love Randa?"

Jack looked down. Michael could tell he'd hit the jackpot.

"Because I don't think this is about Noah's ark," he said pointedly.

Jack still didn't speak. Randa took his hand, and he let her.

"This thing has already killed a lot of people that I presume you loved. You're just spitting on their graves if you let it kill you, too." Michael left that hanging and tried another approach. "You know, you could have a life. You and Randa could have a life together. I know I just met her, but I'd be willing to bet it would never get boring."

Randa smiled and looked embarrassed.

"It's not too late. Get married. Get a house. Get a lawn mower. Have kids. Name them after your brothers." He saw Jack flinch at that. "Look, I don't care if you run away and join the circus. Just don't let this thing win."

"From where I'm sitting, it's already won," Jack said.

"I don't notice a noose around your neck."

"Stick around."

"Jack, take the polygraph," Michael said. "Don't tell them you don't remember. Tell them you didn't do it. And if you pass, then you'll know that I'm telling the truth."

"Don't you mean *when* I pass?"

"Yes. I do."

Jack looked at Randa. He reached up and brushed a tear off her cheek with his thumb. He stared into her eyes for a long time. Michael could see Randa's eyes locked on Jack's, pleading.

"Jack, what could it hurt?" Randa asked. "If you flunk, they can't use it against you."

"I'm not sure it's flunking that he's afraid of," Michael said. He looked at Jack. "The real question is, do you have the guts to live, if you pass?"

Jack didn't speak or look at Michael. Michael stood.

"I'll leave you guys alone," he said. Then, to Jack: "I don't know anything about this woman who died," Michael said, "but if she was your friend, I doubt she would want to be what made you finally give up your life."

Michael's footsteps on the tiled floor punctuated his exit. He reached the door and opened it.

"Michael?"

He stopped. Hearing his name on Jack's lips almost made him shiver. It felt uncomfortably intimate.

Michael turned around. "What?"

"Would you ask Barney Fife to call the GBI and have them send a polygraph examiner?"

Michael smiled and nodded. "I'd be happy to do that."

He left to find the sheriff, his feeling of relief completely eclipsed by a stronger feeling of dread.

CHAPTER 8

Jack passed the polygraph. Apparently he passed it convincingly. Randa overheard the examiner tell the sheriff, "I'd be looking elsewhere." The sheriff was clearly pissed—both that he hadn't solved his big murder case, and that he wasn't going to become the town hero for getting rid of the last Landry.

Even with the polygraph results, the sheriff kept them there for as long as he could; but time was running out and he had to let Jack go or charge him with something. Finally Michael got testy and asked if they were planning to charge Jack with felony gutter repair. Said he had a friend at the ACLU who'd probably be very interested to hear about it. At which point, the sheriff got some religion; he grunted warnings about Jack staying close to home, and then he let them go.

Once they were outside, Michael wasted no time.

"We need someplace to do this. We can't do it at the boardinghouse or the rectory. We have to go someplace where the noise won't attract attention."

"What kind of noise?" Randa asked.

"Trust me," Michael said.

She supposed the answer was obvious. Demonic noise, whatever the hell that meant.

She told Michael about the farm, and he declared it perfect. The demon would be attracted to that place, he said, so it would be easier to get it to manifest itself there. This was not a comforting thought to Randa, but Michael assured her that it was good news. There was no way to get rid of the demon without first tackling it head-on.

"Let me get this straight," Jack said, looking at Michael. "You're saying there's something in me . . . that my body is just a shell and I'm actually this invisible . . . thing . . . that lives there? And I can be displaced by another invisible thing, which happens to be an evil thing . . . that wants to destroy me . . . and it's going to destroy me by making me destroy other people?"

Michael nodded. "Basically."

Jack shook his head. "Why?" he asked. "If there is this entire unseen reality coexisting with us . . . it's entirely unknown to us, and we're so . . . concrete. What would be the point?"

"Jack, if I came home and my house was on fire, I wouldn't stand on the lawn explaining to the firemen that I have all new wiring and nonflammable drapes. What we need to do right now is put out the damned fire."

"How?" Jack asked. "By magic?"

Michael was getting impatient. "I guess so, from your point of view," he said. "Look, you just explained it yourself. It's a metaphysical problem, we have to fight it where it lives. If this doesn't work, you're welcome to come up with your own solution."

"He's right, Jack," Randa said. "Let's just do it."

Michael didn't give Jack time to argue. "I have to go grab a few things," he said. "Randa, you go ahead. Start clearing out one of the bedrooms, take out everything except the furniture. We'll move that when I get there. Jack's riding with me."

Randa nodded.

"Come on," Michael said to Jack, leaving no room for

discussion. Jack followed, apparently resigned to the insanity.

As Randa drove to the farm, it struck her that she was going into this event the same way she lived her life—throwing herself into something that didn't make a damned bit of sense, because there was simply nothing else to do.

They cleared most of the furniture out of the downstairs bedroom. Jack lay down on the bare mattress, and Michael strapped his arms and legs to the bed frame, apologizing for doing so several dozen times.

"Is this too tight?" he asked, checking Jack's straps for the third time.

"I want it tight," Jack said. He glanced at Randa. She knew he was worried about hurting her.

"Do you have water here?" Michael asked.

Jack nodded. "Water, electricity, everything."

Michael left the room, presumably to do something involving water. Randa sat on the bed beside Jack. She kissed him. She could feel his lips quiver.

"Randa . . . what Michael said at the police station . . . I did do something. I didn't kill anyone, but—"

"Don't," she said, shaking her head. "Whatever it was, there's nothing you can do about it now."

"But you need to know—"

"No." She didn't. The last thing she needed right now was something new added to the mix. Whatever he had done, she was sure he was making it worse than it was.

"You can't just bury your head in the sand about who I am," Jack said, insistent.

She kissed him again, mostly to shut him up. "We can talk about it later," she said.

Michael returned with a small bowl of water. He placed it on the nightstand by the bed, where he'd already placed a white candle and a wooden crucifix. He mumbled something and made a small cross in the air, over the water. He took two red books out of a black leather bag; he handed one of them to Randa.

"I need you to follow along and read the responses. The places are marked."

"You're kidding."

"It's just a sentence here and there."

"But . . . isn't another priest supposed to do this?"

"Yes. And we're supposed to have a medical doctor and a couple of assistants just to hold him down. And we're supposed to have the Church's official permission. And we're supposed to have an exorcist who has a hell of a lot more experience than I do, and a cleaner conscience. But we don't. So you've just been ordained."

"I can't say a bunch of God stuff. I don't even know what I believe."

"That's okay," Michael said. "Neither do I."

He positioned her on the left side of the bed and took his place on the right, in front of the nightstand. He opened his book.

"This is the official Rite of Exorcism. Parts of it were written in the third century. The last time it was updated was sometime in the seventeenth century. Basically, it's going to sound ridiculous coming out of my mouth, but it's been known to work."

Michael picked up the bowl of water, dipped his thumb into it and made a cross on Randa's forehead. She was amazed at how comforting the meaningless gesture felt. He did the same thing to Jack, who had no visible reaction one way or the other. All the while, Michael was mumbling words that Randa couldn't make out. She assumed it had something to do with protection. Michael put the water down, crossed himself, told Randa to do the same thing, and they began.

They followed the text for half an hour without deviation. Randa read her responses and tried not to feel like the world's biggest hypocrite. She glanced at Jack a couple of times. His eyes were closed and she wasn't even sure he was awake. She didn't know how these things usually went, but so far *60 Minutes* wasn't missing anything.

"You're wasting your energy, Padre," Jack said suddenly. "You can't put out the fire from inside the burning building."

Randa's breath was shallow and she could feel her heart pounding against her chest. There was a presence in the room. It emanated from Jack, but it didn't end there by any means.

Oh my God . . . there's really something in here . . .

"By the authority of Jesus, I command you," Michael said, his tone stronger. "To what name will you answer?"

"You know my name," Jack said. He chuckled. "You need to learn your own name."

The air was heavy. It felt like a living thing. There was a bad smell to it, like an open garbage can on a hot summer day. She had to struggle not to retch. Michael stopped and took a couple of slow breaths, apparently trying to steady himself against the presence. Randa did the same. It helped a little with the nausea; did nothing for the weakness in her legs.

"Mi casa es tu casa, Padre," Jack said.

"Dígame tu nombre," Michael demanded.

"Esta vez, Padre," Jack said, grinning. "Nadie estará para aggarrarte."

Randa had no idea what it meant, but whatever it was, it didn't seem to faze Michael.

"Tu nombre," he repeated.

"No te recuerdas de mí?" Jack asked, the grin widening.

"You will obey me," Michael said, "by the—"

He stopped. The pressure in the air had grown much worse in an instant, bearing down on them. A pain shot through Randa's head, as if someone had driven a spear through it. She cried out and her book fell to the floor.

The demon laughed—a loud, sickening cackle. Randa managed to look at Michael. His face was locked in a grimace, his teeth clenched. Whatever it was, it had him, too. He was groping for something on the table. The crucifix. He found it; grasped it.

A sound filled the room. Or maybe Randa's head. She couldn't tell where it was coming from. A gruesome symphony—thousands of voices at once, all screaming in utter agony. Souls in complete despair. They existed, somewhere. Randa knew that. The demon was opening a window of their prison, allowing the sound and the feeling to reach out and grab Randa and Michael. Over it all, she could still hear the demon—it had to be a demon—howling with laughter. Enjoying the show.

Michael lifted the crucifix and held it over Jack. He was trying to speak, but could not. Jack's smile turned into an equally hideous frown. He stared at the crucifix with a look of pure hatred. A low and inhuman groan came from somewhere deep in his throat. At the same time, something in the air broke loose, and the pain and the sounds started to fade. Soon they were gone entirely. The only sound in the room was that of Randa and Michael trying to catch their breath.

Suddenly Jack spoke again. "Put . . . it . . . down . . . you . . . fucking . . . pig . . ."

The voice was different now. Not Jack's. It was rough. Grating. Each word seemed to take all the effort he had.

"He . . . doesn't . . . control . . . me . . ."

"He cast you and all like you into the pit," Michael said. "And by His power I command you to return."

"I . . . am . . . not . . . stained . . ." The demon's voice was getting stronger. ". . . by . . . his sacred fucking blood."

"You are not saved by His blood," Michael said. The thing growled again.

"I HATE HIM!" it yelled. The horrible voice filled the room. Randa could feel it vibrate in her body.

"Why?" Michael asked. He was staring intently at Jack.

"WHYYYYY!!??" The demon seemed infuriated by the question.

"There's nothing in Him to hate," Michael said.

"You don't know him!" the demon spat, his words now coming fast and sharp. "You don't know shit about him!"

"I know all I need to know."

"YOU KNOW LIES! HE WAS NO ONE!"

"Then why hate Him?"

"Because, you cocksucking pig! He gets power from you brain-dead slime! You and your fucking fairy tales!"

"Oh, really?" Michael asked. "How does that work?"

"He had no power until you gave it to him! He was no one!"

"How did we give Him power?"

"Thoughts are real, you fucking moron. You don't see the most obvious thing."

Michael didn't respond. Randa looked at him. He seemed to have lost his foothold.

Jack suddenly laughed again, long and loud. Now he was back on top. "And you know it, you weak shit! Your bread is bread and your wine is wine, and there's nobody who's gonna unconditionally save your ass! You're going to stand in front of the same wrath I did, and you're going to get the same fucking amount of mercy!"

Michael was staring at Jack. He seemed lost. Randa's

instincts told her to do something. Anything. She picked up her book again and opened it and read the first thing her eyes landed on.

"God . . . it is an attribute of Yours to have mercy and to forgive . . ." Her voice was trembling, but she kept going. "Hear our prayer, so that this servant of Yours . . ."

". . . who is bound with the chain of sins," Michael said, joining her, "be mercifully freed by the compassion of Your goodness."

Jack's eyes closed and the low growl started again.

There was a sudden loud noise, which Randa recognized too late as the sound of glass shattering. The window nearest her had exploded. She felt a sharp sting on her face; she dropped to the floor and covered her head with her arms. She could hear glass falling all around her. The sound finally stopped, but she was afraid to move. She felt something touch her shoulder and she jumped.

"Randa."

It was Michael. She looked up.

"Are you okay?" he asked.

"I don't know." She put her hand on her face and felt blood. Michael was squinting, trying to see how bad it was.

"I can't tell," he said. "Let's get you out of here."

The room was eerily quiet. Jack watched them leave without comment. Just a demented grin on his face.

They sat on the sofa and Michael dabbed at her face with a wet cloth.

"He missed your eye by an inch."

"Is it deep?"

Michael shook his head. "I don't think it'll leave a scar. Is that the only place he got you?"

"I think so."

"I'm really sorry," he said. "I should have thought about those windows."

"It's not your fault."

"Yeah, it is," he said. He handed her the cloth. "Hold this to it until it stops bleeding. I'm going to go check the barn and see if there's any plywood."

Randa counted the seconds, waiting for Michael to return. She didn't want him out of her sight. He was the only thing standing between her and consummate Evil.

She wrapped herself up in an afghan, though she doubted it would do any good. The cold, clammy air had a completely unnatural feel to it. No earthly warmth was going to penetrate it.

Michael returned without plywood, but he'd found a couple of old army blankets that were heavy enough to do the trick. He took them and a tool kit back into the room. Randa held her breath, waiting for the sound of glass shattering. All she heard was hammering. Michael came out of the room and went into the bathroom without comment, so Randa assumed the mission had been successful.

She tried to calm herself by listening to the steady rain that had begun to fall. There was an occasional rumble of thunder in the distance. Too late in the year for a storm, but Randa didn't want to analyze it. If this thing could control the weather, she didn't want to know about it.

Michael came out of the bathroom, wiping his face with a towel. His hair was wet from the rain. He had taken off all the robes and stoles earlier. Now he was wearing a black shirt and black pants, and there was a piece of white plastic sticking out of his pocket, which Randa assumed went into the neck of the shirt somehow and became the collar. The black looked good on him, and he was even better looking, if possible, without his glasses. Randa hoped he was gay; otherwise it was a crime against all of female humanity that this man had taken a vow of celibacy.

"How do you feel?" Michael asked.

"Physically?"

He nodded.

She thought about it. "Sick," she said. It was the best description she could come up with.

"Yeah, I figured," he said. "I'm sorry."

"Do you want to apologize for the rain forests while you're at it?" Randa asked.

He smiled.

Randa felt herself shiver. "I didn't believe you," she said.

"That's okay. I wouldn't have believed me either." He sat on the arm of the sofa; rubbed his eyes.

"I mean . . . I believed some version of it," Randa said. "I guess I didn't give a lot of thought to what a demon was. I was thinking along the lines of psychotic PMS mixed with amnesia. But this—"

She shivered; pulled the afghan tighter around her.

Michael nodded. "Yeah," he said. "I know."

"Have you ever done this before?"

He nodded again. "Once."

"How did it end?"

"Badly."

He didn't offer any more. He stood.

"I'm going to see if I can find the controls for the furnace," Michael said. "Why don't you see if there's any food in the kitchen."

Food?

"You must be kidding. You could eat?"

"We're going to have to keep our strength up. This isn't going to be over any time soon."

"How long does it usually take?"

"I don't think there is a 'usually.' It's going to be at least a couple of days."

Jesus. A couple of days in the room with this thing? And what if . . .

"You said that other one ended badly—"

"We can't think about that now," he said. "All we can do is deal with what's in front of us."

"But how in God's name is a bunch of ancient gibberish supposed to get rid of this thing? Look at all the people it's killed! And we're going to fight it with words?"

Michael shook his head. "No. Not with words."

"Well, what? Are the Marines going to land any minute?"

"Look," he said, his voice firm, "you go find food, I'll go find heat, and we'll rest for a while and I'll try to explain it to you. Okay?"

She nodded. "Okay." He was going to explain it to her. This should be good.

Randa went into the kitchen and checked the cabinets, where she found a pyramid of cans that looked as if someone had won the Chef Boyardee sweepstakes. She heated a couple of cans of SpaghettiOs and took two bowls of it out into the living room. Michael had a nice blaze going in the fireplace, but the room didn't seem any warmer. Randa put the bowls down on the coffee table.

"Mmmmm boy," Michael said, looking into his bowl.

"Tell yourself there are children starving in Africa."

"Well, I'd send this to them, but I don't think they'd eat it." He picked up his fork and speared a meatball.

"Aren't you going to bless it?" Randa asked.

"There's only so much I can ask of God."

They ate in silence for a moment. The crackling of the fire was not comforting. Neither was the chance to think.

An overview descended on Randa like a shroud. She put her fork down.

"The Devil," she said. "Like life wasn't hard enough with only things we knew about working against us. It makes me want to just . . . give up."

"If you were the Devil, isn't that how you'd want to make people feel?"

"Here's what I don't understand," Randa said. "Why would God allow demons to exist? Why would He allow the Devil to exist? He's God, why doesn't He just sit on them?"

"Well, that's—"

"And don't start rattling off the party line," Randa said, in case that's what he was gearing up for. "I've heard it all. Evil has to exist in order for us to appreciate good. Bullshit. I could appreciate the beauty of a rose or a cloud or a newborn baby without Nazi Germany. And I've heard about how this is just a blink of an eye to God. Well, so what? It's not a blink of an eye to us, and we're the ones who have to live through the pain."

"Maybe you don't need the bad to see the good," Michael said. "But maybe the intensity of the good is multiplied by a trillion, once you see how bad the bad really is."

Randa was not impressed. "Is that what you really believe, or just what you tell people when your collar's round your neck instead of in your pocket?"

"I'm a Jesuit. I don't have to wear a collar or tell anyone anything."

Randa shook her head. "I don't know the first thing about Jesuits. Or any other order, for that matter."

Michael thought for a moment. He smiled a little. "Okay. Here's a story. There were three priests in a room—"

"Is this anything like 'There was a certain man who had two sons . . .'?"

"Oh, shut up," Michael said, laughing. "I get enough shit about my Messiah complex. So, there were three priests sitting in a room. A Franciscan, a Dominican, and a Jesuit. The light went out. The Franciscan said, 'My brothers, let us take this opportunity to consider the debt we owe to our sister, the light.' The Dominican said, 'Yes, but let us also take this opportunity to contemplate the difference between the light and the dark.' And by this time, the Jesuit had found the circuit breaker and flipped the switch."

"That definitely sounds like you," Randa said, smiling. "So, how does it work? What do Jesuits do about all the unanswerable questions?"

"We drink ourselves into oblivion while the Franciscans and the Dominicans are sleeping soundly."

Randa laughed out loud. It felt good. Michael even smiled.

"All right," she said. "Tell me why your words are going to get rid of the demon."

"Because they aren't words."

"Excuse me?"

"It isn't about a bunch of words. It's about the power of ritual."

"What is ritual if it isn't a bunch of words? A bunch of words with candles?"

"Well . . . this is just my personal theory. I think it's focused energy. I think we have the power to affect the . . . unseen. Whatever it is. I think rituals focus energy in a certain way, and it does something that we can't see or understand to the other plane, and whatever it does, it changes something. For lack of a more sophisticated way to put it."

Randa nodded. It made some kind of sense.

"Think about it," Michael said. "Jesus spoke almost entirely in symbols and metaphors. And the last thing He did was ask us to perform a ritual in His memory." He chuckled. "A ritual if you're Protestant. If you're Catholic it's the world's damnedest magic trick. All my life, I've had this fantasy of explaining Mass to a Martian. 'See, we say these words and our deity turns into a little piece of bread, and then we eat Him.' I think he'd be hightailing it for the spaceship before I got to the part about the wine and blood. But, I digress—"

Randa laughed. Michael went on.

"Symbols and rituals obviously have a very high priority in the universe, as far as God is concerned. Down here we place primary importance on things that can be bought and sold and weighed and measured. Symbols and metaphors are for the flaky artists, and rituals are all but extinct. I think we have it exactly backward. I think ritual is a powerful force, and when we acknowledge that, we align ourselves with that power."

Randa got up and moved closer to the fire. "Well, I hope you're right," she said. She shook her head. "I can't believe this. I'm standing here *hoping* the man I'm in love with is demonically possessed. Otherwise, I'm in love with a murderer who's come up with an original excuse."

"You're not in love with a murderer," Michael said.

"I'm not sure it matters. I've been in love with narcissists, commitment phobes, liars, cheaters, you-name-it-aholics. What difference does it make why this one goes down the tubes? At least this will make a good story."

Michael pushed his bowl away.

"You're at least five years too young to be so bitter," he said.

"I thought I'd beat the rush."

There was no point in explaining to him that she was

sure it was a life pattern, destined to continue. He'd probably offer some fucking perspective on her love life—the last thing she was interested in hearing, especially from an avowed celibate.

"It's not just me," she said. "The whole system stinks. Even if you fix him and we ride off into the sunset, in a couple of years we'll be sick of each other and arguing over whose turn it is to unload the dishwasher. And then there are all the people who never find anyone, who don't even get to delude themselves for a couple of years, and spend the rest of their lives weeping at sappy movies and turning horrible books into bestsellers." She stared into the fire. "I tell myself we've just fed ourselves this 'happily-ever-after' myth until we've made ourselves miserable over something that doesn't exist, but it doesn't make sense. If it doesn't exist, why do we all want it so desperately?"

She had a vague sense of being embarrassed at launching such a tirade at a guy she barely knew, but she was too mad to care.

"If there is a God," Randa concluded, "then love is the dirtiest trick He's ever played on us."

Michael was quiet. He stared into his bowl.

"What?" she asked him.

"I think you don't believe that for a minute," he said.

"I know," Randa said. "But I should."

CHAPTER 9

When they went back into the room, Jack appeared to be asleep. Michael buttoned his shirt at the neck and slipped the collar into place. He wasn't going to put the robes back on. They'd be too constricting should he need to move fast. Randa had taken her place and was waiting. The cut on her cheek looked worse than he'd realized, and he felt completely responsible. He didn't know what she did for a living, but he doubted she could afford plastic surgery. Maybe she'd let him pay for it out of Vincent's estate. It seemed appropriate, all things considered.

He took a deep breath and reminded himself that taking a guilt inventory was not going to help him right now.

"We'll start where we left off," he said. Randa nodded. He crossed himself and she followed suit.

Dear God, please let this work.

The room was freezing cold and foul-smelling. Michael tried to call to mind something pleasant, thinking it would give him strength. He remembered the feeling of waking up with his arm around Tess. The warmth of her body next to his. The soft rhythm of her breath. The fresh smell of her hair.

The sound of the demon's cackle made him look up. Jack's eyes were open.

"That's right, pig. Think about your *real* religion."

Michael felt himself shiver. He'd forgotten the filthy thing could read his mind. Official Church teaching said this was impossible, but he had some unofficial news for them.

He tried to wipe his mind clean. The thing was laughing again.

"Padre, I have a joke for you," it said. "God says to Adam, I've got good news and bad news. The good news is, I've given you a brain and a dick. The bad news is, I can't figure out how to make the blood go to both of them at once." He howled, completely amused with himself.

Michael ignored him and began the first prayer.

"God, Creator and Defender of the human race—"

"Oh come on, Padre. Don't be a stiff. You loved that joke. Or did it hit you too close to where you live?"

Michael felt his face flush.

Okay. You knew that was coming. Ignore it. Randa's not even religious, she doesn't care. And she probably doesn't think you're a forty-eight-year-old virgin . . .

He kept going. "You who made man in Your own image—"

"What are you gonna do?" the demon asked. "Chase me off by boring the shit out of me?"

"Look on this your servant, Jack Landry, who is assaulted by the cunning of the unclean spirit—"

"The primeval adversary," the demon said mockingly. "The ancient Enemy of earth . . . Enemy of the faith . . . Enemy of the human race . . . Best Supporting Actor in a Recurring Role . . . and let's not forget Most Likely to Succeed. Is this it? Is this the best you've got to throw at me? Name-calling?"

Michael looked up. Weighed it. Anything the demon

could be tricked into revealing about itself could be used to trap him later. It was worth the digression.

"Okay," Michael said, setting the book down on the nightstand. "Why don't *you* tell me who you are."

"You know who I am."

"I don't know your name."

"And you think I might be stupid enough to tell you?"

"Are you the only one?" Michael asked, trying a different approach.

"Oh, Padre. We are legion. You know that."

"Are you the only one possessing Jack?"

"It doesn't matter, you dumb fuck. It's all the same."

"What's the same?" Michael asked. He glanced at Randa. She was watching, riveted.

"Tell you what," said the demon. "You want to know who I am? Who *we* are? Why don't I give you *our* résumé?"

Something happened. It was as if Michael's mind suddenly became a projection screen and someone flipped a switch to roll the film. He was bombarded by a series of images. Pictures of horror and death. The nightly news without network mercy. He saw starving children with distended stomachs, skeletal bodies of AIDS victims, people infected with the Ebola virus, their internal organs exploding like grenades. Natural disasters. Earthquakes, landslides, floods, fires, blizzards, droughts, hurricanes, tornadoes. Concentration camps: men lined up for the showers; children being wrenched from the arms of sobbing mothers. War-ravaged cities. Wailing children running naked through the shells of bombed-out buildings. Derailed freight cars spewing toxic fumes, poison gas in crowded subways, fourteen-year-olds with Uzis, gunning each other down in the streets, suicide bombers driving cars full of dynamite into mosques, hypodermic needles washing up on pristine beaches, rescue dogs sniffing through the rubble of a day care center that had been blown to bits by fertilizer and diesel fuel mixed with blind rage and raw hatred—the stench of death and destruction and waste and hopelessness. The putrid underbelly of God's allegedly glorious creation. Everything behind the façade.

And then the reel changed, and Michael began to see a montage of mankind's pitiful attempts at defense and protection. Labels on soup cans, airbags in cars, BABY ON BOARD signs, alarm systems, Mace canisters, the surgeon general's warnings, air-popped popcorn, turkey hot dogs, consumer reports, smoke detectors, antiradiation computer screens, earthquake kits, tornado warnings, flash-flood watches, iron lungs, organ transplants, bottled water, nonfat ice cream, rosaries hanging from rearview mirrors, plastic Jesuses on the dash . . .

Pathetic, Michael realized. All our little safeguards and superstitions. Trying to fool ourselves into thinking we have any kind of control. We're the South in the Civil War—too proud to admit that we are greatly outnumbered, poorly armed, and rapidly depleting our meager resources. Just a matter of time before there's nothing to do but saddle up Traveller and ride to Appomattox to admit our defeat. Left with nothing but shame and humiliation, and the war-torn ruins of our souls.

"Where's Jesus, Padre? Conjure Him up and let Him explain why I'm wrong."

"You're wrong because you don't know anything but lies," Michael said. It was a third-grade reflex. Nothing more.

"Who told you that? The Caped Crusader? Tell me, if God created everything, wouldn't that make *Him* the Father of All Lies?"

Before Michael could figure out how to answer, the demon was off on a new track.

"You want me to set you straight about Junior? It's a very simple story. He looked different. The whole world is in a fucking uproar two thousand years later because he was taller than the average first-century Palestinian Jew. Because his hair was lighter than everyone else's and his eyes were blue. A fluke of nature, like a white buffalo calf. It had to *mean* something. He looked different, so he had to be divine. If he'd been just another scruffy little Jew, no one would know his name by now."

"Did they kill Him for having blue eyes?"

"They killed him for being a self-righteous prick."

Bullshit. It's all bullshit.

"Is it, Padre? Then where is He? I'm here. You're here. Where's Superman?"

Michael opened his mouth to speak and realized he had nothing to say. Randa was staring at him, worried.

"In fact," the demon went on, "where has He been all these years? Where was He when your grandfather was fucking a thirteen-year-old girl and she was screaming for His help? Where was He when your mother's brains were splattered all over Peachtree Boulevard? Or when Tallen Landry used the Christmas Eve congregation for target practice?"

He took a break to laugh, then went on.

"I got one even better. Where was He the night you dumped Donna Padera?" He laughed. "You and your famous ego. You thought she was so upset because she couldn't stand the thought of living without you. You might have suspected something if you'd ever bothered to know her any better."

"What are you talking about?" Michael asked. How the hell had Donna Padera gotten into the act?

"Poor Donna. Your first victim. Believed everything you told her. Fine upstanding Catholic boy from a good home, with a rich and famous saint for a grandfather. If

Michael Kinney said it wasn't a sin, then by God, it wasn't a sin. Let's see . . . first it wasn't a sin to jerk you off, because that wasn't really sex. Then it wasn't a sin for her to suck your cock, because it wasn't a sin unless she could get pregnant from it. And then my favorite part. 'We might as well go all the way because if God's going to be mad at us, He's already mad.' " He stopped to laugh. Then stopped laughing. "She didn't want to do any of it, but she wasn't about to lose her prize-catch rich Catholic boy. And you knew it. You used it. You used *her*. Now, tell me. How is that so different from what your grandfather did?"

Michael felt himself reeling. He'd been ready for attacks on his sex life, but it never occurred to him that the bastard would start with high school. He'd made a big mistake by talking to the demon in the first place. He'd broken the cardinal rule of exorcism, and now he was paying for it. He was no longer in control.

He opened the book again and looked for his place.

"Oh no," the demon said. "We're not finished. You haven't told me where your friend was the night you dumped Donna. And I haven't told you why she was so upset that night. I haven't told you that she'd just found out she was pregnant."

Michael stopped breathing.

That can't possibly be true.

"Oh, but I'm afraid it is. She didn't tell you because she didn't want to stand in the way of your hallowed calling. She spent a *lot* of time calling on His Majesty about it, but I guess He was too busy to listen. He didn't seem to be around when she almost bled to death from a botched back-alley abortion. He didn't seem to be around when she had to have a hysterectomy at age seventeen, when all she'd ever wanted was a family." He chuckled.

"Well, *your money* and a family. So what happened, Michael? Where was Captain I-Am-With-You-Always?"

Michael couldn't speak. He couldn't move.

"And where were *you,* for that matter?" He snarled. "Trotting off to show the world how holy you were. You're about as holy as I am. You're a fucking murderer, from a long line of murderers! And *you* call *me* unclean? *You're* gonna cast *me* out? Out? Where do you think *you* are, asshole? You think *you're* out? I've got a news bulletin for you, about what's waiting for you on the other end of your leaky raft!"

Michael forced his legs to move and walked out of the room. Behind him, the demon was laughing hysterically.

He put the book down on the first table he came to. His hands were shaking.

It couldn't be true. Donna would have told him. Surely she would have told him. He might not have ever been in love with her, but they'd always told each other everything. There was no way she wouldn't have told him.

Randa appeared behind him.

"Michael?"

"I'm okay," he said. He took a deep breath. "I need a break. I need to go and do something. Why don't you try to rest, and I'll be back in a couple of hours."

"Okay," she said, clearly puzzled.

"Just stay away from him. Don't go in there, don't talk to him, don't look at him. Stay completely away. All right?"

She nodded. He felt bad about leaving her, but he had to. He couldn't go on with this until he knew the truth.

Donna lived on Myrtle Street in midtown. He knew the house because Vincent had remodeled it, shortly after Donna had married the radiologist. He rang the doorbell and in a few seconds he heard footsteps. He dreaded this like nothing he'd ever dreaded, but it had to be done.

Donna opened the door. It took a moment for Michael's identity to register, probably because she'd never seen him in clerics. When she realized who it was, the smile left her face. She didn't speak.

"May I come in?" he asked.

"Why?"

"I need to talk to you."

"I'm in the phone book."

"I didn't want to do this over the phone."

Something flashed in her eyes, and Michael felt it in his stomach. Did that mean she knew why he was here? Did that mean it was true?

She led him into the living room, but didn't offer him a seat. The room was meticulously detailed with all of Vincent's finest touches, which made being there that much more difficult. The mahogany fireplace was lined with sienna tiles, hand-painted with troubadours on either side. The mantel was lined with expensively framed pictures of Donna's three daughters.

That's right—she has kids! It can't be true.

He glanced at the pictures. Donna was a natural blond. The girls all had dark hair. None of them looked like her, or like each other. The fact that she had kids didn't mean anything. Not if they were all adopted.

"What is this about?" Donna asked. She was clearly uncomfortable.

He knew of no easy way to get into it, and wasn't in the mood to search for one.

"Were you pregnant when we broke up?"

She looked away from him; she brushed her bangs to the side, nervously. It took her a moment to speak. "Who told you?" she asked, her voice trembling.

He didn't answer. Gave himself a minute to take it in. It didn't want to go in. He felt he might throw up.

"Why didn't you tell me?" he asked finally.

"What would have been the point?"

"The point?" He forced himself to keep his voice down. "The point is that I had a right to know."

"Michael, why are you doing this? It was over thirty years ago."

"Well, I'm sorry. I would have gotten upset earlier, but I never heard anything about it until today."

"Who the hell told you? My husband doesn't even know."

"Then what did you tell him about why you couldn't have kids?" Michael asked, seeing an opening to verify the rest of it.

Her eyes blazed. "*Who* told you this? *No one* knows this."

Oh dear God. It's all true.

"Donna, why didn't you tell me? Even if it wasn't a big thing to you—"

"How the hell do you know what it was to me?" Donna half screamed. "You never knew who I was, and you never gave a damn, as long as—" She stopped herself; she took a couple of breaths. Started again, slightly calmer. "What difference would it have made if I'd told you, Michael? You had big plans. What would you have done? Married me?"

He didn't answer. She knew the answer.

"All you would have done is what you're doing now. Barge in here on your morally superior high horse, judging *me*, like it wasn't your fault in the first place!"

She let him sit with it for a moment. She was right. It was entirely his fault, in more ways than one.

"I didn't see any point in both of our lives being ruined," she said.

"Has your life been ruined?" he asked. He tried to make his voice inflectionless. He really wanted to know.

"Not the way you mean," she said. "I didn't get to do it the way I wanted to, but so what? Not many people get to do it the way they wanted to." She hesitated. "You did something worse than ruin this stupid life. You ruined me with God. The great irony." She was starting to cry.

"Donna, I think God knows who to blame," Michael said.

"I don't care who He blames!" she snapped. "All I know is, He punished me and He didn't punish you, and I can never forgive Him for that! And I guess He can't forgive me, either, because I sure as hell don't feel forgiven. Especially not with *you* standing in my living room."

It was his cue to leave, but he couldn't make himself move.

"There's nothing else to say about it, and I'd appreciate it if you'd leave. My husband is going to be here any minute."

Michael nodded. "Okay," he said quietly. He certainly didn't want to cause her any more pain than he already had. He walked toward the door. She didn't follow him. He stopped in the doorway.

"Donna . . . I'm really sorry," he said. "I would have been there for you, if you'd told me."

She looked at him, unimpressed. "Michael, just go. You're not going to use me to ease your conscience."

It was as painful as she'd intended it to be. He left her standing in the living room, staring out the window at the rain.

He drove back to Barton as fast as he dared, given the weather and the condition of his head and heart.

Dear God . . . Dear God . . .

No prayer would form in his mind.

Why would God listen to you?
Is that true? Am I alone with this?
Do you see anybody else? Do you feel anybody else?
But what about the dreams I had?

Do you really think Jesus is a smart-ass in a flannel shirt and jeans? He's not even the guy in the white robe with a lamb in his arms. He was no one. He knew nothing. He taught nothing. He redeemed nothing. He was good-looking and charismatic. Knew how to milk a crowd. He was the ancient Palestinian version of a rock star. All flash, no substance. And now he's gone. He died, he was buried, he rotted, he's gone.

Michael stopped at a gas station and parked by a phone booth. Searched his wallet and found the phone company charge card he never used; dialed Larry's number.

"I'm mad at you," Larry said. "Why didn't you tell me about Vincent?"

"I had a plane to catch."

"Repeat after me: Vincent died, I'm very upset, I can't talk about it now, I'll E-mail you when I get home."

"Look, I'm in the middle of something and I just need a quick favor."

"Okay, but you haven't heard the last of this. What do you need?"

"You mentioned once that there were a couple of physical descriptions of Jesus written by contemporaries."

"Allegedly written by contemporaries. Yeah."

"Do you have them anywhere?"

"In my computer. Want me to fax them to you?"

"No. I want you to read them to me."

"Right now?"

"Right now."

"All right," Larry said. "Let me find the file."

He put the phone down. In a couple of minutes he was back.

"Are you writing something?" Larry asked.

"No."

"Just had one of those sudden middle-of-the-night cravings to know what Jesus looked like?"

"Would you just read it to me?"

"Mikey, have you gone to work for the Franklin Mint? You can tell me."

"Larry—"

"Okay, calm down. Here we go. This was allegedly written by one Publius Lentulus, governor of Judea, to the Roman senate and Tiberius Caesar. It says: 'There has appeared in our times a man of tall stature, beautiful, with a venerable countenance, which they who look on it can both love and fear. His hair is waving and crisp, the color of new wine—' "

"What color is new wine?" Michael asked.

"Well, when my Aunt Bernice made it in her basement, it was sort of a reddish gold."

Michael felt something tighten in his chest.

"Go on," he said.

" 'Color of new wine, with a parting in the middle in the manner of the Nazarenes. His brow is smooth and most serene; his face is without any spot or wrinkle, and glows with a delicate flush. His nose and mouth are of faultless contour . . .' It goes on for a week. Do you need the whole thing?"

"Does it say anything about his eyes?"

" 'His eyes are gray and lively, and change their color.' Here's my favorite part. 'In denunciation he is terrible . . . calm and loving in admonition . . . cheerful but with unimpaired dignity.' "

"All right," Michael said. "What are the chances this is a real description?"

"Depends on who you ask. Most learned people think

this letter is a twelfth-century forgery and there was never any such person as Lentulus or any such office as governor of Judea. Personally, I'm not so sure."

"Why not?"

"In the first place, there are several other apocryphal descriptions that are amazingly similar. In the second place, if you were going to forge a description of Jesus and try to get away with it, would you give him reddish gold hair and blue eyes? And in the third place, it makes sense to me that Jesus would look different. Easier for him to stand out in a crowd. Easier for people to believe that he was somebody special. He could have looked any way God wanted him to look, so why not take advantage of that fact?"

Michael felt a chill go through him.

If he'd been just another scruffy little Jew, no one would know his name by now.

"Okay," Michael said. "Thanks for your help. I have to go. I'll E-mail you."

"You'd better."

Michael hung up.

What does it mean? The dreams are real? The demon's story is true? The guy in the flannel shirt's never said anything to me about who he is. Did he ever say it to anyone, or did they just make it up? The demon has been telling the truth consistently. He told the truth about Donna. Everything he has said about me has been true. Does that mean he's telling the truth about Jesus, too?

He remembered Bob telling him that one of Satan's most powerful tools was confusion. That he'd mix truth with lies until there was no way to know what to believe.

Who am I? What am I? What do I stand for? Who do I serve? Who was Vincent? How bad was he, really? How bad am I, really? How good is God? Where is He? Why isn't

He helping me? Is it too late? Am I past the point of redemption? Where does that leave me? Where does it leave Jack?

Questions continued to pummel him, all the way back to the farm, until he pulled up in front of the house and realized Randa's car was missing. He couldn't think of a single scenario where that was anything other than very bad news. He got out and ran into the house.

He found Randa sitting on the sofa, crying. One side of her face was swollen and bruised. She was holding a cloth to her forehead, where another gash was bleeding. Michael ran to her.

"Oh, God. Randa. What happened?"

"He's gone," she said, trying to stop crying. "He told me he had to go to the bathroom and I thought it was Jack . . . it seemed like Jack, he sounded just like himself and I thought it was him . . . I'm really sorry . . ."

"No, no. It's my fault. I was stupid to leave you here with him. Jesus. How long ago did he leave?"

"I don't know. I hit my head on the wall, I was unconscious for a while. I didn't look at the clock. God, why didn't I think . . ."

"It wasn't your fault."

"We have to find him. He could do anything. We have to find him before he does something we can't get him out of."

It was true. They had to find him, and fast.

"Did he say anything? Besides the bathroom thing?"

"He was talking a lot before I went in there. It sounded like gibberish."

"Can you remember any of it?" Michael asked.

The gibberish could be a clue, Michael reasoned. The demon wanted the showdown. He wouldn't run without leaving Michael a way to find him.

"He was saying that Spanish stuff," Randa said.

"Which stuff?"

"What he was saying before. Nadie estará . . . whatever."

"Nadie estará alla para agarrarte?" Michael asked.

Randa nodded. "Yeah. What does it mean?"

"No one will be there to catch you," Michael said.

"What does *that* mean?"

Michael thought. He tried to put it together with the Spanish the demon had spoken previously. *Sal si puedes.* Get out if you can. No one will be there to catch you. Get out if you can. No one will be there . . .

He's at the Winecoff!

Of course. It made perfect sense. The Winecoff, where he'd killed Michael's family. Where he had tried to kill Michael. He'd probably laughed that night, and sang his little "get out if you can" song. Probably reveled in all the carnage, but he hadn't gotten the one thing he'd really wanted. He hadn't killed Michael. Vincent had been waiting, to catch him. *Nadie estará alla para agarrarte.*

"I know where he is," Michael said.

"Where?"

"Downtown Atlanta."

"How do you know? Oh, who cares. Let's go!"

She stood up. Michael didn't.

"Michael?"

Nine-thirty at night. An empty building. Why? A lot of people on the street. Target practice. Jack has to have a gun. Every male in Georgia over the age of ten has a gun. Is he looking for a good vantage point? For target practice?

"Michael, let's go!" Randa said.

People on the street. Jack with a gun. Me with a book

of prayers. A book of prayers and a dirty past. Dirty present. Dirty soul. People on the street. I can't help them. More blood on my hands.

"Randa, I don't think we should go."

"What? What are you talking about?"

"Look . . . people's lives are at stake. Innocent lives."

"Yes. Like Jack's."

"You know . . . I told you . . . I knew I wasn't a saint, but it's even worse than I thought. I can't do this. I'm wasting my time."

"But if you give up, what hope does he have?"

"There is no hope. That's what I'm trying to tell you. All we can do is call the cops and try to stop him before anyone else gets killed."

Randa stared at him, her eyes filled with disbelief. The disbelief faded into something else. Anger.

"Give me the damned book," she said.

"What?"

"If you won't do it, I'll do it. If there is a God, He doesn't care what sex I am or what I majored in. Just give me the damned book and tell me where Jack is."

"I can't do that."

"You don't know!" she yelled. "You don't have any idea what it feels like! You don't give up on someone you love! You don't just leave them to their fate! You live in your little bubble and you don't have any idea what I'm talking about!"

He did know. And she was right. If it were Tess out there, he wouldn't be calling the cops. He'd fight the damned thing until he won or dropped dead. For all the guilt he'd felt over Tess, it mattered right now. It mattered that he knew what Randa was talking about. Knew, in his soul, what she was feeling. Vincent's words rang in his ears. "Love is a real thing." And his own words. "It's the only thing we have."

He took Randa's hand.

"Come on," he said.

"Where?"

"To find Jack."

He dragged her toward the door.

"But . . . the book . . ." she said.

"To hell with the book."

They didn't need the book. They didn't need words. They didn't need props. If there was any way Jack could be saved, they already had the only thing they needed.

CHAPTER 10

Randa drove them to Atlanta. Michael was quiet; every now and then he mumbled something to himself. Randa had a feeling he was praying. He only spoke out loud to give her directions (*"Spring Street and Peachtree exit—go down to Ellis and turn left, there's a parking lot—"*). She parked in the lot and followed him up the hill to Peachtree. They crossed and headed west. She had asked Michael where they were going. All he'd say was "it's just a building."

Michael came to a dead stop right in front of Macy's. He was wincing as if in physical pain.

"Are you okay?" Randa asked.

It took him a moment to catch his breath. For a moment, Randa was afraid he was having a heart attack.

"My parents died here," he said.

Randa looked around, wondering what he meant. Here in Atlanta? Here on the street in front of Macy's?

He pointed across Ellis, to an old abandoned building.

"He's doing something to me," Michael said. "I don't usually react like this."

"You think Jack is in that building?" Randa asked, still trying to piece it together.

Michael nodded.

"Why would he come here?"

"I don't know. Maybe to make me feel like this."

The pain in his face was so intense it was hard for Randa to look at him. She was trying to figure out what to say when he said "let's go" and started across the street, without waiting for the light to change. She followed him.

The glass doors and windows on the first floor of the building were covered with brown paper. Michael pushed them anyway. When they refused to budge, he looked around. On the other side of the building there was a Chinese restaurant. Neon lights glowed in the window: DINE IN OR TAKE OUT and DELIVERY AVAILABLE.

Michael motioned for her to follow him and went through the door into the restaurant.

The interior was full of small Formica tables, with a takeout counter and cash register in the back. Oriental music, played on some stringed instrument, hung delicately and incongruously in the air. Other than that, the place was silent.

Randa glanced around. Several of the tables had dishes of half-eaten food on them. The table nearest her had plates full of stir-fried rice and cashew chicken. Cups of green tea sat untouched. The entire scene reminded Randa of descriptions she'd read of ghost ships found in the Bermuda triangle. As if the inhabitants had suddenly vanished, leaving all else in place.

She looked at Michael, who was taking it in.

"Anybody here?" he called.

No answer.

He reached down and felt one of the teacups, then stuck his finger into the tea.

"It's barely warm," he said, apparently to himself. "Come on," he said to Randa, and he headed around the counter and into the kitchen.

The kitchen was the same ghost town, even to a large pot of soup on the stove, still simmering over a low flame. Michael turned the burner off.

"Anybody in here?" he called again. Still no reply.

He looked around. There was a narrow corridor that led to a door. He pushed it open. Randa followed as Michael stepped into a small vestibule. There were two doors there. He opened one; it went to the alley outside the building. He pushed the other door, which opened to a set of concrete stairs.

"Fire stairs," Randa said. The irony made her cringe.

"They must have gone this way," Michael said.

"Do you think Jack—"

"Took hostages," Michael said, nodding. "Which means he's probably armed. Which means you're staying here."

"But—"

He shook his head. "I need you here. I need some time upstairs. Put the closed sign on the door and lock it if you can. Stay here and keep an eye out. If cops show up, I'll need some warning."

"But if he has a gun—"

"Randa, I'm going up there. Are you going to help me or not?"

He meant it. She had no choice.

"Okay," she said.

"Someone might have tripped a silent alarm. If you see cops coming, run up these stairs and warn me. I'll be on the eleventh floor, the front room on the Peachtree and Ellis corner."

"How do you know?" Randa asked.

"I know."

He started through the door, then stopped. Looked around. His gaze landed on the counter, where there was a tray with several glasses of water. Michael picked one up. Randa found herself feeling relieved, though she didn't know why. Holy water was hardly going to stop a bullet.

"Good luck," she said. It sounded comical, considering what he was heading into.

He nodded absently. "Go flip the sign now," he called behind, and was gone.

Randa went to the door and turned the sign over. She found the light switch and turned the lights off. The light that spilled in from Peachtree cast weird shadows; she tried to ignore them. She sat in a booth where she had a good view of the door; tried not to cry.

CHAPTER 11

He knew the minute he started up the stairs that he was right. He could feel the presence, by the heaviness in the air and the heaviness in his soul. He had to stop on the third floor, just to come to terms with being in the building. The fire had started here, not more than twenty feet from where he was standing.

On the sixth-floor landing he was hit by another wave of grief, and this time it was paralyzing. Like what he'd felt outside, only worse. Knowing its source gave him no power over it.

He sat on the stairs and cried. Sobbed. Deep, tight sobs that made his throat ache. His breath wouldn't come, and when it did, he started to cough and couldn't stop. When the coughing finally stopped, the sobbing started again. Everything inside him, body and soul, ached until he didn't think he could live through it.

God, why did You let them die? All those innocent people. Why did You punish them for what Vincent did? Families, Christmas shopping. Fathers on business trips. A bunch of high school kids in town for the Junior Assembly... they were probably so excited to be here... their parents were probably thrilled for them to be staying at a big hotel in Atlanta... waiting for them to come home and tell their stories... why, God? Where the hell were You?

No answer. Never any answer to the pain. Never any answer to anything. Just orders.

"*Pack. Move. Keep going.*"

Why? Why should I keep going?

He knew the answer to that. Jack was upstairs, with more innocent victims. *Jack* was an innocent victim. And since God apparently had no interest in saving the innocents, the job had fallen to him.

He picked himself up and started back up the stairs, counting the floors as he went. The stairs were lit only by what little light spilled through the dirty windows. The stairwell smelled strongly of urine. The paint on the walls had flaked off in sheets that had fallen to the floor and now crackled under Michael's feet. The paint on the handrail was peeling badly, too; it broke off in his hand, along with years' worth of dust.

He kept moving. Reached the eleventh floor. He opened the fire door, slowly, and stepped into the hall.

Michael had spent countless hours over the years studying the floor plan of the building in Vincent's scrapbook, trying to figure out how his family could have escaped. He knew the suite of rooms where his family had died was on the other side of the building. He knew Jack was waiting.

He blessed the water, all the while thinking how stupid and childish a gesture it was.

Can't shoot me. I've got holy water.

The hall was littered with food wrappers, old blankets, and other signs of the homeless people who called this hellhole home. The smell of urine was even stronger. Michael ignored it and made his way down the hall.

There were three rooms to the suite, and three doors. They were all closed. Michael chose the middle one, which led to the room that had been the parlor; it accessed both of the bedrooms. The bedroom doors were closed, too. Michael knew which room Jack was in. The room where they had died. He took a moment to center himself.

The light from the hot stretch of Peachtree cast a blue glow into the room. The paint on the walls was peeling, not just in places, but everywhere. Michael looked out the window. What must it have been like? To sit here staring out at safety, at the world going on about its business, while death moved rapidly closer?

Must have felt a lot like I feel right now.

He reached for the knob on the door to the corner room. Turned it. Pushed the door open slowly.

He could shoot me the second I walk through the door. What is there to stop him?

He waited for the sound of gunfire; there was none. He pushed the door open the rest of the way. He saw Jack—or rather, the wretched thing that now controlled Jack—glaring at him with a repulsive smile on his miserable face. In front of him, held in a choke hold, was an elderly Chinese woman. She was gagged with a white linen napkin. Her eyes were filled with raw terror; she was crying softly. Jack was holding the gun to her temple.

"Well, look who's finally here. Did you have to run to New York first and fuck your girlfriend?"

Michael felt himself cringe at the accusation, but forced himself to ignore it. He couldn't afford the distraction. Had to get his bearings. The room was small and hellish. Same peeling paint; same blue light from the street; same strange shadows. There was an odd metallic smell in the room that Michael recognized but couldn't place.

"Too bad you're late. You've already missed a lot of the fun."

The words sent a sick feeling to Michael's stomach. He quickly glanced around the room.

Oh dear God . . .

In the same moment he realized that the smell was blood.

Across the room, lined against the wall, were the hostages from the restaurant. They were all tied and gagged. All shot in the head, lying on flat pillows of pooling crimson. Three of them. A middle-aged Chinese man in an apron. Must have been the cook. A young Chinese woman, college age. Waitress. A man in a suit. And the worst. A little Chinese boy, about ten years old. Probably the grandson of the woman Jack was holding. The kid was wearing jeans and a Batman T-shirt. A Braves cap was lying on the floor in front of him.

Michael looked at Jack, who threw his head back and

laughed. Michael felt a hatred he'd never known he was
capable of. It was all he could do not to charge Jack.
Instead, he went to the victims and started checking
pulses.

"What's wrong, Padre? I sent them to a better place,
didn't I?"

Michael looked up, into the creature's eyes. He saw
the look. Dead. Consumed by hate. Jack was not there.

"You son of a bitch," Michael said, through clenched
teeth.

The thing inside Jack laughed. The living hostage gave
a pitiful moan; it jarred Michael into action. He put the
glass of water down on the floor. Turned to face Jack.
And realized he had no idea what the hell he was going
to do.

*Jesus, what now? The same stuff that has never fazed
him before?*

There was nothing else to do. Michael dipped his fingers into the water and crossed himself.

"In the name of the Father, and of the Son . . ."

"Oh, no," the demon said. "No. We're not going to do
the mumbo-jumbo again. And we need to clear up a few
things, like about who's running the show."

Before Michael could wonder what he meant, it started
again. His psyche was invaded by a sense of futility.
Hopelessness. Pointlessness. The overwhelming impression that everything good and beautiful and holy was just
a façade. Michael tried to fight it by conjuring up an
image the demon couldn't defile.

A rose.

It withers and dies and rots and stinks . . .

A child.

*Who grows into an adult who lives a miserable, useless
life full of pain and heartache, until gradually the body*

begins to break down at the same rate as the hope, and the dreams die and rot just like the body...

"All right!" Michael yelled. "*What* do you *want*?"

The demon laughed. "Oh, I want a lot of things, Padre."

"Let the woman go," Michael said. "And then tell me what it would take to make you leave."

The demon smiled. "We'll get to that. In time."

"No! Now! This is between you and me. Let the lady go."

The demon smiled and motioned toward the open window on the Peachtree side. "That's the very window where your family made their unfortunate exit," he said.

"I know that," Michael said, trying to keep from feeling it.

The demon scooped the hostage up in his arms, like a sack of flour, and moved toward the window. She screamed beneath the gag.

"I thought we'd have a reenactment," he said. "Aren't they all the rage now?"

"No!" Michael yelled. "Stop!"

To his surprise, the thing stopped.

"Look, dammit! I'll do whatever you want me to do," Michael said. "Just put her down!"

"Okay," the demon said.

For a split second, Michael thought it had worked. Then, in one motion, Jack tossed the woman through the open window.

"No!" Michael yelled. He could hear the woman screaming. He ran to the window, in time to see her fall the last few yards before she hit the ground. Cars on Peachtree screeched to a halt. Michael turned away from the window in horror.

"See, I can be reasonable," the demon said. "What else would you like me to do?"

Michael took a few deep breaths, trying to calm his rage down to a level where he could speak.

"What do you think that proved?" he asked, still seething.

"I don't have to prove anything. I was just keeping my half of the bargain. And now you can keep yours."

Michael could feel something change. He began to feel dizzy. The air grew heavy and hot. The smell came back. The room started to spin. He felt the same pressure as before. The same pain shot through his head. He closed his eyes; it was all he could do not to scream. He could feel himself shaking, straining against the pain. It lasted for a full two minutes, and then it was gone, as suddenly as it had appeared.

The smell had changed. The rotten garbage smell was gone, replaced by a strong smell which Michael instantly recognized, from a lifelong fear.

Smoke.

He opened his eyes. The room was much darker, and full of smoke. The air was hot and thick. He couldn't breathe. He dropped down and tried to crawl toward the window. He couldn't see anything through the smoke; didn't know where the window was. He moved in what he thought was the right direction.

This is it. He's killing me.

He heard a sound that he didn't recognize immediately. It seemed to fade into the room. As it got louder, he recognized it as a child crying.

A child? What child?

The smoke grew thinner and he could see the window. But there was something else. He squinted; tried to focus his smoke-filled eyes.

No. It can't be.

There were people by the window. Two women, one

holding a toddler. Two men. All coughing, struggling to breathe. The women were crying. The child was crying.

Christ. No. He can't do this.

But obviously he could. Michael was back there. Or maybe the demon had just made it all materialize. It didn't matter.

"A reenactment. Aren't they all the rage now?"

Vincent. Michael's parents. His grandmother. Himself. He glanced out the window. There was no Ritz-Carlton. Somehow, he was back there. Being forced to live through it. Feel it. Smell it.

Michael tried closing his eyes, but the scene didn't disappear. If anything, it got clearer. There was nothing he could do but watch.

His father and Vincent were throwing a rope made of wet bedsheets out of the window. The other end was tied to the bed frame. They tugged on it to make sure it was tight, then Vincent started down it.

"Send Claire down when I get to the ladder," Vincent said to Michael's father. Matthew nodded. The women were holding on to each other, crying. Laura was rocking Michael in her arms, trying to calm him. They all had to put their heads out the window to breathe, though the smoke-filled air outside wasn't much of an improvement.

Michael's father held the rope for extra security while Vincent climbed. The women watched out the window, their faces tense with fear.

Michael looked at his father. Matthew Kinney, standing there, alive. A man who'd never been anything but a question mark to Michael. Michael had never realized how young Matthew had been when he died. Ridiculously young. And handsome. He looked like a younger version of Vincent. He looked strong in body and spirit. Michael had never imagined his father as strong. He tried to move closer, to be closer to Matthew, but found that he couldn't move at all.

"He made it," Matthew said, watching Vincent through the window. His voice was full of amazement. "We're going to make it."

The women were laughing through their tears.

"Come on, Mother," he said to Claire. "There's no time to spare."

He helped Claire through the window.

"Don't look down," he said. "Use your feet to feel for windowsills."

Claire nodded. Matthew kissed her on the forehead, and she started down the rope. She looked terrified, but she moved quickly. Matthew and Laura watched.

"You're doing fine," Matthew called. "You're almost there. A few more feet." He stopped to cough, and to take a breath.

"I can't believe it," Laura said, laughing, crying. "We're not going to die."

"Come on, let's get you down," Matthew said. "Give me Michael."

Laura handed the child over to Matthew. She kissed them both.

"Don't drop him," she said, her eyes pleading.

"Laura, I'd die before I'd drop him," Matthew said. Michael felt a different kind of pain shoot through him. He could feel the love from this man he'd never known. The love that was about to be ripped away from him.

My God . . . don't make me live through this . . .

Why should He answer your prayer? He didn't answer theirs.

Laura climbed through the window and started down. Matthew watched her disappear.

"You're doing great," Matthew said. "Just keep going. There's a windowsill about two feet below you. Just try to—" Matthew began to look concerned. He seemed to be listening to something Michael couldn't hear.

"No. You can hold on. You *can*, Laura. You *have* to! You're not slipping. No, you're *not*—"

He was cut off by the sound of a scream.

"Nooooo!" he cried. "Laura! Nooooo!"

Michael tried to yell, too, as if it could help. Nothing would come out of his mouth. And then he felt the spinning sensation again, and the pressure. The air around him changed, from searing heat to chilly, moist night air. New smells faded in. Pine trees. Candles. Smoke again, but not as strong. Some sweet smell he didn't recognize. Colors began to break through the darkness and a new scene appeared . . .

Men in long black robes. A fire. Noises. Chants. Moans. Howls. The scene became clearer and Michael was surrounded by frenzied activity. He was in the middle of an orgy.

Opium. That smell is opium. How do I know that?

Dear God, don't make me be here . . .

The men were all paired and grouped and their robes were open down the front and Michael refused to look at what was going on, but their faces were enough to tell him everything.

That's what we look like . . . it's not because they're men or because they're Satan worshipers . . . sex is ugly under any circumstances . . . it's ugly and inhuman and if it were only about procreation we wouldn't want it all the time . . . God created it to humiliate us . . . to keep us in our place and our place is low and disgusting and out of control . . . the good people can rise above it but I'm not one of them . . . I'm one of these depraved animals and that's what I look like . . . I tell myself it's different but it's not . . . I don't love Tess I'm simply justifying my own lust . . . like

*Linda and the red dress . . . there's nothing good in me . . . I
came from this ugliness and it owns me . . .*

And then Michael saw Vincent.

Seventeen-year-old Vincent, but unmistakably Vincent just the same. On the altar in the middle of the circle. A young girl who must be Rebecca beneath him, terrified: screaming, crying, begging. Her pleas were useless, falling to the ground unheard. The look on Vincent's face dissolved any hope Michael had harbored. Vincent was enjoying the hell out of it.

The strange reality shifted and all the sounds faded except for Rebecca's screams and Vincent's heavy breathing . . . and then it all seemed to speed up and Michael felt himself caught in the frenzy . . . and then Vincent's breath became Michael's breath, and somehow Michael was suddenly seventeen again . . . not watching, he was actually back there . . . not in the woods . . . in Donna's basement on the sofa and she was under him and he could feel her mouth on his neck and their breath rose and fell together and the frantic sounds he heard were his own and he could hear Donna calling his name and he didn't answer, didn't stop, didn't slow down and she called more insistently and she was pleading now (*"Michael, pull out! Michael!"*) and he didn't and he *could have*, but he didn't and then it was too late and he heard his own cry and then it became Vincent's and he was back in the woods and now it was Michael, not Vincent, who was on top of Rebecca and inside her as she screamed and her screams just excited him more and he could feel his body exploding with the pleasure of it as he gasped for breath and he could feel the heat of the ceremonial fire on his face and he could smell a mixture of booze and candle wax and semen and incense and somehow every smell seemed to wrap itself around him with slimy fingers and they wrenched the pleasure away and left a shell of self-loathing and then the scene changed again and he saw nothing but a flesh-colored blob . . . it started to take shape and it became a fetus, fully formed, totally human, sucking its thumb . . . and then a sound, a wailing that was coming from the baby, who was being pulled apart, limb by limb, by unseen hands . . . blood filled the scream of his mind, but not before he saw the pain and terror on the innocent face and he knew that the Satan worshipers had nothing to do with it . . . his baby, his fault, his selfishness, his crime . . . and the blood poured over him and he was covered in it and he could feel it hot and sticky and in a blinding flash he saw that he hadn't escaped the ghastly legacy at all . . . born of murderers, he was a murderer himself . . . his soul was blackened beyond repair, beyond redemption and if there *was* a guy in a flannel shirt, He'd been finished with Michael for a long time, wouldn't hear him if he begged for mercy . . . the black hole in his soul was going to be Michael's home for the rest of eternity . . . he heard Donna's pleas again and Rebecca's screams and the baby's, and all the Landrys and their victims and the Ingrams and the people who died in the fire and all the screams reached a crescendo together . . . an ungodly sound . . . the sound of ruin and waste and destruction and hopelessness . . . he was the only person who could have made a dent in the agony and it was too late . . . he joined the scream and he screamed and screamed and finally realized he was back in the room . . . and the demon was howling with laughter.

Michael stopped screaming.

"Where's your hope now, Padre?" the demon asked. "Where's your friend?"

Not here . . . He's not here . . . it must be true . . . no

Jesus . . . just an angry, vengeful God who has it in for me . . . I've been living a lie . . . my whole life is a lie . . .

Michael was crying again. He forced himself to stop. Didn't want to give the demon the satisfaction of seeing it. He was standing in front of the window. He looked out. On the street below, people had gathered around the dead woman. Suddenly he had a new thought.

This is it. This is what I can do. I can offer my life as a penance.

"The truth is in the jump."

This must be what He was talking about.

What He? There is no He.

Doesn't matter. If it's a lie, I don't want to be here anyway.

"If I jump, will you leave?" Michael asked the demon.

The demon laughed. "Good, Padre. Now you're getting the hang of it."

It's a lie. If he just wanted you dead, he'd have killed you a long time ago.

Then what does he want?

Behind him, the demon snickered. "Go on. Do the world a favor. You owe them one, don't you?"

He's right. This is it. My last chance to do the right thing.

No! Don't you see? It's not your body he's after.

What then? My soul? It's too late to worry about that.

It's not too late. Never too late.

Michael sat on the windowsill. Swung one leg over, then the other. The people below were too preoccupied with the dead woman to notice him. They were in for a surprise.

He took a deep breath. He hesitated, as if he were walking out the door for a vacation and wanted to make sure he'd packed everything. Tess flashed through his mind. And Krissy. And Barbara. And Larry. And all the other people who loved him, and would never understand this. Even Annie Poteet. And Randa.

Randa! I can't do this! He'll kill Randa!

Suddenly there was a noise from the hall, and Randa appeared at the door.

"Michael, the cops are coming . . . some lady . . . what happened?" she asked, breathlessly.

Michael forgot all else and motioned Randa away.

"Randa! Go back!" Michael yelled, scrambling back into the room. Too late.

Jack stepped behind her and slammed the door. He grabbed her and held her in front of him, the gun against her head.

"Now, why should she go away, Padre? Are you trying to hog all the fun?"

With the same sudden motion as before, Jack scooped Randa up and started for the window. Michael began to yell, but caught himself.

"What, Padre?" the demon asked. "Should I put her down, too?"

Michael lunged, throwing his full weight at Jack with all the strength he had. He managed to wrench Randa free, and he heard her hit the floor. Heard something else hit the floor. The gun? He glanced around quickly; didn't see it.

Jack forgot about Randa and went for Michael, knocking him to the ground. Michael tried to roll away, but Jack was on him before he could think about it. He could feel Jack's hands around his throat—more power than he could fight. He tried to kick, but Jack had his legs pinned. He couldn't move. He couldn't breathe.

"Jack, let him go!"

Randa's voice, behind them. The demon ignored it.

"I have the gun," Randa said insistently.

Jack loosened his grip on Michael, but left his hands on Michael's throat.

"Isn't that cute? She has the gun."

"I'm not kidding. I won't let you kill Michael."

Her voice was trembling, and Michael knew she realized the full implication of what she was doing. He wanted to tell her not to do it, but if Jack killed him, he'd simply kill Randa next.

"Now come on," the demon said. "You know you're not going to shoot the best fuck you ever had."

"Let him go!" Randa yelled. "I mean it!"

Michael was amazed to feel the hands leave his throat. He had only a second of relief before he realized it had been a trick. The second Randa had relaxed, the demon had gone for her. He knocked her to the ground. Michael heard the gun fall again, but still couldn't tell where it was. He got to his feet. The thing had Randa by the throat. Michael knew it would do no good to try to pull him off. He looked around for anything within his reach. There was a short section of two-by-four lying against the baseboard. He grabbed it, brought it down as hard as he could on the back of Jack's head. Jack gave a sharp cry and released Randa. He turned toward Michael, his eyes blazing with fury. He threw himself at Michael and the two of them hit the floor. Michael tried to roll away, but he was trapped between Jack and the wall. He could feel Jack's rough hands around his throat again. Tighter this time. He couldn't breathe at all.

He managed to get his right hand free, and reached behind him for whatever might be there. His fingertips brushed steel and he realized he could reach the gun.

The gun!

He closed his fingers around it. All he needed was enough strength to aim and pull the trigger.

And what? Shoot Jack?

If I don't, he'll kill me.

So what?

And then he'll kill Randa.

You can't shoot him. You're supposed to be saving him.

I can't save him if I'm dead.

Everything was turning a weird shade of purple, and Michael knew he only had seconds left. He let go of the gun and moved his hand forward, hoping to find the two-by-four. He touched something, but it wasn't wood. Glass. A glass.

The holy water.

He closed his hand around the glass.

Throw it on him.

It won't do anything.

Throw it.

It's just water.

Throw it.

He had one chance. Enough time, enough strength to do one thing. If he chose the gun, he'd live. But Jack would die. If he chose the water . . .

Do it!

His thoughts spun out of control. Started their own war.

. . . it won't work . . . I'm too bad . . .

"It's not about goodness, Michael. It's about faith."

"He was no one."

". . . remind yourself you believe in redemption . . ."

"He looked different . . . a fluke of nature . . ."

". . . something you have to do . . ."

"He wasn't there when I needed Him."

". . . keep going . . ."

". . . it's too late, Padre . . ."

". . . not too late . . . never too late . . ."

"He was no one."

". . . the truth is in the jump . . ."

"He was no one."

". . . something you have to do . . ."

"HE WAS NO ONE!"

". . . the truth is in the jump . . ."

And then he realized something.

This is it! THIS is the jump!

He tightened his grip on the glass. If he chose the glass instead of the gun, he'd be offering his own life as a show of faith. As proof to God. As proof to himself. A complete, conscious choice.

With all the strength he could summon—physically, emotionally, spiritually—Michael picked up the glass and threw the water at Jack.

In Michael's mind, Jack reacted as if he'd been hit in the face with battery acid. In reality, Jack reacted as if he'd been hit in the face with a glass of water. It stunned him just enough for him to loosen his grip on Michael's throat.

"Damn you!" Michael yelled, and not at the demon. He knew he had a split second, no options, and no help. He did the only thing he could think of: he kneed the devil in the groin.

To his complete amazement, it worked. Jack doubled over. Michael grabbed Randa and ran.

They made their way down the filthy stairs as fast as they could, climbing over garbage and loose two-by-fours.

"Where are we going?" Randa asked.

"Just go!" Michael spat, pushing her forward.

There was still no sign of Jack following when they reached the ground floor. Michael pushed the door open and shoved Randa out of it.

"What are you doing?" she yelled.

"You wait here," he said.

"Like hell!"

"There's nothing you can do, and I can't be worrying about your safety."

"What am I supposed to do? Sit out here and be the girl? I flew across the damned country to help him!"

"And you've done a great job so far—"

"Well, what the hell do you think *you've* done?"

Michael grabbed her by the shoulders and all but shook her. "Randa, I wasn't being sarcastic. You've brought him a long way. But I have to do the rest, and you have to let me."

She didn't like it, but she stopped arguing. Folded her arms and walked away.

"Go around front, where the cops are, and stay there," Michael said. Then he heard Jack's footsteps on the stairs, a few floors above him. He closed the door and ran.

At the bottom of the stairs, he opened the fire door and made his way into the dark basement. Without the light from the street, it was almost impossible to see. He needed a place to hide, to buy himself time to think. From the floor plan, he knew there was a subbasement, with stairs in the northwest corner. He groped toward them.

He made his way down the stairs, using the clammy concrete of the wall in place of sight. The subbasement was even darker; he could just make out the shapes of the ancient furnace and boilers. He felt his way around the corner of the furnace and hid there, trying to catch his breath without making a sound.

He knew it wouldn't take Jack long to find him. He could already hear Jack's footsteps in the basement above.

Michael tried to think. He'd been so sure he had it figured out. Why had the voice told him to throw the water if it wasn't going to work? He realized that his lack of breath came from anger as much as from running.

I jumped, dammit! Where the hell were You, on a fucking coffee break?

You're alive, aren't you?

It stopped Michael's train of thought. His mind suddenly flashed on Charlotte's Eskimo story. At the same moment, he heard the familiar voice again.

That's right. If I don't save you the way you think I should, you don't even notice you're still alive.

It was true.

Okay. You're right. But he's on his way, and I don't have a clue what to do next.

No answer.

So I could use one, if it's not too much trouble.

No answer. Of course, no answer. Nothing except the sound of Jack's footsteps on the subbasement stairs.

"Hiding, Padre?" he called. "How appropriate. That's what you do best, isn't it?"

Michael held his breath. He could feel the room fill with the energy of Evil.

This is it. Now he'll kill me.

A sudden force slammed into Michael, pinning him against the furnace. In an instant, all of his senses were bombarded by a vision. First the sounds. Hundreds of voices, jeering, yelling, in a language he couldn't understand. He could see throngs of people—in front of him; below him; they were only a blur, as if he were underwater. There was something warm running down his face; the same metallic smell as before; the taste of blood in his mouth. And over it all, the pain. Agonizing. Unearthly. But the physical pain was nothing compared to the other—the aloneness. Total. Absolute. A black pit with no end. Everything within him cried out in an ancient plea:

Why have You forsaken me?

The pain was so intense, it was all Michael could do not to scream.

And then, as quickly as it had appeared, it was gone. And Michael realized it had not come from the demon.

Had Jesus expected a deal, too?

Didn't that question imply an expectation? In fact, the same expectation as Michael's: "I did what You wanted, so why aren't You here to save me?"

What answer did Jesus get?

None.

Anybody show up to save Him?

No.

And what did He do next, Michael asked himself. He'd said, "Into Your hands I commend my spirit." In that moment, when He could have condemned God with as much justification as anyone in history, instead He announced—to all present, and to generations to come—that He still chose to trust God. There was never a transition, Michael realized. There was simply a choice.

Just like Job, Michael thought. Job, the divinely tormented righteous man, who had demanded that God defend Himself. God appeared in a whirlwind and offered no defense whatsoever; just a lot of questions that boiled down to one: What do you know about running the universe? And Job's answer? "You're right. I'm sorry." Job had sided with God, against himself. Based on nothing. Was that what God wanted from Michael?

Maybe God had not lived up to His end of the deal because there had never been a deal. And maybe that was the entire point. A new thought came to Michael, fully formed.

The jump is not a leap of faith. Not really. It's an acknowledgment that there's a gap between us that nothing can fill. Uncrossable, by any means we understand. All we can do is declare ourselves to be on the

other side. Like Jesus. Like Job. Stop ranting and
demanding an explanation or retribution or justice.
Simply declare: Okay, God. For no damned reason—and
more in SPITE *of You than because of You—I'm with You.*

"All right!" Michael yelled at the ceiling, "But this is
it! This is **all** I've got!"

He stepped out from behind the furnace. His eyes had
adjusted to the darkness and he could see Jack—and the
gun that was pointed straight at him.

Jack cocked the trigger, but Michael was too caught up
in his own anger to care. He threw himself at Jack, grab-
bing his legs. Both men went tumbling to the floor.
Michael heard the gun hit the ground a few feet away.
The physical strength of the demon was now well
matched by the force of Michael's fury—part of it aimed
at the demon, the rest aimed at their common enemy:
God's fucking plan.

Michael had Jack by the throat, and had no doubt that
he could kill Jack right then if he chose to.

"You do whatever you want," he yelled, as if God
were hard of hearing. "I'm not asking for any deal. I'm
telling You that I'm on Your fucking side and nothing
You do to me or let him do to me is going to change it!"

There was a moment where time seemed to stand still;
then Michael's mind began to fill with a sound, like
rushing water. He could feel his body vibrating, as if an
electrical current were pulsing through him. He had a
sense of color—a golden light filling his body and his
mind and, somehow, his soul. He had no visual sense of
color, just a feeling. The inside of his head had a
"copper" feeling—the way a mouth feels with a penny in
it. He loosened his grip on Jack, but continued to hold
him down. Jack was still straining against Michael, with
an enraged look on his contorted face.

Somewhere, in some way that had nothing to do with

auditory senses, he heard the word *now*. It filled him, riding on the electrical current. He opened his mouth and words came out, but he knew they weren't coming from him. Yet, somehow, he also knew he was more than an empty vessel.

"Leave him!" said the voice that came out of Michael. It was no louder than normal conversation, yet the force of its anger was staggering.

"Fuck you!" Jack yelled.

Michael felt a reaction in the electrical force. It intensified. On instinct, Michael moved closer to Jack.

"Leave him!" the voice repeated. Michael had trouble keeping his balance. He could feel his body recoil as if he'd just fired a rifle.

In seconds, there was a wail from Jack. Michael could feel the electrical current in his body intensify, and then he could feel it on the outside, filling the room.

"Jack!"

The scream came from the stairs, and Michael looked up to see Randa.

"What's happening?" she screamed at Michael.

Before Michael could answer, the energy in the room shifted, to something that was the spiritual equivalent of fingernails on a chalkboard. It was not so much a sound as a vibration, and it was accompanied by a crushing pressure that seemed to pull in opposite directions. Michael sensed that he and Randa were caught in the crossfire of a war. He felt completely helpless.

Then, from somewhere, he remembered Bob Curso's words: *"It is through the will that God will save Danny."*

The will.

Fine. But where was Jack's will? What would make him want to live?

Randa.

Michael looked at Randa. She was moving toward

Jack, slowly, fighting the pressure as if she were walking
against the wind of a hurricane.

Michael opened his mouth. Speaking was a major
effort.

"Jack . . . you have to choose . . . we can't do it for
you. . . ." he said.

Jack remained on the ground, still screaming, looking
as if he were being crushed alive under an invisible
boulder. He showed no sign of having heard Michael.

Randa reached for Jack's hand. She couldn't quite
touch him. The force seemed to be more powerful the
closer she got to him.

"Jack . . . take Randa's hand!" Michael managed to
yell. "Do it!"

No reaction, except for the continuing wail.

"Jack!" Randa yelled. "I know you can hear me!" She
caught her breath, then tried again to reach him.

The wail continued, but Michael could see Jack trying
to move his hand.

"That's it!" Michael yelled. "Take her hand!"

Jack's hand began to move toward Randa. Both of
them fighting against the force between them.

Please, God. Help them.

Suddenly Jack seemed to gain strength and break
through the barrier. He grabbed Randa's hand. Michael
knew what it meant. Jack's choice was made, too.

The wail started to recede, as if it were being sucked
out of the room. Michael realized that Jack's mouth was
closed. The wail was coming from somewhere else now.
It continued to recede, until it was gone. With it went the
pressure. Michael fell against the furnace, breathing
hard. Jack collapsed onto the floor. Randa collapsed
beside him.

"Jack!"

Jack looked up at her, rubbing his head as if he were

waking from a deep sleep. When he realized it was Randa beside him, he hugged her.

"Randa!" The voice was clearly Jack's.

Michael was beginning to breathe normally again. He could still feel the electrical current all around him. Suddenly it changed, from a physical feeling to an emotional one. It was a feeling unlike any he had ever experienced—a wave of joy and peace and reassurance and love, as pure as the hate it had banished. It poured over him. Through him.

Michael looked at Randa. She was staring at him, wide-eyed.

Say something. Did you feel it?

"*What was that*?" she asked.

Michael felt his face break into a smile. The feeling had left a glow in its wake, as tangible as the residual slimy coating that the Evil used to leave.

"Where the hell are we?" Jack asked, apparently unaware of the glow.

"I'll tell you later," Michael said. "We need to get out of here."

Randa and Michael helped Jack to his feet. He was still rubbing his head. Michael picked up the gun and put it in the pocket of his jacket.

"Follow me," Michael said to them. "And don't touch anything." He led them up the dark stairs to the back door. He pushed it open with his elbow and looked out. There was a small fenced-in area around the door. The alley was dark and clear.

He motioned for them to follow him. They all stepped out into the alley. There was very little sound, just the crackle of a police radio, vague and filtered from the other side of the building.

"Okay," Michael said, in a low voice. "There's a MARTA entrance right there," he pointed. It was on the other side of the fence that blocked the alley between the Winecoff and the Carnegie building. "The cops are up on Peachtree. We can get on the MARTA and be in Buckhead in ten minutes."

"Hey!"

It came from the Ellis Street side. Michael looked up. The world's largest cop was headed their way.

"Just be quiet and let me handle this," Michael said, simultaneously sending a silent alarm to the guy in the flannel shirt.

You're wearing your collar.

Michael had forgotten. He touched the neck of his shirt to confirm it, and sent up a silent thank you. He stepped forward, toward the cop.

"Officer, I'm Father Riley." No point giving the guy a name he could trace later. "I got a call that a woman had jumped from the Carnegie building."

"A call from who?" the cop asked.

"I don't know. My housekeeper took the message. Someone called the rectory and said for me to come to the alley behind the Winecoff." He pointed to Randa and Jack. "They're from the *Constitution*. We walked up from the Macy's parking lot."

The cop looked at Randa, and his mood changed. "It's not a very exciting story," he said. "Old lady jumped out a window. Probably just found out she had a brain tumor or something."

"Well, maybe you can help us find a distraught relative to quote."

"I'll find you whatever you need," he said, his smile broadening.

Jack was in luck, Michael realized. Nothing more immediately trustworthy than a priest or a beautiful woman, and Jack had one on either side. The cop hadn't even glanced at him.

"Excuse me," Michael said, pretending to be annoyed, "but I think my job has a higher priority rating at the moment."

"Oh, really?" Randa asked, picking up the game beautifully. "Do you have a certain amount of time to say the magic words before God gets impatient and sends her to Hell?"

"I'm not worried about God. I'm worried about the coroner."

The cop stepped in to protect the peace.

"Let me just take him where he needs to go," he said to Randa. "Y'all can wait here and I'll come back and get you."

Randa smiled. "That would be great. Thank you."

He nodded and winked.

"Okay, Father," he said, and turned to lead Michael up the hill. Michael followed. "Do they still call y'all 'Father,' or is that just in the movies?"

"They still call us 'Father.' "

Michael smiled. He glanced down the hill, just in time to see Randa and Jack disappear behind the Carnegie building.

The cop kept talking. "I don't know who coulda called you. Some Catholic looky-loo I guess. But I thought y'all didn't give Last Rites to people who committed suicide. Plus it's a Chinese woman, so I doubt she was Catholic."

"Well, as long as I'm here anyway—"

"You know, Father, you might want to throw some holy water at this building while you're here. It's never been anything but trouble."

Michael smiled. "I have a hunch its luck is going to change."

They had reached the small crowd gathered around the woman.

"Excuse us," the cop said. "Excuse us. Stand back, please."

People looked up and saw the cop and the priest; the crowd parted like the Red Sea. A Hispanic man in a Ritz-Carlton valet parking uniform nodded at Michael.

"Hi, Father," he said.

"Hi," Michael said.

Good. Maybe the cop'll think he's the guy who called me.

Michael patted the man on the shoulder as he walked by, as if they were old friends. Oddly, he realized he wasn't doing it just to sell his story to the cop. It meant something. He wasn't sure what it meant, but it meant something. He felt a connection to the guy that he never would have felt before.

"Father Riley?"

Michael looked up, startled. An elderly man in a navy windbreaker was standing in front of him.

How can he know my fake name?

Michael stared at the guy, trying to stay calm. The guy was in his sixties. White hair. Longish face. Michael looked into his eyes and almost gasped. He would have recognized those eyes anywhere, even without the flannel shirt.

"I'm the one who called you," the man said.

Michael nodded. He felt his heart pounding; it seemed to be somewhere in the general vicinity of his appendix.

My God . . . this is not a dream. . . .

He forced his voice to work. "I know," he was able to say. He took a step closer. "I know who You are," he added.

The man smiled; nodded slightly. "You're getting there," he said.

"Hey, Father!"

Michael turned toward the voice, annoyed by the interruption. It was the cop.

"Coroner's waiting for you," he said.

"I'll be right there," Michael said. He turned back around. The man was gone.

Michael scanned the crowd, but knew there was no point. Knew the man was gone. Just as he knew the man had been there.

CHAPTER 12

Michael was up and packing before dawn. He wanted to get to Manhattan before Tess left for work. He knew she went in late on Fridays, but it was still going to be a push. He was not happy when the phone rang. Someone's untimely crisis was going to make him miss the plane. He answered it anyway.

"Michael, it's Randa. I'm at Jack's, you have to come over here. Hurry."

Michael was at Jack's door in ten minutes. Randa let him in.

"What's going on?" Michael asked, afraid of the answer.

"You have to do something," Randa said. "He didn't sleep at all and he says he's going to turn himself in."

Michael felt himself relax slightly. "Okay," he said. "Where is he?"

Randa nodded toward the back of the apartment.

"Taking a shower," she said. "I guess he wants to be clean when they lynch him."

The bathroom door opened and Jack came out, wearing only a pair of jeans and drying his hair with a towel. He stopped walking when he saw Michael.

"Jack, you are not going to turn yourself in," Michael said, "if I have to sit on you. *You* didn't do anything."

Jack tossed the towel aside. "That's not what you said before."

"What are you talking about?"

"You said it had to be because of something I did. You said I did something to let it in."

"That doesn't make you a murderer."

"Yes, it does. You don't know the whole story. I made a *decision* to kill someone. Ten years ago. It just took me awhile to get around to it."

"What are you talking about?" Michael asked.

"*I* let it in. And that means those people are dead because of me."

"They're dead because of my grandfather!" Michael said. "And his father, and God knows who before that. Your whole life has been a reaction to things you didn't choose. So has mine. And turning yourself in isn't going to bring those people back."

Jack shook his head. "I can't forgive myself," he said.

"Well, luckily that's not your job!"

Michael had spoken so loudly that both Jack and Randa had stared at him in surprise. Michael went on. "Let's say you tell the truth. The truth is *not* that you cold-bloodedly murdered those people. So let's say you and I go to the cops—right now—and tell them the real story. And then what would happen? Anything that has to do with the *truth*? When they lock you up forever or execute you, what would that have to do with the *truth*? After everything we've been through, you're going to let the Devil win? Is that the holy outcome you're after? Or are you just looking for a new place to hide?"

Michael took a moment to breathe, then went on.

"I think all three of us have been hiding, for a long time, behind whatever we could find to use. And I'm all for stepping out into the open. But if you want it to be about the truth, then you have to tell your story to someone who knows the whole context. Except He already knows the story, and He's already judged you and I'm sorry to break this to you, but you've been sentenced to life." Michael looked at Randa. "We all have," he said.

He gave it a moment to sink in, then added, "It's God's version of capital punishment."

CHAPTER 13

Randa sat with Jack on the hill by the duck pond and they watched the ducks. It seemed to have the calming effect on Jack that she'd hoped for. The storm front had moved on, and the midmorning sun shining down on her was just warm enough to offset the chill in the air. Randa was feeling her own strange calmness, but it had nothing to do with the ducks.

Jack hadn't felt it—whatever it was that she and Michael had felt in the basement of the Winecoff. There was no way to explain it to him. She certainly didn't understand it herself. All she knew was that it was like nothing she'd ever felt before. And that it had been the thing that sent the demon back wherever it had come from.

She couldn't think about that now. She'd have the rest of her life to try to figure it out, and at the moment she had other things to worry about. Like the rest of her life.

She'd been up all night, too. She'd come to a conclusion that she didn't like at all. But she knew it was right. Now there was only the matter of announcing it.

She looked at Jack. He was staring at the ducks, mesmerized, lost in his own thoughts. There was no point in putting this off; there wasn't going to be a "good" time.

"Jack, I have to go back to LA," she said.

He didn't answer, or take his eyes off the ducks.

"It's my home," Randa continued. "It's what I chose, and I love it there. I can't stay here because of you. It wouldn't do either of us any good."

"Okay," he said, after a long moment.

Okay? That's it? Okay?

Randa sighed. Another sock in the gut from the Landrys. At least it would be the last.

Maybe he thought she was leaving because of what had happened. It would make sense. After all, any woman in her right mind would probably ditch a guy for killing half a dozen people. But Randa wasn't afraid of him in the least. In some way that was qualitatively different from any other "knowing" she'd ever felt, she knew Jack was okay. She had felt the Evil in that room. She had felt it leave. And she had felt whatever had chased it away. Whatever that force had been, she knew it could be trusted.

"I almost went to school once to learn hotel management," Jack said, his voice devoid of emotion. "Maybe I'll try that again."

"Hotel management?" Randa asked, forcing her voice to remain steady. "Why that?"

Jack shrugged. "I think I'd be good at it," he said. He looked at her. "I don't have a more noble reason."

"You don't need one," Randa said. "Where would you go?"

Jack looked back at the ducks. "I don't know. I'd have to find a place that would take me. And I guess I'd have to find a place that was on a bus route."

Randa looked at him.

"A bus route?" she asked.

"I've heard it's hard to get around LA without a car," he said.

Randa couldn't believe what she was hearing.

"You'd come to LA? With me?"

He looked confused. "I thought you were asking me to," he said.

Randa laughed, which confused Jack even further.

"You don't want me to?" he asked.

She hugged him, still laughing. "I do want you to," she said. "I just can't believe it."

Jack kissed her, then pulled back and looked her in the eyes.

"I'm just worried about one thing," he said. "Do you think I'd be running? Because I don't want to do that."

She shook her head. "Michael will know where we are, and they'd come to him if they wanted to find you."

"Michael talks a good game," Jack said. "But he doesn't have to live with it." He looked back at the pond. "I'll keep my mouth shut," he said. "I'll do that for him. But if they come for me, I'm not going to run."

Randa nodded. The thought of "them" coming for him terrified her, but she loved him even more for what he was saying.

She leaned back against his chest. He put his arms

around her and kissed the back of her head. The irrational calm swallowed her whole, dissolving all thoughts of ugly pasts and precarious futures. She'd spent way too much of her life worrying about the future anyway. And way too much of it nursing her wounds from the past.

She felt her head move with the rhythm of Jack's breath. She felt a chilly breeze on her face. She listened to the silly sound of the ducks.

In some deep part of her, for this self-contained moment, it all made some ridiculous kind of sense.

CHAPTER 14

Michael made it to Tess's apartment a little before ten-thirty. Deneb said she hadn't come down yet, so Michael went upstairs. She was locking her door to leave when he stepped out of the elevator. She looked up; she stared at him, puzzled, then smiled.

"I guess I'm not going to Atlanta today," she said.

"I didn't want to wait until tonight. I have to talk to you."

Her smile vanished.

"It's okay," he said, kissing her. "I just have to tell you what's been going on."

They went back into her apartment and he told her the entire story. When he was done, she was appropriately speechless.

"I don't know what to do with this," she said.

"You don't have to do anything. I just wanted you to know how I came to be . . . where I am."

"And where are you?" she asked. Her voice was shaky.

"It's like a lot of layers have been stripped away," he said. "All I want now is to feel clean, if that's possible." He sighed. "I don't want to resign," he said. "It's not honest. I *want* to be a priest. But I don't want to be a hypocrite and I don't want to hide. So the only thing I can do is tell them the truth."

"What is the truth?" she asked.

"That I'm in love with you."

"If you tell them that, they'll kick you out."

"They'll do whatever they do," he said. "I will have been honest." He stood up, walked to the window, and looked out. "I've been asking myself why I wanted to be a priest, and I don't know the answer. Maybe it was for Vincent. Maybe it was to get out of Vincent's shadow. Maybe I thought I had to pay God back for letting me live through the fire. I don't know." He looked back at her. "I'm not even sure I've ever *been* a priest. I've been a student and I've been a teacher and I've been a magazine editor. I wanted to serve God, but I wanted to do it on my own terms. That's not how it works."

"Well," Tess said quietly, "maybe you should try it again, now that you know that."

"Maybe I should," Michael said, "but I'm not going to." He came back and sat by her again. "If I *am* a priest, no amount of paperwork can take that away from me. And it's not like there's a limit to the places where the world could use some help."

Tess was trying not to cry. "I love you," she said.

He hugged her and didn't let go. "I love you, too," he said. "So much."

Over Tess's shoulder, Michael saw Krissy hovering in the hallway.

"Hi, Krissy," he said. "Did you catch all of that?"

Krissy was beaming. "I got the gist of it," she said, stepping out into the room. "But . . . you guys aren't going to get married, are you?"

Michael smiled and looked at Tess. "I don't know. Are we?"

Tess was wiping tears with the sleeve of her sweater. "I don't know," she said.

"Why?" Michael asked Krissy. "Did you want to be the flower girl?"

"It would make you my stepfather," she said. "It's too weird."

"But it would make an honest woman out of your mother," Michael said.

Krissy laughed. "My mother is already way too honest."

Michael nodded and laughed. "Good point," he said.

Tess got up and started to gather her belongings. "I have to go," she said. "I have a stupid meeting." She looked at Michael. "Will you be here when I get home?"

"Where else would I be?"

Tess kissed them both and left. As soon as Tess was out the door, Krissy turned to Michael.

"So . . . about this white-haired guy at the hotel . . ."

"You've been listening *that* long?"

Krissy ignored that. "Are you positive he was the same guy as the one you saw in your dreams?"

Michael nodded. "Yes."

"Do you think the version in the dream is what He really looked like?"

"I don't think it matters," Michael answered.

"I just wondered if He was cute."

"Krissy, I think He's a little old for you."

She didn't laugh. "If I could believe that story was true . . ."

"*My* story?"

"The whole thing," Krissy said. "I mean, if I could believe there was a God who gave a shit . . . *and* wore jeans . . ." She walked away from Michael, absently pulling on a strand of hair. "I've been thinking a lot about this God thing, ever since you and Mom . . . whatever. I've even tried to pray, but I just feel stupid."

"Come here," Michael said, patting the sofa cushion beside him. "Sit."

She did. Sans wisecrack, amazingly.

"*Pray* is an intimidating word," Michael said. "What if I were the guy in the flannel shirt and we were just sitting here, talking?"

"I'd be scared shitless to be sitting here," Krissy said.

"Well, pretend you're past that."

"Okay." She thought about it. "Well . . . I'd say something like . . . I'd like to get to know You." Her voice was actually trembling, just a bit. "But I can't go sit on a hard bench once a week and be made to feel guilty. And I don't want to be one of those plastic-faced people who go around telling everyone that You love them. And I don't want Amy Grant in my CD collection. So . . . is there any way I could know You that has something to do with who I am?"

She looked at him, suddenly self-conscious.

"Or something like that," she said.

"Okay. And what do you think I'd say?"

"That's *your* job."

Michael shook his head. "It's my universe, I make the rules."

"Okay," Krissy said, relenting. "I think you'd say, 'Well, I'm sorry my rules don't suit you. When you create your own universe, you can behave any way you want to.' "

Michael shook his head. "No," he said. "Try again."

"You'd say, 'What's wrong with Amy Grant? You should wish I was a tenth as happy with you as I am with her. And you call that screeching you listen to *music*?' "

Michael laughed.

Krissy shook her head. "I don't know," she said. "When I've ever imagined Him existing, I only thought of Him as mean, and really pissed at me." She sighed. "I give up," she said. "He's *your* pal. What would He say?"

Michael thought about it for a second. Listened. The answer, whatever its origin, came to him easily. "He'd say . . . 'I tell you what. Do the best you can. Treat other people decently. Treat yourself decently. And the next time you see a pretty sunset, take a moment to look at it. Count the colors. Wonder where it came from. Say "Wow" out loud. And I'll hear you. And I'll consider it a prayer.' "

He kissed her on the forehead.

"Are you sure He'd say that?" Krissy asked, her voice choked with emotion.

"Of course not," Michael said.

Krissy burst into laughter. Michael joined her.

He was not sure in the least. Of what he'd just said, or of anything else.

And then again . . .

He was absolutely positive.

ACKNOWLEDGMENTS

In the five years that I spent writing this book, and in the thirty-five years I spent *getting ready* to write this book, I have accumulated a lot of people to whom I owe a great deal of gratitude.

Bennett Ashley, my agent and friend, is the person who should have me shot if I didn't thank him first: for five years of patient encouragement, and for reading fifteen drafts of every chapter. I owe a considerable debt to Jon Karp, who is far more than I ever dared hope for in an editor; and to Ann Godoff, for having the insight to pair us up. Thanks to both of them for believing in the book so quickly and so thoroughly. I am grateful to everyone at Random House and at Janklow/Nesbit for the tremendous faith they have shown in the book. (I still can't believe you people even let me ride your elevators.) Particular thanks to Jean-Isabel McNutt, for making me look as if I know how to spell and punctuate and for divesting me of some obnoxious pet phrases; and to J.K. Lambert for his beautiful design.

I have been blessed with an amazing assortment of friends, who have gotten me through this endeavor in an amazing assortment of ways. Chief among them are: Mary Crosby; Nancy Lindquist; Babette Isen; Mandonna Chambers; Matt and Moonie Fishburn; Lynn Lantieri; Bonnie Raskin; Miriam Trogdon; Dale Cousins, who runs my life but should be running the country; Stephen Harrison, who inspires me regularly with his music, his faith and, most important, with his seafood gumbo; Dave Marsh and Barbara Carr, who mean more to me than words can say. I owe perhaps the greatest debt of all to Kristen Carr, who changed my life when it was too late for me to thank her in person; I do so now.

My brother (and favorite theologian) Bryant Wilbourne and sister-in-law Jackie Wilbourne have been an endless source of support, both with the book and with my lifelong theological struggle/obsession. Kay Cessna lent me her faith in the early days, when I was making my first wobbly steps back toward a belief of any sort, and has been there for every wobbly step since, with an unearthly amount of kindness and patience.

The following people were generous with time I'm sure they couldn't afford, and helped me with the daunting task of trying to understand and write a priest: Father Pat Bishop; Father Dan Stack; Father George Hunt, S.J., and the staff of *America* magazine; Father Tom Weston, S.J. (I should also add that I shamelessly stole several of Tom's best jokes, and that there are days when his tapes are the only thing standing between me and institutionalization.) Father Larry Estrada provided an assortrment of pastoral insights, Latin and Spanish when I needed them, and some darned good Dodger tickets.

(I'm sure many—if not all—of the above-mentioned Fathers would appreciate my stating that the theological views reflected herein are not necessarily their own.)

Terry Sweeney is a former Jesuit (which is akin to being a former southerner) who spent countless hours helping me understand the life of a Jesuit. He and his wife, Pam, were a font of information, encouragement, and moral support. I can't image this book or my life had I not met them.

I am grateful to the following people, who taught me most of what I know about writing: Elsie Todd, Lou

Catron, Glenn Caron, Dave Marsh, and Mikal Gilmore. Thanks to Mikal also for all the meanderings and life lessons, and for the stories of his family—the strangers who have, for so long, tugged at my heart.

My sister, Barbara Hall, answered all of my how-to-write-a-novel questions, and gave me the single best piece of advice on writing I've ever received: "Just shut up and write the damned thing." I thank her for that, as it has been my mantra. I also thank Sheldon Bull, who spent a lot of time reading, listening, answering questions, and giving me extremely helpful notes.

Thanks to Ed and Lorraine Warren for telling me everything I needed to know about demons; to Mike Smith of the Atlanta Police Department; to Greg Torre of the Georgia Filming Bureau; to Bert Godwin for the tour of the Winecoff Hotel. Sam Heys and Allen B. Goodwin wrote a wonderful book, *The Winecoff Fire*, without which I don't know how I'd have written mine.

These people have also helped me, in many and various ways, and I am grateful to them: Cora Tolentino; Luvy, Luis, Victor, and Linda Gonzalez; Byron Parker and family; Ramsey Brown; Kim Forst; Michelle Sekula and Ric Kersey; Norman Kurlund; Lydia Wills; Grace McGinnis; Karl Weidergott and Steve Kurtz.

A very special thanks to my CompuServe Religion Forum friends, especially to the gang in S14—the assorted collection of atheists, agnostics, rock-and-roll Christians, Lovescreamers, and generic-confused theists. In addition to your friendship and support, I thank you for keeping me honest about the sheer lunacy of my deepest convictions.

Finally, I thank my daughter, Juli, and I thank the guy in the flannel shirt—the two people who simultaneously exhaust me and give me the strength to keep going. The two people I love beyond reason.